The HOUSE on SUNSET LAKE

TASMINA PERRY

First published in 2016 by HEADLINE REVIEW
An imprint of HEADLINE PUBLISHING GROUP

First published in paperback in 2017 by HEADLINE REVIEW
An imprint of HEADLINE PUBLISHING GROUP

6

All characters in this publication are fictitious and any resemblance
to real persons, living or dead, is purely coincidental.

Cataloguing in Publication Data is available from the British Library

ISBN 978 1 4722 0847 7

Typeset in Caslon by Avon DataSet Ltd, Bidford-on-Avon, Warwickshire

Printed and bound in Great Britain by Clays Ltd, St Ives plc

Headline's policy is to use papers that are natural, renewable and recyclable
products and made from wood grown in well-managed forests and other controlled
sources. The logging and manufacturing processes are expected to conform to the
environmental regulations of the country of origin.

HEADLINE PUBLISHING GROUP
An Hachette UK Company
Carmelite House
50 Victoria Embankment
London EC4Y 0DZ

www.headline.co.uk
www.hachette.co.uk

Praise for

The HOUSE on SUNSET LAKE

'One of 2016's best summer reads'
Red

'Seductive and mysterious, this is the perfect novel to while away a summer's afternoon'
Daily Express

'Gripping . . . it's brilliantly written. I loved it'
Daily Mail

'Buried secrets, lost loves, betrayal and heartbreak fuel this intriguing, atmospheric love story with plenty of twists to keep you turning the pages'
Sunday Express S

'Beautifully descriptive and achingly romantic, this absorbing tale is a pure delight. *****'
Heat

'A classic tale of star-crossed lovers – with a dark twist. Vividly told, with plenty of surprises'
Good Housekeeping

'Romance with a side order of suspense'
Glamour

'Atmospheric and engrossing'
Sunday Mirror

'Fantastic reading, an excellent balance of romance and suspense'
Irish Country Living

'A stirring and intoxicating story of love and twisted secrets'
LoveReading

'Mystery, intrigue and romance all come together in one brilliant read'
Fabulous

Praise for

The Last Kiss Goodbye

'Another note-perfect read from Tasmina Perry'
Red

'Romance, adventure, mystery . . . [A] beautifully written and engaging tale'
Heat

'With political intrigue and sweeping romance, this is a compelling read'
Sunday Express

'A great story about lost love, exploration and long-buried secrets. A perfect rainy Sunday read'
Marie Claire

'Impressive'
Glamour

'Set in both the '60s and the present day, this book will keep you hooked as its secrets are revealed'
Fabulous

'Irresistible escapism'
Sunday Mirror

'Her best yet . . . Beautifully written and the romance is subtle but so moving'
That Thing She Reads

'Unputdownable . . . Tasmina Perry keeps you riveted to her books and when you finish one it stays with you for a long time'
Books With Wine and Chocolate

'All-consuming love, buried secrets and beautiful locations . . . A satisfying read with twists and turns and an old-fashioned love story at its heart'
Random Things Through My Letterbox

Tasmina Perry is the *Sunday Times* Top Ten bestselling author of eleven novels. She left a career in law to enter the world of magazine publishing, and went on to become an award-winning writer and contributor to titles such as *Elle*, *Glamour* and *Marie Claire*. In 2004 she launched her own travel and fashion magazine, *Jaunt*, and was editing *InStyle* magazine when she left the industry to write books full time. Her novels have been published in seventeen countries. Tasmina lives with her husband and son in London, where she is at work on her next novel.

By Tasmina Perry

Daddy's Girls
Gold Diggers
Guilty Pleasures
Original Sin
Kiss Heaven Goodbye
Private Lives
Perfect Strangers
Deep Blue Sea
The Proposal
The Last Kiss Goodbye
The House on Sunset Lake

This one's for my dad

Prologue

No one forgets a summer spent at Casa D'Or. You remember them so clearly you don't even need to close your eyes to recall the heavy warm breeze, the smell of azaleas, and the air that sticks to your sun-kissed skin.

People wonder why we stay here when it gets so hot, so humid from June through to September. When the afternoon storms turn the sky as black as a starling's wing and the rain can drench the house in a heartbeat. People ask why we don't leave for the cooler beaches of the north or the cosmopolitan cities of Europe – Paris, London, Rome. But those who ask have never been to Casa D'Or. They have never felt its magic.

But if every summer at Casa D'Or is special, some sparkle just a little brighter than the others. Your memories of them remain just a little more vivid. Like the summer when we built the tiki swing down by the lake and spent the whole of July drinking peach iced tea and jumping into the water. Or when we sailed down the Moon River at dusk and the sunset was so brilliant that it was as if we were surrounded by fire.

But I know, even now, that this summer will outshine them all. For this is the summer that I met you. It's the summer that I felt alive, when I finally understood how love can make you feel: happy, heady, oblivious to the world except the bits that have you in it. How can I ever forget that time you kissed me by the lake, or when you first took my hand in yours, and the way it seemed to slot perfectly into place?

A song is floating through my head – a song from the Summer of Love – and I wonder if this is what they felt like in San Francisco in '67. Drunk on a sense of newness, heady from sex and freedom.

Except I'm not like the hippy chicks or the stoners. I can't parade my feelings for you on a placard outside City Hall. For this is not just a summer of special memories, it is a summer of secrets, which I know makes it fizz with a certain dangerous brand of sparkle.

In my heart I know that it won't end well. The cream always sours, the sun always sets.

I can feel a storm in the air, and dark clouds are gathering over the lake. The light in your room is on – I spot it twinkling across the water, and if I narrow my eyes I can make out your outline tempting me with your forbidden promise. I want to see you before it rains.

Chapter One

Scottish Highlands, New Year's Eve

On the crowded castle ramparts, there was a moment of quiet. Conversation halted, heads tilted, breath was held. And then there it was: a soft chime as the church clock in Munroe village struck twelve.

Whoooosh!

The first rocket hissed into the sky, followed by a swell of cheering and shrieks of delight. Scarlet fireworks popped in the black sky, spidery tendrils floating back to earth as 'Auld Lang Syne' rang out from hidden speakers. The New Year.

All along the stone parapet, people were embracing and kissing, each sharing this moment with a loved one or a handy stranger, each exchanging whispered words or wishes of hope for the future. Everyone except Jim Johnson. He looked down at his watch, then up at the sky. Eighteen and a half minutes, that was how long the pyrotechnics were due to last, and by then the band in the ballroom needed to be in full swing.

'Hey, Jim, amazing party.'

He looked up and shook the proffered hand. Douglas Strand, a big noise in oil and gas, prominent in Scottish politics. The fact that Strand was here for New Year and not on a balcony overlooking Princes Street brought a smile to Jim's face.

'Thanks, Doug,' he said patting Strand on the back. 'Spread the word, huh?'

The man gestured with his tumbler, indicating the crowds of movers and shakers whooping and laughing along the castle roof.

'Doubt I'll need to after tonight,' he said. 'I think everyone who needs to know is already here.'

Jim shook more hands and accepted tipsy hugs as he made his way back down the stairs towards the Great Hall, Munroe's crowning glory, a stunning lobby atrium formed from what had been until only weeks before the castle's cobbled courtyard. Now it was the elegant entrance to the hotel, the cobbles covered with oak and rugs, the ancient walls softened and warmed by drapes, art and concealed lighting. It was a breathtaking introduction to Europe's new destination hotel – and Jim had seen the impact it had on the faces of the guests as they had arrived. The launch had been a success in every way.

So far anyway, he thought, rolling his neck and feeling a little of the tension there ease.

'Celine,' he said, spotting a woman in a red ball gown by the bar. 'Thanks for coming.'

Heads turned as the striking brunette kissed him on the cheek. Celine Wood was pushing forty but she was still one of the most famous models in the world, so it had been a real coup dragging her up to Scotland for the opening.

'Happy New Year. Are you not going out to watch the fireworks?'

'I've come in for a drink. Here, take this, you look as if you need one,' she said, handing him a flute of champagne.

'Cheers,' he said, taking a quick sip. 'I've not slept for forty-eight hours.'

'Well you still look as gorgeous as ever,' she said, wiping a smudge of lipstick from the corner of his mouth. 'Even more gorgeous than Munroe.'

Jim smiled nervously, wondering if Celine Wood was coming on to him. They'd met and possibly flirted before, but Jim was never sure, whenever he met these showbiz sorts, what was standard-issue interaction and what was the green light for something else. He certainly didn't want to make a fool of himself tonight trying to find out.

'Mr Johnson, could I have a word?'

He frowned as the concierge approached.

'There's a rumpus at the front gates.'

'A rumpus?' he said, quickly getting rid of his drink.

Celine didn't take her eyes off him.

'A security issue, sir. I think you should come and deal with it.'

Jim glanced at Celine, who pulled her famously sultry lips into a downwards curve.

'I've got to go,' he said, touching her shoulder.

'You might be needing this later,' she whispered as she pushed something into his pocket. 'Come and find me if you do.'

Pressing his lips together, he buttoned his dinner jacket, and followed the concierge to the manager's office across the hall, allowing himself a quick backwards glance towards Celine. She was already gone from her spot at the bar. Just as well.

He was ushered in front of a TV monitor, all eyes in the room upon him.

'What's wrong?' he asked, looking at the flickering black and white camera footage.

'Problem at the front gate,' said Munroe's head of security. 'This gentleman is a little excitable, shall we say. Says his name is Lord Brodie. Says he wants to come in.'

'Oh God,' muttered Jim, watching the monitor with a sinking feeling.

'Do you know him?' asked the concierge.

'Yes.'

'Should we let him in?'

'Not in that state.'

'So what should we do?'

Jim had spent the past forty-eight hours with people looking to him for answers. Munroe's newly minted general manager, the PR company, the marketing director, communications director and CEO of Omari Hotels, his employers – everyone wanted a little piece of him, and having had so little sleep since he arrived in Scotland two days earlier, he felt as if he was about to snap.

'Call him a taxi, then go to the gate and make sure the cab takes him wherever he wants to go,' he said, already halfway out of the office. 'As long as it's not up here.'

He checked his watch: still six minutes left of the fireworks display. He crossed to the ballroom and checked on the buffet. It had been replenished, the duck, venison, trout all glistening in the candlelight. Good.

He knew he should go and look for the piper who was due to play from the ramparts after the crowds had gone – but no, that could wait a few minutes.

Grabbing an open bottle of champagne, he slipped down a passageway, weaving his way through the castle until he reached a wrought-iron gate that led into Munroe's walled garden. He pushed open the door and stepped inside, grateful to note that he was alone.

'Happy New Year, Jim,' he muttered to himself as he perched on a cold stone bench and saluted the popping fireworks with the bottle before taking a swig. Most people, he knew, would have balked at working over New Year, but Jim had to admit he loved it. The castle was the star tonight, of course, but he had revelled in the attention too, the admiring glances, the back-slapping.

After all, it had only been eighteen months earlier that he'd found this place. He'd been on his way to a grouse shoot, taken a wrong fork in the road, and stumbled across the tumbledown Scottish pile belonging to the elderly lord. As a hotel investment manager with over fifteen years' experience, he had seen Munroe's potential immediately – the picture-perfect position on the edge of a heather-fringed loch – and wasted no time contacting Brodie to see if he would sell. At first the old man had been reluctant to negotiate, but Jim had won him around eventually. And now here it was, just over a year later, the hottest new resort in Europe and the crowning glory of the company's hotel collection.

Drinking champagne from the half-empty bottle, he felt a pang of guilt at turning Richard Brodie away from the party. He resolved to call him tomorrow, invite him to spend a complimentary evening at Munroe. He would even throw in a round of golf, he decided, not quite able to shake the sense that he had not behaved entirely honourably.

Pushing his hand into his pocket, he burrowed around to find what Celine Wood has deposited in there a few minutes earlier. He was half expecting, half hoping that it would be her phone number – on reflection, the way she'd wiped her lipstick from the edge of his mouth had been very suggestive. Instead he held out his palm and looked at the wrap of cocaine nestled in its centre.

It tempted him for a moment, but then he gave a soft snort, thinking better of it. Class A drugs were definitely not the answer.

'I thought it was you disappearing into the darkness,' said a deep, accented voice.

'Simon,' said Jim, standing up and pushing the wrap quickly back into his pocket as he spotted his boss. 'Sorry, just wanted a breather for a moment.'

'Sit back down,' said Simon Desai, waving an impatient hand.

The chairman of the Mumbai-based global conglomerate that owned Omari Hotels unfastened the single button on his dinner jacket and took a seat next to Jim on the bench. Jim couldn't resist a smile of quiet validation. Here he was, on New Year's Eve, shooting the breeze with one of the world's richest men. Admittedly he was only the hired help, but it wasn't a bad place to find yourself the year you were turning forty.

'So you did it,' said Simon finally.

'*We* did it. Without your commitment, we'd still be draining the moat about now.' Although he had spent almost every waking hour on the renovation of Munroe, Jim knew that he had only managed to deliver a fully working luxury hotel because of Simon's willingness to pour money into the project.

He'd often wondered why Simon bothered with boutique hotels. His empire was vast, spanning every industry from steel to fizzy drinks, and Jim was sure that every single one of his other companies was more profitable and less risk than Omari. But as a shower of golden light sprayed across the black sky like an iridescent willow tree, a babble of laughter playing as its backdrop, Jim knew exactly why he did.

'Hotels are magic, Jim,' said Simon, as if he were reading his thoughts. 'Growing up, I slept on a mattress on the floor with my two brothers. There was no running water in our house, no glass in the windows. But the view – you should have seen it.' He sighed softly. 'From our front step you could see the turrets of the Jaipur Palace, the most beautiful hotel in the province, and every night I wondered what it would be like to step inside, how soft the beds would be, what they ate for supper. But after a while it wasn't enough to wonder. I decided to find out for myself what it was like, so I worked for two whole years to afford a night in the smallest room.'

'And was it everything you'd hoped?' smiled Jim.

'It was. I felt like a king. I thought, "What if anyone could have this? What if living like a king was available to everyone, if only for one night?" That's where it all started. Within ten years, I'd bought the Jaipur Palace.'

'You're such an old romantic,' grinned Jim, finishing off the last of the champagne.

'I was a shrewd businessman.' Simon shrugged nostalgically. 'So where next?' he asked a little more brusquely.

Jim cleared his throat. 'Well, there's an excellent property coming on the market in Hvar. Personally, I think it's the new Saint-Tropez. It's beachfront, a twenty-five-acre site . . .'

Simon shook his head. 'We have four of the top properties in Europe, Jim, all within two hours of one another. Where we need to expand is in North America.'

'America's a saturated market.'

'It's a mature market for sure,' said Simon, 'but it's still the biggest travel market in the world.'

'So where were *you* thinking?'

'Somewhere it's warm all year round. When it's five degrees on the Hudson, we want somewhere people from New York and DC can escape to that doesn't involve putting on a goose-down parka.'

'Florida?' suggested Jim. 'Though most of the interesting properties in Miami have been sold, and we'd be paying top dollar for any strip of coast.'

Simon put a hand on his shoulder. 'I'm not interested in those beachfront carbuncles. Look at this,' he said, nodding towards the ramparts. 'Omari properties have history. They are properties of significance.

'I was thinking the Deep South,' he said after another moment. 'Wide terraces, iced tea and linen suits. The things I used to dream about when I was a child. The things that made me feel like a king.'

Jim rubbed his chin, an uncomfortable memory stirring, but Simon was still talking.

'I'm thinking of a grand Deep South plantation house with a mile-long driveway flanked with trees covered with those plants that look like cobwebs.'

'Spanish moss,' said Jim, glancing across.

'So you know exactly the type of property I am looking for,' said Simon, reaching in his pocket for his phone.

Now Jim was really off balance.

'Simon, the fireworks are finishing, I have the bar to check on, I've lost the piper—'

'I'm thinking of a property like this,' Simon said, ignoring Jim's objections and tapping at the screen.

Jim frowned at the image he had called up. 'That's Tara. The house from *Gone with the Wind*,' he said, recognising the iconic plantation house.

'Tell me what you know about this type of house,' said Simon.

Jim felt himself shiver in the cold Scottish night air. 'Well, it's Greek Revival in style. Early nineteenth century. Graceful proportions, low-gabled. They were built as a backlash against British style, hence the pillars, the nod to Greek architecture. They were popular with wealthy Deep South businessmen, cotton growers, which is why they were known as plantation houses. If you look, you can often see the darker side to these properties – slave cottages in the grounds and so on.'

'You know your stuff.'

'I spent a summer living right by one.'

Simon looked up at him with interest. 'Where was that?'

'Just outside Savannah. Georgia,' said Jim, torn between the discomfort he felt and the desire to impress Simon.

'Was it your family's house?'

'Hardly.' He laughed awkwardly.

'But isn't your father a famous writer?' asked Simon. Three years working side by side and this was the first time he had asked about Jim's private life.

'Writers generally can't afford houses like Casa D'Or,' Jim said, looking down at the cold stone beneath his feet.

'Casa D'Or,' repeated Simon. 'What a beautiful name. What does it mean?'

'The House of Gold.'

Simon began typing, and another image appeared on the screen, one that made the alcohol residue burn in Jim's throat.

'Is that it?' he asked. Not waiting for Jim's reply, he pointed at the web page he had called up. '"Casa D'Or was the winter home of David Darling, the American railroad magnate and art collector",' he read aloud. '"Alongside Hearst Castle and the Biltmore, it was considered to be one of the great entertaining houses of the twentieth century. It was sold in the 1940s to the Wyatt family, who have owned it ever since."'

He looked up, his face lit by the light of the screen. Jim had seen that look before: desire.

'Do the Wyatts still own it?'

'As far as I know. But it's been a long while since I was there.'

'But you know these people, the Wyatts?'

Jim paused, took a breath. 'I used to,' he said, stiffening in his seat.

'Do you think they would sell?'

'Simon, it's their family home. You know how sentimental people get about places.'

Simon gave him a level look. 'And I've also seen how quickly sentiment fades away when you open a chequebook.'

'Yes, but . . .'

'But what, Jim?' said Simon. 'Is there something about this place you're not telling me?'

You have no idea, Jim thought, getting to his feet.

'All I'm saying is let's not jump the gun. Casa D'Or isn't the only house in the South. Let me put out feelers and see what else there is. Omari properties have to be the absolute best in class.'

'Precisely,' said Simon, putting the phone back in his pocket. 'Best in class, and if Casa D'Or is being mentioned in the same breath as Hearst Castle and the Biltmore, that excites me.'

Jim could feel his control slipping away.

'Look, the place has history,' he said cautiously. 'There was an accident there once. Someone died . . .'

Simon looked at the younger man directly, unbothered by the concerns he had just heard, the look in his eyes indicating he was only concerned with getting his own way.

'Where do you see your future in this company, James?' he said evenly. It was a straight question, but one loaded with meaning. Simon was a fair employer, but no billionaire got to the top of that golden pyramid without having a streak of ruthlessness. And while Jim had carved out a personal niche in the Omari property portfolio, the first rule of business was that no one was indispensable.

'I love working for Omari,' he said after a moment. 'It's my life.'

Simon nodded. 'You've been here from the start, grown the Omari business. And I want to reward you for your vision and your loyalty.'

'I'm flattered, but—' began Jim.

'No buts. I want to open the best hotel in the Deep South and I want that hotel to be Casa D'Or. Make it happen and I will make you CEO of Omari Hotels.'

Jim could feel his eyes opening wide.

'CEO?'

Simon looked at him, his gaze intense, and for a moment Jim's own eyes sparkled with desire. Then there was a whoop and a cheer from the terrace and the moment was gone. Simon smiled and raised his glass.

'Well, I think you'd better go and find the piper, don't you?'

Chapter Two

He needed new curtains: that was his first thought. Sunlight was leaking in over the top of his Swedish drapes and straight on to his pillow, rousing him much earlier than he had planned. Turn off your phone: that was his second. Jim scrabbled for the mobile buzzing on his bedside table. 'M' read the screen. 'Not now,' he groaned, clicking it off and shoving it under his pillow. He pulled the duvet over his head, but he knew it was too late: he was awake. So much for his idea of sleeping till noon, reading the paper: finally a couple of hours to relax.

Brrring.

Jim groaned again. The doorbell now.

He rolled out of bed, grabbed his dressing gown and shuffled towards the front door, jabbing a finger against the intercom button when he got there.

'What?' he growled, his voice still craggy with sleep.

A voice. Impatient, annoyed.

'Jim, it's me. Let me in.'

Shit. Melissa. He glanced across at the clock above the hob in his open-plan kitchen and rubbed his eyes. Five o'clock? Could it really be that late?

'Crap,' he muttered, pressing the door release. Working over New Year was one thing, but still being in bed when your girlfriend came to see you? Jim was no expert at relationships, but even he knew that was considered a big no-no.

Footsteps coming up the stairs. No time to think of excuses.

'Don't you ever answer your phone?' asked Melissa, striding into the flat.

'I got the late flight from Inverness last night,' replied Jim, stifling a yawn. 'Didn't get home until one, couldn't sleep.'

'Really? You could have fooled me.'

'I'm knackered, Mel. Munroe, the launch . . .'

'I know it's tough.'

He didn't miss the sarcasm.

'Happy New Year,' he said, pulling her in and kissing her softly on the lips. There was a moment's resistance, then he felt her relax.

'I've missed you,' she said simply as she nuzzled into his neck.

Her hair smelled fresh, clean, delicious. It smelled of anxiety and effort and it made him feel guilty. Maybe he should have invited her to Munroe. Then again, he had made it clear from the start that his job had to take priority, and besides, he was taking her to his father's seventieth birthday party that very evening. That meant something, didn't it?

'You look great,' he said, stepping back to look at her. Her pale green dress was fitted and to the knee; her blond hair bounced over her shoulders. It was a look designed to impress his parents, but she still looked incredibly sexy.

'You think? I didn't know how formal this party was going to be.'

'The Hampstead literati aren't known for their dress sense,' he smiled. 'It's either bow ties or moth-eaten cardigans mostly.'

She looked anxious. 'So you think I'm overdressed?'

'I think you look perfect,' said Jim, pulling her closer and whispering, 'Although I can't wait to see you looking underdressed later.'

She untied his dressing gown and pressed against his bare chest, grinning.

'Why does it have to be later?'

It was almost 7.30 by the time the taxi pulled up outside Jim's parents' house in Hampstead, and already the party looked as though it was in full swing. Every light in the property seemed to be switched on, and they could see the outline of guests at each golden window. A particularly decorous holly wreath was hanging on the polished black front door; with the street's faux gaslight reflecting off the frosty pavement, it looked like the front of one of the Christmas cards still standing on Jim's mantelpiece.

'Just grab this a minute, will you?'

Jim handed Melissa the bottle of Scotch, his father's birthday present, as he leaned forward to pay the driver. When he looked back at her, she was already on the street, gazing up at the house.

'Nice place. When did they buy this?' she said as Jim slammed the taxi door shut.

'In the days when you didn't have to work two hundred and fifty years just to afford the deposit. Apologies beforehand if my father tries to snog you, by the way.'

'I've met him before.'

'Yes, but you've never experienced the true horror of what he's like when he's had a drink and he's showing off on home turf,' smiled Jim as he banged the big brass door knocker.

'Darling! So glad you could make it.' Jim's mother stepped forward and air-kissed him, wafting them both with Chanel. Elizabeth Johnson was thinner than the last time he had seen her, possibly a little more drawn, but she was hiding it well in a beaded cocktail dress and the clanging bangles that always sheathed her wrists. 'And Melissa, so lovely to see you again.

'Come through,' she trilled over her shoulder, as if she were guiding them into a strange new building rather than the house where Jim had grown up. 'You know Tony and Claire, of course, and the Gillans are here.'

Jim had no idea who she was talking about, but it was something he was used to. The endlessly shifting literary and arty circles Elizabeth and Bryn Johnson moved in meant that the faces were constantly changing, one leading light or hot name being replaced by another. Only his father remained a fixed point around which everything else revolved.

And there he was, just where Jim had known he would be,

one elbow leaning on the marble fireplace, his free hand gesturing with a half-full glass, an admiring group surrounding him.

'Jimmy!' he bellowed, breaking off mid-anecdote. 'Come on over, my boy, let the dog see the rabbit.'

He seized Jim in a bear hug, slapping him on the back.

'Drink?'

'What are we celebrating?' asked Jim, smiling.

Bryn Johnson looked at him for a second, then burst out into laughter.

'Trust a Johnson to cut straight to the chase. Everyone else has been tiptoeing around the elephant in the room, giving me guff about entering a golden age, telling me how well I look.'

'You do look well.'

'Considering I've just been butchered. Pretty good for a walking corpse, yes.'

He was being provocative; his default setting. In actual fact he did look well, despite his heart attack only four months previously. When Jim remembered his father in that hospital bed, his skin grey, tubes curling out of his nose and chest, he barely looked the same man. He'd always been strong, like a bull in both body and attitude towards life, and it had upset Jim more than he liked to admit to see him lying there weak and vulnerable.

'Dad, you remember Melissa.'

'Of course. We all went to lunch. The duck was very good, if I remember rightly.'

As he stepped forward to kiss her, Melissa blushed. Over

the years, Bryn Johnson's extraordinary good looks had been much remarked upon: the striking blue eyes, the jet-black hair. Even at seventy, he could still have an effect on women.

'For you,' said Melissa, handing over the bottle of Scotch, which Bryn examined with careful eyes.

'Twenty-Five Year Old Talisker single malt. Very nice. It must be my birthday.' He looked at Jim. 'Nothing from you?'

'It's from both of us,' said Jim, shifting uncomfortably. 'The sommelier at Munroe got hold of it for me. It's excellent. A vintage year. Only a few thousand bottles were ever laid down,' said Jim, but his father had already put it on the mantelpiece.

'Francis, Edward, Peter. Come here. I don't think you've met James Johnson. The very fruit of my loins. Isn't he handsome?'

Hasty introductions were made to three men: a publisher, a sculptor and a playwright.

'Are you a writer too?' asked Edward, the wiry white-haired sculptor.

Jim shook his head. 'I work for a property company.'

'Property? I thought it was poetry.'

'He showed tremendous literary potential at university,' said Bryn, interjecting. 'Saul – that's my American agent – wanted to sign him, but Jimmy wouldn't hear of it.'

'That was a long time ago, Dad.'

'Instead he became a wage slave. Scandalous, isn't it?' he

said. His laugh was loud and raucous.

Jim wasn't sure if his comment had been designed to wound. In his black moods, Bryn Johnson could be brutal, merciless, picking at any aspect of your personality until you felt worthless. On the other hand, just a few generous words from him and he pumped you up until you felt full of air. Jim had spent his entire childhood swinging between the two extremes, although these days he found the most hurtful treatment from his father was his ambivalence to the career he had worked so hard for.

'Good turnout,' he said.

'It is my seventieth.'

'Is Ian coming?'

Ian McConnelly was Jim's godfather. A friend of Bryn's from their Cambridge days, he had gone on to have a hugely successful career writing a series of quirky comic novels that were considered the literary successor to P. G. Wodehouse's Jeeves stories, but which Bryn privately dismissed as 'populist crap'.

'I've got to congratulate him on the knighthood. It's amazing,' said Jim, who had been texted the news by his godfather and had been delighted for him.

'Someone at the Palace probably felt sorry for him,' said Bryn with an ill-disguised huff.

'Really?'

'The Alzheimer's.'

'Ian has Alzheimer's?' said Edward, turning round to rejoin the conversation.

'He'd better not have forgotten about the party tonight,' frowned Bryn.

'Dad . . .'

'So who do you think is going to win the Nobel this year?' he continued, turning his attention back to his cronies.

Jim shook his head and tugged Melissa's sleeve.

'Come on, let's get a drink,' he said.

'How about a guided tour of the house?' she replied, slipping her arm through his. 'I want to see your childhood bedroom.'

Jim hadn't been to his parents' house for a few months, but it looked exactly the same as it always did. A whiff of cigar smoke clung to his father's study; the slightly musty smell of old books pervaded the hallways. His old room was also untouched. Piles of vinyl, all in mint condition, he noted, were stacked up under the window. The blue walls were still festooned with posters – the moody black and white graphics of a Joy Division cover, a psychedelic portrait of Hendrix – plus a pinboard full of tickets from the Mud Club, the Camden Palace and Wembley. He tried to remember when he had last been to a gig or a live venue. He'd taken some clients for dinner at Ronnie Scott's a few months earlier, but he wasn't sure if that counted.

Melissa excused herself to the bathroom and Jim went to refill their glasses in the kitchen. His mother was standing at the island filling a glass bowl with cashew nuts. Surprisingly, they were alone.

'Having a good time?' she said without looking up at him.

She never hired outside caterers, said it was a waste of money. As the daughter of an army officer, she had always had a practical, can-do side, even though her husband demanded that they put on a show.

'Dad seems to be enjoying himself.'

'Never happier than when he's surrounded by people he hardly ever sees.'

Jim fished around the fridge looking for a cold beer.

'Sad news about Ian.'

'I know. He's thrilled with his knighthood, though. Although don't bring that up with your father.'

'I did. He seemed touchy.'

'Touchy? He's been like a bear with a sore head ever since it was announced.'

'But Ian's his friend. He should be pleased for him.'

'In theory,' said his mother softly.

'Don't worry, Melissa will massage his ego.' He opened his can with a hiss and took a long, satisfying sip.

'Pretty little thing.'

Jim looked up and observed the sardonic look on his mother's face.

'Any plans for making an honest woman of this one? Or is this just another of your conquests?'

'Mum,' he said.

'I don't see why I can't ask. You're forty this year and you're still no closer to settling down.'

'It's not a race.'

'Just as well.'

He thought about his brush with Celine Wood at the Munroe party. What would he have done if she had slipped him her number? He had never been unfaithful to any of his girlfriends, but even now he was having thoughts.

Elizabeth reached for a bottle of wine and poured herself a glass.

'What is she, Jim? Thirty-four, thirty-five?'

'We've only been dating a year, Mum. Neither marriage nor babies have been mentioned.'

His mother laughed. 'That doesn't mean they're not on her mind.'

The thought of it made his heart sink. It wasn't that he was against a wife and family per se. Until recently he'd felt sorry for his friends who had disappeared into family life; the boys he'd drunk with, played football, skied and white-water-rafted with, but who now he only saw occasionally: the odd brunch in pubs with playgrounds or crèches, where he was lucky to get ten minutes of undisrupted conversation with his mates, thanks to their children acting up. But lately he had been worried about ending up alone. Work filled his life, but not entirely, and apart from Melissa, there seemed to be fewer and fewer people to spend his free time with. But did he want to settle down with her? He wasn't sure.

'Honestly, she seems very nice,' continued his mother. 'She's a solicitor, too. Why are you hanging around?'

'Perhaps because "very nice" isn't what I'm looking for in a woman.'

Elizabeth sipped her wine and looked at him disapprovingly over the rim of her glass.

'What?' asked Jim, feeling uncomfortable under her scrutiny.

'You're not still clinging to that girl, are you?'

'What girl?' said Jim innocently, although he knew exactly what she was talking about.

'Jim, you have the world's worst case of rose-tinted spectacles.'

'Don't try and tell me what I felt,' he said, feeling defensive.

Elizabeth rolled her eyes. 'You met a girl. It didn't work out. Simple as that. Plus you were kids, another lifetime ago almost.'

'And what's that supposed to mean?'

'That you've spent the last twenty years measuring every other woman against *her*.'

Jim shook his head angrily, about to spit out a reply, but Elizabeth reached over and touched his cheek with the back of her hand. It was such an uncharacteristically tender gesture, it stopped Jim in his tracks.

'Oh darling,' she said. 'I just don't want you to let some idealised vision of something that never really was cloud any chance of happiness you might have here in the real world.'

'I'm not.' He looked over at her, then down at the wine bottle. 'Actually, I've been asked to go back to Casa D'Or.'

That was the real reason he hadn't slept the night before. He'd tossed and turned in his bed, his thoughts consumed by the house, by the memories. By her.

'Back? Whatever for?'

'Simon Desai wants to acquire a historical Southern property. I told him about the house and he wants me to buy it. Blank cheque.'

Elizabeth raised her glass to her lips. 'Well, it could be for sale.'

'Really?'

'You heard David Wyatt died recently?'

'I didn't know,' he said with surprise.

Of course there was no reason he should have heard. Wyatt was a wealthy man, celebrated in his own circles, but he wasn't famous, or of any particular note beyond the society pages of north Georgia. Besides, Jim had been working so hard on Munroe, the bomb could have dropped and he wouldn't have noticed.

'I can't imagine anyone in that family will want to hold on to it,' added Elizabeth, picking up a cashew. 'Not after everything that happened there.'

Jim could feel his heart beating harder.

'Who do you think the house went to?'

Elizabeth gave a disinterested shrug. 'The wife?'

There was a moment's silence.

'You do know that Jennifer is married.'

Jennifer. He hadn't heard anyone – least of all his mother – say her name out loud since that far-off summer. He was amazed how unsettled it made him feel, even now.

He knew, of course. Every few months he would do a Google search on Jennifer Wyatt-Gilbert, usually calling up a picture of her at some benefit dinner or society party. So he knew she had married Connor Gilbert, her childhood sweetheart, and that they lived in New York. It no longer bothered him – well, not as much, anyway. Anyone could see Jennifer was leading the life she was destined to lead, and that was one without him in it.

'Yes,' he said, 'I know.'

'Then move on, James.' Elizabeth raised her eyebrows meaningfully as Melissa walked back into the room. 'It's high time, don't you think?'

Chapter Three

They stayed at the party as long as they could, making conversation with whatever writer, actor or architect they were introduced to next. Melissa threw herself into the throng, cosying up to Jill Jenkins, a firebrand old-school feminist, declaring herself a lifelong fan, although Jim had not been aware of her feminist credentials before. Early on in their relationship she had announced that she wanted to give up work the second she got married, and he couldn't remember her ever paying for dinner. He wasn't sure if this made her not a feminist, but he was sometimes confused when it came to women and what they wanted.

When Jim ventured back into the living room to say his goodbyes, Bryn was still holding court by the fireplace. He was in the middle of a heated discussion with a noted TV historian over the role of women in politics and barely noticed when Jim said they were leaving, merely giving him a distracted wave. Jim knew it shouldn't bother him: that was the way his father was – and besides, hadn't he wanted to slip away without fuss or a confrontation? But as always, being ignored, being dismissed so easily, was what cut the most.

Melissa slipped her hand into his as they walked down the quiet street away from the lights of the house. A cab passed them as they turned on to the main road, but Jim didn't raise an arm to stop it. He wanted to keep walking for a while; the numb of the cold on his skin felt good. The houses were even larger here, set back from the road, surrounded by walls and gardens. Was this what happened when you got rich? he wondered. You worked all those years and kissed all those arses and laughed at people's jokes just so you could cocoon yourself inside high walls, hidden and alone? Was that what it was all about? He took a deep breath and let it out in a white cloud.

'Sorry it wasn't much fun,' he said finally. 'That's what it's like when you get a literary crowd together, I'm afraid.'

'I thought it was great. All those brilliant people in one room. Your father, he's amazing, isn't he?'

Jim glanced at her, wondering if she was being ironic, but there was no smile.

'And it was good to see where you grew up,' she added, squeezing his hand a little tighter.

Jim laughed. 'My mum says she's turning my bedroom into a gym.'

'I had that a few months ago.' Melissa smiled back. 'My parents said they were having a clear-out, which is just a polite way of saying they're sick of being a storage facility for all my old stuff.'

'I guess it means we're grown-ups,' he said, feeling a pang of sadness.

'Is that a sign? Being handed all our records back?'

They walked on, their footsteps and the occasional whoosh of a passing car the only sounds.

'So who's Jennifer?' Her voice had a contrived lightness to it.

'Jennifer?'

Jim found himself unconsciously dropping her hand. He buttoned up his coat and started to quicken his pace a little.

'An old family friend.'

There was a pause.

'Just a friend?'

'Well, a sort of girlfriend, though barely. We were thrown together when we went to America one summer, years ago.'

Jim glanced to his side and realised Melissa had stopped walking. He turned, frowning.

'What's up?'

'A sort of girlfriend,' repeated Melissa, her voice hardening. 'I suppose that's how you describe me too.'

He cringed. So she *had* heard the conversation about marriage and babies.

'Mel,' he said, reaching out a hand for her, but she took a step back.

'Don't, Jim,' she said. 'We need to talk about this.'

'Here?' he said, casting an arm towards the road.

'Why not here? Why not now? You've been ducking the question every time I try to bring it up.'

Jim ran a hand through his hair. Clearly there was no getting out of it this time.

'We've been together almost a year,' she said. 'I'm thirty-five, you're almost forty, for God's sake. Are we supposed to carry on behaving like school kids, meeting once, twice a week? You get jumpy when I leave a bloody cardigan at your flat.'

He blew out his cheeks in irritation. 'And what did you have in mind?'

'Something! Anything!' cried Melissa, throwing her hands up. 'Cath moved in with Daniel before Christmas and she only started seeing him six months ago. Nikki's just had her first baby. All my friends are settling down.'

'So now we're keeping up with the Joneses?'

She looked at him, her gaze level: her 'don't screw with me' face.

'Do you know what I did on New Year's Eve, Jim? Do you?'

He sighed. 'You were at Suzanne's dinner party.'

'Wrong,' she hissed, her eyes sparkling with fury in the dark. 'I was on my own, watching some crappy repeat movie with a bottle of wine and a microwave meal for one.'

He frowned. 'But what about the dinner party?'

'There *was* no fucking dinner party.'

'Then why did you tell me there was?'

In the cool moonlight he could see spots of colour rising on her cheeks.

'All my friends were with someone that night – husbands, boyfriends, lovers. That's what you do on New Year's Eve when you love someone. I wasn't going to admit that my boyfriend didn't even want to see me.'

'I did want to see you, Mel. I was working – you knew what I did for a living when we first met. I happen to have a job that means I have to work on nights like that. You know how important Munroe is to me.'

She snorted angrily. 'Oh, I know how important your job is to you, believe me, but don't try to tell me I wasn't there because you weren't allowed to bring a partner.'

'I wasn't!' he cried in frustration.

'So why, when I talked to Annabel Miles at Christmas, did she tell me she was going to Munroe for Hogmanay?'

'Annabel was there because her husband is CEO of Omari. He wasn't working; he was drinking the champagne I had to carry in from the vans.'

Her tone softened. 'Jim, you know and I know that you could have invited me if you'd really wanted to. The fact is that you didn't want me there.'

'Mel, that's not true.'

'But it is, Jim. When it's me or your precious job, the job wins every time. And you know what? I've had enough of being second best. You're not a workaholic. You're just sad. A sad commitment-phobe with Peter Pan syndrome who needs to change his ways or he's going to end up very, very lonely.'

'Peter Pan syndrome?'

'They say Hitler had it.'

Jim laughed incredulously. 'Now you're comparing me to *Hitler*.'

'I'd actually feel sorry for you, Jim, if I wasn't starting to believe I'm wasting my time waiting for you to do something. Relationship, marriage. It's not the bogeyman; it's called growing up. I mean, look where we're just been. Your parents have been married, what, forty-five years, and I bet he's not the easiest man in the world to live with.'

'Two minutes ago you said he was amazing.'

She shook her head and looked back at him. 'Tell me, Jim. Is our relationship going anywhere?'

'I just need time.'

'Then look me in the eye and say that you love me.'

He closed his eyes and realised he couldn't.

He heard her footsteps walking away, getting quieter and quieter until he opened his eyes and called out, 'Melissa, wait!'

'I'm sick of waiting,' she shouted without even turning back.

He watched her figure recede into the distance. He could see the glowing sign of Hampstead tube just beyond, knew he could catch up with her, plead with her, bury her in a flurry of platitudes and promises. But she was right: he knew in his heart of hearts that he wouldn't – couldn't – keep any promises.

He closed his eyes, breathing cold air in and out, picturing the sun on the white stone of Casa D'Or, almost feeling himself back there: the warmth on his skin, the rush of excitement, of anticipation. And of love, true love. His mother had been right: he *had* been measuring every other woman against Jennifer. But as he watched Melissa turn the corner and disappear down the steps to the tube, he knew something else too: he knew he owed it to himself to feel something like that again. He had to try. And there was only one way he could do that. He had to go back to Casa D'Or. He had to get that house, that girl, out of his system.

Chapter Four

Jim slowed the car to a stop as he reached the imposing gates of the Wyatts' family home.

It had taken him a whole hour to get from his hotel in Savannah's historical district to the Isle of Hope, cursing himself for not taking the sat nav option at Hertz. He'd got lost in the city's one-way system, around its warren of park squares and side streets, almost running into the back of a horse-drawn carriage before he'd admitted defeat and asked a traffic warden how to go south. Even when he'd been put on the right highway, the traffic had been terrible, a stop-start hell past strips of nail bars and tyre change shops, until he'd turned off the Truman Parkway and time seemed to slow down again. The streets were wide and shady here, a world away from the grid of tightly packed elegant homes that typified the central historical district. Signs pointed to stables down dusty tracks; clapboard homes hid behind palm trees, picket fences and wide front lawns; and as the road crossed a sweep of freshwater marshland, Jim admired the vivid colours, the bulrushes, the sharp shade of a bowl of limes, against a sky that was a Caribbean blue.

Although he was already late, he turned off the engine and took a moment to think, a creeping sense of unease palpable as he looked up at the stone archway above him. Once scrubbed and honey-coloured, it was now mottled and wrapped in ivy, but he could still read the words 'Casa D'Or' chiselled into the centre.

It was over twenty years since he had last driven down this stretch of road, but he doubted a week had passed without him thinking about it. Casa D'Or was only a house, a collection of wood and brick and slate, but it had loomed so large in his life it had taken on an other-worldly feel, and now, as he glanced in the rear-view mirror of his hire car, his heart beating hard, the years falling away, he could almost see an unlined, hopeful face, hair stiffened by too much gel, his younger self who hadn't wanted to come here in the first place.

It had been Easter 1994 when it had been decided that the Johnson family were to decamp from leafy Hampstead to Savannah, Georgia. No one said as much, but it had been obvious to everyone that the radical change of scene was a last-ditch attempt to revitalise Bryn Johnson's career. His debut novel *All My Fathers*, a blistering polemic about class, sex and power, had been a huge hit, with the literary world hailing him as the voice of the zeitgeist. Riding the wave, lionised and preening, Bryn had taken three years to follow it up, and the resulting book had been self-indulgent and obscure. The literary elite of London and New York still fawned over him, but the public had moved on: sales were 'disappointing', and after diminishing interest for his third and fourth books, Bryn developed a writer's block that had lasted for almost a decade.

His New York agent, Saul Black, had decided something must be done and ordered Bryn to lock himself away and write. He found a small cottage with adjoining boathouse on an acquaintance's estate and bought them all one-way tickets. *Create something*, he had said, *or don't come back.*

Jim snapped back into the present and looked down the drive, an arrow-straight avenue of overhanging trees. Ninety-six live oaks. The Wyatts had always made a great deal of the fact that every one of the trees planted by the original owners of the Casa D'Or estate was still standing, lining the driveway, staring at visitors in silent witness. They had survived hurricane, disease and civil war and it seemed they had managed to survive the last twenty years too. Jim felt their imaginary gaze as he engaged 'drive' and slowly rolled down the unpaved road, swerving to dodge potholes and puddles. He peered up, looking at the wispy grey Spanish moss interlacing the overreaching branches and blocking out the sunlight. He felt as if he had fallen into the rabbit hole, and he wasn't sure if there was going to be a Wonderland at the other end.

As he approached the house, he stabbed a foot hard on the brake, skidding to a stop.

'Bloody hell,' he whispered, opening the door and stepping out.

The house was exactly as he had remembered it – tall windows, a wide terrace running front to back and a high gabled roof that spoke of grandeur, a desire to join a more elegant age – though when he looked closer, Jim could see it was in a fairly advanced state of disrepair. Tiles were missing from the roof, the once proud pillars were grey with bird excrement, the gardens hopelessly parched and overgrown. Even the front steps, once gleaming with their blue and white Italian tiles, were choked with unswept leaves and creeping weeds.

He walked towards it, gravel crunching underneath his feet. It was warm and balmy in Savannah compared with the cold grey winter that Jim had left behind in London, but still he shivered.

Casa D'Or represented the outer limits of his emotions: utter joy and crashing despair. Sometimes he had hated it, wished it had burnt to the ground that night, reduced to ash, but standing here now, he could see it for what it was: just a house, unique and beautiful. And someone had let it fall apart.

'Hello, James.'

He turned to see a tall woman walking towards him, a familiar smile on her face. Marion Wyatt, or Marion Wilson as she had been back then, when she had been Casa D'Or's housekeeper. He'd heard that she had married David Wyatt, her employer – inevitably there had been gossip. He supposed she must be early to mid-fifties: she was certainly still a beautiful woman, with alert dark eyes and smooth coffee-coloured skin. Perhaps a little heavier, and the gamine crop she had sported with such verve twenty years ago was now worn to her shoulders, but the cheekbones and the elegant bearing were still there. He could see how she had caught David's eye.

'Marion,' he grinned, offering a hand. 'So good to see you again. I didn't know you were here. Couldn't see a car.'

'Oh, I parked at the back, by the staff quarters,' she said. 'Old habits, even now.'

'Even though you're lady of the house.'

'I don't know about that.' She smiled as she touched him on the shoulder and led him into the house, where the temperature seemed to drop by twenty degrees.

The first thing that hit him was the smell, a cold, stagnant mustiness that reminded him of churches. The second was the sight of the wide sweeping staircase that dominated the wood-panelled hall. He found himself looking away, not wanting to think about that night, his last night in Georgia. He imagined Sylvia Wyatt's thin body lying on the polished walnut floor like a puppet with broken strings, then took a sharp inhalation of breath, forcing himself not to think about it.

'I thought we'd have lemonade on the terrace, if that suits?' said Marion.

He nodded, grateful to keeping moving and get out of the hall.

As he followed Marion, his eyes darted left, then right,

towards the library and the kitchen. Corners of the thick paisley wallpaper were peeling away from the plaster, the paintwork was cracked, but everything else remained exactly as he remembered it. He could see the black grand piano by the arched windows, pages of sheet music still on its stand; a cookery book open on the farmhouse table, gathering dust.

He knew he should be looking at the house with a developer's eye, working out how much work there was to do and how quickly it could be done, but it was impossible not to think about his last days there. The place looked as if it had been so hastily abandoned that the family had not even stopped to pick up their belongings.

He remembered that night so clearly. The sound of an urgent siren piercing the thick, swampy night air; running round the lake so fast he thought his heart would burst; then his memories dissolved into fragments of noise and images: the red light of the ambulance, the frantic, panicked conversation. Looking back, there hadn't been many people at the scene – Marion, her parents, Jennifer, and the paramedics, – but even now, despite the eerie stillness of the house, he could feel the sense of chaos and despair that had consumed them all.

'I know what you're thinking,' said Marion quietly. 'How did we let it get into this state?'

Jim forced his attention back to her, welcoming the distraction from his thoughts.

'Big properties are my stock in trade. I know how high-maintenance they can be. Unless you have the staff and finance to maintain them on a day-by-day basis, all it takes is one bird's nest in the wrong place, or a split pipe, and it's a downward spiral.' He stopped in his tracks as they reached the back of the house. 'But wow, the view, that view is still amazing.'

For all the grandeur of Casa D'Or's architecture, the terrace had always been its show-stopper. Sweeping and elegant, it faced green lawns that ran down to a forty-acre expanse of water, known as Sunset Lake on account of the early evening light that transformed it, most days, into a pool of liquid copper.

There was a single wrought-iron café table set up under an umbrella, a jug of lemonade beading with condensation. Jim took a glass gratefully and settled into a wicker chair with a creak. Across the lake he could see the boathouse where his father used to work, the cottage where they'd all lived for two long, heady months.

'I was sorry to hear about David.'

'I bet you never expected that, did you?'

'David's passing?'

'No, the fact that I married him.'

Jim shrugged, spread his hands in a 'none of my business' gesture, but he could see Marion was waiting for some sort of response.

'I'm not surprised, no. After that summer, I can see that anyone would need . . .'

'Comfort?'

'I guess so.'

She nodded and looked out over the water.

'After Sylvia died, David went to Charleston. He told us it was to be nearer to work, but we knew he didn't want to be in the house. We were all so worried about him, especially when we didn't see him for three months. When Christmas came around, I hated to think of him on his own, so I went to Charleston with a turkey, determined to cook for him. I only went for an hour or two. I never left.'

'And you never came back here?'

Marion shook her head. 'David used to say, "We'll go back soon." But soon never came. There were too many ghosts. Too many memories. Besides, I think we were both happy to have a fresh start.'

'What about Jennifer?' He was almost afraid to ask.

'She went to New York not long after the funeral.'

'With Connor?'

She nodded. 'Her father had become a recluse. She was lost, bereft, and Connor was there.'

She paused and looked at him more directly.

'So you became a hotshot.' It was said with a note of surprise, and he didn't blame her. He doubted that he would have been anybody's pick for most likely to succeed. Not compared to Connor.

'I work for Omari Hotels. I'm their global investment and project manager.'

'I know, I read your sales pitch.'

Jim sipped his lemonade and seized the opportunity to keep this as professional as possible.

'My boss, Simon Desai, saw Casa D'Or and thought it would be a perfect addition to the Omari portfolio.'

Marion put down her glass, the ice cubes clinking.

'Don't talk about it like a business asset, Jimmy,' she said. 'You know Casa D'Or is more than that. This house has been the Wyatt family home for nearly seventy years. The thought of getting rid of it makes me want to cry.'

'So is it for sale?'

She glanced at him, then sighed. 'I didn't bring you here to play games. Of course it's for sale, although I'll be honest with you, Jim. I don't feel comfortable doing it. You can imagine the whispers about me when David and I got married. People called me a gold-digger, a whore. Part of me thinks that if I sell now, I'm just confirming everything those people believed was true.'

'So you were the sole beneficiary?' He chose his words carefully.

Marion nodded. 'Jennifer didn't want the house. She always made that clear. Not after what happened. And what do I need a place this size for? If I don't do something soon, it's going to fall down of its own accord. David would have understood that, even though he could never quite instruct the realtors himself.'

'Why didn't he?'

Marion gave a low, soft laugh. 'You know there were an awful lot of good memories that happened in this place, not just that one tragedy.'

'How is she?' he asked, trying to keep his voice as level and casual as possible. Marion responded with a soft smile.

'I wondered when you were going to ask. She's still in New York.'

'Does she still sail?'

'Not sure Manhattan's quite as good for sailing as Georgia.'

He looked out at the water. A shame, he thought. She really had loved that boat.

'Are you ever in New York?' said Marion, breaking into his thoughts.

'Quite a lot, actually.'

Marion laughed. 'I miss that word, "actually". You never hear it around here.'

'That's what Jennifer used to say.'

'You should look her up. She's on the Upper East Side. 61st Street, I think. I'll give you the address.'

He nodded politely, knowing he would do nothing of the sort.

'Promise me you'll look after her,' said Marion after a moment.

'Who?' replied Jim, awkwardly.

'The house, of course,' she said, her eyes trailing over the water. 'She has such a dark history. Not just what happened here that summer. But the past. I'll never forget the stories my father used to tell me about the plantation, and how the original owners of this place got so wealthy. Dozens of slaves used to live here, harvesting the fields, working the cotton gins. And since the Georgian landowners couldn't get the workforce from Africa, not legally anyway, they used to smuggle them in, up the creeks all around here.'

She paused and looked at Jim directly.

'Sometimes I think Casa D'Or deserves to fade away. But David was right when he said there were golden times too.' A tear glistened in the corner of her eye.

'So you'll sell?' ventured Jim carefully.

'Yes,' she said, standing up and taking a long look at the house. 'Sometimes you have to know when it's time to let go, no matter how much you love something. Have you ever felt that?'

Jim smiled. But he wasn't at all sure he had. Not yet, anyway.

Chapter Five

Jim stared at Casa D'Or, unfurled on the table in front of him. Only it wasn't Casa D'Or, not any more.

'Thierry, this is an amazing job. Really, truly amazing. I love every inch of it,' he said warmly, looking up into the eyes of the elderly Frenchman.

'They're only plans at the moment, my friend,' Thierry said, smiling. 'I am still struggling with the structure: she was built as a private house, not a hotel, but we will overcome. And yes, I think she will be *trop belle* when we are finished.'

Jim knew it was an understatement. Thierry Dupont was one of the most in-demand architects in the business. At seventy, he was semi-retired but had agreed to the Casa D'Or project as a favour to Jim.

'Now you do know we have a tight schedule on this?'

Thierry gave a Gallic shrug. 'We always need more time, no? But this house has good bones, structurally it is sound.

And with the outbuildings, I think we can extend your room capacity.'

Jim fixed his eyes on the computer screen as Thierry moved his mouse around, slowly spinning a 3D computer image of the house. The picture was only made up of blue lines, the walls and roof transparent, but it was still wonderfully evocative. Jim could see exactly how Thierry was planning on dividing up the existing rooms; he could even zoom inside the entrance hall, giving an idea of how the space would look and feel. This was the part of his job he enjoyed the most. He supposed it was the creative part of him being exercised, the part he'd always thought he'd use for composing songs or writing books. Instead he was here in his New York office, breathing life into an idea, creating a space people could actually move through, a place they could live in. There was a satisfying and creative value in that.

'Thierry, this looks great. Seriously.'

The Frenchman gave an ironic bow. 'I aim to please.'

Jim stared at the image of the entrance, picturing how it had looked all those years ago – and for some reason, all he saw was Sylvia Wyatt, the lady of the house, standing by the fireplace, a look of distaste on her face. Yes, the Johnsons had been the poor neighbours – literally – and Sylvia had always made it clear she didn't think they were good enough for her social circle. At the few parties they had attended, even his father, the great author, had been viewed by Sylvia and her wealthy friends as an object of curious interest, but not quite respect. If Sylvia Wyatt were still alive today, he wondered what she would think of him now. Jim Johnson, CEO of Omari Hotels – or he would be if Casa D'Or was ready for guests by Thanksgiving.

Thierry closed the laptop and rolled the plans into a tube.

'Now, how would you like to take an old man for a drink?'

Jim clapped him on the shoulder and gave it a squeeze.

'I'd love to, but I haven't even unpacked yet. If I don't get back and turn the heating on, I swear the front door will be iced shut when I get there.'

Thierry chuckled. 'I can't believe you've finally moved to New York. I thought you were too much of a diehard Brit to ever leave.'

'It's a temporary thing, Thierry, just until the project is done.'

The Frenchman nodded, but Jim saw a twinkle in his eye that said he didn't quite believe it.

'Thanks again, Thierry. I think Casa D'Or is going to be your best yet,' he said as they walked towards the lift.

'Oh, no doubt about that,' said Thierry, tapping the rolled plans against Jim's chest. 'When a seed is planted with passion, the fruit is always the sweetest.'

The lift doors closed and Jim let out a long breath. He glanced at the clock above the reception desk and realised that their meeting had dragged on for three hours: everyone else had gone home. He walked back to his office, still quietly pleased by its size and grandeur, even though he knew it was all relative. Omari's Manhattan outpost was tiny compared to the London office, taking up just a single floor of the Commodore Tower on 57th, but still Jim loved it. Here at least he was solely in charge, the master of his own destiny, which was exactly how he liked it. Here he could show Simon just how good he was, with no one questioning his decisions or taking credit. Plus he had an amazing corner office with uninterrupted views along Lexington and across to Park. At night, from the twenty-fifth floor, the ebb and flow of the neon traffic far below was mesmerising.

For a moment, he thought of calling Melissa, or at least sending her a text, checking she was all right. He looked down at the street below and shook his head. No, Melissa had been right that night, and it wasn't fair to either of them to prolong it. She'd been half right about something else too. She'd overstepped the mark when she'd suggested that he needed to change, but perhaps he needed *a* change.

He'd been apprehensive about coming to New York. There had been a moment at Heathrow when he'd almost turned back, but he was a grown-up, not the Peter Pan figure Melissa had suggested, and he knew he could handle the Casa D'Or project and whatever emotions it threw up. He had another theory too, that moving away from London, facing the demons of his past, could only help him move forward.

He poured himself an espresso from the machine in the corner and sank down in his ergonomic office chair, tapping casually through his emails: nothing that couldn't wait, messages from colleagues in the London office. Right now he just wanted to grab some Korean takeout – it never got old just how good the to-go food was in New York – and head back to his neglected flat to watch the football. But just then a new email popped into his inbox.

> Re: NetworkMe request from Jennifer Wyatt-Gilbert
> Do you know Jennifer Wyatt-Gilbert? She would like to link with you . . .

It was a standard introduction email from a networking site Jim subscribed to, but this was anything but standard. It was from Jennifer, from *her*. Remembering to breathe, he read and reread the bland form letter, but of course there was nothing personal there except for her name. There was a link button to the right, and Jim hovered over it for a moment. All he had to do was click; what harm could it do? She was just being polite after all, personally acknowledging the letter he'd sent her several weeks earlier.

Jim had written to Jennifer as soon as Marion had agreed to the sale of Casa D'Or. Marion owned the property outright, but Jim wanted the transaction to go through without any hitches, and ultimately he'd decided that it was only right to ask Jennifer's permission to buy the house.

He'd tortured himself for hours with what words to use, drafting and deleting dozens of versions. In the end he'd kept it crisp and to the point, formal and professional. Perhaps too formal. He'd spent so much time on it, he could still remember the final line: *Please advise if you are happy for me to proceed with the acquisition.*

Cold, impersonal words to a girl – a woman – he had once believed his soulmate.

Stupid, he thought, steeling himself. Well, the least he could do was approve her request. He clicked the link button and sat back and took a sip of his coffee.

The mail icon on his desktop flashed red to indicate another incoming message. He jumped forward in his chair.

NetworkMe message: from Jennifer Wyatt-Gilbert
How are you? I hear you're in New York. How are you getting on with Casa D'Or? I know you'll look after her. Jen

Jim felt his body jolt, as if his heart had been wired to a defibrillator and the voltage had just been switched on. He looked at the message knowing he had to respond. There was no way he couldn't, not when he knew she was on the other end of this invisible cyberspace line.

Just looking at the plans now. I think you'd be impressed.
Return message: I'd love to see them.

He rubbed his mouth in hesitation, then tipped back the rest of his espresso to fortify himself.

You should swing by the office.
Where are you based?
57 and Lexington. The Commodore building.
You're round the corner!

Where are you?

Bloomingdale's.

Is that your registered address?

I try to split my time between here and Bergdorf's.

He pushed his shirtsleeves up, sat back in his chair and felt a broad grin creep across his face, followed by a stab of panic.

They still hadn't lost it. The connection, the crackle. He leaned forward and began to type the words that felt natural to write.

Are you free now?

But as his forefinger pressed the send button, it was as if a cold slap of air had sobered him up.

'Shit,' he muttered out loud as the email was fired off into cyberspace. What was he doing? He had opened his heart once before and had it crushed like a tin can under the wheels of a lorry.

There was a minute of excruciating silence before the reassuring ping of another incoming message.

I can be there in ten minutes.

Jim gulped hard, then stared at the screen, seeing his own shadowy reflection in the bright desktop blue.

The office was empty and he felt alone and vulnerable. It was a sensation that gave him a considerable amount of disquiet. Until about two minutes earlier, Jim Johnson had thought he was doing OK. On the cusp of forty, he had all his own hair and could still fit into the same 32-inch jeans he wore in his twenties. He was popular with the opposite sex; even supermodels found him attractive, if New Year's Eve was anything to go by.

A long-forgotten quote popped into his head, something he'd perhaps heard in a school assembly or a church service: *When I became a man, I put away childish things*. Over the past twenty years he had certainly succeeded in that aim. He'd put to bed any silly ideas of being a rock star – he was never going to be the new Thom Yorke or John Lennon – and instead got a proper job. One that was interesting and satisfying, one that paid him a good salary and had genuine prospects and a pension, or so he liked to remind himself in the dark moments when he wondered whether he had made the right life choices.

And he'd moved on from Jennifer Wyatt, although for the longest time that had been easier said than done.

His phone rang and shook him from his thoughts. It was Brad from security.

'Mr Johnson. There's a visitor downstairs for you. Says you're expecting her. Should I send her up?'

'Yes,' he replied, his voice a low and anxious croak, as he braced himself to see her once again.

Chapter Six

'Hello, Jim.'

The lift doors opened and Jennifer stepped out. She hadn't changed a bit. Her hair still shone a glossy chestnut, but it was shorter, a long bob that sat on the shoulders of her expensively tailored coat. There were a few lines around her clear grey eyes and a tiny furrow between her brows, but she was still beautiful, the coltish good looks he remembered matured into something more elegant and spectacular. A distant, forgotten longing stirred, and instantly Jim knew it had been a bad idea emailing her.

'Sorry, hi!' he said enthusiastically, stepping forward. He had meant to give her a confident kiss on the cheek, but panicked at the last moment, thrusting his hand out for a weak handshake before stepping back and taking another moment to observe her. The grey coat was definitely designer, as were the high-heeled shoes, the sort that looked as if they never even hit the pavement. Typically, his one Savile Row suit, the one he had worn for his first couple of days at work, was at the dry cleaner's. The high-street substitute he was wearing today felt cheap and unsuccessful compared to Jennifer's highly groomed and polished look, although he might have been naked given how exposed he felt standing there before her.

'Marion told me you were moving to New York. I was wondering if you were here yet. I saw your profile on NetworkMe . . .'

He wondered if she had looked him up on purpose; he doubted their circles crossed in any other way. The idea gave him a spike of confidence.

'I got your letter. Well, your lawyer's letter. The permission for Casa D'Or. Thank you, it meant a lot,' he said crisply.

'Connor thought I should send something official. Legal.'

'Of course,' said Jim, holding one hand up magnanimously.

Silence rang around the dark, empty office.

'How are you, Jim?' she asked, rubbing her fingers with the thumb of her other hand, twisting her rings, almost as if she were trying to get them off. She was definitely nervous. Jim wished the sight of it would give him some pleasure, but any victory felt hollow as they stood there awkwardly.

'Good, fine,' he said quickly. *Recovered*, he wanted to tell her, searching around for the lines he'd rehearsed all those years ago, the words he would say to her if they ever met again, the things he'd written in the letters that never got sent.

'So, the plans,' she said more brightly. 'I can't wait to see them.'

'Actually, I've got a confession to make.'

'Oh yes?'

'My architect has just taken them. But he can't be far. I can call him, get him to come back . . .'

'Don't do that. You're just going to have to describe them to me yourself.'

'It's going to be awesome,' replied Jim, running his hand through his dark hair.

'Awesome? You've acclimatised already.'

They both gave a little laugh – she still had that beautiful laugh – and Jim felt some of the tension dissolve.

'This is an impressive building,' she said finally. 'I bet you have the corner office too.'

'I do, actually. I've only been here a week, so it's still a novelty. I'd show you round, but there's not much to see.'

'Not in the dark.'

'I know.' He smiled awkwardly, realising that the only light on the entire floor came from his desk lamp. 'Everyone's gone home.'

She didn't say anything for a few moments.

'Well, if you're closing up for the night, we could go for a quick drink. I saw a bar on the corner . . .'

Jim knew the place she meant. A hole in the wall, not her sort of thing at all, but he knew it was better than staying here.

'A drink. Why not?'

Jim grabbed his coat and followed Jennifer back to the elevator before she had a chance to change her mind. The Greek chorus in his head was going mad. 'Don't!' it sang theatrically, but he forced himself to ignore it.

The walk to the bar was short and brisk: New York in March was still shockingly cold, the wind cutting through his London coat with ease. They made a little small talk. He commiserated about her father's death. She admitted that it had been tough, even though they only saw each other a handful of times a year.

It was a typical sports bar, dark except for the glow of a TV above the pool table. The faint scent of beer made it smell sour.

'You know, I should apologise,' said Jim as they found a booth and gave the waitress their order.

'What for?' she asked, slipping off her coat.

'The letter I sent you about Casa D'Or. It was a bit formal.'

'I was just as bad.' She smiled sadly.

'Yes, you were.'

'It was business.'

'Yes, it was,' said Jim, determined to keep his poise.

The waitress returned with their drinks: a bottle of beer for Jim and a glass of white wine for Jennifer.

'I've stayed in a couple of Omari hotels before,' she said finally. 'I had no idea you worked for them. What happened to wanting to be a musician?'

'That was never going to happen. Besides, I like what I do now.'

'Which is what?'

'I buy and develop properties for the Omari group. Not quite pushed through to the board yet, but I'm getting there,' he said, sitting straighter in his seat.

'How long have you been doing that?'

'Fifteen years. I put in a couple of years at J. P. Morgan first. Joined Omari just as Simon Desai was looking to expand his Indian hotels into a global chain.'

'You were in *banking*?' she said, raising one eyebrow.

'Yes,' he said defensively.

There was a moment's silence.

'What?' he asked quickly.

She smiled slowly and looked down at the table. 'I don't know. I didn't think that's the way you'd go.'

'Where did you think I'd go?' he said. Her last words to him were ringing in his head as if they'd been spoken yesterday: *Just go back to England, Jim*. It was an instant dampener on his mood. When he thought about how she'd ended their relationship, he felt as sick and mugged as he had done twenty years earlier.

He'd been willing to give up everything for Jennifer Wyatt – his family, his friends, his life in England – but when it came to the crunch, she had only ever been having fun, playing with his emotions. For weeks afterwards he'd tortured himself with thoughts of what might have happened if Sylvia Wyatt hadn't died that night, but the truth was that Jennifer had already made her decision. She'd picked money and prospects over whatever it was Jim Johnson could or could not offer.

He'd returned to England, summer had faded into autumn, and although he'd felt wretched, he had returned to UCL for his final year, swearing off women, the Students' Union, anything remotely resembling fun. He had found a strange and reassuring solace in work, and nine months later, in possession of a high 2:1 degree, all that hurt, yearning and rejection morphed into pure ambition. He won an entry-level position at one of the City's top banks, and was never going to be rebuffed again.

'I travel the world, I get to stay in fantastic hotels, play golf, go skiing, try out minibars – all in the name of work,' he said expansively as he traced her expression for any sign of guilt or regret.

'It's worked out well for you,' she said softly.

'So far, so good,' he said, swirling the beer around the bottle. 'What about you?' he added, looking at her more directly.

She gave a gentle laugh.

'What?' said Jim kindly.

'Nothing,' she said with a wave of her hand. 'It's just a forty thing. Wondering what I've done with my life, what I'm going to do with my life . . .'

Jim wanted to tell her that from this angle it looked as if she had done pretty well for herself. Of course he'd Googled the address that Marion Wyatt had given him, Street Viewed it in fact. He had worked in property long enough to recognise twenty million dollars' worth of real estate when he saw it.

'Forty is the new twenty-five. Look at me, moving to New York.'

'You were always going to be brilliant,' she said, not taking her eyes off his.

'And so are you. You have a degree from Wellesley, you're

super-connected, and you're one of the smartest people I know, not to mention having the best taste on the whole of the East Coast.'

'I should hire you as my PR.'

'No, *I* should hire *you.*' He realised he was only half joking, and a knowing dart passed between them.

'And how is Connor?'

He watched her flush. She had such pale skin, any colour in her cheeks was obvious.

'He's good.'

'Still in finance?'

'Property, funnily enough. Maybe you two should get together.'

Jim didn't say anything. He'd always disliked Connor Gilbert, and not just because he had been Jennifer's boyfriend. He was arrogant and cocky, seemed to imagine himself at the centre of the universe – that appeared to be the standard personality type in Georgian society circles back then – but there was something else about Connor he didn't like, something he couldn't quite put his finger on.

'How long have you been married now?'

She pressed her hands together. 'Eighteen years.'

'In New York that's sort of like a golden anniversary, isn't it?'

'You're thinking of Hollywood.'

'What about kids? I bet you've got a whole brood of them.'

Jennifer finished off her wine, which he noticed she'd drunk very quickly.

'No. But I have a dog,' she said more playfully.

Jim detected a hint of sadness in her casual remark and decided not to pursue it. He'd once sat next to a former girlfriend at a dinner party and over the cheese and quince course she had shared the horrors of her IVF experiences with him, presumably from the comfort of her position as a mother of three children, perhaps to make him feel a little bit guilty that she had wasted eighteen months of her early thirties trying to get him to commit before she had finally moved on and married an accountant called Colin.

'I don't even have dogs,' he grinned, trying to lighten the mood.

She glanced down at his left hand. 'So is there a Mrs Jim Johnson?'

'Apparently I'm married to my job.'

'Did you come over with anyone?'

'An excellent relocation service.'

'A girlfriend, partner?' She was definitely fishing for personal information.

'I'm single, actually. There was someone, recently. It didn't work out. So if you know anyone . . .' He laughed a little too enthusiastically.

'Yes, I do know someone,' she said quickly. 'I should set you up . . .'

'I was joking.'

She pulled her phone from her bag and studied the screen.

'What?'

'Nothing. But I should probably go.'

'We've just sat down.'

'You were on your way home,' she said, waving her hand. He liked her nail polish. Dark pink. Sexy, but not obviously so. He'd always liked that about her. 'I'll get the bill,' she added with more conviction.

Jim felt a wave of panic. He didn't want her to go. There were so many things he wanted to say, so many questions he wanted to ask, but once she stood up and walked out of the bar, there was a strong chance he would never see her again. After all, they'd discussed Casa D'Or, and in a city of ten million people, what were the chances of them bumping into each other?

'So who is she?' he said, groping around the silence.

'Who?'

'The friend you were going to set me up with.'

'She's called Sarah. British. Works at Whizzfeed, the website.'

'What's she like?'

'You mean is she hot?' smiled Jennifer, looking at him from under her long lashes.

'I'm nothing if not predictable,' he laughed, knowing it was both a terrible and yet brilliant idea. If he was to date Jennifer's friend, there would be parties, double dates, invitations to the Hamptons; he'd be with another woman, sure, but he'd also be with her.

Yes, he had to push on with this idea, as ridiculous as it sounded.

'You'll like her,' said Jennifer, after a moment. 'She's fun.

Give me your number and I'll set it up,' she added as she left a twenty-dollar bill on a silver tray.

He followed her out, up the iron steps back on to the street. A few spots of rain fell from the sky, and she pulled her collar up around her neck. Soon she would be home. Connor would be waiting. He imagined a couple of little yappy dogs jumping up at the door as she came in.

'Where do you live?' she asked, giving him a slow, rueful smile.

'I've got a flat in the West Village.'

'A flat?'

'OK, apartment. In fact, back home we'd call it a bedsit. I'd heard Manhattan houses were small, but there is literally about a foot either side of my bed.'

'I'm heading the other way . . .'

'Let me call you a cab,' he said, stepping into the street and raising his arm to call a taxi to a stop.

She turned to face him, pulling her coat a little tighter across her chest. Jim couldn't help noticing how the soft grey of the wool was exactly the same shade as her eyes. And in that moment, he was blind to everything else around him.

'It's been really good to see you, Jim,' she said softly as she opened the door and climbed in. 'We should do it again.'

'We could meet for breakfast or something,' he said, wondering if she had been feeling any of the emotions he'd been experiencing over the last hour.

'Breakfast?' she said wryly.

'Power breakfast. Isn't that what New Yorkers do?'

'Maybe back in the eighties,' she laughed as the taxi door slammed shut.

'Lunch, then,' he said, knocking on the window, hoping that she could hear him.

She nodded and smiled, a big, wide-open smile, and he wasn't sure if it was spots of rain on the window or whether her eyes had a sparkle.

As the taxi moved off into traffic, he stood and watched until she disappeared from sight, knowing in a closed-off corner of his heart that he had just unlocked a Pandora's box that should never have been opened.

Chapter Seven

1994

The taxi stopped outside the white pillars of Casa D'Or and the driver took a minute to stare up at its grandeur.

'Great place,' he whistled through his teeth, turning off the engine and getting out for a closer look. 'Is this a hotel or something?'

'It's a house,' said Jennifer, fumbling around in her purse for a twenty-dollar bill, feeling a suddenly flurry of nerves.

She stepped out of the taxi and waited on the front steps as the driver popped the trunk and lugged out her two heavy suitcases.

'You have a nice day now,' he grinned as she pushed the money into his palm, adding an extra five dollars. Taxis expected a good tip when they turned up at Casa D'Or.

Jennifer released a small sigh as her own gaze locked on the house, its tall white pillars and seven chimneys that stretched into the cloudless blue sky. As she inhaled slowly, the smell of the glorious gardens just feet away from her filled her lungs, the scent of antique roses and delphiniums as sweet as it was heady.

'Home sweet home,' she whispered, but as she closed her eyes, a knot of anxiety tightened in her belly.

Catching a plane to Savannah had seemed such a good idea twenty-four hours earlier. She'd had enough of New York: the city, the Hamptons, where she'd spent a weekend squashed into a three-bedroom beachfront cottage with fourteen other girls. It had not been the summer idyll she had imagined, the one that had been sold to her by her college room-mate, Amanda. Instead Manhattan had been hot and hectic, and Long Island had been no better.

She'd been lying on her camp bed, trying to ignore the smell of weed, the music and the screams of her friends flirting with the boys from the house next door, when she'd had the radical thought that she didn't need to stay there.

A standby ticket had cost her two hundred bucks, the flight had taken just a couple of hours, and the noise and pace of the metropolis had been left behind her for the more simple life she'd never even known she craved. If only it was that easy, she thought, pushing her key into the lock and walking into the grand wood-panelled hall.

Her mother was coming down the sweeping staircase that took centre-stage in the entrance at the exact moment of her arrival.

'Jennifer. What on earth . . . ?' said Sylvia Wyatt, her

delicate features betraying no sign of disbelief except for a slight widening of her eyes.

'Surprise,' grinned Jennifer, dropping her suitcases on the walnut floor, hoping to raise some reaction from her mother. She did not expect an embrace – her mother had never been anything other than brittle and cool – but as Sylvia Wyatt stood motionless at the bottom of her stairs, back straight, one hand resting on the curve of the banister, even Jennifer was surprised at the coldness of her response. If she was glad to see her recently graduated daughter back from college and the city, she certainly didn't look it.

'You were supposed to be in New York till the twentieth,' she said crisply, her eyes noting the two suitcases by Jennifer's feet.

'I know. I just thought, why be there when I could be here . . .'

'You could have let us know.'

'It was a spur-of-the-moment decision,' said Jennifer, feeling herself curl under the heat of the late Southern afternoon and her mother's expression of being inconvenienced.

'Your father will be pleased to see you,' Sylvia replied finally.

'Is he home?'

'Just now. He's on the terrace.'

Jennifer felt her spirits perk up. She ran through the house, past the dining room, the kitchen and the sun-filled solarium, and saw the familiar figure of her father standing on the back terrace overlooking the lake.

He turned and saw her, and his face broke into a grin and he held his arms open for her to run into.

'What's this?' he laughed as they gave each other a tight hug.

'I'm back.'

'So I see,' he said, pulling away and throwing his arm around her shoulder. 'What is it? A flying visit? How long have we got you for? You know, I think we have some celebration cake left over from the Fourth of July. Sylvia, find Marion. See what treats we have for our daughter.'

'I missed you,' said Jennifer honestly, perching on a chair.

'You mean Connor's back from the Caribbean,' he winked, taking off his panama hat.

Her boyfriend had spent the past three weeks sailing around the British Virgin Islands. It was pretty much Jennifer's dream vacation – sailing was what had bonded her and Connor in the first place – but it was to be a boys' trip after his graduation from Harvard, and she had not been invited.

'Yes, he got back a couple of days ago, but that's not why I'm here.'

'You can admit it,' scoffed her father. 'These are your glory days.'

'What glory days?'

'Love, romance.'

'I can't believe I'm discussing relationships with my dad,' she grinned, enjoying the gentle teasing from her father. David Wyatt had been a fairly absent figure during her childhood; his job – heading up a collection of businesses including a paper mill and a food packaging company – meant that he left the house early and worked late. But when he was at Casa D'Or, his very presence warmed the house like a log fire.

'So how's work? The gallery?'

Jennifer did not want to have this discussion, not yet, and was grateful to hear the distracting sounds of a tray behind them. She looked up as Marion, their housekeeper, put an assortment of cold drinks, along with a plate of cookies and muffins, on the table.

'I just pulled a few bits and pieces together,' she said, smiling warmly.

'Thanks. You didn't need to,' said Jennifer, enjoying the sound of Marion's syrupy Southern accent. The sound of home.

Her eyes drifted across the lake to the house on the other shore. It was a smaller property than Casa D'Or, with a jetty and a boathouse that jutted out into the water. There were two types of homeowner in Savannah: families like the Wyatts who lived in the city all year round, and others for whom the area was just a temporary home, a pit stop to escape the winter months and cold, snowy weather of the north. The Lake House belonged to one of the latter, the Sittenfields, a New York family whom the locals referred to as the snow birds, on account of their seasonal migration.

'Is someone staying at the Sittenfields' house? I think there's someone in the boathouse,' she said, squinting through the heat shimmering over the water.

'Old habits die hard,' replied her father. When she was a

kid, the neighbours used to give her a fistful of dollars for watching the house over the summer. She'd treated her responsibility very seriously and taken up her sentry point on the pontoon, with a good book and a soda for company.

'Yes. Some family from England,' he said as her mother appeared on the terrace.

Sylvia looked different from a few minutes earlier, as if she had brushed her hair and refastened the cream silk scarf that was tied around her neck.

'Are we talking about the people in the Lake House?' she said as she took a chair under the shade of the parasol.

'Who are they?' asked Jennifer, taking a welcome sip of iced tea.

'You can find out later,' replied David. 'I met them yesterday and invited them round.'

'Invited them round?' asked Sylvia, looking alarmed. 'When?'

'Tonight. Just for drinks,' said David casually. 'He's a writer, here with his wife. There's a son, too, about your age, Jen.'

'It's Jennifer's first night home . . .'

'I didn't know that,' snorted David.

'You should have asked me before inviting strangers over.' Sylvia was making her displeasure obvious.

'Then why don't we make it sociable? Get Connor to come too, his parents. Have a little drinks party. A welcome home for our daughter.'

Sylvia gave a sigh but looked mollified at the suggestion

of expanding the event, although Jennifer could think of nothing worse. In fact she knew that the shit was going to hit the fan.

She went upstairs to her room at the back of the house. Nothing had changed in the three months since she had last visited home. The window seat was still lined with the assortment of cuddly toys from her childhood that she had never been able to throw out. A pile of books sat by her bed where she had left them; some loose revision notes were still on her desk, along with an exam timetable and a handful of pens stuffed into an old jam jar. She remembered how anxious she'd been, about to return to college for her final semester, but looking back, she couldn't understand what she'd been so worried about. They'd been simpler times. Much simpler, she thought, unpacking her case and putting her clothes in neat piles on the candy-striped duvet: the smart black skirts, the silk blouses, the clear-lensed black-framed glasses. The art gallerist's wardrobe she would no longer be needing.

She showered, dried her short brown hair and changed into her favourite gingham sundress, then picked up the phone to call Connor. There was no escaping the conversation, not when her mother had already called his parents and invited them round. She rehearsed some dialogue in her head as her hand cradled the receiver, disturbed only by a deep baritone, smooth, well-spoken, British, from the hall.

She frowned as the voice called again.

'Hello. Is anyone there?'

She could not hear any footsteps coming to greet their caller, so she went downstairs and saw three people collected in the hall. An older but attractive man, notable by his sheer size – at least six foot three tall, and broad, extending his hand as Jennifer reached the bottom of the stairs.

'Bryn Johnson. My wife Elizabeth and son James. Your father's expecting us. The door was open.'

He had a bullish confidence, but he was the sort of man who could get away with it. Jennifer thought her mother would dislike him on sight.

'Yes, of course. You're at the Lake House. It's nice to meet you. Come through,' she replied, guiding them to the back of the house.

The terrace had been transformed, as if someone had waved a magic wand since she had last been here an hour earlier. The garden lights had been turned on so that cones of soft yellow twinkled across the lawns. The table had been set with a starched white tablecloth and the best cutlery. A huge vase of creamy hydrangeas sat proudly in the middle, alongside two softly glowing hurricane lanterns. She knew their guests would be impressed, although for her mother this was little more than a picnic.

'Bryn. Good to see you again,' said David, hurrying to greet them. 'How's the writing going?'

The group made polite conversation that largely consisted of David telling the Johnsons about the history of the house. How it had been in the Wyatt family since the 1940s although it had been built a hundred years before that, when a wealthy family from Pennsylvania came to exploit the rich farmland and the legalised slavery in Georgia. The plantation had over two thousand acres of land in those days, with peach orchards, pecan groves, and fields of rice and cotton that stretched for miles around, although the Wyatts only owned two hundred acres now.

'Do you still have the peach orchards?' asked Elizabeth Johnson, almost swooning.

'Not any more,' said David, shaking his head. 'Most of the farming crops are gone, but we've got the woods, the paddocks and the swamps. The tidal creek over there runs into the Wilmington. And you've seen the lake.'

Jennifer glanced at her watch. The Gilberts had said they would be here at eight; it was close to that now. To distract herself, she listened to Bryn Johnson wax lyrical about his writing career.

'I consider myself to be in exile,' he said expansively, eager to insert his own narrative into the conversation. 'All the greats did it. Hemingway, Fitzgerald, Neruda, although the only thing we're escaping from is the British weather,' he added with a rich laugh.

'How are you enjoying Savannah?' said Jennifer, turning to the son.

'We've only just got here,' he said with a casual shrug of the shoulders.

'Jim would rather be bar-hopping with friends around Europe round now,' interrupted Bryn.

'Interrailing,' corrected Jim Johnson.

Bryn scoffed. 'I love the way young people make it sound like a cultural endeavour, when really all they want is to score cheap girls and cheaper booze in the sunshine.'

'Savannah might not be Europe, but it has its own charms,' smiled David, noticing the younger man scowl.

Marion brought drinks and canapés on to the terrace and the group made small talk. The sun was beginning to set, turning the lake a glorious liquid bronze and daubing the back of the house in the soft golden light that had inspired its name.

Her parents drifted down the lawn to show Bryn and Elizabeth their prize azaleas, leaving Jennifer alone with Jim Johnson. She took a few moments to observe him. The younger man was less obviously handsome than his father. His mouth had a slight downturned moodiness. His hair was a couple of shades lighter than Bryn's jet-black crown; a long fringe fell fashionably to one side of his face. There was stubble on his chin and his hands were thrust in the pockets of his jeans as he slouched in his chair. She'd seen these sorts of boys before at college, the tortured artists who lured girls into bed with promises of poems and song lyrics in their honour but rarely delivered anything beyond unreliability and eventual heartbreak.

'So you don't want to be here?' she said, trying to make conversation but suspecting it might be tricky.

'Not really,' he said sullenly.

'Have you ever been to Greece?'

'No. Have you?'

'I did a tour of Europe the summer before college,' she nodded.

'Of course you did,' he grunted.

'What's that supposed to mean?' She frowned back.

'That's what girls like you do, isn't it,' he replied with a shrug. 'Grand Tour, study art history, work in a smart little gallery . . .'

His handful of words had infuriated her.

'I didn't realise I was so predictable,' she said, putting her glass of iced tea down.

'Am I right?'

She wasn't sure, but she swore she saw a faint smile pull at his lips.

'I was interning in a gallery in New York, but I left. Happy now?' she said with as much dignity as she could manage.

'So what happened?'

'I didn't like it,' she said slowly.

'Good.'

'What's wrong with art galleries?' she said, suddenly defensive of the career she had rejected.

'They're the ultimate conjuring trick. Rich people selling stuff to other rich people. I thought it would be perfect for you.'

She felt her back straighten even more.

'I went to work in a gallery because I majored in art history.'

'And here's me thinking that university was supposed to expand our horizons, not limit us to the choices we made at eighteen.'

She resisted the urge to shake her head. It would have been nice having someone her own age living next door, but Jim Johnson was pompous and insufferable.

She was almost looking forward to the Gilberts' arrival, when her wish was granted and she heard movement behind her.

Carolyn Gilbert appeared first on the terrace. She was a classic trophy wife, a former caterer who had landed one of her clients, Robert Gilbert, one of the city's richest financiers. Everyone pretended not to remember her celebrity as a local beauty queen. Today, in a blue patterned tunic, flanked by her handsome husband and son, the one-time Miss Southern Dream looked like the ultimate WASP.

Connor smiled when he saw Jennifer, but she noticed there was a tightness to his expression. She regretted not having got round to a telephone conversation earlier, but hoped that the presence of the Johnsons might stop any sort of confrontation. Mr and Mrs Gilbert were far too polite for that.

'Sweetheart,' he said, kissing her formally on the cheek. Aware of Jim Johnson watching them, she wished that Connor had behaved a bit more demonstratively, so she took her boyfriend's hand and did not let it go as she said hello to his mother and father.

Sylvia almost ran up the lawn when she saw them, and ordered Marion to bring the food to the table.

'I'm so glad you could come over. It's just something casual, a little finger buffet, but I thought it would be nice to get everyone together now the kids are back. One last summer before they fly the coop, right?'

Robert Gilbert glanced at Jennifer and she didn't miss his look of disapproval. Oh God, she thought, feeling her heart hammer, knowing what was coming, knowing she needed a glass of that Cabernet Sauvignon that had just been brought out in a large, tempting carafe.

It was another hour before the subject was brought up, although she suspected that her mother, who had seated herself next to Robert during supper, had been discussing it with him throughout the meal. Every now and then Sylvia would glance across towards her daughter, her mouth disappearing into an even thinner and tighter line as she huddled back into her conversation.

'Can we have a word, Jennifer?' asked Robert as the supper dissolved into drinks and people stood up from the table.

Connor's father was a tall man; in any circumstances he always seemed to be looking down at people, but Jennifer knew she was in for a telling-off.

'I spoke to Lucian at the gallery this afternoon, after we heard that you'd come back to Savannah. He said it hadn't worked out between you.'

The heat of the day had dissipated, but Jennifer felt suddenly warm.

'It didn't, no,' she said, taking a fortifying swig of wine. If she was totally honest, she was surprised her resignation from her internship at one of the most prestigious galleries in New York, a position Robert had secured through his network of contacts, had taken so long to be made known.

'So you just *gave up*,' said Robert archly.

'I didn't think there was much point being there when I knew it wasn't for me,' she said honestly. 'I knew there'd be a dozen girls desperate for the chance to work there and I was just taking up someone else's place . . .'

It was another moment before she felt her mother at her side. She could feel the heat of Sylvia's displeasure radiating off her.

'Your father and I were under the impression that you were going back. We assumed you were home for just a couple of days.'

'I was unhappy, Mother. I'm not sure New York is for me,' she said simply.

'I see,' said Sylvia before exchanging a look with Robert.

'I don't want you to think me ungrateful. It was so kind of you to sort the internship out, and it was an amazing opportunity, but . . .'

He looked down at her, and Jennifer lost the ability to speak.

'Life isn't all about enjoying yourself,' he said, shaking his head, then walked away to rejoin his wife, who glanced over at Jennifer, one hand holding a glass of wine, the other clutched to her chest.

Her mother stayed rooted to the spot and gave her a cool stare.

'So what are your plans now?' she asked crisply. 'When will you be returning to New York?'

Jennifer knew what she was really saying. Connor's new job, an entry-level position at Goldman Sachs in New York, started in a few weeks.

'I thought I'd hang out in Savannah for a little while,' she said vaguely.

'And do what?' asked her mother, her pale cheeks reddening noticeably.

She heard a sound to her left and saw that Bryn Johnson was listening to them.

'Kids have got to find themselves,' he smiled, popping a honey-roasted pecan into his mouth and taking a few steps forward to join the conversation. 'After Cambridge, I bummed around London, Paris with my little notebook, writing down my thoughts, lines of poetry, observations. I didn't know if I wanted to be the new T. S. Eliot, Hemingway or Joseph Pulitzer, but what I had was a passion to write, and until I'd let that percolate, I didn't have any purpose. Passion and purpose, the two things you need in life to be successful,' he said, winking at them both.

'Let her percolate this summer,' he added, directing his attention towards Sylvia. 'She won't regret it.'

Jennifer grinned at him, welcoming the relief in the tension. Sylvia looked less impressed and excused herself to go and refill her glass.

'Speaking of aimless youth, have you seen my son?' Bryn said, looking around. Darkness had fallen quickly, and the grounds of Casa D'Or disappeared into the shadows.

'I think he's gone back to watch the football,' smiled

Elizabeth Johnson, joining them.

Bryn snorted. 'No idea what the appeal is in the World Cup after England failed to qualify. And tell me, why on earth is America hosting the tournament when you don't even play?'

'He's gone back to the Lake House?' said Jennifer, glancing around for him.

'I'm sure he meant to say goodbye,' said his mother apologetically.

'Which way did he go?' said Jennifer, frowning. She hadn't seen him leave through the terrace, and the French doors were shut.

'The quick way, no doubt,' smiled his mother, sipping her gin and tonic and pointing towards the water.

'Excuse me,' muttered Jennifer under her breath as she grabbed one of the hurricane lamps from the table and walked towards the lake, her pace quickening over the manicured lawn.

The grass underfoot began to get longer and squelchier the closer she got to the water. It was darker out here too. Little light from the house made it this far. She could hear the evening breeze blowing through the bulrushes and she spotted an outline retreating in the night.

'Jim, stop!' she shouted.

He halted and turned around. He didn't say anything, just stood there motionless as she ran towards him, his face becoming clearer in the light of her hurricane lamp.

'Don't go that way,' she said when she reached him.

'Why not?' He looked at her through the soft amber glow. They were just a few feet apart now, and his eyes seemed to challenge her.

'Gators. You sometimes get them around here.'

'*Alligators?*' he said with a low, soft laugh. 'I thought this place was civilised.'

The moon was out now, and a shaft of silvery light caught his face. For a second he looked like a movie star, like a black-and-white James Dean still she'd had pinned on her wall at college, although she was not going to tell him that.

'You get them all around here,' she said, aware of the nervous tremor that had suddenly appeared in her voice. 'From Texas to the Carolinas. This is the South, and sometimes it can be wild,' she added, keeping her voice low.

'Do they bite?'

'The females are the worst,' she said, folding her arms defiantly in front of her.

'It's often the way,' he replied with the hint of a smile.

Jennifer gave him a stern look. 'They're lazy predators, but if the mothers have got hatchlings with them, or if they're hungry, you wouldn't last a minute. They've got teeth the size of a Tic Tac packet.'

'And I'm guessing you wouldn't come and save me.'

She resisted the urge to shake her head. He was so arrogant, she was half minded to let him carry on tramping around the lake.

'You just don't want to be out there in the dark,' she said firmly, thrusting her hands in her pockets as she felt a sudden chill. 'I suggest you go that way,' she added, motioning towards a path that led away from the lake, around the side of Casa D'Or and back towards the road.

She returned to the party without another word, and when she turned back to check which way he had taken, she smiled with satisfaction to see that he had heeded her advice.

Chapter Eight

Connor and Jennifer were not the only ones who had returned to Savannah after college had finished. The city was full of old friends in limbo, and one of them, Jeanne Bosko, was throwing a party in a bar on Broughton Street.

'I thought your birthday was in April,' shouted Jennifer over the noise of the band. Jeanne had been one of her best friends at Our Sacred Hearts, the private school she had attended in Savannah, although she had not seen her properly for more than a year. Their closeness had dwindled over the time they had been away at different colleges, the familiarity of friendship rubbed away to the point that she knew very little about Jeanne's life now, although she was fairly sure that the other girl had already had her twenty-first birthday.

'It was,' said the brunette at her side. She was wearing a fifties prom dress and a big pair of diamanté glasses. Jennifer wasn't sure whether they were for comic effect or not. 'Then I got all sentimental and decided to throw a party back home.

You know, a celebration for finishing college and all that, but I guess that turned out to be ironic.'

'Why ironic?'

Jeanne gave her an incredulous look. 'You don't think this is so fucking depressing? We are officially the most unemployable graduates in a generation. Here I am, valedictorian of my university, and I'm working at the Seven Eleven. The college careers service did not prepare me for the Big Gulp.'

Jennifer gave a sympathetic sigh. Jeanne had been the scholarship kid at school, the school secretary's kid who had won friends right across Sacred Hearts with her humour and smarts. But when her father had died in her final year and her GPA had suffered, she had gone to the community college rather than an Ivy League one.

'I see Connor has a job on Wall Street,' Jeanne said cynically.

'You know Connor.'

'Was it the Harvard old boys' network, or did Daddy make a call?'

'Purely on account of his own genius,' Jennifer giggled. 'Or at least that's what he's been going around telling everyone.'

Jeanne sipped her beer through a straw and looked up mischievously.

'So you two are still together, huh?'

Jennifer grinned and nodded, aware that she was a little embarrassed by the idea.

'And are we going to be seeing a big fat rock on that little finger any time soon?' grinned her friend, nudging her elbow.

'I'm not even twenty-one yet, Jeanne. This is 1994, not 1894.'

'Connor is the sort that wants to get the pesky business of finding a wife out of the way so he can concentrate on conquering the world. Expect a proposal, my friend. And speaking of twenty-firsts, where's my invitation to yours? Or is it being held at a Hamptons beach house or on a yacht in Saint-Tropez, close friends, family and celebrities only?'

'I don't know yet. The plan was to be in New York, but I'm not sure that's going to happen. I want to stay in Savannah for a while.'

'Does Connor know this? I overheard him telling someone that he's bought a loft in somewhere called Tribeca. Never heard of it myself, but apparently all the Wall Street douchebags are crazy for it, and he's going to make a million bucks on it by flipping it in two years' time.'

'Well I'm glad you know more about my boyfriend's future plans than I do.'

'So how's it going to work? Connor's in New York. You're staying here . . .'

Jennifer shrugged. 'We've been at different colleges for three years and it's worked out.'

'Wellesley is thirty miles from Harvard. That's not a long-distance relationship; it just makes it slightly inconvenient for impromptu sex.'

Jeanne took off her glasses and looked at Jennifer wide-eyed.

'I've just had the most amazing idea.'

'Tell me,' said Jennifer slowly.

'You're back in Savannah. I'm looking for a flatmate. It's a small room and the walls are thin, but I can provide earplugs for when I'm entertaining, and I get a twenty-five per cent discount on groceries from the Seven Eleven.'

'An offer I can't refuse, then,' Jennifer grinned as both girls dissolved into laughter.

'What's so funny?' said Connor returning from the bar with two bottles of beer. Some foamy liquid had spilt on his chinos and he didn't look amused.

'Sex,' said Jeanne, pulling her straightest of faces.

'I turn my back for a second and the dirty talk begins, huh?' he said, wiping the beer off his pants.

'Actually we were talking about the labour market and the employability of our peers in a recession,' said Jennifer, giving him a playful smile.

'Oh yeah?'

'We were.'

'I think you'll find we have been out of recession for six economic quarters now,' said Connor, perching on a bar stool. 'The people who haven't got jobs simply don't want to work. There are plenty of opportunities around for graduates if you've got a decent resumé.'

'Tell that to my mom, who's wondering why I have twenty thousand dollars' worth of debt only to be dishing out Twinkies to truckers.'

'I didn't mean you,' said Connor unconvincingly. 'Jen says you were valedictorian of . . . where was it you went? Maybe you can get to an Ivy League for a masters.'

'And who's going to pay for that? The Seven Eleven?'

'You'll find a great job soon, I promise,' said Jennifer, putting a reassuring hand on her friend's shoulder.

'And can you magic up a hot guy while you're at it? The only reason I had a frigging party was to try and score,' Jeanne said, putting another straw into a second cup of beer and drinking through both.

'Some British guy has moved in next door to Jennifer,' suggested Connor after a moment. 'Maybe she could introduce you. He seems like your type.'

'Is he cute?' asked Jeanne.

'He's got the pretty poet vibe going on.'

'A sexy slacker,' said Jeanne, clasping her hands together. 'I like nothing better than a man with no purpose other than to pleasure me in bed.'

'I thought slackers, you know, were all on heroin,' said Connor with a frown.

'Some of the rock lot might dabble, but generally their drug of choice is weed. I find it makes men compliant to my demands,' said Jeanne theatrically.

'Do you think your neighbour is on heroin?' asked Connor, turning to Jennifer. 'He told my mother he was in a band.'

Jennifer laughed, but found herself annoyed at his bigotry. 'That doesn't mean he's on drugs, Connor.'

'How do you know? Never trust a man with facial hair, that's what I say. You know he's trying to hide something.'

'On that note, I'm telling the DJ to change the music,' said

Jeanne, jumping off her stool. 'I want Nirvana, I want something nihilistic,' she declared.

'What are we doing here?' said Connor as soon as she'd gone.

'Celebrating graduation,' sighed Jennifer, still irritated with him.

He looked at her disapprovingly. 'You know, I'm surprised you're still friends with the likes of Jeanne,' he said finally.

'Why?' she said, taken aback.

'Come on, Jen. You have nothing in common. Look around. There are only a few people here from school; the rest, I've no idea who these people are. Nor do I want to. I feel like I'm in the mosh pit. I feel unclean.'

Jennifer resisted the urge to shake her head. Connor had always had a tendency to be snobbish. It was one of the things she liked least about him, the thing she had tried to pull him up on, or ignore, but it seemed to have got worse since he had been at Harvard, where he had worked hard to befriend the grandest students.

'Maybe you should get to know some of them. Maybe you need to know a few more people other than your Harvard lot and your sailing buddies.'

'What do I want to know these people for?' he asked with genuine bemusement.

'You can be friends with people, Connor, for reasons other than what they can do for you.'

'Your idealism is very sweet, but increasingly naïve.' He pushed a lock of hair behind her ear.

'Naïve?'

'You think that you have things in common with Jeanne just because she was in the same class as you for five years. You think that British guy isn't on drugs just because he has a fancy English accent. You think you can walk out of an extremely prestigious internship in New York just because you didn't like it.'

'I knew something was bugging you.'

'Well, we need to talk about it.'

'OK, let's talk.'

He took a pause for dramatic effect.

'Look, my parents are incredibly disappointed. They might not have shown it on Monday, but they were so embarrassed by what happened.'

'It wasn't my proudest moment, Connor, but it was hideous. No one spoke to me, the other interns were bitches. You know, they pulled a sixteen-foot papier-mâché vagina out of storage, dusted it off, hiked the price up by seventy-five per cent and sold it to this Hong Kong couple. They were laughing even before the couple had left the gallery. It was the only time I saw any of them raise a smile.'

'I agree, that was very unprofessional. But my parents buy a lot of art from Lucian, which is probably why he's agreed to have you back. A proper assistant's job this time. Turns out they actually liked you. Thought you looked the part.'

Jennifer took a deep breath, knowing this was the time to tell him.

'I'm not going back to New York, Connor,' she said.

'Why not?'

'Because it's not for me.'

'Not for me?' His brow furrowed in bemusement.

'I know it's the thing we are all supposed to do. Move to the city, make our name, fame, money. But why? We live in one of the greatest cities in the world. It's beautiful, it's always warm, our friends, our family are here . . .'

'Friends? We're in a basement bar surrounded by losers.'

'You love it too, Connor, or else why are you here?'

'Because I live here. For now,' he added pointedly.

'You love Savannah as much as I do. I know you're hungry to succeed, but your father built a fortune without going further than fifty miles out of the city.'

'He's in finance,' Connor said in a measured and level voice. 'The money markets are the new gold rush. My father's done well, but to achieve my potential, I have to be in the financial centre of the world, and right now, that place is New York.'

The passion in his eyes made her smile. If his snobbery was something she disliked, his singular confidence and self-belief had always been attractive.

'You can't sail in New York,' she said playfully.

'Manhattan is an island. Besides, I'll be too busy for hobbies. Do you know how hard they work you at Goldman's?'

'Life isn't all about work,' she sighed. She'd seen it with friends at her own college. Sucked into a cycle of thinking that achievement was everything, they had left Wellesley straight for New York without even considering other options.

'But you need work in your life, otherwise you're rudderless. That's something you need to think about, Jen.'

'I do want to work, Connor. I just need to decide what it is I want to do, and I think I want to do whatever it is here, in our home town.'

His brow creased. 'What are you saying, Jen? I start work in three weeks' time. I have an apartment. I thought, you know, we could talk about you moving in at some point.' He made it sound as if he was doing her a favour.

'We can still make it work. It's just a two-hour flight . . .'

'I'm not listening to this. Someone needs to talk some sense into you.' His voice had returned to its arrogant and dismissive tone.

'Fine. It's your turn to go to the bar.'

'No, it's your turn to go to the bar,' he corrected. 'I'll have a bourbon. I need it after this conversation. And then we're leaving. Randy Chubb is having drinks at his parents' house on Lafayette before they head to Maine.'

'OK,' muttered Jennifer as she slid off her stool and headed to the bar, which was about three deep in thirsty party guests. Glancing back, she saw Connor surveying the room with contempt and wondered, not for the first time, what she actually saw in him.

Screw you, she thought with a spike of rebellion, and made for the door.

Chapter Nine

It was dark by the time she got outside, but she always enjoyed walking the streets of Savannah at this time. It was true that there was a certain eeriness to the city when the light fell from the sky, the noise of the traffic retreated as you left the main streets and the Spanish moss in the trees rustled in the warm evening breeze, but she always felt safe and at home.

She tucked her cardigan and bag under her arm as she walked away from Broughton, weaving her way through the quiet streets of the historic district, not really knowing where she was going, just wanting a little space for her thoughts after her conversation with Connor.

Jennifer did not consider herself to be a stubborn person, but she did not want to back down from where she stood on returning to New York. She felt certain that the city was not right for her, that it was too fast, too crazy, too concerned with the things she really wasn't bothered about: money, power and status.

Jeanne's offer of sharing an apartment was an exciting one. She hadn't been to her friend's place before, and could imagine it was nothing close to the levels of comfort she was used to; even as a student she had been allocated one of the best rooms at Wellesley, and it certainly wouldn't compare to living at Casa D'Or. But her family home meant living with her mother, and after being back in the city less than a week, she was quickly remembering how difficult Sylvia could be. Her disapproval was more corrosive than Connor's offhanded remarks, and the pointed silences and withering looks were beginning to grind Jennifer down. She found herself tiptoeing around the house, marshalling her own silence as if she were in a library or place of worship. She didn't want to be seen and not heard. She wanted to be not seen and not heard.

At least Savannah was still as beautiful as ever, she thought, as a horse and carriage tour trundled past, hooves clattering on the road, tourists waving as it disappeared around a corner. Most people she knew at college had been desperate to leave their home towns and reinvent themselves in New York, Boston or LA. But they hadn't been from Savannah, which tonight looked particularly glorious.

Soft light glowed from the windows of the grand houses that lined the grassy squares; rocking chairs on porches swayed gently in the perfumed breeze. Jennifer imagined herself living in a town house in the historic district; somewhere cosier than Casa D'Or but with all its unique Southern flavour. She imagined a house with a raspberry-red door and a balcony she could step out on to and drink her French vanilla coffee and smell the magnolia bushes in the garden.

She was almost at Forsyth Park now, one of her favourite places of all. She always thought of it as the heart of the city – the perfect spot to read or relax and watch the world go by – and its grand fountain, with its arches of glittering spray, still dazzled her even though she had seen it a thousand times.

She paused as the red and blue flashing lights of a police car drove past. Her heartbeat quickened as for one crazy and paranoid moment she wondered if Connor had sent someone to look for her. The vehicle stopped a few feet in front of her, pulling over an old red pickup truck that was driving the wrong way up a one-way street. She couldn't resist having a look at what was going on.

The driver of the truck got out and stood under one of Savannah's old street lamps. Jennifer knew that she recognised him, but for a second she couldn't place from where. Then it struck her. It was Jim Johnson from the Lake House. The policeman had also got out of his car and was approaching him. Jennifer quickened her pace, reaching Jim just behind the officer.

The policeman spoke first. 'This is a one-way street . . .'

'I'm sorry,' began Jim, thrusting his hands into his pockets sheepishly. 'I didn't know . . .'

Jennifer caught his eye, then turned her attention to the officer.

'It's totally my fault,' she said, leaping to Jim's defence. 'My friend is over from England and offered to pick me up.

I gave him directions to follow because he's only just got into town. I told him to come this way.'

'You told him to come this way?' repeated the police officer, looking down at her sceptically.

'Yes. Jennifer Wyatt, by the way,' she said, knowing that her family's name carried some weight around town. She thrust her hand forward. The officer didn't shake it.

'Your friend was still driving down the street the wrong way. It's his responsibility as the driver to check where he is going,' he said firmly.

'I realise that, Officer,' said Jim, giving Jennifer a quick look.

'I'm so sorry, Jim,' said Jennifer, feeling herself getting sucked into the role she had decided to play. 'I should have just got a taxi or walked home rather than asking you to ferry me around the whole time. You're on holiday after all.'

'Driver's licence,' said the police officer resignedly.

Jim pulled his wallet out of his pocket, rifled through some dollar bills and pulled out a crumpled piece of paper, which he handed over. Somehow Jennifer was surprised he carried it on him, and even more surprised when he went to the glove compartment of the truck and produced the insurance document as well.

The policeman gave the papers a glance and then paused for a moment, as if he was deciding what to do, before tapping Jim on the arm with them.

'Next time you fancy playing the white knight and picking your girl up from the city, make sure you check which way you're going, no matter what she tells you, OK?'

'I will,' said Jim, giving the officer a charming contrite smile.

The policeman got back in his car and gave them both a look before shaking his head and driving away.

They stood on the pavement in silence for a few moments.

'He has a difficult wife,' said Jennifer finally, watching the tail lights of the police car fade from view.

'How do you know?' said Jim, leaning on the open door of the truck.

'There was sympathy in his eyes when I said I'd insisted you pick me up.'

'So you're the white knight in this situation,' said Jim, raising one of his brows.

'I think I helped back there,' she said with a slow grin.

'Thank you,' he said after a moment. 'For saving me from the county jail,' he added, not entirely seriously.

They stayed rooted to their respective spots.

'So what are you doing downtown?'

'Checking it out,' shrugged Jim.

'I thought you weren't interested in the delights of Savannah?'

'I figured, seeing as I'm here . . .'

'You want a native to show you the sights?' she asked him impulsively.

'Are you offering?'

'So long as you let me drive,' she said as an inviting and sweet-smelling breeze whistled down the street.

'Why don't we walk?' he suggested.

'OK,' she replied without even thinking.

She led him east, mindful that they should not venture too far north towards Broughton Street; she had no desire to see Connor again this evening, especially not when she was with Jim Johnson. They threaded through the back streets of the historic district, now draped in twilight, just the glow from the street lamps lighting up the city. She pointed out some of the city's most notable buildings, the slim white stuccoed town house that had been the childhood home of one of her favourite writers, Flannery O'Connor; the grand Andrew Low house on Abercorn Street; and Poetter Hall, the beautiful redbrick Romanesque revival jewel that was now home to the Savannah College of Art and Design. She told him about the history of the city and its links to England, how it had been colonised by the British general James Oglethorpe, who brought over some of London's poor in the hope of giving them a fresh start; and she explained that the tangle of grey feathery fibre draped from every tree branch was Spanish moss, a tropical flowering plant that was surrounded by myth and legend.

In return, Jim explained what had brought the family to Savannah. His father was apparently a big literary name in England, but had been unable to replicate his success after an early hit, published when Jim was young. He had been sent here by his agent to write his comeback book, and Jim had been persuaded to accompany his parents. The deal was that he would spend two months in Savannah, keeping his mother company whilst his father wrote, and in return they were going to buy him an Interrail ticket to travel around Europe before college started again in October. Jim was obviously looking forward to this trip, but reading between the lines, Jennifer could also tell that he was keen for his father to get his career back on track.

He described how he had been pulled out of private school aged thirteen, when the money for school fees ran out. How he'd gone to university in London so that he could live at home and make his student grant go further, funnelling his spare time and money into his music. It was when he talked about this that his face really came alive.

He told her how he got his first guitar for his twelfth birthday and had over the years taught himself the clarinet, the piano, even an instrument called the sitar, and how he had paid for his last vacation to the South of France by busking all the way down from London to Nice. His heroes were Nick Drake and John Martyn, names that didn't mean a great deal to Jennifer but whose music she made a note to listen to. He'd already written more than thirty songs; he wanted to send them off to a record company but wasn't quite sure he had nailed the killer track that would land him a record deal. He wanted to write a novel too, and had already done some short stories, but unfavourable comparisons to his father's genius put him off devoting more time to it.

Everything about Jim Johnson was different – his accent, his intellectual, exotically bohemian background, his references to his London life: a pub that used to be frequented by highwaymen, school trips to the Houses of Parliament that sounded as if they were straight out of a history book – and perhaps that was why he was so easy to open up to.

'So what have you been doing in town tonight?' he asked as the conversation lulled.

'At a friend's party,' she replied, thoughts of Connor making her grimace.

'Wasn't it any good?'

'No, it was fun. I had a bit of a row with my boyfriend, that's all.'

'Connor.'

'He doesn't like my friends.'

'Why not?'

'He thinks that if you don't want to work on Wall Street you don't have any ambition,' she said, feeling slightly traitorous.

'You're not a Yuppie,' he said simply.

'Is that meant to be a compliment?' she laughed.

'Absolutely.'

One word, but it made her feel good. It was another moment before he spoke again.

'So what is the story with Connor?'

'The story?'

'How long have you been together?'

'Since I was sixteen. We met in school.'

'And it lasted all the way through uni?' he asked incredulously.

'I was at an all-women college.'

'Connor's suggestion?' teased Jim. Jennifer didn't like to admit that it was.

'What about you?' she asked as casually as she could.

'There's Emma. She's cool.'

Jennifer tried to imagine what Emma looked like. She'd be pretty; flowery little dress and big shoes, glasses maybe. She didn't want to know any more and let the matter drop.

'I don't suppose I could hitch a ride home,' she said, putting her cardigan over her shoulders.

'You've saved me from alligators and the long arm of the law. I think I owe you a lift to Casa D'Or at the very least.'

They looped back round to the pickup truck, an ancient relic that had come with the Lake House, and Jim opened the door for her to hop in. But as the engine gunned to a start, she realised that she did not want the night to end.

'You know, a tour of the city wouldn't be complete without seeing one more thing,' she said, feeling a little provocative.

'Where should we go?'

'I'm not saying. Not yet,' she smiled.

They drove for about ten minutes out of the historic district of the city. The old truck didn't have air conditioning, and Jim rolled down the windows. They sat in a contented silence.

'Where are we?' asked Jim after Jennifer directed him to stop.

'The Bonaventura cemetery,' she revealed.

'Cheerful,' he said with a nervous laugh. 'Is this the bit where you reveal you're a serial killer?'

'Don't worry. You're safe. Very few serials are female.'

They got out and walked up to a pair of big iron gates. Beyond, they could see the shapes and shadows in the cemetery lit by the glow of the moon.

'I love this place,' said Jennifer, peering through the grille in the darkness. 'Have you read the book *Midnight in the Garden of Good and Evil*?' Jim shook his head. 'The cover is a picture of a statue in the grounds.'

'What's the book about?'

'A murder. I'll lend you a copy.'

Jim gave a low, slow laugh.

'What?'

'Nothing,' he said as his bare arm brushed against hers. 'You're just not what I expected.'

They stood there, arms laced through the iron gate, although Jennifer made sure that they didn't touch again.

'You know, I think we could climb over this thing if you want to give me the full tour.'

Jennifer turned to him and smiled. 'You're really up for breaking into a cemetery in the most haunted city in America?'

'Is it?'

She nodded. 'They say everyone in Savannah has a great ghost story.'

'What about you? Tell me about your spectral encounters.'

She smiled. 'I'm still waiting for something to happen. I guess that's the story of my life.'

He looked at her as if he was really interested in her. His eyes were the most extraordinary colour, a greyish-green not dissimilar from the colour of Spanish moss, she mused, deciding that her first impression, that Bryn Johnson was the most good-looking member of the Johnson family, was wrong.

'So what is it you want to do?'

'I don't know. That's why I've come home. To think about it.'

'Tell me your dreams,' he said, nudging her playfully.

'Easy, tiger,' she smiled.

'I'm serious. Where do you see yourself when you're thirty?'

Jennifer tried hard to picture it, but she could not. She had actually given the question a lot of thought over the past few weeks. She saw glimpses of her future self when she was working in the art gallery, a joyless salesperson in black Issey Miyake, and knew that was not the path she wanted to take.

'Married, I suppose,' she said, wanting to give some response.

'You don't just want to be a wife,' he scoffed. 'You're far too interesting for that. Come on, blue-sky thinking. When did you last see someone do something and think, "I'd love to do that"?'

Jennifer thought for a moment.

'You know that new Tom Hanks movie that comes out this weekend? They filmed some of it right here in Chippawa Square a few months ago. I liked going down to watch that.'

'So you want to be a film director?' replied Jim without any hint of amusement.

'I don't know. It's a ridiculous dream,' she said. Some things were too big to fantasise about. To say them out loud sounded arrogant at best, laughable at least. 'I did a few video production classes at college and loved it, but I wouldn't know where to start.'

'Get a camcorder and start shooting. Savannah is so photogenic, it's crying out to be in a movie.'

'I'd need actors and stuff. Where do I find them?'

'You can use real people.'

'You mean like *The Real World*?'

'Maybe,' he smiled. 'Film your friends this summer. Connor and everyone he doesn't approve of. You could call it *Yuppies and Bums*. And when you go and collect your Oscar, I can say I knew you back when and then bribe you into letting me do the soundtrack for your next movie.'

'You'll be Jim Johnson, rock star, by then.'

'With a bit of luck.'

'You'll have to write me a song.'

'If you play your cards right.' He grinned and gave her a look that made her shiver, a look that told her it was time to go home.

As they turned around, away from the railings, an old couple walked past them hand in hand. The woman, with her silver hair and big glasses, smiled at her, a conspiratorial and wistful look that made Jennifer feel guilty and uncomfortable. For even though they were by a cemetery, she could see the romance in this situation and wondered how it had happened. After all, it was just a few hours earlier that she had quite disliked Jim Johnson. Enough to reject Connor's idea of setting him up with Jeanne, although now that she had discovered he was funny and sharp and interesting, she still wasn't sure that she wanted to fix him up with Jeanne or any of her friends.

'We should go back,' she said, and he nodded in agreement.

They made small talk on the way home, and when he stopped the truck outside Casa D'Or, there was an awkward moment when they sat there in silence.

'You've convinced me of Savannah's charms,' he said, defusing the tension. 'We should do it again. Maybe see that Tom Hanks movie you were talking about.'

She wasn't sure if she was excited or disappointed as he got out of the driver's seat and came round to open the door for her.

She reminded herself it was perfectly natural, desirable even, to have friends of the opposite sex, especially ones who were visitors in your hometown, ones you wanted to make feel welcome. And yet she felt gloriously rebellious and shamefully traitorous as she turned around, gave him her most encouraging smile, and said, 'Yes, that would be nice.'

Chapter Ten

The marina at the Isle of Hope was one of Jennifer's favourite places in the world. Just a short bicycle ride away from her house, it was not huge, with just a handful of boats moored along the slips, but the people were friendly, the sunsets were glorious and the access to the rivers, tidal creeks and coastline was good. Her own twenty-two-foot cruiser, *Sparkling Tinkerbell*, her father's nickname for her as a child, had been moored there ever since he had given it to her for her eighteenth birthday. It was small enough to keep by the creek at Casa D'Or, but she liked to berth at the marina, where there was a friendly community of sailing enthusiasts who had been teaching her how to tie knots and improve her seamanship since she was small.

Back when she was growing up, she used to come here with her father. As an only child whose school was several miles away and who had few local friends, she regarded David Wyatt as a great pal as well as a parent. His increasing workload meant he didn't come down as much any more, but Jennifer still used it as a place to escape and forget her worries. She liked nothing better than taking *Sparkling Tinkerbell* out along the intercoastal waterway, with an ice bucket full of soda, snaking along the rivers and estuaries of the Georgian coast, north to Hilton Head or even as far as Jekyll Island, listening to the sound of the water and the squawking of the pelicans and egrets that circled overhead.

Today she had taken the boat down the Back River. There was much romance and adventure attached to this part of the world, which was one of the reasons why Jennifer loved it so much. It was said that the Spanish had come here looking for gold and instead had found a string of islands so beautiful they had called them the Golden Isles. Back River was also known as Moon River, after the song from her favourite movie, *Breakfast at Tiffany's*. Local legend had it that the song's lyricist, Johnny Mercer, had lived on its banks and it had inspired him. Today she had let the boat just drift with its open sails, her tape recorder blasting out the song. Once or twice, an image of Jim Johnson strumming away on his guitar had popped into her mind, but she had successfully stamped it out and instead concentrated not on the romance of the song but on the sense of adventure contained within the lyrics; the two drifters who were off to see the world.

She thought about sailing to Casa D'Or but decided against it. Docking back at the marina, she wiped her forehead with the back of her hand. It was a hot day; she could feel sweat dripping down her temple and her stash of soda had been depleted. She squinted in the bright light, and when her vision refocused, she could see Connor standing on the pontoon, one hand thrust in the pocket of his chinos, the other shielding his face from the bright early-afternoon sun.

Her heart sank and she knew it wasn't the disappointment of being back on dry land. They hadn't spoken since the night before, when she had walked out of Jeanne's party, and she knew it was not the sort of behaviour he would take well.

'Hi,' she said, tying up the boat and not looking at him.

'Here, let me help,' he said, which surprised her.

He took her hand as she stepped off the boat. They stood there for a moment, not speaking.

'I'm sorry about last night,' she said eventually. She didn't particularly want to apologise, but it seemed the natural thing to do.

'I'm sorry too,' he said, trying to catch her gaze.

'You're sorry?' She smiled slowly, aware that she was teasing him.

'I was rude about your friends. I shouldn't have been. And I know you don't like Randy. We didn't have to go to his drinks, but you should have told me you were leaving. I was worried about you running off like that.'

She looked at him, expecting his voice to have a hectoring note of disapproval, but instead she heard genuine concern.

'I'm going to have to call you my runaway girl,' he added, teasing her.

'What are you doing here?' she asked, feeling everything soften.

'Looking for you.'

He said it with such honesty that she felt a sudden pang of affection for him.

'Want a ride home?'

'I've got my bicycle.'

'We can come back for it later. Come on, let me take you for lunch.'

They drove into the city, and it was such a hot day that Connor suggested somewhere by the water. They headed to River Street, past the old cotton mills and the paddle steamers moored at the dock, and found a diner that served jambalaya and key lime pie. Jennifer wasn't sure that the two dishes went together, but the morning's sailing had made her ravenous.

Connor was solicitous from the moment they had got into his sports car to sitting down for lunch, deferring to her choice on everything from restaurant to aperitif. She thought it distinctly out of character but found herself enjoying the afternoon and his company.

'I've written a letter to your parents apologising for the business with the gallery,' said Jennifer, wanting to clear some of the awkward stuff out of the way.

'My dad didn't become successful wasting his time on things that weren't going to materialise into anything,' said Connor with a shrug. 'I can see why you left New York. We all can.'

The waitress appeared with two sweet teas and Connor took a sip.

'I've been thinking. If I come back to Savannah every fortnight and you to fly to New York every two or three weeks, we'll still see each other almost every weekend. I reckon I can put eighteen months in at Goldman's and then I can strike out on my own. Hedge funds, property . . . I can be more flexible with location when I own my own company.'

She knew that for Connor, this was an incredibly sweet gesture. His own version of buying a fluffy puppy to say 'I love you'.

She looked up and grinned at him.

'How about you?' he said more guardedly. 'Have you had a chance to think about things?'

'I want to make a documentary.'

'A documentary?' He didn't say it unkindly, but it still reminded her of a teacher who had just been told by a five-year-old pupil that he wanted to be an astronaut.

'Visual arts was the bit I liked most about my course,' she replied cautiously. 'Besides, I think we are living through interesting times, the fallout from the crazy eighties. We've got friends who've graduated summa cum laude working in gas stations; have been brought up to think that one in two marriages ending in divorce is normal. We haven't really got anything to rebel against any more, so we just get cynical, *resigned* to it all. I thought it was worth recording.'

Connor's face had softened into something that almost resembled pride.

'You've thought about this then.' He smiled.

'I was out on the water this morning and couldn't think of anything else.'

She felt a wave of relief wash over her, as if she had been transported back to the ways things used to be before they went off to college, when Connor was the perfect gent, the only grown-up she had met in a sea of silly boys who just wanted to get their hands in her panties and then tell all their friends about it.

The waitress brought their food and they started picking at it.

'Where did all this come from, then?'

Under the circumstances, the way they'd been getting on so well for the past hour, she decided not to tell him it was Jim Johnson's idea and that they had concocted her life plan on a moonlit walk after she had abandoned Connor in the bar.

'Don't you think it's a good idea? A plan, at least,' she said, avoiding the question.

'Have you even got a video camera?' he asked sceptically. Jennifer didn't blame him. She'd met girls who were seriously into film at college; intense students with posters of Jim Jarmusch films on their walls and a working knowledge of Czechoslovakian cinematic history. Her own favourite movies were *When Harry Met Sally* and *Moonstruck*.

'Not yet.'

'Come on then,' he said, wiping his chin with his napkin. 'It's time to go shopping.'

They went to an electronics store at the mall and Connor paid for her brand-new Sony camcorder. He insisted. He would be working at Goldman Sachs within the month; he would be earning and wanted to treat her.

She opened the box on the car ride back to Casa D'Or, stroked the smooth black casing, and it felt like the start of something good.

It was late afternoon by the time they approached the house, and lazy peach light was streaming through the leaves of the live oaks along the drive.

'Why don't you pick up an overnight bag and come back to my parents'?' he offered.

'Are they going to be at home?'

'They're entertaining tonight. But we could go to the guest cottage.'

'When they're entertaining, aren't you supposed to put in an appearance?'

'Then how about you come tomorrow instead? Bring that.' He smiled, motioning at the camcorder. 'Maybe we can have a little fun with it,' he added as Jennifer slapped him playfully on the wrist.

Connor parked the car outside the house. As he switched off the engine, Jennifer could hear noises from inside.

She hesitated for a moment and glanced at Connor as she got out of the car.

In the still, sticky summer air, she could hear it quite distinctly. The raised yet controlled voice of her father; her mother's more malevolent and hysterical screams.

Connor got out of the car and stood with Jennifer in solidarity on the steps of Casa D'Or.

'Let's go,' he said softly.

'I can't.' She couldn't just drive off and leave her parents to it. She didn't want to go into the house either, but when she heard something smash, she took a deep breath and opened the door.

It was as if she were witnessing a picture on freeze frame. Her mother stood motionless, clenched white fingers raised to her face. Her father glanced over towards Jennifer. The expression on his face was tired and frustrated.

She heard Sylvia take a sharp inhalation of breath. Tension quivered around the room. Then her mother dropped her arms to her sides, crossed the hall to the walnut cabinet and snatched up a set of car keys, striding towards the front door without another word, not even glancing in her daughter's direction.

Jennifer watched her go, watched her pause for a moment when she saw Connor standing there, and although she could no longer see her mother's face, she imagined it flushing with anger and shame to be caught out like this.

'Let her go,' said her father, pre-empting Jennifer's next question. 'She's just had another one of her turns. She'll be back soon.'

Jennifer bit down on her lip, memories of her childhood flooding back to haunt her. Feelings of fear and guilt, and anxiety. Even when she was old enough to understand that her mother had changeable and unpredictable moods, she still wondered what she had done to make her behave like this, wondered what she had done to upset her and how she could have been better. Thoughts that were going around her head at that very moment.

She heard her mother's car gun off in the distance and then the soft sound of footsteps coming up the steps. Connor put his arm around her shoulders and squeezed her reassuringly close.

Her father was already headed upstairs.

'I'm going to read,' he said, his voice drained of any life or emotion.

'Come back to mine,' said Connor, as David Wyatt turned back and nodded his approval.

Jennifer agreed, knowing that at least her boyfriend had seen all this before, and understood.

Chapter Eleven

David Wyatt had taken a pragmatic approach to his daughter's unemployment and a deal had been struck. He would support the idea of her making a documentary and would continue to pay her the allowance he had given her whilst she was at college. He had emphasised that it was only a temporary arrangement; in fact he had given her a deadline of the end of the summer, at which point Jennifer had to do something with her creative body of work: use it to find a job in the media, or submit it to film festivals to gauge whether it – and by implication, she – had any artistic merit.

The summer suddenly felt full of promise, and Jim Johnson had offered to help with the filming. It made sense to turn down Jeanne's offer of a room in her apartment and instead Jennifer started seeing her Lake House neighbour every day. Once Connor had left Savannah for New York, Jennifer had felt a little guilty about seeing so much of her new friend, but two heads were better than one, and Jim had a lot of good ideas. Sometimes they made their creative brainstorms sociable; she'd had her first crack at a shooting script over ice cream and soda after they had been to see a matinee performance of *Forrest Gump*.

She'd started videoing her friends almost immediately after Connor had bought her the camera, and had been surprised how many people were keen to get involved, confirming Jim's view that everybody liked the opportunity to talk about themselves.

Today she was at the Lake House with Jim, watching the tapes of everything she had filmed so far. It was a particularly hot and sticky afternoon, the sort of day when she loved to go sailing, but with the clock ticking, it made more sense to stay out of the sun and do some work.

Bryn Johnson came into the main house smoking a cigar. According to Jim, his father usually worked in the boathouse at the end of the pontoon, but he was clearly taking a break. He had grown a stubbly beard since the last time Jennifer had seen him and reminded her of Ernest Hemingway, which was almost certainly the look he was after.

'Where's your mother?' he asked.

'Gone swimming,' said Jim from his reclined position on the floor, not even looking up from the television.

Bryn paused and watched what they were doing.

'What's this then?' he said, pointing at the screen.

'Jen's documentary,' replied Jim. There was a note of pride in his voice that made Jennifer feel more confident in front of his celebrated father.

Bryn perched on the end of the wicker sofa and blew a smoke ring as Jennifer resisted the urge to cough.

'Elizabeth mentioned you'd been filming. Let's have a look, then.'

'Dad, please.'

Jennifer was glad that Jim had picked up on her embarrassment. 'They're just video interviews,' she said, both horrified and secretly thrilled at the idea that an author, a famous author, would want to have a look at her work.

'Come on, don't be shy. I know what that feels like.'

'Yeah, right,' replied Jim under his breath.

'I do. Creativity of any description is deeply personal. The only person to see my book before it goes to my editor is my agent, Saul, and even then he has to prise it from my fingertips.'

They sat in silence as they watched Connor's friend Randy Chubb speak of his place at Harvard Law School and his plans to make partner on a Wall Street firm by thirty.

'Let me guess,' said Bryn, stubbing his cigar out on a saucer. 'His father is a prominent Savannah attorney.'

'How did you know?' asked Jennifer with surprise.

Bryn dismissed her question and looked thoughtful.

'So what's your narrative then?' he asked, making himself comfortable in a chair.

'It's a documentary, not a movie, Dad,' replied Jim, sitting up straighter.

'I worked on *World in Action* for six months in my twenties. Fantastic training for novel writing. You're still telling a story, you still need themes, a *point*, otherwise you'll spend twelve months in the editing suite, sifting through the rubble, wondering why a few dozen interviews with a bunch of twenty-year-olds doesn't make ten minutes of compelling television.'

'Dad, I thought you had a book to write.' Jim obviously wanted to get rid of his father.

'What's it called, this documentary?'

'*Friends*,' replied Jennifer. 'Although I read there's a sitcom coming out with that name, so maybe I'll have to change it.'

Bryn grunted as if the title didn't meet with his approval.

'How about *Hopes and Dreams*?' he said dramatically, sweeping his hand in front of his face as if he were imagining the name made up in lights. 'Why do we do what we do?' he continued expansively. 'To what degree is free will involved in our adolescent career choices, or are we in fact obligated or influenced to make certain professional decisions because of our parents?'

Jennifer nodded thoughtfully as Jim spoke up.

'So what are you saying? We need to get back to everyone we've interviewed and ask to speak to their parents?'

'That's exactly what I'm saying,' said Bryn as he ambled back towards the open porch doors.

'Thanks,' shouted Jennifer after him.

Bryn lifted his hand languorously and waved without even turning back.

Jennifer switched off the VHS machine and took out her tape.

'I should go home.'

It was almost five o'clock and her mother would be back from the country club. Sylvia was always in a spiky mood when she came back from the club, especially if she had lost her tennis match. Jennifer would much rather hang out at the Lake House with Jim, but she knew that her mother would start asking too many questions if she did.

'I'll walk you home,' said Jim.

The afternoon was hot and sultry. There was a complete absence of breeze – even the birds seemed to have stopped singing and had retired for quiet siestas in the treetops – and it made the short walk from the Lake House back to Casa D'Or exhausting.

'Do you ever use your pool?' asked Jim as they skirted the edge of the lake.

She smiled and knew what he was hinting at.

'We don't use it much. I think my mother finds it vulgar.'

'I thought she was playing tennis.'

'I'm not sure she'll appreciate coming back to find you dive-bombing in the deep end.'

'You don't get on, do you?'

Jennifer's smile was more regretful this time.

'I'm not sure my mother wanted children,' she said honestly.

She looked at him and wanted to take back what she had just said. It felt traitorous to discuss it, but it was a thought that had gnawed away at her for years, and it was good to finally share it with someone she trusted. There had to be some reason for her mother's remoteness, her complete lack of interest. Jennifer remembered bringing home Christmas decorations that she had made at school, stars crayoned in violet, red and blue that had been quietly thrown away rather than put on the tree, presumably because they did not fit in with Sylvia's silver and Tiffany-blue colour scheme. The sailing competitions that Jennifer had entered but Sylvia had not bothered to turn up to. She could hear her mother's voice now – 'Sailing is not very feminine, now is it?' – even when she won trophies and medals and everyone was cheering her name.

Jennifer hadn't ever been sure what her mother wanted from her, and certainly not now.

'Don't be daft,' said Jim reassuringly.

Jennifer looked at him unconvinced.

'You know what you should do,' suggested Jim as they approached the house.

'What?' she asked, knowing that whatever came out of his mouth was generally good.

'You should interview yourself for the documentary. I'll do it. And then you can interview your mum. Maybe that way you'll find out what makes her tick.'

Jennifer wasn't sure about the idea of capturing herself on celluloid, but she had to admit it was an interesting suggestion.

'Your father's great,' she said, wanting to divert the conversation away from her mother. 'It must be wonderful growing up in such a creative house.'

'His ego is bigger than China.' He smiled back.

'That's not entirely unexpected. How's his book going?'

Jim gave a snort. 'He's in that boathouse a lot, but we're not exactly sure how much he's getting done. One minute he says he's writing the definitive tome about the history of slavery, the next it's a deconstruction of the American Dream. Personally I think he should write a schlocky airport thriller and be done with it.'

He grinned at her, and at that exact moment Jennifer felt a gust of something warm and joyful and good, even though the air was still.

'So how's Emma?' She suddenly wanted to know.

'I don't know,' said Jim with a shrug.

'You don't know?' said Jennifer, feeling oddly excited at this news.

'I'll see her in September. If she hasn't moved on, if I haven't . . . well, we'll take it from there.'

'I wonder if Connor is talking about me like that,' she smiled.

'I doubt it. When are you seeing him next?'

'I'm flying to New York tomorrow.'

'Oh.'

She looked at his expression for any sign of disappointment but she could see none.

'Do you think it's going to work? This long-distance thing?'

'I'm quite looking forward to it. I like the idea of being able to write letters.'

'Love letters,' he teased.

She blushed. 'I'm not sure Connor will be into the idea of it, though.'

'I see him as more of a fax man,' agreed Jim, smiling. 'But

you're right. Letters are good,' he said softly. 'You can send me some when I'm back in London.'

She looked up and could see Sylvia on the terrace. She was wearing her tennis dress and was shielding her eyes as she looked across the lake, as if she was tracking them.

'You don't have to come in,' she said, with gentle warning.

'No pool, then?'

'We've got a lake right here,' she grinned.

'All right,' he said as he began to pull off his T-shirt and jeans.

'What are you doing?' she shouted.

'Having fun!' he yelled, running towards the water and diving in.

Jennifer shook her head and started laughing, but she could almost feel a laser beam of frostiness emanating from the terrace. Raising her hand to wave goodbye to her friend, she turned and hurried back to Casa D'Or.

Sylvia had gone into the kitchen by the time she arrived at the house. She was standing by the sink, sipping some water from a tumbler.

'I got you something from the city,' she said without any enthusiasm, motioning to a bag from one of Savannah's smartest boutiques.

Jennifer crossed the room and took out the garment from the folds of tissue paper. A teal-blue silk dress fluttered from her fingertips.

'It's beautiful,' she said.

'I thought you could take it to New York,' Sylvia said crisply.

Jennifer looked at her, wondering if it was the right moment to ask her to be interviewed for her documentary, but Sylvia had already put the tumbler on the countertop.

'I'd better go and have a shower,' she said, and Jennifer decided to leave her request for another day.

Chapter Twelve

'So why's it called Labor Day, if everybody has a holiday?' asked Jim on the other end of the receiver.

'We're celebrating why people work and the contributions they make to the prosperity of our country,' replied Jennifer, tucking her phone under her chin and staring out of the window towards the Lake House. 'And it's sort of the last official day of summer, so I guess it's reminding some people that they've got to go back to work.'

'Will there be turkey?'

'You're thinking of Thanksgiving.'

'So what happens?'

'There'll be beer. Lots of people spend the weekend at the beach.'

'Is that what you're doing?'

'I've been invited to Tybee Island on Saturday.'

'Sounds fun.'

'You can come if you want.' She said it as casually as she

could, but she felt as if she had just flashed her breasts at him through the window. Other than when she had been in New York or Connor had come down for the weekend, she'd seen Jim most days, but it was the documentary that generally gave them an excuse to be together, and without it, the invitation of just a trip to the beach made her feel eager and exposed, even though she was sure he'd been fishing for an invite. 'My friend Jeanne is getting a few people together. It will be fun and casual.'

'Well, I'm all for witnessing great American traditions.'

'We're meeting at the beach at two. It's about an hour's drive away.'

'Then how about I pick you up in the truck at one?'

Tybee Island was to the north of the city. Jennifer always thought of it as Savannah's Coney Island, a bit faded, but with its own retro charm. It had a lighthouse and miles of golden sand, and thousands of ordinary families came here every summer to eat hot dogs and have fun. It was the sort of place that her mother disapproved of, just as Jennifer knew she would disapprove of her spending Labor Day weekend with Jim Johnson.

In the event, David Wyatt had announced that he was taking her mother off for lunch in the city. Their argument a few weeks earlier, when Sylvia had screamed at David and stormed out of the house, had not been mentioned again, but he had been working particularly long hours at the office ever since. Jennifer didn't blame him for sometimes wanting to keep out of the house, but she had still been pleased when he had told her with a particularly mischievous wink that they were off out, 'just the two of us', as if relations between them had thawed.

She'd called Jim after they had gone, and his pickup truck pulled up outside Casa D'Or a few minutes later. Marion was having the entire weekend off to visit her parents in Augusta but had left the fridge stuffed with pies and salads, and marinated catfish that just needed to be griddled. Jennifer liberated some cornbread, cookies and cake from the pantry and smuggled the cool box loaded with beers out of the house.

She'd taken particular care with her appearance, telling herself it was difficult choosing something to wear when the weather might change. She had chosen white shorts and a yellow T-shirt and some leather sandals that she had picked up in the South of France the summer before. A waterproof windcheater was stashed in the straw basket that would get absolutely soaked if it decided to rain.

'Where's Connor this weekend?' asked Jim as she got into the truck.

'Being macho and volunteering to work. He says it's very competitive at the firm. Apparently going into the office on Labor Day is going to give him a professional advantage.'

'Something smells good.' He grinned, changing the subject.

'That will be Marion's coconut cake,' she said.

'No, I think it's your hair.'

'I thought it was Southern gents who had all the charm.'

He gave her a mischievous glance across the cabin. Not

for the first time, she felt a little flutter of something as he looked at her. She wasn't sure what it was. Excitement. Promise. A frisson of guilt that they were spending so much time together. Whatever it was, Jennifer had become an expert on not dwelling on it. As an about-to-be-twenty-one-year-old woman, she was absolutely capable of having a very good-looking, fun and interesting male friend.

'You do realise you've only got eleven days left of my sparkling company,' Jim said as they headed north, music blaring from the cassette machine.

Jennifer stared out of the window and didn't say anything for a few moments. It seemed as if they had talked about everything that summer: their likes, dislikes, hopes and fears, music, sailing, Boston and London – everything had been up for discussion except the fact that the Johnson family were shortly to fly home.

'Why are you going back so early?' she said as casually as she could. 'You mentioned that you weren't sure about going Interrailing any more but I thought college didn't start for another month. Can't you stay here?'

'My ticket is non-refundable, non-transferable, non-changeable, which is another way of saying cheap, although not so cheap that my parents can afford to buy me another. Besides, the Sittenfields want their house back.'

She wanted to tell him there was another way. There was plenty of room at Casa D'Or, and a small trust fund kicking in on her twenty-first birthday in ten days' time meant she would be able to buy him a replacement ticket home. It was the least she could do after all his help on her documentary.

But she was too embarrassed to suggest it.

'My twenty-first party will have to be your unofficial send-off, then,' she said, sounding more subdued.

'You can do me a little speech and everything,' he teased.

'Sure. I was even thinking of a shower of confetti coming down from the sky with your name written on every petal.'

'Very funny. How about you just buy me a drink tonight?'

'There should be loads of beers at the beach party,' she said, feeling her cheeks colour.

'Excellent,' he replied and turned the tape player up loud.

Jennifer knew that it was supposed to be a fun day, but she couldn't help feeling out of sorts. Labor Day was always bittersweet, the sense of an ending in the air. Jim played cassette tapes for the rest of the journey, sharing new music he had discovered and liked; bands with names like Pulp, Oasis and Blur, Brits who were giving a kick in the teeth to American grunge, he explained with a note of national pride. He hoped this summer had been worthwhile if for no other reason than to improve her taste in music. She wanted to tell him how amazing it had been, how sad she was that it was almost over, but she stayed quiet.

Her mood picked up by the time they got to the island. Most people were already at the beach, assembled in a knot around a pile of baskets and ice boxes and footballs. There were at least twenty in the group, and at first glance, Jennifer realised she knew about half of them. They were Jeanne's crowd, not her own; nice people from school, and a few she had met at the party at the start of the summer.

They played volleyball and sunbathed. Jim mixed in easily. Too easily, she noted with annoyance when Tina, a petite curvy blonde and a friend of Jeanne's new flatmate, asked him to apply some tanning oil to her back, and he readily accepted.

As the light fell out of the sky, they made a makeshift fire pit on the beach and collected driftwood to burn. Everyone cheered as the flames roared into the air and the mauve twilight seemed to gift the night more magic.

'Time for s'mores,' someone shouted.

'What's a s'more?' asked Jim, fetching his guitar from their pile of stuff.

'A campfire tradition,' replied Tina, getting up to find a jumper and sitting herself down next to Jim when she returned.

'Grab a prong, my friend,' said Jeanne, handing him a skewer.

He stabbed his fork into a huge marshmallow and put it into the fire.

'There's an art to it,' continued Jeanne. 'Some people like them burned and incinerated; some people just want to warm them up a bit, but the best is when you get them golden and roasted.'

'Just like this,' said Jim, carefully removing his mallow from the top of the flame. He was about to pop it into his mouth when Tina stopped him.

'That's not a s'more,' she said, moving closer. 'You need a graham cracker and a piece of chocolate.' She demonstrated her recipe with the ingredients she had to hand. 'Then you get your marshmallow and sandwich it together with another cracker, and there you have it. Delicious,' she said, reaching over and feeding it directly into Jim's mouth.

Jennifer felt as if she'd been tasered. Her entire body was in shock as she watched Tina lick a remnant of white goo from her hand suggestively. She couldn't believe how the woman was making a campfire tradition into an artful seduction. She flashed a look over at Jeanne, who registered a faint, resigned disapproval before standing up and waving a bottle of beer in the air.

'I think it's time we played a game,' she announced.

A murmur of unwillingness rippled around the circle until she instructed their school friend Pete to get the shot glasses.

'In honour of this being our School's Out Forever summer . . . we should play Most Likely.'

'What? Like a yearbook?' asked a voice in the growing darkness.

'Exactly like a yearbook, except with added tequila,' confirmed Jeanne.

Jim started strumming his guitar softly.

'How does this work then? We don't do yearbooks in England.'

'I think up a category, and then we all have to decide who's most likely to do that thing. If someone votes for you, you have to drink a shot. I like to think of it as punishment for potential and accomplishment.'

Jim laughed, and Jennifer watched him for a moment. She liked his smile, she always had done. He looked quite beautiful in the twilight, she thought, remembering back to the first night they had met, by the lake. She felt something in her heart, a yearning for something she had not yet had or was ever likely to have.

As her gaze trailed around the circle, she could see Tina looking at him too and wished that Jim would just put the guitar down. He needed no help attracting female attention as it was, and there was something about the way Tina was looking at him that made Jennifer's back stiffen. The pretty blonde looked tiny and lovely and vulnerable bundled up in her sweater, although to men, Jennifer knew she would look like a sex kitten.

'Do you want another s'more?' asked Jennifer, edging towards her friend. She knew that it was not the most tempting offer she could make, but she felt on red alert; that he was in the proximity of a predator and she had to stop him from getting caught.

'Cheers,' he smiled.

She toasted a marshmallow until it was brown and crisp, but as she sandwiched it between two graham crackers, the biscuits disintegrated, leaving a crumbled mess.

'I'm sorry,' she said as he put his guitar down and took the broken s'more from her.

'It all tastes the same,' he said reassuringly, but Jennifer noticed that Tina was looking over triumphantly.

Shot glasses were dispensed and filled up around the circle.

'Most likely to be President in 2030,' began Jeanne.

There was a chorus of groans, and everyone decided that

the prospect of becoming even the manager of a Gap store seemed depressingly remote right now.

'OK, OK,' said Jeanne. 'I get the message. You want me to spice it up a bit.'

The categories came thick and fast.

'Most like to have hot monkey sex tonight,' said Jeanne, getting more and more drunk by the minute. Even when she was not being nominated for a category she took a shot of tequila anyway.

Most people pointed at Rory and Gail, two of Jeanne's neighbours who had spent half the afternoon making out on the beach.

'I vote for Jim,' smiled Tina suggestively.

Jennifer noticed her friend blush. Her own heart was thumping a little harder. Was Tina offering him a invitation? she wondered, hoping that Jim had been looking the other way or not listening. She took a shot of tequila even though she had not been picked by anyone, and prayed for the game to finish.

'Most likely to get married . . . to one another,' said Jeanne with a hint of mischief.

Jennifer looked around the circle. She was very drunk now. Having been voted most likely to end up on the *New York Post*'s Page Six and most likely to have a respectable job by Christmas, she'd had way too much tequila, and hadn't drunk enough water in the heat of the day or eaten enough of the cake or cornbread.

She wondered where to cast her vote.

Jeanne had been coyly flirting with Pete all afternoon and

she thought they would make a great couple if only Jeanne would stop playing at being 'one of the boys'. But she didn't want to embarrass her friend and in the end chose Rory and Gail, who picked up the entire bottle of tequila and said they were going home to bed.

'Jim and Jen. That's who I think are most likely to get married,' said Jeanne from the other side of the campfire, waving a marshmallow on a stick. 'You two are so sickeningly cute and gorgeous.'

'Well, I wouldn't mind a Green Card,' said Jim, grinning, then downing his shot.

'You old romantic,' Jennifer said, trying to hide her nerves. A flutter of awkwardness passed between them. Spots of rain began to fall.

'You're kidding,' shrieked Jeanne, jumping to her feet and grabbing her blanket.

Within a minute it was raining hard. Everyone sprang into action, collecting their things and running barefoot from the beach, the sand growing colder and wetter under their feet by the second.

There were a few hotels and bars along the boardwalk. People seemed to be heading towards a neon-lit bar across the street, but Jim and Jennifer were right by the truck.

'Jump in,' said Jim, hurrying to get the door open as a crack of thunder rumbled through the sky.

They sat in the cabin, dripping wet. There was a strange tension in the air that was making Jennifer nervous.

'I should probably get back,' she said finally.

'Well, I'm not sure I can drive us,' he confessed. 'Shouldn't have won "Most likely to be on the front cover of *Rolling Stone* magazine". It was a slippery slope after that.'

'I wondered when you'd start bragging about that, pretty boy.'

'They appreciated the music,' he chided.

They listened to the shower pound against the windscreen.

'Why don't we sit it out? Go for a drink with the others?'

'No, I should really get back,' she said, thinking of her mother. Besides, she had no intention of seeing Tina again, could imagine her cornering Jim at the bar and didn't even want to think where that might lead.

He glanced in his rear-view mirror and then jumped out of the truck. Jennifer shouted after him, but he was in the middle of the road, trying to hail a taxi in the pouring rain.

A cab screeched to a stop. Jim ran back, locked up the truck and helped Jennifer load her basket into the cab. As they set off, she gazed out of the window. The weather felt like a portent that all the good times she'd had over the summer were coming to a close.

'Rains more than I thought it would around here,' said Jim.

'Atlantic hurricane season,' she explained. 'I mean, we don't often get hit in Savannah, but it's peak time around now.'

They were soon back at Casa D'Or, and as the house grew closer and closer at the end of the long drive, she felt a sense of a ticking clock, an urgency to do something though she didn't know what.

Jim was only in Savannah for one more weekend, and

besides, Connor was coming back for her twenty-first. And then he would be gone.

'You know, I've never really thanked you,' she said, feeling more and more sentimental.

'What for?'

'I think I might have been pressured back to New York if it wasn't for you and your idea of the documentary.'

'You're no pushover. I had nothing to do with it. I should be thanking you for keeping me company all summer. At least I can now put "documentary research assistant" on my CV, because I haven't got anything else to go on there beyond "enthusiastic drinker" and "Students' Union darts champion".'

'Darts?'

'I'll have to show you sometime.'

They sat there, just a couple of feet apart, and looked at each other.

'You are going to keep in touch, Wyatt,' he said, not moving his gaze.

'I know I am. It's you I'm worried about. Once you get back to college and your friends and Emma—'

'Emma's gone. I told you,' he said without his usual good humour. 'It was never really that serious, if I'm honest. In fact, it was never really anything at all.'

Jennifer frowned in puzzlement. 'It was never really anything?'

'I only said it because, you know, you had . . . have Connor. And I wasn't sure if you'd want to be friends if you thought I was single. You might have thought I was just after you.'

'After you?' she said, feeling a little gallop in her heart.

'You know. *Liked you.*'

She could feel her cheeks burning hot.

'I wouldn't think that. We've always been just friends.'

'Of course,' he said quickly.

The taxi stopped and Jennifer got out. Well that's it then, she thought as she rifled in her bag for some money. When she looked up, the taxi was heading off down the drive and Jim was standing next to her in the dark.

'What are you doing?'

'I can walk from here,' he said, looking embarrassed.

The rain had stopped. It was as if the thunder had pushed the clouds out of the sky and let the creamy moon spill its light over the grounds.

He shoved his hands into his pockets and lingered.

'Do you want to come in?'

'But your mum bites . . .'

Jennifer glanced back towards the house. There was little sign of life inside, just the faint glow of a lamp that had been left on somewhere. She racked her brain for another suggestion of something to do.

'Most likely to be on the front cover of *Rolling Stone* . . .' she said, quite easily imagining his handsome face on the cover of a magazine. 'And you've still not written me a song.'

'Most likely to get married,' he said, raising a brow.

'Sorry if the thought of it is so hideous.' She laughed, trying to deflect the tension, telling herself that they were just having fun, just teasing each other.

'It's not, actually.' He said it so matter-of-factly, without embarrassment. 'In fact we should make a pact, right here, right now. If we get to forty and neither one of us is married, we should, you know. Do it.'

'Do what?'

'Get married.'

She looked away and gulped. She could feel her heart racing but told herself that it was just a joke, that the suggestion didn't really mean anything.

'Do we have to be unmarried, or does being divorced count?' she said, struggling to keep a lightness in her voice, struggling to hide how exciting this suggestion was to her. 'Because you'll be a rock star by then and on your third marriage . . .'

'We just have to be single. Which means if you're very lucky, you might get a window of opportunity . . .'

'Between *Playboy* models?'

He didn't take his eyes away from her.

'You think I'm that shallow?'

'Absolutely, you're a man.'

He took a step towards her and her heart started to thud harder, as if a glimmer of light had presented itself on the horizon.

'But you'll be a famous film director by then. Running around with all these handsome young actors, won't spare a minute for your old mate Jim Johnson, the gnarly rock star.'

'I'll always have time for you,' she said with a surge of courage.

'You'd better.'

He looked at her with those eyes that were sometimes green, sometimes grey, and she knew right then that all she wanted to do was kiss him. That all she had wanted to do all summer was kiss him.

He pushed a lock of her hair behind her ear and their lips were so close she could smell the light whiff of beer on his breath. The mood shifted, the air vibrated, a shiver of possibility made her whole body prickle and she knew that from nowhere had come a night that she would remember for ever.

Instinctively she closed her eyes, willing him to come even closer, but as she felt his lips brush hers, she heard a noise behind her. The sound of the front door of Casa D'Or.

Her eyes snapped open and she turned and saw her mother, back-lit in the doorway of the house.

Jennifer could almost hear the pin pricking her little bubble of happiness. *Pop.*

Sylvia walked to the edge of the steps.

'I think you had better come inside,' she said coolly, not even acknowledging Jim's presence.

Jennifer glanced at Jim and muttered a goodbye, then ran up the steps, tripping as she reached the top. Too embarrassed to even turn around to see if he was still watching, she disappeared inside the house.

Silence settled around the dimly lit hall.

Sylvia looked immaculate in her expensive navy dressing gown. It was made of silk and chiffon and had the effect of making her look like a formidable Hollywood star.

'Where have you been?' she asked, crossing her arms in front of her.

'The beach,' said Jennifer, looking down at her still-damp-from-the-rain shorts and T-shirt.

'You know Connor phoned the house this evening. He wanted to know where you were and I didn't know what to tell him.'

'I was with friends,' she said, feeling herself wilt under her mother's gaze.

'Really,' replied Sylvia tightly.

A sliver of moonlight shone in through the skylight window, and for a moment Jennifer thought her mother looked like the wicked queen from some wintry fantasy land. Her skin was as white as alabaster, her expression frozen in quiet contempt. She was waiting for the tension in the room to rise. Jennifer knew the script. Her mother would lift her fingers to her temples. Her voice would start to tremble with rage, climbing in pitch; her nostrils would flare and her eyes blaze.

Sylvia Wyatt was quite terrifying when she was angry – and from a young age, Jennifer had worked out that the best way to deal with it was to avoid her mother's fits entirely, either by not upsetting her in the first place, or by getting out of the way of her fury.

Now, however, Sylvia released her arms and her expression softened.

'You wanted to interview me for your documentary,' she said finally.

'Yes,' replied Jennifer cautiously. She had mentioned the subject a couple of times over the past few weeks. On both occasions it was when her mother had seemed most relaxed and happy; once after a victorious game of tennis, another time when a particularly flattering photograph of her had appeared in one of Savannah's society magazines.

'Why don't we do it now? Your father has gone to a party at Matthew and Brooke Lane's house, but I had a headache and decided to come home.'

Jennifer frowned in puzzlement, but her mother pretended not to notice.

'Come with me,' she instructed.

Jennifer followed her up the long sweep of staircase. Her camcorder was on her dressing table, so she grabbed it and caught up with her mother, who had gone up to the next floor, to a part of the house used only for storage. They went into a room in the far wing that contained Sylvia's winter clothes. The weather in Savannah rarely dipped below ten degrees even on dark December evenings, but it was here that she kept her riding boots and cashmere coats, the heavy wool dresses she would take on trips to Europe, her fur stoles and leather gloves, an Aladdin's cave of feminine treasures that David Wyatt rarely ventured into.

The room was in the eaves of the house. It was dark up here, with only a small light on the ceiling. There was a window seat at one end, underneath an arched panel of glass that looked out on to the swimming pool, shining turquoise in the night. Jennifer crossed the room to sit down as Sylvia picked up a hat box and opened it. Jennifer could barely see its contents; it appeared to be full of papers and knick-knacks, the sort of memory box that people kept for no reason other than nostalgia. It surprised her, as her mother had never appeared the sentimental sort.

Sylvia pulled out a book of the small, glossy hardback variety, with the words *Charleston Design* on the cover.

'You want to know about me, about my life, about my hopes and dreams for my child?' she asked, clutching it to her chest. 'This book was my bible. I found it in a thrift store in Alabama, when I was a couple of years younger than you are now. No idea how it got there. Not much call for interior design in my home town, I can tell you. But the world inside this book . . . It was a million miles away from the place I grew up.'

Jennifer was taken aback by this personal revelation. She knew very little about her mother's background and family. Jennifer's grandparents had died before she was born, and there was a sister, Donna, whom Jennifer had apparently met, though her memories of her were so faint, she wondered if she had only imagined them. Donna was alluded to infrequently, a cautionary tale that involved drink and multiple partners and drifting around the world, but very little information had ever been revealed beyond the fact that Sylvia had grown up on a farm in Alabama and was to all intents and purposes an orphan.

'This book brought me to Charleston. I came to learn about design and I fell in love with the city and the art of making things beautiful. And then I fell in love with Ethan Jamieson.'

She opened the book carefully, pulled out a loose photograph from within its pages and handed it to Jennifer. It was an old black-and-white snap, poorly developed and faded at the edges. But despite the quality of the picture, there was no denying the beauty of the subject.

'Is this him?' asked Jennifer quietly, too transfixed to even pick up her camcorder. He had dark hair and piercing eyes that reminded her a little of Jim.

Sylvia nodded and took the photo back.

'I was twenty years old when I met him. I was living the life,' she said with a soft, nostalgic smile. 'I had an apartment above an antique store on King Street. I was young, pretty. There were a lot of offers of dates and nights out, and I enjoyed the attention. I'd met your father by this point too; we'd been on a couple of dates and I liked him.'

Jennifer knew that her father and mother had met at a party in Charleston over Christmas, but not even her father had elaborated on those scant details.

'Ethan was exciting,' she said with what sounded almost like disapproval. 'Not just the best-looking guy in the room, maybe the most handsome man in the whole of Charleston. He was twenty-two, just graduated from Brown. He was a photographer and an incredibly talented one. Charleston was still segregated at this point. Legislation had been passed but it was slow to move, so Ethan was out there doing his bit for racial equality. He drank in bars that the coloured folk used to drink in, took pictures of the racial divides that still existed in the city and exhibited them in New York, Washington to show the ruling elite what was still going on. He was exotic, dynamic, and I loved his passion. In comparison, your father seemed a little dull and ordinary and I stopped taking his calls.'

Sylvia paused as if she were composing herself. Jennifer could only clutch her camcorder and stare at her. She couldn't remember a time when her mother had spoken so openly or expansively and wondered how difficult it must be for her.

'We dated for three months, Ethan and I. And then we didn't. It turns out he had a girlfriend in Washington the whole time,' she said, her voice returning to its usual brisk efficiency. 'The joke, unfortunately, was on me, although a few weeks later I ran into your father again. I didn't deserve a second chance but he gave me one. He moved back to Savannah, I came with him and we were married twelve months later.'

'Did you ever see Ethan again?' asked Jennifer quietly.

'I read a story in the paper a few years ago. "Charleston war photographer dies". It was Ethan. I looked into it. I thought maybe a bomb in Sudan or Iraq might have killed him. But he drank himself to death. He died alone, a divorced, penniless alcoholic in Mount Pleasant.'

Sylvia walked slowly towards her daughter, and for a moment Jennifer's heart was hammering as she wondered what she was going to do. But she just sat down next to her.

'My point,' she said in the most steady and even voice, 'is that the exciting option is not always the right one, however it might seem at the time. My point is that love, lust,' she added with emphasis, 'can be more intoxicating than liquor, and like alcohol, it can make us choose unwisely.'

Her face became steely. 'I keep a photo of Ethan to remind myself of that. To remind myself how things could have been. How things could have turned out for me and my child.'

She touched Jennifer tenderly on the arm.

'Connor is a good boy. He's smart and generous and he's prepared to wait for you to decide what you want to do. You do love him?' she asked, meeting her daughter's gaze, challenging her to defy her.

Jennifer didn't feel as if she knew anything any more and just nodded. It seemed to placate her mother.

'You know each other inside and out and you can have a good life with him,' she continued. 'Jim Johnson is handsome, exciting, I will admit that. But who is he other than some boy from England who's going to break your heart once he goes back to London? He's not your future. I spoke to his parents and he's still planning on going around Europe in the fall. Did you imagine he was going to stay here in Savannah with you?'

Jennifer didn't have any reply for her mother. She was too overwhelmed even to speak.

'Am I not right?' urged Sylvia.

And as her memories of Jim Johnson outside the house faded from her consciousness, and her mother gripped her hand with an emotion that could only be described as love, Jennifer found herself agreeing with her.

Chapter Thirteen

2015

Jim looked at his watch, then across at the door, wondering how long it was polite to wait before he could just get up and go.

A blind date. What had he been thinking of? So he wasn't up there with Jack Nicholson in the little-black-book stakes, but he was a popular guy by anyone's measure. The pretty maître d' had definitely seated him at one of the better tables in the restaurant, and kept looking and smiling more than had probably been advised in the customer service handbook. No, Jim didn't need setting up, he reminded himself. Besides which, he was off women. Melissa had transitioned through the silent treatment phase, and had contacted him twice in the past week to tell him that not only was he an arsehole, he still had her *The Good Wife* box set at his flat and please could he FedEx it back as a matter of urgency. In addition, as the new de facto head of the Omari group in the US, he had a whole new inbox of headaches to deal with: planning and zoning issues; VIP customers at their Santa Barbara resort; even a personnel issue when a sous chef had disappeared with a juicing machine.

He watched the people on the sidewalk opposite, a crowd of suits and high-end dresses, presumably heading to a gallery opening. The bar he'd chosen was right across from the Chelsea market, in the heart of arty Manhattan. Twenty years ago, this area would have been no-go, home to junkies and working girls, the gutters overflowing. Now it abounded with galleries and artfully distressed bars just like this one.

'Another?'

He looked up, momentarily thrown. The maître d' smiled, nodding at the glass in front of him.

'Another beer?'

'Sure. No, actually I'd better . . . Maybe later.'

'No probs,' she said with a coquettish smile. 'I can wait.'

I can't, he thought, glancing at his watch and realising that if he slipped out of here now, he might be able to squeeze in a run and still be back in time for *Homeland*.

He was just about to summon the bill when an attractive redhead came in from the cold. She loosened the scarf around her neck and looked around, meeting his gaze. Since his entanglement with Jennifer all those years ago, he had come to realise that his new type was not quite so obviously beautiful women, his reasoning being that they were less likely to leave him, but there was no denying that Sarah Huxley was an absolute knockout.

He put his wallet back in his pocket and looked at her hopefully.

'Jim?' she asked with a broad red-lipped smile.

He nodded gratefully. 'How did you guess?'

'Google takes out the guesswork. I'm Sarah, by the way,' she said breathlessly. 'Sorry I'm late. Bloody subway's useless. What are we drinking?'

Jim laughed, holding up his beer bottle. 'Well I've just had—'

'Great, two more of those,' she said to the maître d', dumping her bag on the floor.

'I suppose this is better than Tinder,' she grinned, slipping her brown coat off to reveal a cherry-coloured dress.

'I've not joined the digital dating age.'

'Get with the programme, Grandad.'

He was touchy these days about age jibes, but Sarah said it with such a sense of fun, he didn't take offence.

'So how long have you been in New York?'

'Three weeks. What about you?'

'Three years.'

'And you're a reporter?'

She nodded. 'I came over on a graduate scheme for one of the tabloids, but I liked it and stayed. Now I'm on the news desk at Whizzfeed.'

'The website? I thought it was all lists and pictures of fluffy kittens.'

'We've got a news team of thirty-five, and a bigger investigations department than *Newsweek*.'

'What story are you working on this week?'

'The top ten places to buy doughnuts in New York City.'

Jim looked at her with bemusement before she burst out laughing.

'I'm kidding.'

'You've got the filthiest laugh since Sid James, do you know that?'

'And I can't tell you how good it is to speak to someone who knows who Sid James actually is, even if he was about twenty years before my time.'

He made a mental calculation of her age, but didn't do it discreetly enough.

'I'm twenty-seven,' she smiled playfully. 'What about you?'

'Older,' he replied, swirling his beer around his bottle.

'Are you the same age as Jennifer?'

'More or less.'

'Is that how you know each other? You were contemporaries?' she asked, fishing for information.

'We were neighbours in Savannah for one summer about twenty years ago. I hadn't seen her for years until I moved to New York.'

'Did you have a fling?' she asked bluntly.

'A fling?'

'Back in Savannah. Was she a holiday romance?'

'She was a friend. A good friend. What about you? How did you meet her?' he asked, grateful to steer the conversation away from him.

'Some swanky charity event,' smiled Sarah. 'I'd been sent to cover it for the parties section of the website. I was on my own, didn't know a soul. I was loitering by the buffet wondering when I could leave when Jennifer came over and introduced herself. Turns out she organised the event and still managed to be the friendliest person in the room. You don't often get that in New York society circles.'

Jim gave a soft smile. 'That sounds like Jen.'

'We kept in touch. I helped her promote the charity. Somewhere along the line we became friends. She says she likes the British sense of humour. Maybe I remind her of you.' Sarah grinned.

Jim ordered them both another drink.

'So do you know Connor?' he asked, his turn to mine for information.

Sarah groaned and Jim felt a sense of satisfaction.

'You're a fan, then?'

'I don't really know him, but I don't like to see Jen when she's around him. She treads on eggshells. I don't think life with him is easy.'

Jim could feel his heart beating harder.

'His business troubles aren't helping.'

'Connor? I thought he was King of the Hill.'

'Sure, that's what he wants everyone to think. But businessmen like that . . . Well, a lot of it is just a con trick, isn't it?'

'You think Connor's business is in trouble?'

Sarah hesitated as if she didn't want to say any more.

'I heard a rumour at work that he's thrown all his chips in with some developer and that the project is in trouble.

I broached it with Jen and she reluctantly told me how worried they were. She was even talking about using the inheritance from her dad to tide him over.'

'But I always got the sense that Connor came from money,' he frowned. 'I mean, isn't his father loaded?'

'Not after Lehman Brothers,' replied Sarah.

Jim had never really understood what Connor's father had done. Something in finance as he recalled – or had he just assumed? Certainly during that hot summer Connor had made sure everyone was aware that his daddy had a yacht, a big house and a Cessna jet. But Sarah was right: often in those circumstances it was just a matter of moving paper around, keeping all the plates spinning. And when they crashed down, they could bring others with them.

'Maybe I should speak to her,' said Jim.

'Don't,' said Sarah, shaking her head. 'I shouldn't have said anything. Jen's proud, I don't think she'd appreciate me gossiping.'

'It's not gossip when it's your friends.'

She looked meaningfully at him. 'Please?'

He thought about it for a moment.

'Sure. I won't say anything. I owe her a favour anyway.'

'What for?'

Jim gave her a crooked smile.

'For you, of course.'

The air was cold when Jim and Sarah stepped out into the street. They had been talking for two hours – more, in fact –

laughing for most of it. Jim couldn't remember having enjoyed a night out so much for ages. Sarah was funny, clever, mischievous. Her eyes danced everywhere, as if she were always looking for the next adventure, and as their conversation progressed and the more they revealed of themselves to each other, the less Jim found himself thinking about work, how he should be home catching up on his emails. The less he found himself thinking about Jennifer.

'So are you going to walk me to the subway?' asked Sarah, pulling up her collar.

'You're not getting a cab?'

'Sitting in traffic drives me nuts. Besides, I've got to keep in shape for Barry's.'

'Barry's?' he said, feeling a spike of jealousy about another man.

'Barry's Bootcamp. It's a class I go to. It's hard-core.'

'So you're keeping fit to keep up with keep-fit.'

'Why don't you come?'

'When is it?'

'Six a.m.'

'Welcome to New York.'

His stomach rumbled and he realised he hadn't eaten anything since lunch.

'How about we get something to eat?' he suggested.

'I've got a better idea. My friend is DJ-ing tonight.'

'It's Tuesday,' he said, struggling to remember the last time he'd gone clubbing, let alone on a week night.

'So? Come on. You'll love it. It's a load of retro stuff.'

* * *

They got a cab to a dive bar in Brooklyn. The place was full of men with beards and plaid shirts. Jim checked his suit jacket in at the cloakroom and ordered a double vodka. Sarah seemed to know everyone. Within half an hour, so did he.

A couple called Justin and Ashley invited them to their cabin in the Adirondacks for the weekend. A travel blogger called Cara offered to do a piece on the Omari group, which Jim politely said he'd think about, until Sarah pointed out that her site had more traffic than Condé Nast Traveller.

Sarah dragged him up to dance, and after the amount he'd had to drink, he was happy to oblige, singing along to everything the DJ threw at them, from Snoop Dogg to Sonic Youth. If he noticed that Sarah didn't know the words, he tried not to register it.

'I love this old stuff,' she said, throwing her head back and laughing out loud. Her hair tossed back like a matador's cape, and when she settled her arms around the back of Jim's neck, it seemed like the most natural place for them to be.

'Are you going to kiss me, then, or am I going to have to make the first move?' she whispered into his ear.

Her lips were only inches away from his now. Jim felt his skin tingle as they moved closer together until they were kissing; soft and sensual at first, becoming firmer and more passionate. Finally, they came up for air, both grinning like schoolchildren caught behind the bike sheds.

'People are going to start staring,' he smiled as they pulled apart. 'The British are supposed to have such a stiff upper lip after all.'

'Then we'd better find somewhere more private,' she smiled as she took his hand and led him out of the club and back to her apartment in Brooklyn.

Chapter Fourteen

Jim had never liked the Hamptons. Or rather, he disliked the idea of it: a glittering enclave created exclusively for the use of the rich. Before today, admittedly, he had never visited Long Island, but he had mixed with plenty of people who had houses there. As a rule, they were the sort of people who boasted about their Upper East Side lateral conversion or their 'cottage' in Mustique.

'Isn't it pretty, though?' said Sarah, peering out of the window of the car. 'It's like Walt Disney created a perfect version of what America should look like.'

She was certainly right about that. The houses passing on either side were perfect: sweeping lawns, picket fences, the Stars and Stripes hanging from the porches of beautifully rendered colonial cottages. Scaled-up versions, of course: hidden at the rear of these cute white clapboard fantasies would be pools and tennis courts and glass extensions filled with art and angular furniture. But from the front they were all nodding blue and pink hydrangeas and Americana shining in the sun.

'I just wish you didn't have to be a millionaire to live here. That's why I love hotels so much: the places we build might be expensive, but at least everyone can go and stay there.'

Sarah raised an eyebrow. 'I had no idea the Omari luxury hotel group was so socialist.'

He laughed. Sarah had a way of managing to cut through his defences. He needed something to calm his nerves, as he was dreading reaching their destination. They were heading to White Dune, the East Hampton estate owned by Connor Gilbert, Jennifer's husband. Apparently the couple held a swish party at their house every Memorial Day, and Jim knew that that in itself was going to be difficult. He didn't like Connor, never had, but meeting him for the first time in twenty years at his thirty-million-dollar estate wasn't going to make him any more humble.

'You OK?'

'Sure, just trying to find my way through all this bling.'

They were passing through Bridgehampton, a small village with a cute ice cream parlour, a pizza shop, even a thrift store, which made the mind boggle. The rest of the single main street seemed to be taken up with art galleries, flash interiors outlets and fashion boutiques. Sarah reached over and squeezed his knee.

'Don't worry, my darling,' she said in a fair impression of Katharine Hepburn's clipped vowels. 'One day, all this will be yours.'

Jim smiled across at her. He was glad she was here; it would certainly make the coming ordeal more bearable. But the truth was, he was also feeling tense because this was their first official outing as a couple. They had been seeing each other now for close to two months. After that electric first date, they had spent almost all their spare time together, much to Jim's surprise. His plan, of course, had been to start seeing Sarah as a way of seeing more of Jennifer. In that regard, it had been an abject failure. He had seen Jennifer only once in the past six or seven weeks, and only then briefly for a drink before he and Sarah headed off to the movies. The truth was, there just hadn't been enough time. The Casa D'Or project was well under way, the marketing people already circulating a glossy press release to build interest and excitement, and he was settling into his new life in Manhattan. But it was also that he liked Sarah. They had settled into an easy relationship that was refreshing in its lack of complexity. They went out. They had fun. The sex was great and Jim even found himself calling when he said he would.

He glanced over at her and she winked. He liked her. A lot.

'Christ, is this where they live?'

They had turned off the Montauk Highway – a rather grand name for what was really just a two-lane road cutting through wineries and dunes, with the occasional large house – and on to an unmarked stretch of blacktop punctuated here and there by a hump of white wind-blown sand. Neither of them, however, was paying much attention to the road.

If the houses in Southampton and Water Mill had looked like overgrown cottages, the houses out here looked like full-blown mansions. The architecture paid lip service to the colonial style, yes, but there was no mistaking the grandeur of these dwellings: long drives, landscaped gardens and extensive outbuildings to house the spa or the stables or the 'playroom'.

'To think I've got a degree from sodding Cambridge and I live in a rent-controlled flat in Brooklyn. What do you think all these people do for a living?' said Sarah, with a trace of bitterness. 'They're twenty mil minimum; even if you're a banker, how do you scrape together the cash for that? I mean, these are second homes – they don't even come here most of the year.'

'Money begets money,' said Jim. 'If you start with Grandad's oil millions, Daddy turns it into stock-market billions and then you sit around waiting for the dot-com wave to mature. Unless it's all just paper,' he added.

Sarah nodded. 'Unless it's all just paper. But don't go throwing that into conversation with Connor, OK? I wasn't supposed to tell you about it; Jennifer told me in confidence.'

'Don't worry, I'm not planning on talking to Connor at all if I can help it.'

'Good idea.'

There was a security guard waiting at the end of the drive holding a clipboard. They gave their names and were waved through. At the end of the drive, a uniformed parking attendant took Jim's keys: you couldn't be expected to have to park your own Mercedes, even if it did come from Hertz for the weekend.

Jim looked up at the house. It was a huge two-storey building with tall windows, and honeysuckle climbing up the immaculate whitewashed siding.

'I'm sure he has a really small penis,' whispered Sarah, and they both started to laugh.

A butler opened the door and they were immediately presented with a drink that looked like fruit punch.

The hall was cavernous, with tasteful modern art on the expansive white walls. Jim looked around, working out which architect and interior designer they were likely to have used; the immaculately tasteful use of distressed white oak, copper and mirrors had the hallmark of one particularly exclusive company he had worked with.

'This way, I think,' said Sarah, following the noise of the laughter, the rumble of voices and the chink of glassware.

Jim took a swallow of his cocktail. This whole scenario reminded him vividly of the first time the Johnsons had visited Casa D'Or for a drinks party. Forced into a shirt and one of his father's ties, he had skulked behind his mother and father, scowling and sullen, but had been secretly overawed by the wealth and privilege he'd been surrounded by. Blue bloods who could trace their line back to the *Mayflower*, rich in oil and stocks and communications, they dressed for dinner and for each other. Jim hated everything it stood for, connections and snobbery, but had secretly been impressed by it.

They stepped out from the shadow of the house on to the

deck. Directly in front of them was an infinity pool that connected with its neat visual trick to the ocean. There were at least two dozen people standing around in small groups, chatting and drinking. Jim was used to mixing in these circles. He thought of himself with Simon Desai on New Year's Eve, the conversation that had brought him here, and knew he could keep up. In these circumstances, he would usually seek out the person who had invited him, wait for them to connect him with a handful of others, and then let his charm and banter do the rest.

He saw her face almost immediately, and she had seen him. The crowd seemed to melt away as she moved towards them.

'Sarah, Jim.' She was wearing a floaty blue dress that fell almost to the floor; her dark hair had been pinned up on her head. In a sea of blow-dries, Botox and expensive gowns, she looked more natural and lovely than ever. 'So glad you could make it out.'

She and Sarah embraced. 'Jen, this place is amazing! I want to live here for ever.'

'You wouldn't say that if you had to mow the lawns.' Jennifer grinned back.

Jim smiled, trying to imagine the spectacle of Jennifer Wyatt-Gilbert pushing an old-fashioned rotary mower back and forth across the grass.

'And what are you chuckling about?'

'Oh, just happy to be here,' said Jim, leaning in for a brief kiss. 'Sarah's right, this place . . . whoa!'

He pushed his sunglasses up, as if to check his eyes were

working correctly. Behind the pool was a gently sloping lawn; behind that, a low tangle of scrub, then dazzling white sand and beyond that, the sea.

'It's an amazing party,' he said, sighing at the view and accepting a glass of champagne.

'Well, we invite everyone at the start of summer so that they'll come and spend at the fund-raisers we host over the season,' she whispered playfully. 'Come on. Let me introduce you to a few people. And don't believe anyone who says they bought in the Hamptons before the area was fashionable.'

Jim found himself enjoying the party more than he'd thought he would. He met Chesters, Millies and Jensens; there was even a red-faced woman named Muffy. They were all wealthy, smug and patronising, but they were also masters of small talk, which allowed him to settle back and soak it all in.

'You're in property, Jim?' said a tall, thin man called Cooper. 'Very wise in this day and age. Where's the up-and-coming area at the moment?'

'Jamaica,' said Jim, sensing a chance for some mischief.

'The Caribbean?'

'No, Jamaica, Queens. The pocket right around the AirTrain,' he added, ignoring Sarah's look. 'If you have any spare cash, I'd snap up anything you can lay your hands on. It's solid pre-war stock, near the airport, and the hipsters are moving in. And where the hipsters go . . . Look at Brooklyn. Can't buy a fourth-floor walk-up for less than a mil in Williamsburg any more.'

Cooper nodded sagely and conversation moved on to the rising costs of running a car in the city. Sarah raised a laugh by suggesting they all chip in for a minivan and take it in turns to pop to Whole Foods. Eventually she and Jim detached themselves and drifted down towards the pool.

'You know Cooper will be ordering his realtor to buy some crack house in Queens by Monday,' said Sarah, settling into a big egg-shaped love seat. 'But I don't know any hipsters moving into Sutphin Boulevard.'

'I was yanking his chain a little, but if you're prepared to take a punt, it's not a bad call – assuming you can afford to wait for the upswing. Manhattan's not getting any bigger, people are going to move out, especially people with young families.'

Sarah sat swishing her feet back and forth.

'And what about you?' she said. 'You have any plans to move out and have a family?'

He cut his eyes across at her. Was this a variation on Melissa's babies and wedding bells speech?

'Sarah, I've only just moved to the city . . .'

She looked at him. 'But Jim, I need to know that you're serious about *us*.'

Her face was stony, then a twinkle appeared in her eyes, then she laughed her Sid James laugh.

'You're a devil in the sack, but don't flatter yourself that you're husband material. You've got the big four-oh coming up; isn't it about time you bought a Harley?'

'Isn't thirty-nine a bit young for a mid-life crisis?'

'Our executive editor, Ryan? One Friday lunchtime, he went out and got a tattoo of a shark. We all laughed, until the following Monday when he didn't turn up for work. We got a postcard from him a month later saying he'd moved to the Cayman Islands and was working as a diving instructor.'

'That's a classic.'

'Yeah, but Ryan was thirty-six and had a wife and two-year-old daughter. Don't know if they got a postcard too.'

Jim laughed. 'I'm not sure thirty-six counts as middle age,' he said pointedly.

'Should we go for a nosy around this place?' said Sarah, standing up. 'I thought I saw Karlie Kloss by the buffet. Besides, I want to take a picture of the lobster thermidor for Instagram.'

As Sarah picked up her shoes, Jim felt a tap on his shoulder. He turned, but too fast, slipping in Sarah's wet footprints. A voice he immediately recognised spoke, a hand gripping his elbow, steadying him.

'Don't want anyone drowning, do we?'

Embarrassed, Jim straightened and forced a smile.

'Thanks, Connor,' he said. 'Not quite the way I imagined making my entrance.'

Connor Gilbert laughed. His hair was streaked with grey, he had deep lines across his forehead, but there was no mistaking him. Whereas most of his contemporaries had filled out a little since their twenties, Connor's lineback physique had become leaner.

'You look great,' said Jim honestly, extending his hand and

immediately regretting it: Connor Gilbert was one of those people who felt the need to crush your knuckle bones by way of a greeting.

'Yoga and vitamins,' Connor said off-handedly. 'Been a long time, Jimmy,' he added, slightly too loudly. 'You haven't changed a bit.'

Jim wasn't sure he meant it as a compliment.

'This is Sarah . . .' he began, then suddenly remembered they were already acquainted.

'I know this little lady,' said Connor, reaching over to give Sarah an awkward hug. Jim knew she wouldn't exactly be overjoyed to be referred to as a 'little lady', either.

'So how's things?' he said. 'Jennifer says you're working for Simon Desai. I hear his finances ain't what they were.'

Jim felt his anger rising.

'Really? Well don't believe all you hear, Connor.'

'I thought you were going to be a rock star?'

'Teenage kicks,' he answered, although the music reference was lost on Connor.

Connor turned to Sarah. 'Could you excuse us for a few moments?' he said, indicating that she was no longer welcome.

When she had gone, they were both silent for a few seconds.

'So how did it feel then, Johnson? Did it give you all the satisfaction you thought it would?'

'I'm not sure what you're talking about, Connor,' said Jim, not moving his gaze from the other man's.

'Buying Casa D'Or. A master class in petty point-scoring if ever I saw one.'

'No,' said Jim emphatically. 'It wasn't a point score. We were looking for a house in the South. We looked at Casa D'Or. I happen to think it needed saving.'

'Needed saving!' scoffed Connor. 'Is that how you're justifying it to yourself when you're trying to sleep at night? You leave Savannah under a cloud. You come back and rub salt into the wound after everything that happened. Sylvia Wyatt *died* in that house, Jim, and you write to Jennifer asking for permission to turn it into a pleasure palace. If that's not the most fucking immoral and insensitive thing I have heard in the property business, I don't know what is.'

Jim felt angered that Connor had taken the moral high ground. He felt sure that men like Connor didn't get to be as rich or successful as he had without making some ruthless decisions. The truth was, though, he knew the other man had a point.

'I know you're here in the city now, Johnson, I know you've even seen Jen once or twice.' Connor put his glass of champagne down on a table and looked Jim directly in the eye. 'But if you mention that house to her, if you mention the family name in any of the marketing material, if you bring her anywhere near that place, involve her in any way, then I will do everything I can in my power to make things difficult in Savannah. Do you understand?'

'You don't need to threaten me, Connor,' said Jim coolly. 'I've only ever had Jen's best interests at heart.'

'Really? You've got no idea what Jennifer's best interests

are,' Connor said coldly. 'You did your best to sabotage our relationship, pit Jennifer against her family. And when she fell apart after what happened, where were you to pick up the pieces?'

I was sent away, thought Jim, clenching his hand into a fist.

Just go back to England, Jim. If you are truly my friend, you should do what is right for all of us and not contact me again.

Connor shook his head, glaring at Jim. Then, with a snort of disgust, he turned and stalked back towards the house.

'Shit,' whispered Jim under his breath. He felt the same way he used to after trying to lock horns with his father as a young man: like he'd just been run over.

He looked around for Sarah, but she was locked in conversation with a supermodel. He didn't feel she would welcome an interruption, not when she was probably trying to secure an interview or a story for Whizzfeed.

He picked up the glass of champagne that Connor had left behind and knocked the dregs down his throat. Then he wiped his mouth with the back of his hand and left the pool area through a side gate that led to the beach, letting the party noise fade behind him.

The light had fallen out of the sky and the horizon was streaked peach and violet. As he got closer to the water, he could hear the sound of the waves crashing against the shore.

A sobering thought hit him. No matter what he felt about Connor – and right from the start he had never liked him – there was no denying that he loved Jennifer. And for that, he felt like a cuckoo in the nest just being here.

He kicked at a stone with his toe, then bent to pick it up. Flat and round, it felt good in his hand. Whipping his arm sideways, he threw the pebble, spinning it with his index finger, watching with satisfaction as it hopped once, twice . . . four . . . no, five times across the water before disappearing with a plop.

'You tried to teach me to do that, do you remember?' said a voice behind him.

He turned around and saw Jennifer standing there, holding a glass.

'I never could get it, though, could I?'

Jim took a step towards her. The sea roared on to the beach and sucked a raft of pebbles out to its depths

'What are you doing out here?' he said finally.

'Coming to bring you in.'

'Don't be daft, I'm just getting some air.'

'So how rude was Connor to you?' she asked, searching around for words.

He frowned.

'You were talking. Heatedly . . .'

'We were just chatting.' He shrugged.

'That's what Connor said.' She looked at him dubiously. 'But I know him better than that.'

Jennifer's soft face smiled at him. He remembered the first time they had been alone together, in the dark, by the water, the first night he had gone to Casa D'Or. He'd been dazzled by her. She was pretty – beautiful, even – but in the short time he had been at that supper party, he'd guessed at her many beguiling layers. Jennifer Wyatt was at once the lost girl, the rich girl, the tomboy and the swan. She had spent her whole life doing what other people had told her, and yet with a quiet sense of will she was determined to strike out on her own.

'He doesn't think I should be developing Casa D'Or,' said Jim, knowing he couldn't hide things from her. 'Is that what you think?'

'It's too late to object now.' She smiled slowly. 'I got an email from Marion. She said they're already recruiting for staff to start at Thanksgiving.'

'It was never my intention to hurt you, Jen.'

'I know that. I always have. Despite everything, I love Casa D'Or. I don't want it to become a mausoleum, and I know you'll breathe life back into the place. I think it deserves that.'

'Well, I'm sorry,' he replied.

'I'm sorry too. Connor . . . he's going through some things at the moment.'

He knew it was his opportunity to bring it up.

'Work?'

She puffed out her cheeks, then looked away.

'Nothing. Just his latest condo development is more complicated than he thought.'

Jim nodded. It was the big risk in any development project: the time it took and how long you could afford to keep going. Buildings had a way of throwing you endless curveballs: foundations built on unseen mining work, attics that had become home to protected creatures that couldn't be moved. Ancient masonry, subsidence, termites – there were hundreds of variables that could hold up a build, and that was before you got to the legal problems of ownership, planning consent and any number of local protests that could bubble up. It was always about how soon you could deliver. The longer it took, the more it cost.

'How complicated?'

She didn't speak.

'Jen, tell me. I might be able to help.'

'He'd like that.' She smiled grimly. 'Besides, I'm sure he'll work it out.'

He took a step towards her.

'Jen, I know people. I might be able to point him towards someone, maybe pull in a favour.'

'No,' she said, shaking her head.

'Too proud?'

'Not me. Connor.'

'Besides, I'd be the last person he'd take help from, right?'

'Your words, not mine,' she smiled.

She looked at him for a long moment, then threw back the last of her drink.

'Come on,' she said. 'Let's get back to the party.'

Jim shook his head. 'I think it'd be better if Sarah and I pushed off.'

'Pushed off? You've both had a drink, it's two hours back to the city. You're staying over as planned, and that's the last I'll hear of it. If you leave, it will only make things more awkward.

Besides, I don't go to the trouble of matchmaking if I can't enjoy watching the results.'

Jim grinned awkwardly.

'How's it going?' she said after a moment. Her words came out quite stiffly, but Jim tried not to read too much into it.

'With Sarah? She's nice. You were right.'

'Only nice?'

He wasn't sure if she was teasing him. He didn't smile back.

'She's fun,' he said finally, deciding that sounded the best balance of being complimentary and yet non-committal. Besides, it was entirely honest.

'Oh yes?'

'A gentleman never tells,' he said, holding up his hands.

'You're no fun.' She grinned slowly, swinging her arms by her sides.

'Let's just say I can't decide if the age gap keeps me young or makes me feel very old,' he said, finally letting his guard down. 'I told her the first gig I'd ever been to was the Nelson Mandela tribute at Wembley. She said she was there too; the only difference was she was *in utero*.'

In his line of vision he could see Sarah walking towards them, coltish legs in tailored shorts striding across the sand. He felt guilty about the quip he had just made, and turned his attention back to Jennifer.

'I like her. Thank you,' he said as his girlfriend got closer. 'I forgot how lonely New York can be. So it's good to have someone around. And I always knew you had impeccable taste in everything.'

'I wondered where you'd got to,' said Sarah, her eyes darting between Jim and Jennifer. 'Is everything OK?'

'Connor was just being Connor,' said Jennifer.

She diplomatically stepped back and let Sarah stand between them. The younger woman's broad smile was a little tighter than usual. As she took her spot, she folded her arms protectively across her chest.

'I was just stopping Jim from fleeing, because you two are staying here tonight. Best room in the house, although if there's any more bad behaviour from Connor, we'll be in separate bedrooms.'

Sarah's look of fear softened to something more reassured, and Jim took her hand.

'Now come on,' said Jennifer. 'Cooper has been telling me all about a zingy new property hot spot you put him on to, and I want in.'

Jim laughed and followed her back across the sand.

Chapter Fifteen

Gently Jim lifted Sarah's arm and slid out of bed, tiptoeing across the floor to the bathroom. Closing the door, he ran water into his hands and splashed it on his face. He looked rough, his complexion pallid.

The rest of the evening had actually been surprisingly fun. Once he'd loosened up, Cooper had shown he had a nice line in anecdotes about the celebrities who dined in the Japanese restaurant he owned downtown. Jim had also found himself in demand as a dance partner once the cheesy disco began on the terrace – one of the pampered wives declaring, 'It's like dancing with Mr Darcy.' Clearly one handsome Englishman was as good as any other after a few appletinis, but at least it allowed Jim to relax a little. He was still angry about his confrontation with Connor by the swimming pool; in the sober light of day, and taking his own guilt out of the equation, he knew that Connor had been spoiling for a fight for the past twenty years and was using the Omari development of

Casa D'Or as a rod to beat him with. And with good reason. After all, as far as he was concerned, Jim had tried to pinch his girlfriend off him. Jim and Jennifer had fallen in love, but Connor was never going to see it like that.

Stretching, Jim left the en suite and returned to the bedroom. Sarah had rolled over and kicked off the sheet in her semi-slumber and now lay temptingly naked. Part of him wanted to slide back in next to her and wake her up, but he knew where that would lead. Last night he had avoided sex by blaming his reluctance on the heavy consumption of alcohol; this morning there would be no excuses, but he felt uncomfortable about doing anything so intimate in Jennifer's house, even if they were in a distant wing.

He stepped outside, squinting at the brightness. Nothing better for a hangover than a blinding flash of sun. Slowly his eyes adjusted to the glare and he leaned on the rail, taking in the view. It was even more impressive from the second floor. From here you could see the whole sweep of the beach, and apart from a small group of gulls picking at the sand, it was deserted. Then he saw movement in the water; not quite deserted, then. Someone was on a paddleboard, heading back towards the beach.

Jim watched as the figure paddled closer, turning from a silhouette to a man in a wetsuit to a recognisable person. It was Connor; there was no mistaking his height. Plus who else would be out on a private beach at six in the morning?

As quietly as he could, he scooped up his jeans and a T-shirt from his overnight bag, put them on, and headed for the door. For himself, Jim would rather never speak to the man again, but for Jennifer's sake he knew he had to try to make peace with Connor – and there was never going to be a better time than now, when he was on his own.

He padded barefoot downstairs. A few wrong turns and he was out on the terrace, walking down the decking ramp to the beach just as Connor was carrying his board up from the sea.

'How was it?' he called.

Connor looked at him, then glanced towards the house. He saw he had no option but to reply.

'Water's still pretty cool this time of year. But it's OK. Quiet.' He propped the board against the walkway's rail and unzipped his suit. 'What are you doing up so early?'

'Couldn't sleep, I guess.'

Neither of them said anything for a few moments.

'Look, I wanted to reiterate what I said last night. About Jen and Casa D'Or.'

Connor shrugged. 'Sure. Do what you've gotta do. Just know that Jennifer's a good person, she'd never make you feel bad, and that shit with the house . . . it's upset her, that's all. Stirred up things she'd rather forget. We'd all rather forget.'

'I understand. And I'm sorry.'

Connor let out a long breath, glancing at Jim.

'And I should apologise too. Shouldn't have gone so crazy at you,' he said begrudgingly. 'You know what parties are like. Stressful.'

Jim was surprised to hear any sort of apology.

'Jen said the condo development is all a bit high-maintenance at the moment.'

'Did she?' Connor said disapprovingly.

'I tell you, I've been there a dozen times. Japanese knotweed almost brought one development we were working on to its knees.'

Connor looked at him for a moment, as if he were weighing things up.

'It's just a liquidity thing. I need to do a bit of refinancing. It will be fine.'

'Will it?' He wanted to push him for an answer. He knew men like Connor would sooner be admitted to the asylum than own up to failure or weakness, but Connor's fortunes affected Jennifer's life too. He remembered his own teenage years. When royalties from his father's book had dried up, the estate agents came round to value the house, and he was pulled out of his fee-paying school to go to the comprehensive down the road.

'What is your point, Jim?'

'No point,' he replied. 'I'm just wondering if there is anything I can do to help.'

Connor gave a loud sarcastic bellow. 'Ha. I bet you're loving this. First buying Casa D'Or, and now you're offering to open the Omari contacts book.'

'I wouldn't wish cash-flow problems on any developer,' Jim said honestly.

'Right.'

'What is it you need?'

A look of anger crossed Connor's face. Jim sensed he had overstepped the mark. The great Connor Gilbert didn't need to go cap in hand to some hotel employee.

'Try a few dozen more billionaires in Manhattan within the next eighteen months.'

'How many have you sold?'

'Some,' he said cautiously.

'But not enough,' said Jim, filling in the gaps.

'Sales have plateaued. There are bigger, shinier developments in the city. I thought Manhattan had the highest number of billionaires per capita in any city in the world. Apparently that's not enough to sustain the number of high-net-worth developments.'

'Anything I can do? I mean, if it's bridging finance you need . . .'

'What are you doing, Johnson? Your girlfriend's dirty work? Looking for a scoop for the business pages of that trivia site she works for?'

'Believe me when I say that anything I can offer is purely to help an old friend.'

Connor hesitated, then sat down on the walkway.

'My finance team are calling it a cash-flow crisis, but I guess you know what that means.'

Jim nodded and sat down next to him. It was a polite way of saying the money had run out and the banks were refusing to lend any more, or worse, calling in the debt. He'd seen it so many times in rival companies: an entire resort development in Dubai had once gone belly-up because there was a sudden inexplicable shortage of sand. Sand was everywhere, of course, but not the right kind, the kind required for making flexible levelling compound. There just wasn't any in the country at the time they needed it, so the building stalled, causing a domino effect that cost the investors millions and meant that the project still stood windowless and empty, the desert slowly blowing in.

'How far in are you?' asked Jim as gently as he could.

Connor barked out a hollow laugh. 'That's the irony; it's seventy-five per cent done.' He turned to Jim, the weariness apparent on his face. 'I'll level with you. We overplayed our hand, told everyone it was under control when it wasn't, missed one too many payment deadlines, I guess. Now when I tell the banks it's ready to go, they don't believe us and I can't really blame them. But – man, you should see it. When it's finished, it will be one of the finest places to live in the city.'

'What do you need?'

He named a figure. Jim didn't blanch. He knew the business well enough to have worked it out.

'Could you not sell some assets?'

'Like our family home?'

'No, I wasn't suggesting that.'

'Yes you were. You've seen this place, must know how much it's worth.'

'It would liquidate some cash . . .'

'It would kill Jennifer to sell this place.'

'Do you think Jen is that interested in money, in the trappings of it all?'

'Is that what she told you?' Connor said, flashing him a fiery look. Then his expression softened and he looked genuinely upset. 'Our city house belongs to a family trust. I could never get rid of this place. Jen loves it. It's the one place where she's happy. By the water. I just don't want her to have to go through leaving another family home that she cares about.'

'I know,' said Jim quietly, silently acknowledging that for once, he and Connor were in complete agreement.

'How interested do you think Simon would be in investing?' Connor's expression was stoic, proud, but the hint of desperation was obvious. Jim didn't like to point out that he had been belittling Simon Desai just the night before, hinting at his financial problems. But he could only imagine how difficult it was for Connor to have this conversation. And he had been telling the truth when he said he didn't want to point-score.

'I don't know,' he said honestly. 'He's avoided ultra-luxe residential investments in New York in the past. Thinks the market's saturated. But I can ask him.'

He watched Connor's shoulders slump. He didn't like the man, but it was impossible not to feel sympathy for everything he was going through.

'I have two hotels,' Connor said finally. 'Through a separate investment vehicle. I don't want to sell either of them, but if I don't raise the capital to salvage the condo project, then I'm in danger of losing everything.'

'Where are they?'

'One is in New York. The other is in the Caribbean. Would you be interested in having a look?'

'Tell me about the Caribbean resort.'

Connor puffed out his cheeks. 'It's on the island of Baruda. Do you know it?'

It was Jim's job to know the industry inside out, the best resorts, the hot spots with buzz. But there were so many thousands of hotels in the world, it was hard to keep abreast of everything. The Caribbean in particular had a raft of hotels with ever-changing names and ownership.

'It's called The RedReef Club. I bought it three years ago. It's not as deluxe as any Omari resort, but it's a wonderful spot, private beach access, fifteen minutes by seaplane to the international airport on Turks and Caicos. You could do something interesting with it.'

'Do you have a sales prospectus?'

'Until five minutes ago, it wasn't even for sale.'

'Well send me something,' Jim said, and for the first time in twenty years, he and Connor looked at each other with something approaching solidarity.

Chapter Sixteen

'Here. Just pull over here.' Jim leaned forward and stuffed a twenty through the Plexiglas screen behind the driver. The cab slid to a halt next to the elderly couple standing at the kerb. His parents, he realised with a sudden shock.

He sighed to himself as he jumped out of the taxi. He had planned to get there early – punctuality was one of Bryn's personal bugbears – but it seemed they had second-guessed him.

'Hey there,' he said, closing the door and embracing them both awkwardly. 'I did say one, didn't I?'

'Your father likes to be on time, you know that,' said Elizabeth briskly. She was wearing a bright blue trench coat, tightly knotted at the waist, and had clearly taken advantage of one of New York's many blow-dry bars.

'Saul used to bring me here,' said Bryn with a scowl, nodding at the door of 21. 'Thought we could have gone somewhere different.'

Jim smiled politely. 'I didn't know. Besides, I thought you'd like it. It's a New York institution.'

He ushered them inside, wondering what his mother would have to say about the restaurant's quirky interior – hundreds of model aeroplanes, trucks and other ephemera hanging from the roof beams – but she didn't have a chance to comment as Gerry, the maître d', swept forward and greeted Bryn like an old friend.

'And this must be Mrs Johnson, a great pleasure.'

'This is our son James,' said Elizabeth. 'He lives here now.'

'Really?' said Gerry. 'I hope we'll be seeing you regularly.'

Jim smiled, biting back the observation that he had been to 21 for dinner twice in the last two months and no one had got terribly excited.

Gerry escorted the group to a curved booth, Jim and Bryn on the ends, Elizabeth in the middle.

'So, happy birthday,' smiled Elizabeth.

'It's not until Sunday.'

'I know, but we're here to celebrate.'

'I really appreciate you coming over. Shame you can't stay until the big day.'

'You don't want your parents hanging around your fortieth birthday party.'

'I'm not having a party,' he laughed. 'Not when I've got a hotel to get opened by November.'

'Melissa would have planned a party for you,' said Elizabeth, raising a brow.

'I'm not sure a fortieth birthday is anything to celebrate.

I'm just going to have a quiet dinner. Maybe go to the cinema. See if there are any reruns of *The Best Exotic Marigold Hotel* anywhere.'

His mother smiled cynically and began to tell him about all the things they had done since they had arrived in New York the evening before: dinner with friends, then cocktails at their hotel.

'Salman picked us up from the airport,' said Bryn pointedly.

Jim knew there was no point reminding them that he had offered to collect them but had been told they were going straight out for dinner.

'Have you seen Saul yet?'

Saul Black, his father's New York agent, was long retired. Bryn would never have admitted it, but Saul was responsible for his change in fortune. Their stay in Savannah resulted in Bryn's biggest hit – the multi-million-selling novel *College*, which was conceived and part-written at the Lake House.

'We've only been in the country twenty-four hours,' said Bryn, back on his short fuse.

'You should go and see him, Jim,' said Elizabeth softly. 'He'd love to see you. Do you remember the superhero pen he gave you when he came to London one time?'

'The pen is mightier than the sword. I think that was what he told me when I tried to hit him with a plastic light sabre.'

Elizabeth fished about in her small handbag, drew out an address book and began copying something on to a piece of paper.

'I'm not going to tell him you'll pop round if you won't, if you're too busy. But it would be lovely if you could go and see him.'

'I'm not completely chained to my desk, you know.'

'Try,' she pressed as the waiter came to take their order.

'So your father has something to announce,' said Elizabeth, evidently tiring of the subject.

'Announce?' Bryn harrumphed, glowering at Elizabeth, but Jim could detect a smile under the frown. 'You make it sound like I'm abdicating or something,' he grumbled. 'Just some nonsense in the honours list.'

'It is not nonsense,' said Elizabeth. 'It's about bloody time, if you ask me.'

Jim looked from one parent to the other. 'Well?' he prompted.

'CBE,' said Bryn bluntly.

'Isn't it marvellous?' trilled Elizabeth, beaming. Jim wasn't sure he'd ever seen his mother smile that widely.

'That's amazing, Dad,' he said, leaning across and clutching Bryn's hand. 'Seriously, it's really well deserved. I'm proud of you.'

Bryn met his eyes for a long moment, then glanced away. 'Lot of rubbish really,' he said. Jim saw that his mother was about to object, so he jumped in first.

'So do you have to go to the palace? Is there a presentation?'

'Not a presentation, an *investiture*,' said Elizabeth, with evident pride. 'It's very formal. They've sent a list of acceptable attire and a guide to the etiquette on the day.'

'Wow, part of the establishment now, Dad?'

'I'd turn it down if I thought it'd make a blind bit of difference,' Bryn snorted.

'Why should you turn it down?' said Elizabeth. 'You're a pioneer, you've changed the face of English literature . . .'

'I'm really thrilled for you. It's brilliant. We should have a party,' suggested Jim. 'I'm due a visit back to London. Maybe we can hire out Wheeler's or Wiltons.' They were two of his father's favourite restaurants.

'Actually, we thought we'd have a party here.'

'In New York?' frowned Jim.

His mother leaned forward and placed both hands on the table.

'Your father's had a very exciting opportunity come his way.'

'I don't know about exciting,' he blustered. 'But it's an opportunity and it's good to try different things.'

'What opportunity?'

'I've been offered a visiting fellowship at Columbia. Just for a semester, although we'll see how it goes.'

'Teaching?'

'I like to think of it as *inspiring*. You know, Martin Amis did it for a little while at Manchester University. The job can be so solitary sometimes.'

'So we're moving over,' added Elizabeth.

'Fantastic,' said Jim, not entirely sure how he really felt about it. He had spent a lifetime living in Bryn Johnson's shadow. Growing up, he'd lost track of the number of times he'd simply been introduced as 'Jim, Bryn Johnson's son', as if he didn't actually exist in his own right. Even when he had moved into the corporate field, his father's reputation still preceded him: the bankers and politicians he met, who all liked to consider themselves well read and literary, seemed to take him that little bit more seriously when they connected his surname to the great prize-winning writer. But in New York, he didn't have that baggage. No one cared where you came from, only where you were going.

'We can keep an eye on you,' added Bryn.

'Right,' he said, taking a large gulp of his gin and tonic.

'You know your mother and I lived here for a while before you were born?'

'Really? I didn't.'

'Yes, carefree times,' Bryn said, a smile creeping on to his face. 'It was just a few weeks. We were real beatniks, living in a cold-water flat off Washington Square. Everyone was a poet or an artist, everyone playing bongos, all the girls wearing smocks. It was glorious.'

'And we went out to Sagaponack to stay with your editor friend,' Elizabeth added. 'It was just the most beautiful place on earth.'

'Back when the right sort of people lived in the Hamptons . . . These days I hear it's all financiers and businessmen. All bought with ill-gotten gains from exploiting the peasants.'

'So who are you going for dinner with on your birthday?' asked his mother, changing the subject.

'Just a few friends.'

'That's nice, I'm glad you're managing to meet people. It's not easy at your age.' She didn't say it unkindly, but it still irked him.

'Is Simon going?' asked Bryn, tasting the wine that the sommelier had brought over.

'Don't be daft, Dad.'

'Well, you can invite him to my investiture party. Or did we decide it was going to be another seventieth birthday party?'

'Both,' said Elizabeth, turning to Jim. 'We should be able to get a contribution from your father's publishers, so if you've got any suggestions about venues, somewhere nice, then let me know.'

'We don't need Jim's help on that. We can have it at the club . . . So how's work?' his father asked.

'Good. Busy.'

'How often are you in Savannah?'

'Once every couple of weeks.'

'Is it still the same?'

'It's much buzzier. Lots of chic shops on Broughton Street.'

'What about Casa D'Or?'

'It's beginning to look a lot like its old self. It was very run down when we bought it. The Lake House has been sold too. The Sittenfields both died. A young family has it now. Anyway, we're having a party too. A launch party. I should be able to swing an invite for Mr and Mrs Bryn Johnson CBE.'

'Have you seen her?'

His mother's expression had cooled. Jim watched her flash a look of disapproval to his father and he knew what they both were thinking. Under the circumstances, he thought it best just to say no.

Chapter Seventeen

Circling down from a cloudless sky, it looked like a child's drawing of a desert island. Lush green strips of palm, ringed by ivory beaches and lapped by azure sea. All clichés had to begin with a truth somewhere, thought Jim, shifting in his seat to peer further out of the Gulfstream's window, so perhaps the Turks and Caicos islands had been the inspiration for those countless images of paradise: endless white sand, coconut trees, maybe even a girl called Friday.

Of course, Jim was the sidekick today. Simon had decided to fly out to see the RedReef development in person – hence the private jet – and Jim was really only going along as a go-between, a middleman to oil the wheels between Simon as the potential buyer and the vendor of RedReef, Connor Gilbert's investment vehicle, CJI. Perhaps he had oversold the 'old friends' dynamic between him and Connor, but in all honesty, it could work for everyone. The resort would be a good fit for Simon's portfolio and a quick sale would be a dream solution to Connor's cash-flow problems. Plus it meant that Jim got a couple of days in the sunshine, which was never a chore.

'RedReef,' said Connor's lawyer, Lance Freer. 'Even sounds pretty, doesn't it?'

'When did you buy it?' asked Simon, looking out of the porthole. They had been in the air for over three hours and had made convivial conversation throughout, but now Jim could see Simon shifting the conversation to a more professional footing.

'Three years ago,' replied Connor stiffly.

'Not long,' Simon said thoughtfully, still staring out of the glass.

'Long enough to know the dangers of diversifying too far out of sectors I don't have much experience in,' added Connor with more modesty than Jim had ever heard from him before.

Simon nodded as if this was an acceptable answer.

A shiny black car met them on the far side of customs and drove them the short distance to a jetty, where a sleek motor launch was waiting.

'It will only take twenty minutes,' said Connor, leading the way up the gangplank. 'Plus it's the best way to approach RedReef: absolutely spectacular, as you will see.'

Jim breathed a sigh of relief as the boat drew closer to Baruda. The sea had been a dazzling emerald for some distance from the shore, but as they neared the island, the vivid colour faded until it was gin clear, which only served to show off the pink-tinged whiteness of the sand. Connor hadn't been wrong about the beauty of his resort, and for that Jim could be thankful; it had certainly been a risk inviting Simon out here sight unseen.

A uniformed waiter had been standing on the aft deck ready with cocktails for the VIP guests, and Jim had winced as Connor quickly gulped his down and gestured for another.

'When in Rome, eh?' he grinned.

Connor had been a ball of nervous energy ever since they had met at Teterboro airport in New Jersey for the flight, and had tried to steady himself with champagne on the plane. Jim was no psychologist, but even he knew that communicating your desperation to a potential buyer was a poor strategy.

As the boat docked at a wooden quayside, Connor offered Simon a hand to step up on to the jetty.

'Welcome to RedReef,' he said, sweeping an arm grandly towards the complex. 'The finest luxury destination in the Caribbean.'

He really didn't need the hyperbole. The resort did all the talking for itself. Built around a glistening lagoon, it was made up of a series of stand-alone villas, each facing the water, many with their own strip of private beach. Painted in candy colours, they had a traditional Caribbean feel. The shabby-chic look was intentional, noted Jim, taking in the deceptively high finish.

'I thought we'd get you settled into your suites, then I'll get Udo, the general manager, to give you the tour.'

* * *

As Jim and Simon travelled round the resort in a golf cart, Jim made a mental inventory. He could see Simon taking in the same details: the spa, restaurant, beachside bar and water sports centre. The fine details of the hotel – the bright hand-crafted Creole bed linens, the outdoor showers, the wood-panelled library stocked with books about the island – were all well done to produce an effect that was chic, casual and comfortable. The only problem was that it did not fit into Omari's aesthetic at all.

'So what do you think?' asked Jim when Connor and the general manager had left them alone.

'It's a good location, that much I can see. But it's not an Omari. It's too rustic, too basic,' Simon said, echoing Jim's own concerns. 'We'd have to pull it down and start again. The spec is good, but not the best, and the best is everything Omari represents.'

'That Omari represents,' said Jim slowly.

Simon frowned.

'I've had an idea for a while, but coming here has brought it to the table.'

Simon was listening with interest.

'I think we need to create a spin-off brand from Omari. A junior Omari. A feeder for the main brand, which represents the very best – and the highest price points – that the hotel industry has to offer.'

'Keep talking.'

Jim's thoughts gained momentum. 'You know the client demographic of the Omari hotels – CEOs, high-net-worths

– but I think there's a class of luxury traveller that doesn't want anything too lavish. I'm dating a girl at the moment. She's twenty-seven and she likes the nice things in life, but it's feeling the sand between her toes and drinking green organic smoothies that matter to her. She wants a ceiling fan, not air con; fresh, simple food, not complicated Michelin-starred meals.'

'So we're aiming at millennials?'

Jim had been a long-time admirer of Chris Blackwell's Island Outpost chain. Yes, its properties were luxurious, but they also had a bohemian hipness to them that appealed to rock stars and supermodels, and he could see the Omari group launching something similar.

'I just think there is an opportunity for us in the market, a younger, lo-fi brand that uses the luxury of nature, and RedReef would be perfect as our debut resort. It needs very little work, purely cosmetic stuff. It closes anyway for hurricane season in a couple of weeks. We can do a soft launch in December, give the new brand a fanfare after we've opened Casa D'Or.'

'Ambitious.'

'You know me.'

Simon rubbed his chin thoughtfully. 'What do you think about the low occupancy rates?'

'Well there's obviously room for improvement, but that's one of the reasons why this hotel interests me.'

'And the lack of an international airport on the island?'

'Being a little bit off the beaten tracks fits in with the ethos of the brand.'

'Our new brand,' smiled Simon, looking at Jim with pride.

'If I get the green light . . . If you trust me.'

'When my beverage company launches a new drink, of course I try it. But I don't design the can, or concoct the flavour. I have a team that I trust to do that, and with Omari, if you believe this is the right property to kick-start a new diffusion brand, then I will support you, provided your decisions are professional ones, not sentimental.'

'Sentimental?'

'Connor is a childhood friend, Jim. I do my research too. I know his New York business is in trouble. I know this is essentially a fire sale.'

'I knew Connor when I was twenty and I wouldn't call him a friend,' said Jim, feeling as if he had been caught out. 'But I happen to think RedReef represents an incredible opportunity for us to do something different.'

Simon nodded, and Jim felt a palpable sense of relief.

'I want you to negotiate hard on price. He's desperate. We need to take advantage of that.'

Jim smiled unconvincingly as Simon glanced at his watch, making it clear that their conversation was over.

'I'm going back to my room. Catch up on emails.'

'Do you ever stop?'

'Remember the shack in Jaipur, Jimmy. I didn't get from there to here sitting back and watching the sunset.' Simon smiled, lifting his hand to wave goodnight, and disappeared in the direction of his suite.

Jim grabbed a beer and wandered down to the shore,

enjoying the sour sensation of the cold drink on his tongue. He had never been one for beach holidays. His perfect vacation was motorcycling along a stretch of coast or scuba diving in the warm waters of Thailand or Australia rather than lazing on a sunlounger pretending to read. But as his mind drifted to whether he too should be checking his emails or making some calls, he admitted to himself that he'd forgotten how to relax. The act of doing nothing had been filed away under self-indulgent and prohibited, a problem that he suspected was exacerbated by being surrounded by people who lived life in exactly the same way.

He tried to remember the last time he had been scuba diving, but the answer, for the moment, eluded him. Somewhere over the course of time, work had become inseparable from being somewhere hot and sunny. He didn't go anywhere these days without doing a site visit, researching an area for commercial opportunities or at the very least sitting on a veranda with his laptop.

Squinting up, he saw a teenage boy, maybe twelve or thirteen.

'Coconut, boss?' The smiling youth had already cracked one open, with a straw poking from the hole.

Jim gestured to his beer. 'Got a drink, thanks,' he said.

'No, no,' said the kid. 'Alcohol's no good for you in the sun. You need real refreshment. And coconut only two American dollar.'

Jim liked the kid's moxie and handed him a five. His name was Victor and he had been working the beach since he was old enough to walk: jewellery, sunglasses, rugs, anything he could lay his hands on.

'Beats paying tax, I guess,' smiled Jim.

'Oh no,' said Victor. 'I still pay tax, everyone does. Unless you want to wake up with a rock tied to your feet.'

Jim turned as he heard Connor call him. He circled back to the beachside bar, where Connor was waiting for him.

'I hope you like seafood. I've ordered the *fruits de mer* platter,' he said, sitting back in his Adirondack chair.

'You sure you really want to sell this place?' said Jim. 'I mean . . .' he waved his glass in the air, 'it is pretty special.'

'No choice,' said Connor. 'It's this or . . . Well, there isn't really an alternative.'

'Does Jennifer know we're here? You said she had issues about Casa D'Or. I don't want any more awkwardness.'

'That was different,' said Connor, not looking at him.

'I'm grateful for this,' he said after another moment. 'You know I really don't want my business to go the way of my father's.'

'What happened there?' asked Jim, remembering how Robert Gilbert had been the Deep South hotshot.

Connor shrugged. 'He took his eye off the ball. He never really managed to leave the eighties, didn't understand the global economy, wanted to keep doing business in Charleston in the clubs and on the golf course. Got too comfortable. Started enjoying moments like this a bit too much.'

'Isn't that what it's all about?' said Jim.

'He lost his business, his marriage when my mother decided

to divorce him. I'm not sure that was worth the daily pina coladas, are you?'

'Connor, sometimes you have to remind yourself how lucky you are. You're got your health, a property empire, a beautiful wife . . .' He tried not to linger on the last words of that sentence.

'A wife with a chronic drink problem,' Connor said quietly. 'Maybe you can help solve that next. She seems to listen to what you say.' That familiar challenge was back in his eyes.

'Drink problem?'

Jim frowned. From his observations, Jennifer seemed to have the perfect life now. The Hamptons estate, the New York town house, the society profile and the sideline in philanthropy. At the Memorial Day party, people had waxed lyrical about what a wonderful woman she was. The millions she quietly raised for charity – smaller and more unfashionable causes than say the ballet or the opera, Jim had noted with some degree of pride. They had been bittersweet observations, of course, that she lived such a seemingly happy existence without him in it. But ultimately all he cared about, had ever cared about, was Jennifer's safety and happiness.

'I don't understand.'

'Have you not noticed the exuberance with which she drinks martinis?' replied Connor, lifting a brow. 'Although that's only the half of it. It's the vodka bottles hidden in her boot collection you have to worry about. I've tried doctors, shrinks, even suggested getting her out of the country, maybe Europe somewhere.'

'You think it's that bad?' asked Jim with panic.

Connor laughed mirthlessly. '*She* wouldn't say so. It's more common than you'd think, especially in our perfect world. And of course Jennifer has certain things she is drinking to forget.'

Jim stayed silent.

'You know we never had children,' said Connor, so quietly that he almost didn't hear him. 'We tried. There were two miscarriages, and an ectopic pregnancy, but no baby.'

'I'm sorry.'

He thought about his old friend's warm way with people. She would have been a wonderful mother.

'Jen nearly died with that ectopic pregnancy. There was blood . . . so much blood. It was a long night, but she got through it, and the next morning she cried so much I thought she would never stop. I held her and told her it didn't matter, that the two of us was enough, and that was when she told me how guilty she felt.'

'Guilty?'

'She told me that she'd had an abortion when she was twenty-one and that the miscarriages, the ectopic pregnancy, were a punishment for what she had done.'

Jim took a second to process it.

'She had an abortion when she was twenty-one?' he said slowly, unable to hide the quaver in his voice.

Connor sat back in his chair and looked at him.

'I had to work that one out too, Jim,' he said evenly. 'Couldn't understand. I mean, I loved her. She loved me. We were living in New York together by that point. Why would she abort our baby when she knew how serious we were about each other? She admitted it in the end. It was because she didn't know if it was my baby. Or yours.'

He knocked back the rest of his beer and tossed the bottle on the sand.

'So, if you've wondered why I've hated you for twenty years, that's why. If you wonder why Jen drinks so much, why she doesn't like to see you too often . . . It all makes sense now, doesn't it? And while I'm grateful, really grateful, that you're throwing me a lifeline here, buying RedReef, helping me get my finances in order . . . well, it's really the very least that you owe me.'

Chapter Eighteen

1994

Casa D'Or had been transformed into a fairy-tale palace, a Gatsby dream, for Jennifer's twenty-first birthday party. Three days earlier, a team of four carpenters had arrived, and under Sylvia Wyatt's strict instructions had built a stage by the shores of the lake where tonight one of Savannah's best jazz bands was playing a medley of soft, soulful songs. Four hundred guests milled around the gardens, lit up by thousands of fairy lights: her parents' smart Savannah circle, a considerable number of her father's business contacts. 'Everyone will want to keep on doing business with you, just to come back to Casa D'Or,' she'd overheard her mother reason when they were compiling the guest list.

At least fifty of the partygoers were her own friends. Some had even made the journey down from New York, although Jennifer had been disappointed by how few of her college friends had shown up. She'd sent over thirty invitations to her favourite people from Wellesley, but the excuses had trickled in and some hadn't even bothered to reply at all. It was almost as if the past three years at university hadn't existed, as if the people she had once cared about had forgotten about her already.

Jennifer accepted a glass of champagne from the waiter as she glanced around the party wondering where to go next. She had been inundated by well-wishers all evening and was looking forward to a few moments of time out when Jeanne approached her, smiling.

'This is a seriously smart party,' grinned her friend, linking her arm through Jennifer's. 'I feel as if I'm on the set of a Hepburn movie.'

'Audrey or Katharine?' said Jennifer, glad to have a reassuring presence by her side.

'Usually I'm a Katharine kinda girl, but tonight looks like *Sabrina*.'

'I love that movie,' said Jennifer, smiling as she remembered the classic Billy Wilder film about two brothers competing for the love of their chauffeur's beautiful daughter.

'And how's your own little love triangle getting on?' said Jeanne, nudging her friend gently with her elbow.

'What love triangle?' asked Jennifer, trying not to blush.

'Oh come on,' Jeanne said, holding her hands up in the air. 'You've still not told me if anything happened between you and Jim Johnson at the beach the other night.'

'Nothing happened.'

'He was moon-eyed after you all day and I'd usually just write that off as another Jennifer Wyatt admirer, but you like him too, admit it.'

Jennifer looked away, not wanting to talk about it. It had been ten days since their trip to Tybee Island, and she had not seen or spoken to Jim since. Part of her was glad that he was out of sight, if not out of mind.

Her mother had been a changed woman since their conversation. She had taken Jennifer out for lunch, and tennis, and whilst they had been shopping in downtown Savannah the day before, she had treated her to a beautiful gold hummingbird necklace, which she had presented to her with the warmest of embraces.

But still, Jennifer had spent the past week and a half feeling sad and empty. It just didn't make sense that Jim wasn't around any more. He hadn't called her or popped round, even when her mother had left for a trip downtown or to the country club. It was almost as if he wasn't there, as if she had dreamed him. The one time she had seen the red pickup truck drive past the entrance to Casa D'Or, her heart had stopped as the driver had waved, only for her to realise that it was Bryn Johnson and not his son.

Getting ready for the party that evening, she had found herself staring out of her bedroom window towards the Lake House, wondering whether he would turn up to say goodbye.

She wasn't sure what part of Jim's vanishing trick had hurt the most: that the frisson of attraction between them outside

Casa D'Or had been a lie, some meaningless consequence of the amount they'd had to drink, or the fact that he was about to slip out of her life for ever and she wouldn't get to see him again.

She felt tears come to her eyes at the thought of it.

'Hey, what's the matter?' said Jeanne, noticing that her friend was upset.

'Nothing,' she said quickly.

Jeanne peered at her over the rim of her glasses with a look that said she was not going to take no for an answer.

'Look, we almost kissed. But we haven't seen each other since and he's going home tomorrow.'

'Why haven't you seen him?'

'He hasn't got in touch. But it's for the best. I have Connor; Jim's going back to London. It was a friendship that got complicated. That's all.'

'There's nothing *that's all* about the way he looks at you, Jen. Or the way you glow when you're with him.'

'That'll just be the sunburn,' she said, not wanting to be persuaded.

'Is he here?'

'No. And that speaks volumes, doesn't it?'

'There you are, darling,' said David Wyatt, touching her on the shoulder. 'I've apparently paid for the best jazz band in Savannah, and my own daughter hasn't even given me the honour of a dance.'

'Of course,' smiled Jennifer, allowing her father to whisk her off in the yellow cloud of chiffon of her dress.

She rested her hand on his shoulder and allowed him to twirl her round, feeling joyful and safe.

'Are you enjoying yourself?'

'It's a wonderful party.'

'I know you don't really like being the centre of attention. If it all gets a bit much, I can go and smoke my cigar near the fire alarm and we can make them all go away.'

'Mum seems to be enjoying herself,' smiled Jennifer, looking across the dance floor to where her mother was talking to Bryn Johnson and even laughing.

David gave a soft conspiratorial laugh, as if they both understood how hard Sylvia was to live with.

The band started to play 'The Shadow of Your Smile', and Jennifer listened wistfully to its lyrics.

'I don't believe it,' said her father, stopping dancing. 'She came.'

'Who?'

'Your aunt. Your aunt Donna.'

Jennifer turned round to follow her father's line of sight. A blonde woman was standing at the French doors that led from the house to the terrace. She was taller than Sylvia, but still slim, although an obvious boob job made her look very top heavy. Her hair was a harsher shade than her mother's elegant do, but there was no mistaking that the two women were related.

'Did Mom invite her?' said Jennifer with surprise, wondering if her mother's mood had really improved that much.

'I did,' said David with an expression that told her he was wondering if it had been such a good idea.

'And you've told Mom . . .'

'Not exactly,' said her father with a frown. 'Look. I have no living family any more. Neither does your mother, with the exception of Donna. I just thought it was important that you meet. Your mother might not have any desire to see her sister, but Donna is still family, and now you're twenty-one, it's up to you to make those sort of decisions yourself.'

'What are we waiting for, then?' said Jennifer, giving her father a grateful squeeze, both excited and nervous about speaking to her aunt.

Donna's expression melted into joy and relief when she saw them. She took Jennifer's face between her hands and beamed.

'Look at you,' she said with a note of sadness.

'Thank you for coming,' said David. 'Is your husband with you?'

'Frank's probably still outside gaping at the size of the house,' she said with a strong Southern accent.

'I didn't know you were married,' said Jennifer.

'We don't know a lot about each other's lives,' Donna said regretfully. 'I think that's why your father invited me this evening.'

'Where's your mother?' asked David briskly. He was the most poised and confident man she knew, but Jennifer detected a reticence in his voice. It was just like her father to want to mend the rift between his wife and her sister, but they all knew that Sylvia might react unpredictably to the situation.

They both glanced around but could no longer see her.

'I'll go and find her,' said David. 'Jen, you show Donna around the party.'

'Wow,' said Donna, rooted to the spot. 'I knew it was going to be lovely, but this place . . .'

'We didn't buy it,' said Jen modestly. 'It's been in our family for years. My great-grandfather bought it and everyone else has just tried to keep it going ever since.'

'Lordy, the pressure's on you then, the next generation, to keep it all going.'

Jennifer smiled uncomfortably. She'd never really considered it before, but perhaps there was a financial imperative in her mother's belief that Connor was perfect for her. Jennifer knew that her father had struggled throughout the recession; she couldn't pretend she hadn't noticed that they didn't live quite as lavishly as they once had.

Only five or six years before, Casa D'Or had had a full-time staff of five. Marion's parents, Jeffrey and Dolores Wilson, were the chaffeur and cook respectively; Marion was an unofficial sous chef and housekeeper; a gardener and estate manager were also on the payroll. But when the Wilsons retired, replacements were never recruited, and over time, the other members of staff also disappeared, a state of affairs that was in sharp contrast to the Gilbert family, who in addition to a fully staffed house north of the city had homes in Lyford Cay and on the Côte d'Azur as well.

Jennifer didn't want to dwell on all that tonight and linked her arm through her aunt's to show her around.

Donna was as warm as her mother was cool. As they walked around Casa D'Or, swapping stories about their lives, Jennifer wondered why she had always been portrayed as such a family cautionary tale. The reasons for Donna and Sylvia's estrangement had always been unspecified. There were rumours of drink and gambling, but speaking to her aunt about her job as a restaurant supervisor in Pensacola and her travels around the world on the cruise ships, Jennifer could just see a nice ordinary lady whose only weakness – as she explained herself when she told Jennifer that her new husband Frank, circulating somewhere around the party, was in fact her fourth – was her poor taste in men.

Jennifer took Donna upstairs for the best view from the house. Her parents' master suite had the biggest terrace, with sweeping views of the grounds, but feeling sure that her mother would be annoyed at anyone going into her room uninvited, she took Donna to the top floor, into her favourite part of the house.

'You're going to love this,' she grinned as she led her to a cupola on the rooftop.

'What's this?' said Donna, sounding like a gleeful child.

Jennifer opened a small door and they stepped out on to a platform that surrounded the circular room.

'It's a widow's walk,' she said, inhaling the balmy night air. 'Lots of houses on the coast have them. Apparently they were for the ladies of the house, so they could come out and look for their mariner husbands returning from sea.'

'And I take it some of them never came back.'

'I guess,' said Jennifer, glancing towards the Lake House. 'I guess it makes it either the saddest or the most romantic part of the house.'

Donna leaned on the balcony and looked wistfully out into the fairy-light-studded darkness.

'Why don't you and my mother speak?' asked Jennifer quietly.

'I don't know. I tried,' Donna said with a sad laugh. 'She moved to Charleston and fell off the radar. We didn't even know where she was. We'd get the odd Christmas card as if to tell us, I'm out here, I'm all right, but there was never any number to call or address to get back in touch.'

'Who's we?' asked Jennifer, puzzled.

'Our parents. Your grandmom and grandpop.'

She frowned. 'But I thought they died when Mom was eighteen.'

'No,' said Donna, shaking her head. 'It was a long time after that. Sylvia had married your father but you hadn't been born.'

'What happened?' said Jennifer, not sure that she was following correctly. 'I thought they died in a car crash.'

'Car crash?' said Donna with surprise. 'No, they'd been in poor health for a long time. We were dirt-poor, with no money for medical bills, so I nursed them both for a couple of years. I suppose that's why I was angry with Sylvia for so long, for not doing her bit. But she had a new life by then. The life she always wanted. If there's one thing about my sister, it's that she's unsentimental, especially when it comes to getting what she wants. Just ask Ethan Jamieson.'

'Ethan Jamieson?' repeated Jennifer. The name was familiar. She was certain it was the man whose photograph her mother had showed her. Sylvia Wyatt's lost love. 'The war photographer she met in Charleston?'

'War photographer?' said Donna in surprise. 'No, Ethan was Sylvia's high school sweetheart. They were madly in love and I'm not surprised. He was the most handsome guy you ever did see. But when Sylva hit twenty, she wasn't hanging around Dixie any more. I'm not sure Ethan's job in the timber yard cut it either. She left town, left Ethan and never came back to either of them again.'

Jennifer went quiet, betrayed by the lies her mother had spun. Not just the other night, when she had shown her the photo of Ethan; her whole life, what little Jennifer knew of it, had been a convincingly told fiction.

'I should get back to the party and find Frank before he gets up to any mischief,' Donna said. 'I just wanted to have a proper chat with you. I hope it's the first of many.'

'I should come down to Pensacola.'

'You should.' Donna broke out into a grin. 'We've got beaches as white as sugar, and Frank's got a bar. We make the meanest margaritas. Do you have a boyfriend?'

Jennifer nodded.

'Bring him for a weekend. We'll have so much fun.'

Jennifer couldn't imagine Connor in a bar in Pensacola, but she said yes anyway.

Donna gave her niece a tight hug, and for a moment

Jennifer was lost in a cloud of blond curls.

'I'm so glad I came,' she said, pulling away. 'When your papa invited me, I wasn't going to accept, not after all this time, but Frank says it's never too late to say I love you.'

As Jennifer climbed through the small door back into the house, she had a feeling that her aunt was wrong.

Chapter Nineteen

After a few minutes spent chatting to Donna's husband Frank, Jennifer snaked her way around the side of the house to the far reaches of the back garden, where the party crowds had thinned.

She needed a few moments of quiet. She was not naturally gregarious, so being the centre of attention, making small talk with the dozens of family friends her parents had invited, felt quite exhausting. Besides, she needed some space to think. Donna's revelations had shocked her. Her mother was a complicated woman, but she couldn't believe she had told so many lies. Perhaps Sylvia had been embarrassed about her background, and her family's poverty, but her story about Ethan Jamieson – assuming Donna had been telling the truth – was a complete fabrication.

She was by the pavilion now, which looked like a beautiful antique bird cage in the dark. It was soothing out here, and thoughts of her mother started to dissolve, until the sight of the Lake House taunted her again.

You have to go and say goodbye, she told herself, downing the flute of champagne she had brought with her.

A tear ran down her cheek as she spotted a light on in the house. She imagined Jim packing, his music on loud. She wondered if he was looking across the lake too, watching the lights of the party and feeling as sad and regretful as she was. She doubted it.

Jim Johnson had a wild and passionate heart – it was one of the things she liked most about him. When he cared, he cared deeply; whether it was about his music, or an opinion, he was prepared to put himself out there. He was not the type of guy to let awkwardness or embarrassment stop him from doing something, unless it was the sort of embarrassment that stemmed from regret.

The moon shimmered across the water and she felt her shoulders sag. She had escaped New York at the beginning of the summer to get some clarity in her life, but now, two months later, things seemed more confused than ever.

'Hey.' She heard a voice behind her and turned round, her heart thudding with hope. She was disappointed to see that it was Connor.

'What are you doing out here?' She laughed awkwardly.

'Looking for you,' he said, taking a step towards her in the pavilion.

The space between them seemed to contract. It was an oppressively hot night, but the air seemed to have been sucked out of the tiny glass building. She felt uncomfortable being in such a close, confined space with him, and pushed her hair back behind her ear.

'Great party.'

'My mom would have settled for nothing less,' she smiled.

'Marion told me you decorated the terrace yourself. It looks good.'

'I didn't think men noticed things like that,' she teased.

'Well I did, and I'm proud of you.'

'I wanted it to look photogenic. I did some filming for the documentary.'

'About the documentary,' he said guardedly. 'I've got some news.'

She felt her mood lift. The last time she had been in New York, Connor had told her about his new friends and acquaintances in the city, one of whom was a film editor who had worked on all sorts of exciting projects and had offered to help Jennifer cut her documentary together. She had hours of footage, was happy with the interviews but Bryn Johnson had been right when he had said that without structure and editing, her tapes were just rambling introspection. Jennifer had been thrilled when Connor said he would set up a meeting, and had been waiting all week for at least a name or contact number where she could reach him.

'Your friend, the editor. Did you speak to him?' she asked breathlessly.

Connor paused.

'Well, I spoke to a friend. Another friend.'

'Is he an editor too?' she asked. She was aware that the

clock was ticking. David Wyatt was already making noises about ending her allowance, and Jennifer planned to enter her film into three competitions whose deadlines were fast approaching.

'I haven't even done a rough cut yet, and if your friend can't help me, then I need to find someone else as quickly as I can.'

Connor took another step forward.

'Look, Jen. I'm not being funny, but entering festivals is amateur stuff. What you really want is a job in the industry, and I think I've just sorted you out.'

She didn't agree with what he was saying but still felt her brow crease with curiosity.

'You've met David Clarke. On my course; we watched the rowing with him once. His brother Richard owns a production company. Makes very successful short films. Anyway, I mentioned you to him and he wants to talk to you. Thinks he might have something.'

'What sort of films?' she asked suspiciously. She had never known Connor to have any friends that worked in the creative industries, and now he seemed to have lots of them.

'Films,' he shrugged. 'For the corporate sector. Did something very interesting recently for one of the big oil companies, some video presentation as part of their sales prospectus.'

'Oh,' she said, feeling herself deflate.

'What did you expect?' he said, frowning. 'An internship with Spielberg? Look, this is where the money is, right here.' He pointed to the ground for emphasis. 'Corporate videos. The printed word is dead – within ten years, once this internet thing really takes off, we are all going to consume our information visually. Films, pictures, razzle-dazzle.'

Jennifer felt herself become emotional.

'Connor, this isn't the sort of film-making I had in mind. If you could get in touch with your editor friend, that would be amazing,' she said, but he clearly wasn't listening.

'To be honest, Jen, when you first told me about this documentary idea, I thought it was a bit ridiculous,' he said dismissively. 'But I've come to realise that actually it's brilliant. Go and learn the trade with Richard Clarke, then we can set up on our own. Video marketing. I can tout for business with the banks. You can do the creative side. We can own the financial marketing sector by the new millennium.'

She started to shake her head. Her breathing was shallow and she felt trapped inside the confines of the pavilion.

'Connor, have you not been listening to a word I've said this summer?'

He held up a hand. 'I admit it. The gig is in New York. Of course it is. Everything is in New York. I know you hated it at Lucian's, but I think you hated working in a gallery and it coloured your view of the city. This will be different,' he said with a smooth reassurance that she almost believed.

'We should probably talk about this another time,' she said, not even looking at him.

'No, I think we should talk about it now,' he said with quiet, steely authority.

He was close enough to take her hands, and guided them to his chest.

'I love you,' he said. 'I love you and I want us to be together in New York. I want to be with you. We belong together.'

An unusual hesitancy appeared in his voice. Connor was never anything other than one hundred per cent confident, but right now there was something different, and it scared her.

He let go of her hands and reached into his pocket. Her heart was pounding as he produced a small black velvet box, and she knew this wasn't any old twenty-first-birthday present.

'I know we're young,' he said lifting the lid of the box. 'I know in an ideal world we might wait a while, but when you know, you know, right? Doesn't matter if you're twenty-one or forty-one.'

She looked down at a dazzling oval diamond, flecked with blue and silver in the soft moonlight. It was a beautiful stone, a beautiful ring, but her heart felt heavy as she gazed at it.

'Jennifer Wyatt, will you marry me?' Connor said, an increasingly confident smile pulling at his lips.

'Wow,' she said finally, her voice a croak.

'I chose it myself, but we can change it if you'd prefer a cushion or emerald cut.'

She took a sharp intake of breath and steadied herself. Then she put her hand over the velvet box and shut the lid with the palm of her hand. For a moment she just looked at him, hoping he would get the message, hoping that she wouldn't have to say anything, but his expression soured, demanding that she explain herself.

'I can't, Connor.'

'Why?' he asked incredulously.

She knew she couldn't say anything without it sounding hurtful. Besides, she didn't even know the answer herself.

'I'm just not ready for this.'

Connor's nostrils trembled as he cleared his throat.

'I'm only asking you to marry me,' he replied, obviously thrown. 'We don't have to walk down the aisle just yet. It can be a long engagement. My brother was engaged to Vanessa for three years before they got married.'

'And divorced another three years after that,' she said cynically.

The silence seemed to stretch out for ever.

'Do you still love me?' he asked finally.

Jennifer closed her eyes. There was no easy answer to that question. Perhaps she did love Connor. She certainly used to. Countless times she had felt a smug happiness when she had visited him at college, and they had watched the football, or the rowing. He'd stood behind her and put his arms around her waist and she'd known what other girls were thinking: how lucky she was to be dating the handsome Connor Gilbert, to be wearing his letterman's sweater, to be going home with him at night. She hadn't felt like that in a long time, though. Not this year, certainly, when exams and revisions had kept them apart most weekends, and she hadn't really missed him.

It was not the first time she'd thought their relationship was one of convenient geography and timing. They had gone to the same school, were on the same sailing circuit, went to college in the same state. But finishing Harvard seemed to have given Connor additional purpose and taken his life off in another direction; he was moving faster and travelling further away from her, and she didn't want to follow him on the journey.

'Connor, this is just such a surprise,' she said, trying to explain herself.

'Do you love me?' he repeated.

'Yes,' she whispered, because it seemed the easiest response. She certainly didn't want to create a scene at her own birthday party, and she was aware of guests drifting down towards the pavilion.

He suddenly looked less despondent. 'So you'll at least think about it?'

'Of course I will.'

'Are you coming back to the house, then?' he said more briskly.

'I was just taking time out here for a few minutes.'

'Don't be too long,' he said, his mouth a firm, tight line as he put the ring box back into his jacket pocket and walked back to Casa D'Or without another word.

Chapter Twenty

Jennifer watched Connor's figure recede towards the brightness of the house and she felt wretched inside.

'Crap,' she whispered under her breath, but she wasn't really sure who or what she was referring to.

She didn't know why she had just said no to him. It certainly didn't feel right to accept his proposal of marriage. Jennifer had never been the sort of dreamy, romantic girl who had spent her whole life fantasising about this moment. But as she took a moment to think about why she had turned him down, she knew that she should have been feeling love and hope in her heart when she had opened that velvet box, not dread, and for that she had made exactly the right decision.

Fireflies were dancing in the darkness like tiny showers of gold, miniature meteors. On any other night Jennifer would have watched them with joy and wonder, but she just wanted to get back to the house.

Already the crowds had begun to thin. Ten o'clock, she discovered, glancing at her watch. The oldest guests would be dispersing first; others would mutter about babysitters and early starts. Her fun friends like Jeanne and Pete could possibly be relied upon to party into the night, so too the out-of-towners billeted in a nearby hotel, although Sylvia had told Jennifer that she expected the party to be over by midnight, and she did not doubt her mother would have Casa D'Or cleared by then.

A cooler breeze began to ripple through the trees, and Jennifer decided to go inside for a cardigan.

Threading through the guests, she walked up the steps on to the terrace, not looking where she was going until she walked into someone who steadied her with a hand.

'Jim,' she said, gasping in surprise. 'You're here!'

'Well, you did invite me.'

She started to laugh nervously.

'I should have known you'd be fashionably late.'

'I don't know it's too fashionable in these parts. Southern manners and all,' he grinned.

'Have a drink. Have champagne,' she said, taking a glass from a passing waiter and thrusting it giddily into his hands.

'Happy birthday,' he said, not taking his eyes from her.

'A big day. I can now officially buy alcohol.'

'It's a strange old country, the United States of America,' he said, shaking his head and smiling. 'You can buy a gun at sixteen, but you have to wait until you're twenty-one to get a beer.'

'We have our quirks,' she said, still thrilled that he was here.

'I got you something,' he said, handing her a small packet wrapped in Barbie paper.

'Cute,' she said, taking it from him.

'I thought so.'

'Can I open it?'

'No,' he said unconvincingly.

'I'm going to open it,' she smiled, her eyes taunting him.

There was no card, and once she had ripped off the gift wrap, a cassette tape sat in her hand.

'A mix tape?'

It was a question, because she wasn't sure. It was of the blank cassette variety, but it could have been a recording of the sounds of Savannah, or a soundtrack for her documentary, for all she knew.

'I prefer the English vernacular. A compilation tape. I think it gives it the gravitas it deserves.'

A piece of file paper folded into quarters accompanied the tape. She opened it, and recognised Jim's bold capital letters.

'Twenty-one songs,' she said out loud.

Jim's cheeks coloured a little. 'There's some good stuff on there,' he shrugged. 'Stuff I thought you might like. Songs to make you happy, songs to make you feel sad, songs to make you feel like you can conquer the world.'

'Music can do that,' she said quietly.

'You're learning.'

Her eyes trailed down to read the playlist, but Jim touched the paper awkwardly.

'Don't look at it now. Not when there's free champagne to drink.'

He didn't meet her gaze, and suddenly she felt a jolt of excitement, a suggestion that the mix tape contained something that was perhaps of significance. Thoughts that he didn't want to share, not yet, not in public. The idea was so exciting, she felt butterflies in her belly.

'When are you leaving?' she asked quickly.

'Tomorrow night. We're flying to New York. Dad's got a meeting with his agent. We're flying home the day after.'

'Maybe we can do something,' she said tentatively.

'We leave for the airport at six.'

She wasn't sure if he was rebuffing her or subtly suggesting a time.

She steeled herself and opened her mouth.

'I need to tell you something, and then I need to ask you something.' A voice in her head spoke the words she wanted to say first. *Connor has proposed to me. But I am in love with you, Jim Johnson, and I need to know if I am feeling all these things by myself.*

A deep baritone interrupted her thoughts.

'And here's the birthday girl,' said a voice she recognised, accompanied by a heavy hand on her shoulder.

She turned and saw Bryn Johnson. In her highest heels she was almost as tall as him, and inches away from his purple claret-stained lips.

'Wonderful party, Jennifer. I've just met a senator.'

He took a canapé from a passing tray.

'Are you going to miss us, then?' he asked mischievously.

She could smell the alcohol on his breath and wished that he would leave.

'I just want to put this gift somewhere safe,' she said, interrupting him. 'I won't be a minute,' she added, fixing her attention on Jim.

She pushed her way through the crowd, up the sweeping hall staircase, then looked back, trying to catch Jim's eye, wanting to reassure him that she would be back almost instantly. Instead she saw Connor, and she felt guilty, furtive, with the mix tape in her hands. Connor mouthed some words to her, and she smiled as brightly as she could, nodding to indicate that she would be back in a moment, and ran the final ten steps to vanish out of view.

She relaxed when she reached her bedroom and closed the door, kicking off her high heels for a few moments, enjoying the sensation of having her feet liberated. Perching on the edge of her bed, she opened the piece of paper again, her eyes scanning the list, her heart looking for secret meanings in the titles.

There were a few tracks she recognised. Happy tunes like De La Soul's 'The Magic Number', which they had played in the truck; others were more soulful fare. Thankfully there was nothing sexually suggestive – no 'Let's Get It On' or 'Feel Like Makin' Love' – or had that left her strangely disappointed?

Her eyes drifted to the bottom of the page, and she stopped in her tracks.

'Oceans' – Jim Johnson.

She almost laughed out loud as she realised that Jim had

written a song for her. Her heart was beating hard as she remembered that night in Savannah by the Bonaventura cemetery.

You'll have to write me a song.

If you play your cards right.

He had been flirting with her even then, but Jennifer had not allowed herself to believe it. She could see now what she had been denying all summer. She hadn't spent time with Jim because of her documentary; she had done the documentary because of him. And yes, she had found a creative passion, something that she loved, that she could see herself doing professionally one day, but it had been Jim by her side, cajoling and inspiring her, that had made it so special.

She took a deep, steadying breath and decided she would not be missed downstairs for another few minutes.

There was a small tape player on her desk and she slotted the mix tape inside. Her finger pressed the fast forward button and she ran the tape until she reached the song she was looking for. The track before, an REM number, faded out, and then it was Jim's song.

There was a simple guitar intro, then other instruments were laid on top. A piano, and something with a soft and haunting timbre that made the hairs on the back of her neck stand on end. Jennifer knew little about music, about music production, but she could recognise the effort that had gone into the recording.

He was singing now, and she immediately realised how good he was. His voice was delicate, but it had a depth and strength that was mesmerising. She listened to each word as he painted a picture, a story with his lyrics.

Never knew how big the ocean was
So wide it makes me blue
But I won't let it stop me
From thinking about you . . .

Emotion shivered in her throat, tears welling in her eyes as she felt, for the first time in her life, beautiful and loved. Although her looks were often commented on, she had never really felt desirable. Connor made few remarks about her appearance these days; her mother was generally only critical.

But right now, it was impossible for Jennifer to deny that Jim was speaking to her through his song, and as she closed her eyes, lost in the warmth of his words, she knew that all she wanted was to be with him, to feel his arms around her, his lips on hers. She didn't care that he was leaving tomorrow, because if she could right a whole summer of wrongs – denial and fear and naïvety, all those things that had stopped her from acting on her desire – then perhaps they could work out a way of being together. An ocean didn't have to come between them.

She wanted to listen to every word, every bar, but she knew that she had heard enough. Her finger pushed the stop button and she stood up with a renewed sense of purpose.

She knew that her mother would go mad about her daughter starting a relationship with the boy next door, but Jennifer didn't care any more. Sylvia had lied to her and manipulated her, but she wasn't going to let her hold her back any longer.

As Jennifer descended the long, sweeping staircase, she saw David Wyatt at the bottom, beaming at her. He held out his hand, palm upwards, as if he wanted her to place her hand in his. She smiled at her beloved father, although she was impatient. She wanted to find Jim, and from her vantage point on the stairs, her eyes surveyed the crowd, trying to search him out.

'We've been looking everywhere for you,' said David as she reached the bottom step. It was a further moment before she noticed that more people were assembled in the hall than had been there ten minutes earlier. Her mother, very upright, was standing next to Connor, locked in clandestine conversation. Jennifer met their gaze and they both smiled, but she felt a sudden ominous sense that something was happening that she did not yet know about.

She heard the noise of the party fade as her father tapped a spoon against his wine glass.

'I was going to say a few words to wish my beautiful daughter the happiest of days,' he began. 'But it appears that we are celebrating more than Jenny's twenty-first this evening.'

He beckoned towards Connor, who stepped forward, proud, triumphant, as the words rang in Jennifer's head and the room seemed to spin.

'Please raise your glasses to Jennifer and her boyfriend Connor, who have just got engaged . . .'

The whole party erupted into applause. Glasses were

clinked, and in the distance Jennifer could hear the sound of champagne corks popping. The cacophony of sound faded as her vision homed in on one face in the crowd. Jim Johnson was standing at the back of the room, a full head taller than everyone else. Their eyes met, but his expression was flat, unreadable, and then he turned away and disappeared out of the front door that was open like a portal into the darkness.

Jennifer took a step forward, but in her haste she fell into Connor's arms. He caught her and didn't let go. There had been times when his bulk, his solidity, was safe and reassuring, but now his grip felt like a vice.

'Are you OK?' he whispered through her hair.

She pulled away so she could look at him directly. Her face was so close to his that she could see the pores on his nose and her own reflection in the darkness of his eyes.

'I never said yes,' she said, so quietly that no one else could hear her.

'We can talk about this later,' he said, his hands still gripping her arms.

She glanced away and could see her mother watching, her satisfied smile taunting her.

'Pumpkin, I am so happy for you,' said her father as she pulled away from Connor. She tried to smile as brightly as she could, but she could feel tears stinging the backs of her eyes. She loved her father so much, but really, did he know her so little?

'Who told you?' she said, trying desperately to hold it together.

'Connor asked for my permission weeks ago, but I didn't know when it was going to happen. Then your mother said he asked you just a few minutes ago in the pavilion and you said yes.'

Jennifer pushed her front teeth down into her lip and nodded tightly.

'Excuse me a moment,' she said, ignoring the well-wishers who lunged forward to offer their congratulations.

She took big gulps of air as she stepped outside. It was a warm night, and as she breathed, it was as if there was no oxygen in the air. Her eyes scanned the gardens at the front of the house. Lights studded along the edge of the drive gave just enough illumination so that she could make out movement, a figure who was almost at the gate of Casa D'Or's walled garden.

She knew it was him and began to run. One heel twisted under her, making her stagger, so she kicked off her shoes and hopped on to the lawn, sprinting faster across the soft grass.

'Wait!'

Jim turned round, both hands thrust in his pockets.

She was panting slightly when she reached him, trying to compose herself, not knowing what to say.

A car drove past them, its bright headlights almost blinding them, and they stepped out of the way as it disappeared down the drive. They were standing in front of a long line of cars, an overflow parking lot for the party guests. One of them was Jim's red pickup truck. She knew that the second he got in, revved the engine and drove off, she would almost certainly never see him again.

A soft breeze rustled through the live oaks, and in the distance she could hear the jazz band striking up an inappropriately playful tune.

'Don't go,' she said finally.

'I was only ever going to pop in,' he said, thumbing his hand in the direction of the house. 'You know, to give you your present.'

'I loved it,' she said, aware of the solitary tear rolling down her cheek. 'The song you wrote.'

Jim nodded tightly. 'You said you wanted a song,' he said, not even looking at her.

'The words, the lyrics were beautiful.'

'Well maybe there's a writer in me yet.' He laughed sarcastically. 'My dad will be pleased.'

'Jim, I need to tell you something—'

'Congratulations, by the way,' he said, pre-empting her speech. 'I'm really happy for you.' Now he was looking at her directly, without flinching, and for a second she wondered if he meant it.

'I don't know what happened in there. We had a row, Connor proposed . . . my dad announced it . . .'

'But you said yes?' His voice skirted between hope and disappointment.

'No. Not really . . .'

'Not really?' he challenged her.

'I said I needed to think about it.'

'That's not the impression your father gave.'

'My mother told him I said yes. She lied.' More tears were trickling down her face.

'Why?'

'I don't know. Perhaps she wants me to marry Connor. He's rich.'

'And what do you want, Jen?' He looked away, and she could see the profile of his face, his neck, his Adam's apple moving up and down in his throat.

'I want to be with you,' she said quietly.

The corners of his mouth curled and softened into a smile. His eyes seemed to sparkle. He stepped forward, and she held her breath as the space between them compressed. She closed her eyes, happy, delirious, dizzy, their kiss everything she'd hoped it would be.

'Shit, there's people coming,' he said with a low, throaty laugh.

'Over here.' She grabbed his hand and pulled him towards the stables.

They ran inside the huge barn. Jennifer groped around in the darkness for the light switch but couldn't find it. There were tiles missing from the roof, and the bright beams from a silvery full moon gave the space a beautiful natural light.

'A hayloft,' he smiled, cornering her against the wall. 'Are we going to get jumped on by a wild animal?'

'Here's hoping,' she whispered as he kissed her again, more passionately this time.

'You know I think we're trapped in here,' he said as his

mouth pulled momentarily away from hers.

'We're just going . . . to have to stay . . . for a while longer then,' she said between kisses as he took his cue and started to unbutton the pearl buttons on her dress. They moved across to a hay bale, huge cubes of straw that were a perfect makeshift bed. His hands slid down the slim curves of her waist as he kissed her neck.

She lay back on the bale, impatient and hungry for him. The straw was scratchy, but the dress was a soft protective layer and she slipped it off her shoulders so that it was like a thin blanket for them to lie on. She shuddered as Jim swooped down to kiss her belly, then groaned as he cupped her breast, teasing it out of her lacy bra and sucking her nipple as his hand stroked between her thighs.

She used her palms to ease off her panties, the thin fabric curling down over her thighs. Jim paused to unbuckle his trousers and unbutton his shirt, and then he lay on top of her and kissed her some more, slowly, deeply, his firm torso pressing against her. She parted her legs, and he eased himself inside her. She curled her legs around him and grabbed his hair, arching her back as a sweet, intense pressure built and built and then crescendoed, toppling over into a white-hot crashing wave of release.

'Happy birthday,' he whispered as they collapsed exhausted on the hay. And as Jennifer looked up at the moonlight, she didn't just feel another year older; she felt reborn.

Chapter Twenty-One

A cool breeze blowing over her naked body woke her. Jennifer's eyes blinked open, and for a moment she didn't know where she was. Another second and she registered something irritating her skin: straw. Her mind felt dull – a hangover – and there was someone lying next to her: Jim.

Jennifer's next thought was that this was not good. She was half naked, her dress completely unbuttoned; one breast had popped out from its bra cup, her panties were off and missing in action.

But as she turned her head and looked at Jim, she felt a reckless wave of happiness and desire. Last night had been incredible, and she still couldn't believe that her body had felt all those things that it had, right there on the hay. The sex had been passionate and impatient. She remembered him kissing her until she had fallen asleep, and her chin still felt sore from the roughness of his stubble.

She took a moment to observe him. He was still snoozing

and looked quite angelic – that beautiful profile and long lashes wasted on a man. She wanted to kiss him again, but a distant squawk of early birds somewhere in the oak trees warned her that dawn was coming, and they did not want to get caught. Not like this.

Glancing at her watch, she saw that it was almost six a.m. Trying to stop herself from panicking, she sat up carefully, adjusted her bra and began to fasten her dress. When she was decent, she nudged Jim from his slumber. He stirred slowly.

'Hey,' he said, touching her bare arm and stroking the skin with his fingertip.

'We should go, before things get awkward,' she said with quiet urgency.

'I'd say we're past that point already, wouldn't you?' He smiled lazily, putting both hands behind his head. 'The party's over. We're past being missed, so we're in no rush to get anywhere.'

His casualness did nothing to calm her. 'My parents will be going mad, and I don't know what Connor is going to think.'

'Do you care?'

Panic began to consume her.

'Jim, they're going to be worried about me.'

He sat up on the straw. 'Don't you think they know?' he said simply.

She sighed deeply and acknowledged that he had a point. They had not been disturbed; no search party, as far as she was aware, had been sent out.

'What are we going to do?' she said finally.

'What do you want to do?' asked Jim, his eyes not leaving hers.

She knew what he was really asking her. What was she going to do with her life? Which direction was she going to take? Was she going to accept the life mapped out for her, or pick some exciting, uncharted new course?

Her own mini rebellions over the summer – leaving the art gallery in New York, coming home to Savannah, making her documentary – suddenly seemed quite superficial, as Jim dared her to make a decision.

'Our timing's been lousy, hasn't it?' she said.

'It's not great. We could have had a lot of nights like last night if only . . .'

'If only . . .'

'I should have kissed you at the cemetery.'

'You were too busy calling me a serial killer.'

'There were a dozen times I could've have kissed you. I just didn't. I was scared of being turned down, so I never even tried. I thought it was better to have your friendship than risk being rejected.'

'It was still the best summer of my life. Last night, when you kissed me, I was so happy. It was what I wanted, what I've wanted for a long time. But everything seems so complicated. I mean, you're leaving Savannah. Tonight.'

'I don't have to,' he said quietly.

She felt a surge of hope.

'You'd stay?'

'You might be able to twist my arm,' he grinned.

'What are you going to do, though? Delay your ticket for a week or two? You have college to get back to at the end of the month.'

'Not necessarily,' he said more seriously.

'What are you saying?'

'I'm saying that we can be happy, Jen. Me and you. Together.'

'In an ideal world, yes.'

He shook his head and looked angry.

'We can create whatever world we want for ourselves, make choices to let that happen.'

'And when your visa runs out in three months, you'll be kicked out of the country, with no college place, resentful of me because we didn't think about the practicalities . . .'

'There's ways around all that,' he said, not looking at her.

What was he saying? she wondered to herself. She felt a flood of butterflies at the possibility in his words.

'Jim, you can't quit college. I won't let you.'

'Then come to England with me. We can get a place in London. I can study, you can study, work. I don't know. What I do know is that I can't get on that plane and leave you here.'

'I guess I'd better go and talk to Connor, then,' she teased, feeling as if she had let the brakes off and could freewheel to a life with Jim Johnson.

'You know the National Film School, just outside London, is amazing. There are studios in Shepperton and Pinewood. Soho is chock-full of production companies and editing suites . . .'

'You've got a real knack, you know.'

'For what?'

'For making life seem exciting and full of possibilities.'

'People talk about being trapped, but we generally make cages for ourselves. Sometimes you just have to know when to say no and when you've got to say yes.'

'Yes,' she whispered as he kissed her.

Afterwards Jen found her panties and put them on, and as she watched Jim button his shirt, she felt buoyed and happy. She could hear voices out in the field and she knew that Marion, who lived in a small cottage next to the stables, would be up, and that she had to return to the house quickly.

They made hasty plans. A voice in her head reminded her that half of Savannah thought she was marrying Connor Gilbert, but as Jim made a check list of what they had to do, it all felt so easy, like ticking off a shopping list.

For his part, Jim was going to tell his parents that he was not returning to London. Not that evening, not yet. Friends of the Sittenfields were arriving at the Lake House at the end of the week, so there was no possibility of staying on there. Besides, they both knew how difficult it would be remaining so close to Casa D'Or. They decided it might be an idea for them to leave Savannah for a few days until they decided what to do next.

Jennifer instantly thought of her aunt Donna. Pensacola wasn't too far from Georgia, and she imagined sunset beach walks with Jim along the Floridian sands.

'Do you want me to come with you?' said Jim as they loitered at the barn door.

'Like that will make it easier.' She smiled grimly. 'I'll deal with it. You see if you can extend your plane ticket. We should meet up again later this afternoon.'

The door shut with a creak behind them. Jennifer cringed with embarrassment as she saw that Jim's pickup was one of the few vehicles left on the drive. She didn't kiss him goodbye. Simply walked back towards the house with purpose. She turned round once and saw that he was sitting in the truck. As the engine growled to life, he gave her a wink that gave her a spring in her step.

Chapter Twenty-Two

The house was still and quiet. Grey-blue early-morning light filtered through the windows. Jennifer still had a fuzzy head, so she crept into the kitchen to get a glass of water. The sound of the water trickling out of the taps was as soothing as the liquid slipping down her throat. She was hungry too, and went over to the fridge to see what was in there. It opened with a pop, and light illuminated a dizzy array of leftovers: cold hams and miniature tarts.

'Back so soon?' said a voice behind her.

Jennifer gasped and pushed the fridge door shut. She was not surprised to see her mother standing at the kitchen door in her negligee, her arms folded across her chest. In the cool light and without make-up, Sylvia looked deathly pale. Her face was expressionless, which only added to her ghoulishness.

Jennifer clutched her glass of water like a talisman. For a second she wished that she had taken Jim up on his offer to come with her, but she knew she had to face this alone.

'I was just going to bed,' she said, standing a little straighter.

'You didn't say goodbye to anyone at the party. Not one person,' said her mother coolly.

'I'm sorry . . .'

'I'm sorry,' her mother mimicked. 'Do you know how embarrassed Connor was?'

'I'll speak to him later.'

'If he'll even see you.'

Jennifer pressed her lips together and willed herself to stay strong.

'I have to see him. We need to talk.'

'I can't say I like the sound of that, but I suppose, under the circumstances, he might forgive you.'

'Forgive me?'

'You and Jim Johnson. One final fling before he goes home. Getting it out of your system.'

'I'm in love with Jim,' she said defiantly.

Sylvia gave a mirthless laugh. 'Grow up,' she hissed cruelly. 'You have sexual desire. That's all.'

'It's more than that,' said Jennifer, trying to keep her voice steady. 'Much more. He's not going back to England. He's staying here and we are going to be together.'

'You've gone mad.'

'I have never felt more clear-minded,' she replied, telling herself she could not weaken, could not turn back now.

'You're right, you should go to bed. Get some sleep. I'm sure you need it,' her mother said tartly. 'And when you wake up, you will go and find Connor – your fiancé – and do your damnedest to make it up with him.'

'You told Dad that I'd accepted Connor's proposal, didn't you?' She was testing her mother, but Sylvia's expression barely cracked. There was no sign of surprise at Jennifer's comment, just a slight hardening of her expression.

'You needed a little push. That's all.'

'This is my life,' Jennifer said, thumping her fist against her chest. 'Not a move in your game of social-ambition chess.'

'It's not my fault that you don't know what you want. Don't see good opportunities when they hit you in the face. Instead you go tramping around with that boy from next door, who, believe me, won't be quite so attentive now that he's finally got you into bed.'

'I'm not listening to this.'

'No, don't,' said her mother, composing herself. 'Go to bed. Things will be clearer when you've had some sleep. I know you'll make the right decision.' And she turned and walked back upstairs.

Jennifer stayed in the kitchen for a little while, half expecting David to come down and add his thoughts about the situation. But as she sat and finished her glass of water, she realised that her father hadn't woken. She was glad about that. Didn't want to see him. She remembered his proud, smiling face as he made the announcement about her engagement, and suddenly she felt cheap. Her feelings for Jim were still as intense as they had been the night before – hell, she almost blushed when she thought about the thrilling, secret places that he had kissed her – but still, she'd had sex with another man whilst in a relationship with someone else, and that was wrong.

She crept upstairs to bed and tried to get some sleep. It wasn't difficult, because she was so tired, and when she woke, sunlight was streaming through the shutters and she could hear the sound of the events team disassembling the stage and clearing up the mess from the night before.

The clock on her dressing table told her it was eleven o'clock. Her father would be at work now, and she knew that her mother would keep her distance, at least until Jennifer had done as she was told. She swung her feet out of bed and walked to the window. Sylvia and Marion were directing four men to take stage scaffolding through the side garden. Jennifer watched for a moment from the edge of the window, to keep out of view, and then went for a shower. A piece of hay fell out of her hair and she smiled, although only for a moment. Anxiety did that to you.

She sat on the edge of the bed in her dressing gown, towelling her damp hair, then threw the towel down, knowing she couldn't procrastinate any longer.

She got dressed and put on her shoes – Jennifer hated the telephone at the best of times, so she wanted to feel as formal and armour-plated as possible when she called Connor – then looked at the phone sitting ominously on her bedside table. Her heart beating hard, she picked up the receiver.

A female voice answered after a few rings. She recognised Carolyn Gilbert's sugary tones immediately.

'It's Jennifer,' she said quickly, her heart thumping so

furiously now she thought it would jump right out of her chest. 'Is Connor there?'

'Jennifer . . .'

If she was expecting instant frostiness, she was mistaken.

'I didn't get the chance to say congratulations last night. How are you feeling?'

'Feeling?' she asked weakly.

'The food poisoning!' Carolyn said with surprise. 'You know I always try and avoid shrimp, but I trusted those caterers. I recommended them to your mother, in fact, but I'm going to give them a wide berth from now on. What terrible, terrible timing. Everyone wanted to wish you well, but your momma said you were in the bathroom . . . She was very discreet about it, though, so don't you go worrying.'

'I'm all right now,' Jennifer said, imagining her mother covering her tracks.

'Good, because Connor's daddy and I want to take you out for dinner tonight. To celebrate properly.'

'Is Connor there?' she said, wanting to wind this conversation up as quickly as possible. She felt bad enough as it was, and didn't want to add lying to Mrs Gilbert to her list of sins.

'He's gone for a run. He'll be back soon. You should come round. I'm sure you two have plenty to talk about. Lots of planning. I'm just heading out, so it will be nice and private for you.'

'Let him know I'm coming,' she said, knowing that she had to get the thing done.

* * *

Connor's parents lived on the other side of the city, north of Hilton Head Island, officially across the border into South Carolina. Jennifer took the bridge across the Savannah River, but the traffic was bad and it took over an hour to get to their luxurious family home, a European-style estate with flourishes of French chateau that appealed to Carolyn Gilbert's more flamboyant tastes.

Jennifer sat in her car in front of the house. Her palms were sweaty and she knew it was not from the heat of the midday sun.

She tried to focus on all the things she could do with Jim once all this was over. She imagined a road trip to Florida. Cumberland Island would be beautiful at this time of year, and Jim would love the haunting wilderness of the Okefenokee swamps, where they could take kayaks out into the canals and spot alligators and wildfowl.

She couldn't wait to revisit London either. She had been twice before: once on a family holiday when her mother had been disappointed not to be able to go into Buckingham Palace, and another time on a school trip when they had been shunted around from gallery to heritage site – Westminster Abbey, St Paul's Cathedral and Trafalgar Square. She had loved every single second of it: the city's regal grandeur and its eccentricities, its red telephone boxes and black taxis, the ancient pubs that looked as if they were about to topple over, and the grand gilded stores – Fortnum & Mason, Harrods – that made her feel like a heroine in a Regency romance novel. But she looked forward to a different type of stay in the city.

One where she was a local. Where she could go out to study or work, then come home to an apartment – a flat, they liked to call them in England – where she would huddle next to Jim on cold, rainy nights, an idea that seemed so cosy and seductive that she wished she was there now.

Her shoes crunched on the gravel drive as she got out of the car. She wiped her damp palms on her skirt and walked up the limestone steps to the enormous front door. The housekeeper told her that Connor was in the library, and then silently disappeared.

Jennifer moved through the house, treading carefully so that her shoes didn't make a sound on the floor. The library was in a far wing. Like Casa D'Or, the Gilberts' grand home was built on the banks of a river, and as she pushed open the door, she could see a glimmer of water in the distance. No lights were on, and the room had a cold and gloomy pall. She could just make out Connor sitting in a wing-backed chair that looked out over the grounds.

Words deserted her. She was glad when he spoke first.

'I'm surprised you've got the balls to come here,' he said, throwing the magazine he was reading down on the desk.

'You're right. And I'm surprised you even want to see me.'

'I don't,' he said simply, getting to his feet. The expression on his face made her feel very cheap. 'Was it good then? As good as you imagined?'

'Connor, please . . .'

'Do you expect me not to be angry? My girlfriend leaves her own twenty-first, the party at which we were supposed to be celebrating our engagement, and disappears into the night with the rock star,' he said, his words full of sarcasm and scorn.

'He's my friend. I left the party just for a moment, just to say goodbye.'

'And then you fucked him,' he said, his lip curling into a sneer.

She wasn't going to deny what had happened; she was sick of lying.

'I didn't mean it to happen like that . . .'

'How thoughtful of you. It's lucky for you your mother did such a good job covering for you, otherwise the whole party would have seen you for the slut that you are.'

'Is that what you think of me?' she said, her whole body trembling.

'You know, the reason I am so . . . set back by this,' he said, choosing his words carefully, 'is because I do still love you. Stupid, isn't it? Despite how you've treated me, your family and I still love you, except you don't respect me, not one little bit.'

'I do respect you, Connor. I just . . . I just developed feelings for someone else.'

She could hear him take a deep inhalation of breath. His eyes closed. He looked furious.

'When is he going back to London?'

'Soon,' she said quietly.

'Good,' he said, opening his eyes and fixing them on Jennifer.

'I'm going with him.'

His eyes almost popped in surprise.

'What?'

'I'm going to apply to film school. In London. I want to be with him.'

He shook his head as if he couldn't quite believe what she was saying.

'Wait,' he said. 'I am prepared to forgive you, and you want to run off to London with him.'

'I'm sorry.'

'Sorry?' he repeated, taking an aggressive step forward. 'You bitch. You absolute fucking whore.'

His hand was coiled in a fist. He raised it and she thought he was going to hit her, but after one terrifying moment he slammed it through the air in frustration.

'Get out!' he roared as she held her handbag in front of her like a shield. 'Did you not hear me?' He picked up his magazine and hurled it across the room. 'I said get out.'

Jennifer turned and fled. As she stepped out into the humid air, she was aware that her decision to set her life on a new course had been irrevocably made. All that remained now was to go back to Jim and tell him.

Chapter Twenty-Three

2015

The room was only half dark; Jim's minimalist blinds looked good and offered privacy from prying eyes, but against the glare of New York's setting sun, they were close to useless. He carried a glass of water towards the bed, stepping over the screwed-up tissues scattered across the floor like little rosebuds.

'Here you go, medicine for the patient,' he said, sitting on the edge of the mattress. Sarah had obviously been going down with something when she had come round the night before, but it had quickly developed into a full-blown cold overnight; so much so that she'd had the day off work and had still been in bed when Jim had returned home from the office.

Sarah groaned and turned over, shielding her eyes. Her cheeks were as red as her nose, and her hair was sticking out at all angles. She took the pill from Jim and dutifully swallowed.

'Thanks, babe,' she croaked. 'Sorry to be such a pain.'

'Don't be daft, you can't help getting sick, can you?'

Sarah made a half-hearted effort to smile, then collapsed back on to the pillows. 'But I'm sick in *your* flat. I'm cramping your style.'

Jim smiled. 'Well I *was* planning on throwing a party later, but Hugh Hefner and Tommy Lee have called in sick too.'

'You should go out,' she said, propping herself up with a pillow. 'By the sounds of it, Jen needs cheering up.'

Jim felt guilty for sharing Connor's confidences. He hadn't told Sarah everything, of course. Hadn't told her most things, in fact: Jennifer's pregnancies, the drinking. But he had wanted to see his old friend socially and felt awkward meeting her alone after everything Connor had said. He'd suggested the four of them go out for dinner, but when Sarah had dragged her heels, blaming her workload and the addition of the Hamptons summer social circuit to her reporting brief, he'd pushed the issue, saying that Jennifer needed 'a fun night out'.

'We can reschedule,' he said, handing her another tissue.

'Connor's booked Domina,' she said, shaking her head and blowing her nose noisily. 'It's properly difficult to get a table there. Go on, go. Tell them that funny story about Celine Wood giving you drugs. Besides, you've got Tivo in the bedroom and I want to catch up with *Dancing with the Stars*.'

Jim hadn't seen Connor since Baruda, three weeks earlier, although they had spoken on the phone. The sale of RedReef was now going through and everything was in the hands of the lawyers. Simon had taken Jim out for dinner to congratulate him on the idea of an Omari diffusion brand, and when he confided that the wheels were in motion to make Jim CEO of the entire hotel group when Casa D'Or was finished, Jim believed that there had been some karma in trying to help Connor, or more specifically Jennifer, out.

Domina had apparently only been open a week. As Jim arrived, several couples who had made the social faux pas of just turning up on the night to ask for a table were being told by a frosty-looking platinum blonde that they were now taking bookings for six months' time. Their own table was, meanwhile, not quite ready. He went to the bar and saw Jennifer sitting there alone, one black-trousered leg elegantly crossed over the other, a bronze pump dangling from her tanned foot. It looked so casual: the outfit, her dark hair pinned up, a flash of gold at wrist and neck, like she had just thrown it all on in a rush.

'Hey,' he smiled, giving her an awkward peck on the cheek. 'Where's Connor?'

'Not coming.' She held her phone up and looked piqued. 'He's just called. He's out with investors and the meeting has finished but now they want to go on somewhere.'

She said it as though she didn't believe it, but Jim knew the form of these things. Appointments turned to dinner and drinks, then private clubs, even strip joints – macho pleasures in the name of business – and you were generally beholden to the person holding the purse strings. By that logic he wondered if Connor's priority shouldn't be seeing him this evening, but being here alone with Jennifer looking like a goddess, he couldn't help giving a silent prayer of thanks to the bankers who had taken Connor for a night on the tiles.

'Where's Sarah?' asked Jennifer, putting her phone in her bag and looking around.

'Ill. Bad cold,' he said awkwardly. 'I didn't cancel earlier because we thought she was going to be all right, but when I left, she was doing a fairly accurate impression of Rudolph the Red-Nosed Reindeer.'

'I hope she's OK,' said Jennifer with concern. 'You shouldn't be here.'

'Actually, she seemed pretty determined to have a night in watching the telly alone.'

'Such are your charms,' she quipped.

'So it's just us.'

'Me, you, the uptight staff.'

'I noticed that,' he said, as the bartender gazed determinedly through him.

'Do you want to stay here?' she whispered.

'There's about a dozen people who give a shit about places like this clamouring to get in at the door.'

'Then we should do our bit for the community and give them our table,' she smiled, finishing her drink and picking up her clutch bag.

As they left, Jim approached an anxious-looking man in the atrium.

'Give the name Connor Gilbert at reception and have a nice night with your girl,' he said.

When he got out on to the street, Jennifer was waiting for him. He wondered if they had been too rash in leaving. Maybe she just wanted to go home.

'Fancy grabbing some pizza?' Not his best line.

'Pizza?'

'You know, big, round, tomatoes and cheese on the top. Tend to be the size of dinner plates in London, coffee tables in New York.'

'You're on.'

'How about here?' he said pointing at a typical by-the-slice pizza parlour.

People were staring as they waited by the counter. If Jennifer noticed, she pretended not to. Jim ordered a full-size cheese pie and handed over twenty dollars. On the street, he opened the box and handed her a slice, gooey strings of hot mozzarella stretching out as he pulled it from the round.

'You look like Holly Golightly,' he grinned, thinking of the famous scene in *Breakfast at Tiffany's*.

'She was eating a doughnut,' Jennifer quipped back.

'To the sound of "Moon River",' said Jim quietly, without even thinking.

'Is that our soundtrack?'

'Maybe,' he replied as a string of cheese burned the back of his hand. 'Shit,' he said, shaking it.

'Are you OK?' She pulled a tissue out of her bag and handed it to him. 'Pizza pies. Not the easiest thing to eat in the street. We should have stuck to Krispy Kremes.'

'What am I going to do with this?' he laughed, balancing the brown box on his free hand.

'Why don't we finish it at mine? We're just round the corner. You haven't seen our house yet.'

* * *

The Wyatt-Gilbert residence was a town house on 61st Street. It had a shiny black door, a run of arched windows and a plastic surgeon next door, or so said the discreet gold sign on the brickwork. The whole street reeked of money, as did the fragrant smell of expensive candles when Jennifer let him into the hall.

A shaggy copper-coloured dog ran up to them. Jim wasn't much of a pet person, but this one was cute. It jumped up at him, excited by the smell of the pizza.

'Mars Bar, get down.'

'Your dog is called Mars Bar?' He laughed.

'I'll get some plates,' she said, already in the kitchen.

Jim peered down the long corridor, mentally comparing it to his own one-bedroom walk-up in the Village. In his line of vision he could see a Picasso and an elevator door, as if to emphasise how far apart their lives had become; or perhaps it was that they had maintained the status quo from when they had first met.

He turned left, to the room nearest him, and went in. A living room, the sort of space realtors called 'the snug'. More expensive art and, on a sideboard, a row of photographs of the happy couple. A tasteful black-and-white of their wedding day that was so hard to look at he had to move away.

He sat down and balanced the pizza box on his lap, nervous of getting tomato sauce on the pale green sofa. Jennifer came through with two plates, then went to the drinks cabinet and took out a pair of glasses.

'Red or white?' she asked.

'Neither,' he said carefully. 'Don't bother opening a bottle just for me.'

'I'm having a drink,' she said.

'Coffee,' he said as light-heartedly as he could. 'I'll go and brew up if you like.'

She put the glasses back down on the cabinet and Jim felt a note of relief, as if a moment of danger had passed.

She went to make coffee. When she came back, she sat in the chair opposite him and curled her fingers around her cup.

'How long have you lived here?' he asked.

'Ten years.'

'It's a real grown-up house,' he smiled, thinking of himself at thirty, the proud new owner of a maisonette in Kentish Town, his first step on the housing ladder. The scales had since fallen from his eyes about the London housing market. He was older, wiser. He had made sacrifices in his professional life, chasing money and position rather than the creative fulfilment he knew he would have got as a musician. And yet he guessed that short of winning the lottery, that maisonette would be as high as he ever got on the property ladder.

'And here we are, all grown up,' she said, stroking Mars Bar, who had come and plonked himself down between them.

'You make it sound as if we've changed.'

'Haven't we?' she smiled, looking up.

'I still feel the same as I did when I was twenty. Although I'll see a really bad photo of myself in a trade magazine and think, who the hell is that? Sarah told me the other day that it was time to retire my Converse All Stars. I thought she meant because they were knackered. On reflection, she probably thinks they make me look a bit sad.'

'You'll still be cool at sixty, Jim Johnson. I can see it now. Sharp suits, a beautiful woman on your arm, and a cigarette dangling out of your mouth.'

'You make me sound like an ageing gigolo. That wasn't what I had in mind when you interviewed me at twenty.'

'Interview?'

'The documentary. Or have you forgotten?'

'The documentary.' She cringed, throwing her hands behind her head. 'Did I really think I was going to be the new Martin Scorsese?'

'Now that would have been impressive. A Savannah gangster movie. What happened to it?' he said more seriously.

'Nothing,' she said honestly. She puffed out her cheeks and looked at him. 'I was living in New York by the Christmas. It's hard to make a documentary about your home-town friends when you're hundreds of miles away from them.'

'You never applied to film school?'

She gave him a sad smile. 'I thought about it. But I'd missed the next year's intake, and by the following year I was married. A housewife at twenty-three. I didn't imagine that when I filmed myself for the documentary either.' Her cheeks flushed with embarrassment.

'It's very fashionable being a domestic goddess,' he said, trying to make her feel better. 'I know loads of women with high-powered jobs in London. Get them drunk and they'll tell you that all they want to do is give up work and spend the day in the gym and on the school run.'

'Is that how far feminism has really come?'

'What I'm saying is that there's nothing wrong with wanting to stay at home.'

'Well, I always seem to be busy. Decorating the loft, selling the loft, buying this place. When I look back and wonder where the time went, I guess I've probably spent most of it in ABC Carpet and Home. And the charities. They keep me very busy. In fact there was something I meant to ask you. I'm doing an event for a Brooklyn animal shelter at Christmas. We need prizes for an auction. Any chance of a two-night stay in an Omari hotel?'

'You can have a week in any of our resorts in the world, food and drink included,' he said, happy to help.

'Have you still got it?' he asked after another moment.

'What?'

'The documentary.'

'Somewhere,' she said cautiously.

'Go and have a look,' he encouraged her.

'Now?'

'I want to see this cool guy you remember.'

She hesitated for a moment, then gave him that big warm smile and disappeared upstairs.

He looked around, taking in the details of the house. He had always believed that there was nothing more revealing than being in someone's personal space. So often it was a perfect reflection of themselves. He thought about the homes of his friends back in London; his football pals with their small children and their terraced houses, toys everywhere, vaguely managed chaos and an air of comfortable neglect. Or his own flat, with its Swedish furniture; wilfully independent, a design-conscious space for one.

He grabbed a coffee table book – something about Parisian interiors – and started to flick through it as he waited for Jennifer to return, but she didn't come back.

'Where is she?' he whispered to Mars Bar, who got up, tail wagging, and disappeared out of the room.

Jim smiled to himself and got up.

'Jen,' he shouted.

He could see Mars Bars' tail disappearing up the stairs and followed him.

'Jen?'

'In here,' came a muffled reply.

He passed the master bedroom: huge bed, plump pillows. Thankfully she wasn't in there.

'Top floor,' she shouted.

He located her voice in a smaller room, where she was rifling through a long run of storage cupboards.

'Here,' she said bashfully, pulling out a big white box marked *Sony*. She lifted out a camcorder and popped out a tape from the player.

'I'm not sure I'm ready for this,' he grimaced. 'Have you got a video recorder?'

'You're joking. This place is so high-tech you need a computer science degree to work the television.'

'We can watch it on the camcorder,' he suggested.

They sat on the end of the bed and Jennifer switched it on.

'There's hours of stuff,' she laughed.

'We'd better get comfortable then,' he said as colour images flickered on to the screen. He instantly recognised their afternoon on the beach, the s'mores and the bonfire and the setting sun. 'Bloody hell, I was slim.'

'We all were. I didn't have to do spinning class three times a week to look like that.'

'Your friend with the diamanté glasses. I liked her. What was she called?'

'Jeanne.' She smiled wistfully.

'Do you keep in touch?'

'We lost contact over the years.'

'Then get back in touch. There's no excuses these days with social media.'

'I can't contact someone out of the blue.'

'You found me on the internet.'

'That was different. That was professional.'

Jim registered a disappointed sinking feeling but he didn't want to show it.

'It's weird, I remember that afternoon as if it was yesterday. It's a bit like how I can remember every song lyric from every record I bought in the eighties, but ask me what I had for lunch today and I couldn't tell you.'

'Maybe it's because everything was so new and exciting and hopeful when we were young. It's like printing memories with better ink,' she smiled.

'It's such a shame you never did anything with this, Jen,' said Jim after a few minutes. 'It's still not too late, you know.'

'Don't be silly. Who's going to be interested in a housewife's old home video?'

'It's a social snapshot of Generation X at the height of their disillusionment,' he replied as she gave him a playful tap on the shoulder.

'I know what you should do with these tapes,' he said, an idea slowly percolating.

Jennifer frowned anxiously. 'What?'

'You should get in touch with all these people and interview them again. This footage is great, but as it is, it's all conjecture. People don't want to just hear that Johnny Boy wants to be an astronaut or a stockbroker. They want to see if he makes it.'

'Nice try, but I'm not sure there's a place for TV like this any more. Not when people have got a heap of nostalgia on their own Facebook page.'

'Facebook isn't about nostalgia,' said Jim ruefully. 'It's just people boasting about the best one per cent of their lives. Your documentary is about hopes, dreams, disappointments. Come on, Jen. Think about it. All the kids in this film were twenty, twenty-one when you filmed it. Now you're revisiting them twenty-one years later. And hey, look, you can even interview my dad,' he said as Bryn Johnson flickered into the picture, pompous, expansive, as if he were hosting his own late-night arts programme, enjoying his moment on camera. 'He's just landed a visiting professorship at Columbia. Says he wants to rent a place on Washington Square. I told him it's not like it was during the sixties out there, but he wouldn't listen; he thinks it'll be all Breton tops and Ban the Bomb.'

'It's easy to keep living in the past, though, isn't it?' said Jennifer, switching off the camcorder. 'Nicer to remember yourself when everything was an opportunity rather than a disappointment. When you had no responsibilities. Time is a great airbrush; you can edit out all the bad bits.'

'Do you ever think about us?' he asked, sensing his own moment for reminiscing. It was a question he'd been wanting to ask all night.

'I need a drink,' she said, standing up.

He looked at her and noticed that, despite the coffee, her eyes were not quite focused. How long had she been at Domina before he'd arrived? he wondered, remembering what Connor had said in Baruda.

'Wait,' he said, stopping her from leaving. 'That summer. Do you ever think about it?'

'Sometimes. A lot lately,' she said quietly. She looked at him hopefully, seeking reassurance that she had not been having these thoughts alone.

'So do I,' nodded Jim in solidarity. 'I think about what would have happened if you'd picked me and not Connor. How our lives might have turned out differently.'

'It wasn't a case of picking one over the other,' she said, sitting back down.

'You did,' said Jim, desperate to make his thoughts heard. 'You told me to go back to England. You said that if I cared about you, I should get on the plane and not contact you again.

And then you moved to New York with Connor.'

'I was grieving,' she said, not looking at him.

'Not when you wrote me the letter.'

She didn't say anything.

Memories flooded back in Technicolor. He'd also written to her once he'd returned to England, but she hadn't replied. He didn't blame her.

'I almost didn't get on the plane that day. And looking back, I shouldn't have done. I should have fought for you. I should have been there for you. I never stop asking myself the question: what would have happened if I'd gone back?'

'I'd have made the same choice,' said Jennifer evenly. 'Staying with Connor, moving to New York, I knew that was what my mother would have wanted. I suppose it was my way of saying sorry.'

'But she was dead.'

'That's right. And if it wasn't for me, she might still be alive. I hated myself because of what happened that night,' she said quietly. 'I also knew that if I had you in my life, if I was constantly reminded of why I was fighting with my mother that night on the stairs, I wouldn't just keep on hating myself, I'd end up hating you too. And I never wanted that.'

She puffed out her cheeks and didn't look at him.

'Over the years I've made my own sort of peace with what happened. As for me and you, we had a perfect summer, a perfect love affair frozen in time. Because if you hadn't left Savannah, if we had stayed together, we'd have ended up like all those couples in Domina who don't have anything to say to each other except their thoughts about the tasting menu. As it is, we were and always will be incredible.'

'Is that what you honestly think? Has life really made you that cynical? We were perfect for each other.'

'I'm married, Jim,' she said, the tone of her voice hardening. 'Connor loves me. He's always been so good to me.'

'And I never had the chance,' Jim replied with passion.

He paused before he proceeded.

'I know about the pregnancy,' he said finally. He knew he might never get another chance to say everything he wanted to say to her, but he hadn't been able to forget what Connor had revealed in Baruda. 'Connor told me. He told me about the abortion.'

'He never should have done that,' she said, her voice hardening as a tear slipped down her cheek.

Jim reached over to touch her hand, but as she flinched away, Jim felt a wave of sorrow that made him lose his breath. A sorrow for what was, what they had lost and what never could be.

'You'd better go,' Jennifer said. 'My husband will be back soon.'

'Jen, please. We've waited twenty years to talk about this.'

'Just go,' she repeated, her voice getting even more steely.

Jim nodded grimly at the irony of it, at the painful reality of history repeating itself, and left the house without another word.

Chapter Twenty-Four

'So do you think you can pull it off?' Jim looked at Nina Scott, one of New York's top travel industry publicists as she sat in the boardroom outlining her plans for the Casa D'Or launch in November.

'I can pull off the best launch party of the millennium if you can promise me the place is going to be finished in time. I've been burned too many times by hoteliers wanting the big splash but having to settle for a soft launch because the swimming pool hasn't been tiled.'

'It will be finished,' said Jim with determination. 'Everything is on schedule. All I need is for you to get me lots of big celebrity names and acres of lovely media coverage. If you do, there's a presidential suite at any of the Omari hotels with your name on it for a night.'

'Well, I've put out some feelers and people are already biting my hand off for an invite. I thought it might be a question of who we can get down to Savannah, but I think it's going to be how many people we have to let down.'

'Seems Simon was right about the number of people with Scarlett O'Hara fantasies,' said Jim, flicking through the media pack.

'Speaking of feisty belles,' added Nina, 'an agent from Elan Models called me up yesterday. Seems they've got wind of the party and Celine Wood, a very old friend of yours apparently, wants to know if she can be on the guest list. She said to call her.'

'Did she now?' said Jim, smiling as he sipped his coffee.

'An old friend, hey?'

'Not like that.'

'I wondered. I don't doubt how popular you are with the ladies, although I read in *People* magazine the other day that she's going out with Richie Hawkins, the rock star, now. So long as you don't have any *emotional* objections, I can put him down as her plus one.'

'Mr Johnson, I have your ten o'clock call holding,' said Jim's executive assistant, popping her head around the door.

'Put him through to my office in a moment,' replied Jim, finishing off his coffee.

He wound up his meeting with Nina and went back to his office. He had always wondered what it would be like to be the boss, and had figured it would be an easy life of long lunches and hand-shaking deals. In reality he sometimes felt like a juggler, keeping all these balls in the air, switching lanes from one project to another.

Not only was he overseeing the Casa D'Or launch, he was

still keeping his eye on the rest of the Omari chain, not to mention his new pet project that had been jump-started to life. The RedReef resort acquisition had been rushed through, and with it had come dozens of meetings for creating the Omari diffusion brand. They'd come up with the name Santai for the spin-off, a Far Eastern word meaning 'relax', which he hoped would also become the byword for the new chain. He was still mulling over the idea of an electronics ban for guests from the moment they checked in.

He sat down at his desk and put some headphones on; at least modern technology had made things easier for his juggling act, he reminded himself as he prepared himself for his Skype call.

'Gregor, how are you?' he asked as a flickering image appeared on his monitor.

Gregor Bentley was the new RedReef general manager, transferred just a couple of weeks earlier from the Omari resort in Phuket. In Jim's mind he had been the perfect recruit for their new Caribbean Santai property, having a CV that included many years' service at one of the top Barbados hotels.

The RedReef was currently closed for both the hurricane season and refurbishment, but Gregor and his team had been hard at work getting the property ready for the December soft launch, and had been keeping Jim up to date with improvements in twice-weekly calls.

Gregor didn't respond immediately to Jim's casual greeting, and Jim instantly detected that something was wrong.

'What is it?' he asked quickly as his assistant brought him another cup of coffee.

'There was a problem last night,' replied Gregor, his brown face creasing with concern.

Jim's mind went into overdrive wondering what it might be.

'Daniel Verrander is in hospital,' continued his colleague. Daniel was Gregor's number two, who had also just started at RedReef.

Jim had faith in the hotel's new executive team. Before his official appointment as RedReef's general manager, Gregor had alluded to certain difficulties about working in the Caribbean and was keen to get his own team on board. Jim had agreed; he'd been in the business long enough to know how a corrupt management could fleece profits, and it had been one explanation for why RedReef had not previously been a flourishing business.

'Hospital? Why?' he asked anxiously.

'He was jumped leaving the hotel last night. He's fine. He will be. He has cracked ribs, a broken arm, bruising.'

'Do we know who did it?' asked Jim with rising panic. A violent attack at RedReef was not good news, least of all for poor Daniel Verrander. He pictured the hotel's number two, a strapping, no-nonsense man. 'You don't grow up in Kingston, Jamaica without being able to look after yourself,' Daniel had told Jim on his most recent visit to RedReef. It must have taken a group of assailants to inflict that sort of injury, thought Jim with concern.

'We're not certain, but we have an idea,' said Gregor cautiously.

He paused a moment before he continued.

'It looks like RedReef has been in the pocket of a local crime mob for a long time,' he explained soberly.

'Protection money?' asked Jim, feeling the sunshine drain from his day.

'I think they've taken at least a million dollars from the hotel in the last year alone.'

'Shit. No wonder it's not making any money.'

'Daniel was on to it. He's had experience of this sort of thing before. In fact he had already started weeding out members of staff he thought were involved.'

'*Staff* were involved?' said Jim, almost spilling his coffee.

'Not directly, but it looks like some people were reporting hotel earnings to the mob boss so he knew how much they could extort. Daniel finished his shift last night and left the hotel,' he continued. 'At some point on his way home he was jumped by a gang. He was found by a tourist in a pretty bad way. We had him airlifted to the hospital in Provo last night. I didn't want to contact you until we knew more.'

'But he's OK?' said Jim, wanting assurances.

'He's shaken up pretty badly, which I think was the idea. It was a warning for sure.'

Jim took a sip of his coffee to help him think.

'Who are this crime gang? Do we know?'

'It's headed up by someone called Marshall Roberts. Nasty piece of work. Lives on Baruda.'

'And no one has had any contact with him?'

'Not sure Daniel had the chance, no.'

'Fuck,' muttered Jim under his breath.

'What do you want us to do, Jim? Carry on paying?'

'No,' he replied passionately. 'The hotel will never be owned by us, not really, if we don't face them down.'

'And who's going to do that?'

Jim could tell that Gregor was rattled.

'I will,' he said without even thinking about it.

'So you're going to come over?' asked Gregor with a note of relief.

'Yes,' he said grimly. 'Though first I need to go and speak to someone. Find out what he knows.'

'Who?' replied his Caribbean colleague.

'The man who stitched us up over this bloody acquisition,' said Jim, not even caring that he was talking out of turn. 'The man who sold us RedReef. Connor Gilbert.'

I'm going to strangle him, then I'm going to sue him – in that order, thought Jim, pushing the car faster now he was turning away from the Montauk Highway and on to the tangle of exclusive roads.

He couldn't remember being so angry in a long time. He was angry with Connor Gilbert – furious – but most of all he was angry with himself. Of course he'd listened to Simon's warnings not to be sentimental about the RedReef deal, but he hadn't really paid attention and had pushed the deal through without the right due diligence. Yes, they'd examined the profit-and-loss account and researched the potential of the resort comparative to other hotels in the area, but they hadn't done their homework where it counted. Hadn't spoken to enough people on the ground, hadn't listened to the warning bells: the mutterings among the staff about problems with supply chains; hell, even the boy on the beach who'd talked about taxes.

Jim hadn't got to where he was in the company without being hard-headed, but he'd let his feelings for Jennifer and his desire to help her cloud his judgement, and now he was paying the price. RedReef would never be profitable while it was still in the clutches of a mob gang. And if RedReef failed, it might take his career prospects with it. He'd worked too hard, sacrificed too much – any life outside the office, relationship, friends, hobbies – to have it all fall down now.

But even though he knew he was culpable for the whole mess, Jim couldn't help but feel that he had been royally stitched up by Connor Gilbert. Connor was no fool. He'd have known what was going on, why the hotel was running at a loss, and had used the oldest psychological business game in the book, pretending that RedReef was the one asset he wanted to keep hold of, that he was getting rid of it because he absolutely had to.

Once Jim had been tipped off by Gregor about what was going on, he'd done some investigations of his own, and discovered that local 'businessman' Marshall Roberts controlled everything in Baruda, and demanded a vast protection fee to allow anything in or out of the complex. Not so much as a bag of ice cubes would reach RedReef until they coughed up the cash.

Baruda was governed by a local council, but the mayor was unable or unwilling to lift a finger against Roberts, and without the help of the authorities, the situation would not change for RedReef or the handful of other similar businesses on the island until Roberts was brought down.

Hurtling down the beach road, Jim rolled down the window of the car he had rented to get to the Hamptons, in an attempt to let the warm breeze calm him down. The mood he was in, he was half minded to commit a crime of his own – the premeditated murder of Connor Gilbert. He'd spent all morning after his conversation with Gregor Bentley trying to track the bastard down. His assistant claimed he was in meetings all day, but any requests for him to call Jim back had gone unanswered. In the end, Jim had called Jennifer. It had been an awkward conversation – the last time they had spoken was the evening at her house – but he had kept it polite, the tension between them had disappeared and she had eventually confirmed that Connor had gone to the Hamptons to meet a potential client, and would be back the following day.

Jim didn't really know why he'd decided to drive out there to confront Connor. He guessed that he just wanted to do something to start resolving the mess. Remembering something Connor had said to him at the Memorial Day weekend – 'sometimes I just like to play hookey and come paddle-boarding' – Jim had visions of him on top of his board, the carefree entrepreneur enjoying the fruits of his unscrupulous business, and wanted to knock him into the sea.

A business lunch he could not put off, and collecting the hire car, meant that it was late afternoon by the time he reached Beach Lane. The sun was beginning to dip in the sky, but it was still hot. Jim had no idea where Connor was meeting his business associate, but he figured that if he was returning to the city the next day, he would be staying the night at the beach house.

He pulled up outside the enormous gates that fronted the house and pressed the intercom. There was no response, but he recognised Connor's Ferrari sitting in the drive. He tried Connor's mobile again, but still there was nothing.

Cursing under his breath, he looked around for a place to park. His hire car didn't have the requisite permits to stop near the beach, but he was going to have to take his chances with the police. He hadn't driven all this way to turn back now.

He parked the car in the shadow of a sand dune and walked the fifty yards to the entrance to the beach. He kicked off his shoes and socks and stalked across the hot sand, his vision fixed towards the sea, looking for a paddleboarder, but there was no one in the water except a couple of teenagers playing by the shore.

He turned round and looked at the proud line of beach houses that lined the edge of the sand.

'Sod it,' he muttered, walking towards the picket fence that separated the grounds of the Wyatt-Gilbert house from the beach. Even from this distance he could see that the glass doors were open, which meant that someone was at home. If Connor wasn't going to let him in through the front door, he was going to have to go to Plan B.

As he stalked towards the house, the thought did occur to him that he was more likely to be arrested for trespassing than being able to resolve the RedReef mess. Part of him wondered if he should just call Simon and come clean about what was going on. Simon was one of the wealthiest men in the world. Money meant power, power meant influence; perhaps he could exert some pressure on the mayor to shut Marshall Roberts' operation down. A promise to fund an international airport on Baruda would certainly do it.

But deep down Jim knew that he had to sort this mess out on his own. Besides which, if Simon got to hear about the situation, Jim was more likely to get fired than bag a promotion, which was what had brought him to New York in the first place.

Who are you kidding? he told himself. He'd come to New York to be closer to Jennifer. The one woman he had loved unceasingly for twenty years.

What had he thought would happen once he got here? That Jennifer would fall madly back in love with him – though he doubted she'd had any genuine feelings for him in the first place – that she would divorce Connor and fall into Jim's arms? No. Jim had been living in New York for six months now – had this woman shown the slightest interest in him? Had she given him any sign that she was ready to be swept off her feet by some ex-lover? No, she hadn't. In fact she had set

Jim up with one of her friends, and had dispatched him from their one intimate night out with the words, 'My husband will be home soon'.

It was time to grow up, he thought, putting his shoes and socks back on, not wanting to meet Connor looking like a surfer.

He could hear music now coming from the house. Glancing around to check that he wasn't being watched, he moved closer, stopping at the rear entrance – the wooden walkway where Connor had left his paddleboard that morning. Now he had an uninterrupted view across the pool to the back of the house. And there, backlit in all his glory, was Connor Gilbert, wrapped in a robe, a glass in one hand, apparently dancing to an old Dire Straits song.

'Idiot,' Jim muttered, imagining the look of shock and panic on Connor's face when he knocked on the window.

He had just reached the decking when he froze. Jennifer had walked into view, her back to the window. He gasped: she was wearing only black lingerie, with panties that barely covered her buttocks. She came up behind Connor and put her arms around him, undoing his robe and pulling it off his shoulders. He turned, grinning, kissing her bare shoulder as she tossed her dark hair.

It was painful to watch, but Jim couldn't take his eyes off them. Connor was unclipping her bra now and lifting her on to the table. She lay back, her legs parting instinctively, and Connor stepped closer, disappearing almost from view between her thighs. Jim watched the top of his head moving in a slow, intimate rhythm. The music drowned any other noise, but Jim could imagine Jennifer's soft moans of pleasure as her husband's tongue dipped inside her.

He missed a breath as he realised how badly he'd misjudged everything. He had always found some consolation in the idea that Jennifer didn't really love Connor. They were a couple thrown together by circumstance, bound by guilt and convention.

But here they were now, fucking on a table like young lovers. Jim shifted his position to keep out of view, a voice in his head telling him that he should just leave. Jennifer was climaxing now, arching on the table, her head tipping back in urgent desire, hair cascading like a waterfall. And it was then that he noticed something, and a sick, heavy feeling welled in his stomach. As Connor withdrew himself, his wife coiled upwards to a sitting position, then slid off the table and turned round to face the beach, snaking her arms upwards to stretch out her naked post-coital body. And Jim knew for certain that the woman he was watching was not Jennifer.

Chapter Twenty-Five

Justin and Ashley were getting married, and Jim had been invited as Sarah's plus one. The ceremony itself had been at three o'clock at City Hall, with the guests transported to the reception in Williamsburg in a fleet of beaten-up pickup trucks that reminded him of his old mode of transport in Savannah. Sitting on a hay bale with a dozen beautiful, bohemian-looking guests, Jim enjoyed the sun on his face as they crossed Brooklyn Bridge. He put his sunglasses on as he watched the bride and groom kissing on the opposite bale, grinning at how blissfully happy they looked. Justin had grown his beard for the occasion, and in waistcoat, tweed trousers and boots he reminded Jim of an Amish potato farmer. His bride, a picture of lovely simplicity in a long floaty cream gown and floral crown, was unable to take her eyes off her new husband. Jim found himself hoping that he too could be that happy one day.

'Wow, look at this place,' said Sarah when they arrived at the reception venue. It was an enormous loft stretching the entire length of the warehouse building. There were twinkling fairy lights everywhere, and long tables dressed with white linen, seasonal blooms and tea lights in Mason jars that spilled more soft light about the stark industrial space.

'I didn't think a hipster wedding would be so tasteful,' whispered Jim, gazing around the cavernous room.

'What were you expecting?'

'I don't know. Maybe something a little less conventional. More craft beer, less champagne,' he said, letting a waiter serve him a glass of ice-cold Moët.

'Well, you did come by pickup truck.'

'I was hoping for a skateboard.'

'Well, the speeches have apparently been dispensed with. That's left-field. Instead we're being invited to view a photo montage on the mezzanine.'

'A photo montage?'

'A visual expression of their love for each other and everyone involved in the wedding.'

They both giggled and looked for where they were sitting. Jim found his name written on a square of brown recycled cardboard, which also contained instructions to 'post pictures of our wedding to #ashandjustietheknot'. He wondered who he would be sitting next to for the next two hours and glanced at the surrounding names. He didn't recognise any of them, and felt weary at the prospect of having to be perky and sociable. At least the drink was flowing freely, he thought, taking another glass of fizz.

In the event, they had Patrick and Bryony and Alex and

Joanna for company. They were all around Sarah's age. Conversation was the Brooklyn equivalent of house prices and schools; Patrick and Bryony told them at great length about their own wedding, being held in a barn in upstate New York in three weeks' time. Bryony gave Sarah a Pinterest link in case she was interested in their inspiration.

As the day went on, and their farm-to-table main course turned to dairy-free dessert, Jim found himself wishing that he was somewhere else. It was a lovely wedding, and he was genuinely happy for Ashley and Justin, but surrounded by happy – dare he say it, smug – couples, he couldn't help thinking of Connor and Jennifer's relationship. It had been three days since he had seen Connor and the unknown woman in flagrante, and he still hadn't worked out what to do about it. The only thing he knew with absolute certainty was that Jennifer did not deserve to be treated like that.

But what was the alternative? If he told her that Connor was having an affair, it would look suspiciously peevish after their heart-to-heart at the townhouse. And could Jennifer cope with the idea of Connor and another woman? 'Connor loves me. Connor looks after me.' These were ideas she held on to like a talisman; was it better for her not to know?

'So is this a trend or something?' smiled Jim, reclining in his chair as coffee was served. He was glad of the caffeine, knew he needed it to sober up. He hadn't had lunch, and his cashew milk smoothie breakfast, whipped up by Sarah that morning, had done little to soak up the alcohol.

'What do you mean?' asked Bryony, fiddling with her fiancé's ear lobe.

'Getting married in your twenties.'

'Why do you say that?' said Bryony with bemusement.

'You guys, Ashley and Justin . . . When I was twenty-seven, I was still chasing girls around nightclubs.'

'I thought you were doing that until you met me,' laughed Sarah, settling her arm over the back of his chair.

Bryony smiled thinly and touched Patrick on the forearm, her gratitude at having dodged men like Jim Johnson obvious to see.

'You two aren't married, I take it,' said Alex, putting his chocolate dinner mint to one side.

Sarah shook her head. 'British. Cultural thing. We just like having lots of sex, don't we, darling?'

'Grand old age of forty and never taken the plunge,' said Jim, holding his hands up earnestly, voicing what everyone was thinking.

'You've *never* been married,' said Bryony with genuine interest. 'Is it an ideological thing?' she added, sipping her champagne.

'I believe in marriage when you love someone, when you're absolutely convinced that you've found your soulmate. I'm just not sure you can say that with absolute conviction in your twenties. *I* couldn't anyway,' he added quickly.

A thought nagged at him. Deep down he knew he was lying. Lying to himself. He thought of himself at twenty. Madly in love with Jennifer Wyatt, willing to do anything for her. Move to Savannah to be with her permanently, invite her to live in London to be with him. Marry her. Have a family.

'Maybe you were just too busy having fun to find the idea of commitment attractive,' said Bryony pointedly, clearly having taken his remarks as a personal attack.

Jim was drunk and feeling cavalier. The group were making him feel every one of his forty years, and he didn't like being lectured by a bunch of twenty-somethings.

'I think it's important to have fun,' he said with a shrug. 'Take it from an old man . . . you've got to make mistakes, find out who you are, what you like, and yes, get all the meaningless sex out of your system. Because you don't want to be doing that when you've got a ring on your finger.'

Other people were now listening to their conversation, but Jim was in full flow.

'The other day I found out that the husband of a good friend of mine is having an affair,' he continued expansively. 'They got married young. Almost straight out of college. Fast-forward to her forties and she thinks she's got the happy marriage, the perfect husband, when really he's off shagging his secretary in the Hamptons. You have to ask yourself, Bryony, is that because he didn't do enough catting around in his twenties? Does he think he missed out?'

He reached for his drink to conclude his point, but he miscalculated and the flute tipped over. Champagne trickled under the gold-sprayed twigs that festooned the table.

Sarah picked up the glass and got to her feet.

'Right then, how about we break up this party and go

outside? There is an amazing terrace out there and you can see the whole Manhattan skyline.'

She ushered him out on to a huge decked area with the whole cityscape, backlit by the golden dusk, set out before them.

'Did I overstep the mark?' he said, feeling the fresh air sober him up like a slap.

'They were smug and irritating, but it wasn't exactly appropriate to suggest they shouldn't be getting married at their age – my age,' she said pointedly. 'Especially when their wedding is in less than a month.'

'I'm doing them a favour. I'm focusing their minds,' he said, taking another champagne from a passing waiter.

Sarah took it straight off him.

'What's got into you?' she asked firmly.

'A tough week.'

He hadn't seen her properly in days. The Hamptons beat meant she was out of the city a lot, and problems at work – RedReef, and a few niggles with the Casa D'Or project – had kept him busy in the office.

'Want to talk about it?'

'I've been fucked over by Connor,' he said, looking at her.

'In what way?' said Sarah slowly.

He spent the next ten minutes telling her about RedReef and Marshall Roberts' crime operation.

'I assume you didn't know anything about this.'

'What do you think?'

'And what are you going to do about it?'

'I'm flying to Baruda tomorrow to sort it out.'

'How?'

'I have an appointment with Marshall Roberts and we're going to talk about it,' he said, not wanting to dwell on what he had in store.

'Jim, this is ridiculous. You could end up being thrown to the sharks.'

'Like 007,' he smiled grimly.

'You're Jim Johnson, not James bloody Bond. This is serious. Are you at least going to take some security with you?' Her news reporter instincts were kicking in.

'Know any Caribbean sharpshooters?' He shrugged. 'I'm not very handy with nunchucks.'

Sarah leaned on the balcony and looked out towards the skyline.

'And your friend whose husband is having an affair . . . Three guesses who that is.'

'One guess,' said Jim, taking a spot next to her.

'How do you know?'

'I went to their beach house to confront Connor. I saw him having sex with another woman.'

'Bastard.'

'I can think of a dozen stronger words for him than that . . . Do I tell her?' he asked after another moment.

'I'd want to know.'

'Would you?' queried Jim.

Sarah didn't respond.

'The truth. Such a noble word, right?' said Jim slowly. 'I remember asking my dad to tell me what it meant once, and he said, "It's what's right." But is it right for Jennifer to be told what Connor is up to? Isn't a better truth for her just not to know?'

'She deserves to be happy,' Sarah said firmly.

'I'm not sure she'll let herself be.'

Neither of them said anything for a few moments.

'I know how she can be happy. How you can be happy too,' Sarah said. Her voice was low and the mood between them shifted and saddened. Jim had a sudden sense of an ending, like the last whispers of summer in the September evening air.

'You were right back there, you know,' she said, motioning back into the wedding reception. 'You do need to play the field, kiss a lot of frogs, make mistakes, get your heart broken . . . You also need to know the difference between settling down and settling for someone.'

Another momentary silence.

'Me and you, Jim . . . I'm not daft, you know. I know how you feel about Jennifer. I thought in the beginning that I could win you round, but we're seven, eight months into this relationship and I don't see your eyes shine any less brightly when someone mentions her name.'

'Sarah, come on. Jennifer is my friend. That's all. My first love, yes, so we'll always have a connection, but time moves on, people move on.'

'Do they?'

'Yes,' he said more passionately.

'I'm just not sure this is a good idea any more,' she said finally.

There was a long pause as Jim let the implication of her words sink in.

'What are you saying here, Sarah?'

'When I told my mate I was dating a forty-year-old, she warned me there'd be baggage, but I didn't realise it would be a whole rucksack full of love for the one that got away.'

'You're being too emotional,' said Jim, trying to sound firm. 'We've had a drink, we're at a wedding. Right now everyone is feeling a bit inadequate compared to the great love that is Justin and Ashley.' He smiled at her, but she didn't smile back.

'Sarah, you know I think you're amazing . . .' he said softly.

'I do. I'm just not Jennifer Wyatt.'

He couldn't deny it any more. She deserved a lot more than platitudes. Another shift in the tension, and a soft, resigned solidarity shimmered between them. Sarah Huxley really was an amazing woman, he thought sadly.

'Tell her how you feel,' she said, looking out across the Hudson.

'She's married,' he reminded her.

'To an absolute tosser who's shagging around behind her back. Look, Jim. I've seen the way you two are together and I feel like a spare part whenever I'm with you both. Why do you think I always try and put off seeing her with you? But I'm not finishing with you for you not to do anything about this. That way we'll all end up bloody miserable.'

'I can't,' he said. 'It's her business, she's got to work it out herself.'

'Grow a set of fucking balls, Jim. You can fly to the

Caribbean tomorrow to negotiate with a gangster but you can't tell the woman you love how you feel about her. I know about the backstory, I know why she chose Connor in the first place, and if she still can't see what's in front of her eyes, if she still says no, if she wants to stay with that dick-swinging Gordon Gekko, then so be it. But at least you'll know once and for all. At least if you tell her, you'll be able to finally move on.'

Jim felt stunned into silence.

'Just go, Jim. Just go and do it,' she said, her voice hardening. 'I spoke to her at Pilates on Thursday. She's going to be at some art dinner at the Met this evening.'

Jim took her hand and spun her round and put his arms around her. As she looked up at him, her eyes were sparkling with tears.

'Don't go feeling sorry for me. I have enough of that from this lot thinking I'm dating Grandad. Now go on, piss off. If you make my mascara run, I'll have no option but to set Bryony on you.'

Chapter Twenty-Six

He left the wedding and stepped out on to the deserted street. As he raised his hand for a cab, there was a roll of thunder like a portent, fat droplets stippling the sidewalk. He waved both arms like a man drowning, but car after car hissed past.

He thought about Sarah's words. Settling, not settling down: that was what Jennifer had done with Connor. He'd been a coward back then, leaving Jennifer to her grief and a consolation relationship with Connor. As for Jennifer herself, she'd said she'd have made the same choice, picked Connor if Jim had come back for her, but what if he'd made her braver; made her face her fears and guilt and demons? Made her choose love not death?

Finally a taxi stopped. He jumped in and directed it to New York's famous museum. The rain was sheeting down as it stopped outside the wide expanse of marble steps. Jim lifted his jacket over his head to protect himself from the weather.

Security was on the door.

'Shit,' he muttered, wondering how difficult it would be to get in. A couple in cocktail attire were running down the wet steps. The woman slipped and Jim caught hold of her hand.

'Thank you.' She squinted through the rain.

'I need to get in there. I need to tell someone how much I love them. I don't suppose you still have your invitation on you?' he grinned, his hair sticking to his forehead like glue.

Her companion put his hand into the pocket of his dinner jacket and pulled out a stiff white piece of card.

'Good luck, pal,' he laughed, and they ran off to get a taxi.

Jim rubbed the top of his head to shake off the excess moisture. People were already leaving, huddling under umbrellas as he ran up the steps, waving his invitation at a pair of disinterested security guards.

Pushing against the tide of people, he threaded his way into the high marble hall. *Please don't let her have left.* He scanned the crowd, looking for her but seeing only dowdy women and men in dark suits.

Then his heart skipped a beat as he spotted her across the room. Her dress was bronze, shimmering. She was smiling as someone in a dinner jacket talked animatedly to her, but the smile didn't reach her eyes.

This wasn't Jennifer, he realised; it never had been. He could vividly remember her running barefoot by the creek. The smear of dirt on her cheek, the scratches along her ankles from brambles. Had it not been for her mother's death, Jim felt sure that she wouldn't have ended up leading a life like this.

She was as tall as many of the men in the room, and as her

eyes drifted away from her acquaintance, they locked with Jim's across the heads of the thinning crowd. He nervously flattened his wet hair and started weaving through the guests to get to her.

'Jim. What are you doing here?'

His heart was racing, but he knew he had to go through with this.

'I'm here to tell you something. Something I should have told you twenty years ago.'

The warmth faded from her smile.

'What is it?'

'I'm in love with you, Jen,' he said simply.

A dialogue had gone on over and over in his head in the cab on the way here, but now that he was standing in front of her, it was quite simple, and with those first ice-breaking words he felt braver and bolder than ever.

'I've loved you for twenty years and I've been on my own ever since, because no one can ever match up to you.'

Her face crumpled. 'But you're not alone, Jim. What about Sarah?'

'Sarah knows,' he replied, shaking his head. 'Sarah was the one who told me to come and finally be honest about how I feel.'

Jennifer looked at him sceptically.

'Look, we're not together any more. We can't be. I only asked you to set me up with someone as a way to keep in touch with you. And that's the problem. Sarah is a great girl, but she's not you.'

She closed her eyes, breathed in through her nose.

'Jim, I'm married. You know that.'

He knew his next words were a risk.

'He doesn't deserve you, Jen . . .'

'That's not for you to decide,' she said, blinking hard.

'Isn't it?'

'No.'

As she spoke, her eyes flickered fearfully to the side, and Jim didn't need to turn to know that Connor was behind him. He watched the other man take in the scene.

'What's going on here? Jim, I know you want to speak to me about RedReef, but really, this isn't the time or the place.'

Jim knew there was no turning back now.

'Tell Jennifer where you were on Tuesday, Connor.'

Connor blanched, eyes flicking to his wife.

'I was in meetings all day.'

'Out of town?'

'Yes, in Southampton if you must know. A client of mine has a place out there.' There was a quaver of anxiety in his voice. 'Look, what's going on?'

Jim glared at him. 'I thought you'd have more balls than that.'

He saw Connor's back stiffen, but he ignored it and turned to Jennifer.

'When he finally tells you where he was, I think you'll understand what I'm saying. Why you deserve better than him.'

Jennifer looked at Connor. 'What's he talking about? Tell me.'

Connor stepped forward and put a possessive hand on his wife's shoulder.

'We'll talk later. Right now, I think Jimmy was just leaving.'

Jim's eyes locked with Jennifer's once more.

'Am I, Jen?'

He stretched out a hand towards her. This was the moment, the moment when it would all change or come crashing down. Time seemed to stop, Jennifer's gaze locked on his fingers . . .

'Jennifer.'

Connor's voice was deep, authoritative. Jim had the sense that it was the tone he used when she wasn't doing as she was told, when she was threatening to step out of line.

'Jen?'

Her eyes flickered to his, then down to the floor, and Jim knew it was over. He had been so sure, so convinced, but no. She had made her choice. And it wasn't him. Again.

'Fine,' he said quietly, turning and heading for the door. 'I've got the message.'

Somewhere in the distance he could hear the band playing an instrumental version of 'Come Fly With Me'. He yanked his top button open, pulled his tie loose and stepped out into the night, feeling the cold through his soaked jacket for the first time. It didn't matter; the rain was still coming down anyway. He tipped his head back, feeling the drops on his face.

He walked slowly down the steps, moving into a new life,

one without her. It was almost as if the universe was conspiring to taunt him. He saw a bus go past advertising the latest kids' movie, watched a couple stepping into a taxi, laughing. He must move forward. Make these simple images part of his life too. Not with Jennifer or with Sarah, but perhaps there was someone else out there who could one day make him happy.

'Taxi, sir?'

Jim looked round. A uniformed attendant was standing at the kerb, sheltered under an umbrella.

'Sure, why not?'

The man whistled, and two yellow cabs materialised from the traffic.

Now the taxis are stopping, thought Jim.

'Wait!'

Her voice was muffled by the hiss of the rain and the traffic.

'Jim, wait.'

He turned around and saw her, the bronze of her dress shining at the top of the steps.

They stood motionless for a moment, then Jennifer took a tentative step forward. Shoulders still hunched, he walked towards her.

'We need to talk,' she said.

'Just the weather for it.'

'I knew who Connor was with on Tuesday. Well, I guessed. Some interior designer who's been working on the condo project. I just confronted him. He didn't deny it.'

'You knew he was having an affair?'

She shook her head. 'I'd found a few texts, some emails,

but I never said anything because I knew that I was in the wrong too.'

'Why were you in the wrong?' he asked, his heart beating fast.

'Because of you, Jim.'

Jim felt his heart might break. Did she mean it?

'You never . . .' He faltered. 'You didn't say anything.'

'Every time we were together, I hoped that the day, the night would end another way. I was kidding myself, of course – I mean, you'd even asked me to set you up with someone – but every time we met, or spoke or texted, I was hoping you'd give me a sign that we could go back. Go back to what we were.'

He couldn't believe what she was saying.

'*You* wanted something to happen?'

'I wanted more than being just your friend. I always have. When you came back to the house, when we watched the tapes together and I remembered how happy we were, I wanted to say something, do something, but—'

'Will you just shut up and let me kiss you?' he interrupted. He reached up, touching her cheek, pushing her wet hair from her face, then leaned in and kissed her. Soft, sensual, perfect. He grabbed her hand.

'Let's go,' he said, leading her down the wet steps.

The official with the umbrella was watching them. With the hint of a smile, he blew his whistle and called them a cab.

Chapter Twenty-Seven

Jim woke and felt his eyes flutter open with a sense of contentment. He turned and saw Jennifer's back – pale, lightly freckled – and gave a soft happy snort as he tried to remember every detail of the night before.

'You awake?' he asked softly.

'Finally, I'm in Jim Johnson's bed,' she said, shifting position so that she faced him.

'That's what all the girls say.'

He propped himself on one elbow to look at her. The daylight creeping through the window spotlit her face, and he could see the faint lines around her eyes and the twin creases behind her brows. Jennifer Wyatt wasn't a young woman any more – to an outsider, Sarah Huxley and her pretty, fresh-faced friends were more obviously attractive – but Jim touched her cheek and thought she had never looked more lovely.

'What a night,' she said, lying back and looking at the ceiling. 'But I should probably phone Sarah.'

Jim shook his head, not wanting to spoil the moment. He hoped she wouldn't mention Connor. She didn't.

'So are we going to stay in bed all day and make up for lost time, or does duty call for Omari's head honcho?'

'I'd like nothing better,' said Jim, propping himself up with a pillow and glancing at his diver's watch, 'but I've got to be on a flight in – bloody hell, in four hours.'

'Plenty of time. Where are you going?'

'Baruda. Caribbean.'

He didn't want to give out any more details than that. Sarah might have understood the lengths he had to go to to sort out RedReef, but he suspected Jennifer would go into a blind panic at the thought of him meeting Marshall Roberts.

'And I should probably go and see Connor,' she said, her voice turning more serious. 'It's time I finally got this sorted.'

Jim didn't say anything. He'd done and said enough. Of course he was happy that Jennifer was here in his bed, but there was no satisfaction in being the catalyst for the end of her marriage, no matter how much he disliked Connor. He tried to tell himself that he had done the right thing in finally following his heart and telling Jennifer how he felt. Tried to make himself feel better with the thought that there were no kids involved, that Sarah had finished with him, and that Connor was cheating on Jennifer anyway. But still, he'd pulled the rug out from someone else's life, and however much they deserved it, he knew it was a crappy thing to do.

'You know, Connor and I should have divorced years ago. I've always consoled myself with the thought that he loved me.

But I soon saw that I was just another possession, like a boat or a plane, or a fancy Swiss watch, and our marriage was just another tick-box on the list of his life's conquests. A suitable girl that fitted into his life. But, a bit like the boat and the plane and the watch, you get tired of the shiny things. They lose their appeal and so you trade up; you get the slicker, smarter model. You can't do that with a marriage, though. Not unless you want to lose fifty per cent of everything you've worked for. So you do it quietly. Not so quietly that I didn't find out. I knew about the lingerie model, the leggy blonde realtor and the journalist from Bloomberg, and each time he bought me a diamond and said it wouldn't happen again. Each time I believed him, and when he did have another affair, I thought deep down that I deserved it.'

'You didn't deserve anything like that, Jen.'

'When are you back from the Caribbean?' she said, taking his hand.

'It's just a quick trip. I'm back tomorrow. And then it's Johnson family party time. My father's CBE celebration, his aren't-you-all-pleased-to-see-me shindig. It's at some swanky private members' club. Old-school variety. Three-line whip,' he grinned. 'You should come. There'll be a free copy of his new book at least.'

'I'm not sure,' she replied. 'I think we should give ourselves a little breathing space to sort things out. It's over between me and Connor, in fact I'm going to check into a hotel this afternoon. But he's still my husband.'

'A hotel? You can stay here.'

'Breathing space. Just for a little while,' she grinned.

'OK. Let's keep a respectable distance. For now, anyway.' He leaned in to kiss her. 'Although I'm not sure how long is respectable these days,' he said, moving his lips down to her shoulder. 'A day, a week . . .'

Jennifer gave a soft, sexy laugh. 'I'm not sure how long I can resist you,' she said, wrapping her arms around him.

Jim rolled her over so that she was on her stomach. He gently brushed her hair off her neck and kissed the top of her spine, moving slowly down.

'Look at this,' he said, stroking the dark groove where her spine disappeared between the twin mounds of her buttocks. 'You have a mole. A diamond-shaped mole.' He wondered whether Connor had noticed the landmarks of her body.

'Have I?' she smiled, turning over.

He kissed her belly, her breasts, lingering over one nipple, then the other, sucking, tasting her, sweet and delicious. She moaned and parted her legs and they made love again, more slowly than the night before.

'I can't believe I have to walk the streets of New York in this dress,' she smiled after they had showered. 'You know I've even left my coat at the Met.'

'Borrow something of mine,' he offered.

'You're a six-foot guy.'

'Not so much taller than you.'

He padded to the wardrobe, sifting through his rack of clothes. He glanced back at her. She had folded her arms across her naked body and was smiling at him playfully.

'This should be interesting,' she laughed.

He took a pair of black trousers from his favourite suit and handed them to her.

'Slimmest cut I've got,' he said, reaching for a belt and T-shirt. 'So much so that I can't quite get into them . . .'

He watched her dress, gathering the trousers around her waist with the belt.

'So now I look like a crazy person rather than a hooker,' she said, studying her reflection in the full-length mirror.

'Oi, they're Saint Laurent.'

Once Jim was dressed too, he packed a bag and got his passport.

'Right then.'

'I thought you were going to say righty-ho,' she teased him.

'And of course in the movie of our lives I'd be played by Hugh Grant . . . So when am I going to see you again?' he asked, threading his arms around the back of her neck.

'I'll call you,' she said, and this time he believed her.

Chapter Twenty-Eight

Jim looked out of the window of the cab, willing it to go faster. It wasn't the car's fault, of course, just good old-fashioned Manhattan gridlock in all its maddening stop-go glory. Jennifer had been correct that he had plenty of time to make his flight, but Jim had an errand to run before heading to the airport: he had to meet Saul Black, his father's agent.

'Can you take West 48th, get across to Fifth?' he said, leaning forward. 'I think it'll be less solid this time of day.'

Listen to me, he thought as the driver made the turn. Native New Yorker already.

Saul's home was in the Upper East Side, and Jim's smile faded as he realised they were about to pass near to Jennifer's town house – or rather, Connor's house as it would be, once Jennifer moved out. Jim imagined him at home, drinking his coffee, stewing, hating Jim, and wanted to get out of this part of the city as quickly as he could.

He had received the summons to go and see Saul a couple

of weeks earlier. His mother had been pestering him to visit his father's old agent for months, but somehow Jim had never got round to it. He'd been at the office late one night when a call came in from Saul himself.

'I've got something for your father,' he'd instructed in his booming voice. 'I need you to give it to him before the party.'

With everything that had been going on with RedReef, Jim still hadn't got round to seeing Saul, but as his father's party was the following day, he knew he needed to make it happen. He hadn't imagined for one moment that he'd be leaving Jennifer Wyatt in his bed. There was a certain irony to the situation: his visit to Saul's was about to bring him full circle. After all, if it hadn't been for his father's agent suggesting Casa D'Or as a writer's retreat, the Johnsons would never have met the Wyatt family, and Jim would never have crossed paths with Jennifer.

He smiled to himself. Saul had always been such a man about town, a larger-than-life character; his booming Brooklyn accent and unflappable personality ever present during Jim's formative years. Dinner was often interrupted when Bryn had to take a call from New York, which almost always ended in shouting or laughter or both, and whenever Saul was in London, he'd be at the Hampstead house for dinner and shop talk into the early hours.

At last they pulled up outside an Upper East Side co-op. Jim knew the street well. Simon had a couple of blocks up here in the Desai residential portfolio, and they had even played with the idea of turning one of them into a deluxe hotel along the lines of the Mark and the Carlyle before they had received a deluge of objections from the wealthy residents nearby. Saul was probably one of them.

Jim announced himself to the doorman, who directed him to a lift, gold, with a tiny plush velvet seat inside, that made Jim feel as if he had gone back in time to the fifties. He rode to the eighth floor and rang the bell. A Far Eastern lady dressed in a navy tunic and slacks, an outfit he recognised as a carer's, greeted him at the door, and Jim was ushered through.

He heard the noise first – a deep, long buzz – and then Saul appeared round the corner in a wheelchair. Jim was momentarily shocked to see him. He was old, thin and so frail that the chair seemed to drown him. But beyond that he was the same old Saul. His hair was now white, but still wild like a cartoon professor's, the same mischievous brown eyes twinkling through heavy seventies-style glasses.

'Hey, Jimmy!' he cried, swivelling the chair to face him. 'How d'ya like the place, huh?'

What had once been a glitzy reception room, the scene of many drunken debates between Bryn and his agent, had been stripped and rearranged into what was obviously a living space, with a desk and a narrow bed and a large TV set in the corner.

'It . . . it has character,' said Jim.

Saul laughed loud enough to shake the windows.

'I brought the bed in here. I spend so much time in it I thought I might as well have the big window, the light,' he said, bringing the wheelchair closer to Jim. 'Look at you.' He smiled, studying him. 'All grown up. It's good to see you, kid.'

'It's great to see you too, Saul.'

'I'm surprised you remember me,' he grinned, adjusting his spectacles.

'You came round to our house at least twice a year until I was nearly twenty-one. Of course I bloody remember you.'

Saul laughed. 'Hey, Lucille, fetch us a couple of drinks, wouldya?'

Jim was taken aback. 'Saul, it's not even lunchtime . . .'

'I got a fifty-year-old Scotch in the cabinet. Better drink it, whatever time of day it is, before they confiscate it.'

'Confiscate it?'

'I'm moving into a home. Me!'

He gestured to an armchair as Lucille brought over a couple of measures of whisky.

'Lucille's become a grandmom, haven't you, Lou?' said Saul. 'So she's leaving me to help her own family. I haven't got it in me to start with someone new, and I got to face it: an eighth-floor apartment ain't the best place in the world for someone who lives in one of these.' He tapped his hand against the side of the wheelchair.

'I'm sure it will be social. Plenty of ladies to chase.' Jim smiled.

'That remains to be seen,' snorted Saul. 'Can't do more than about two miles an hour in this, so let's hope they got a few with bad hips. Anyway . . .' He raised his glass towards Jim. 'Good health, huh?'

Jim sipped the Scotch and grimaced.

'Pretty smooth,' laughed Saul, catching the expression. 'I

thought you'd be used to the good stuff now you've got that snazzy job with Simon Desai. And you can tell your boss that if he ever wants to sell his memoirs, I know five publishers that would have them like that.'

He clicked his fingers together in a slow but exaggerated gesture. Jim tried not to notice how much his hands were shaking.

'Once an agent, always an agent, eh, Saul?'

'You know I was still executive chairman of the agency until a couple of years ago. Problems started when I could barely walk to the boardroom, let along chair it. How's your father?'

'Good. You've heard about his CBE?'

'Who hasn't?'

'Never knowingly hides his light under a bushel, my father. Are you looking forward to the party?'

'I'm not coming,' replied Saul, glancing away.

'Not coming?' said Jim incredulously. It was hard to imagine that Saul would want to miss being in the thick of a literary soirée.

'I'm busy.'

'Saul, come on. From where I'm sitting, you don't appear to be living in party central.'

'Lucille's night off, isn't it.'

'Then come with me. I can pick you up, take you to the venue . . . You'll know everyone there.'

'Precisely,' he said quietly.

He took another swig of his Scotch.

'You know, I was someone once, Jim. Someone who made careers, who people listened to. And the truth is, the older you get, the more people should listen to you. But it doesn't work like that. They listen to you but they're not interested in what you've got to say.'

'Saul, don't be silly.'

'Your father will have half of the beau monde at his party and I don't want them to see me like this. I want them to remember me as I was. Racing to Elaine's or Michael's with the hottest manuscript in town in my briefcase and the prettiest girl in town on my arm. Not some old guy in a wheelchair they have to give five minutes' polite chit-chat to.'

'Saul, everyone will be thrilled to see you.'

'The wise man knows when to bow out,' he said quietly.

Jim wanted to tell him that until a couple of days ago he would have said the same thing, but now he believed that you had to play your hand as long as possible, but Saul had already wheeled his chair over to the bookcase.

'I've got something for him,' he said, more briskly.

'My father?'

'I got Lucille to sort a gift. She's better at that sort of thing than me. I think she got him some fancy case of wine. But then I found this as well,' he said, struggling to lift something heavy off the shelf.

'Here, let me help,' said Jim, going over.

'When you move outta place after fifty years, there's always one hell of a clear-out.' Saul handed him a thick white envelope. 'We found this.'

'What is it?' asked Jim, feeling the weight of it in his hands.

There was a twinkle in Saul's eye.

'Your father's first draft manuscript of *College*.'

'You kept it?'

'He came to see me in New York, Christmas 1994. I was always the first person to see his work, and with your father, I never knew what to expect,. I was particularly nervous that meeting,' he said, shaking his frail head. 'I knew it was my final throw of the dice with him. If going to Savannah wasn't going to help him find his writer's mojo, then I didn't know what I was going to do. But . . .' He paused and looked away, lost in thought. 'But I had nothing to worry about. I read it straight after he'd gone and couldn't put it down until I'd finished it. I knew I had an important piece of fiction in my hands.'

'And that's it,' said Jim, nodding towards the envelope.

'The only original version in existence, I guess. Could have sold it, might have paid for one of those stair-lift things, but screw it, eh?'

'This changed our lives, you know.'

'I'm glad,' said Saul, nodding sagely. 'Give it to him at the party, huh?'

'Are you sure I can't tempt you to come? It would mean a lot if you were there.'

'I'll catch up with him some other time,' Saul replied in a voice that suggested he wouldn't.

'I've got to go,' Jim said, knowing that time was ticking. 'I'm on a flight that leaves in two hours.'

'Tell your father I love him, all right?'

'Now you're getting mawkish.'

'I mean it.'

Jim nodded and left the apartment, glad that he had made the time to visit.

Chapter Twenty-Nine

Jim hesitated for only a moment as Gregor Bentley parked outside a large white villa on the outskirts of Baruda's main town, St Sebastian.

'Right, I'm going in,' he said with more confidence than he felt, turning to Gregor and unfastening his seat belt, knowing that now was as good a time as any.

'Are you sure you don't want us to come with you?' asked Gregor, turning to the two burly men sitting in the back seat.

Jim still hadn't been introduced to them properly. Gregor had described them as security. They hadn't said a word on the journey over to Marshall Roberts' house, and Jim didn't doubt they were both carrying guns hidden in their socks or underpants.

He wondered if his younger self might have seen some sort of glamour in this situation, imagined he was in *Ocean's Eleven*, but the truth was he was frightened. Here he was, about to go and negotiate with a known mobster, a dangerous and ruthless man who thought nothing of extortion and violence when it was a means to his own ends.

Even an hour earlier, he had felt calm, had seen it merely as a problem he had to get efficiently out of the way. Perhaps his night with Jennifer had buoyed him, given him a little armour plating. But standing here in the hot Caribbean sun, he realised the folly of what he was about to do. He was about to go into Marshall Roberts' house, and there was the possibility that he might not come out again.

Just as life was getting interesting, he thought grimly, thinking of Jennifer in his bed, a montage of images flashing suddenly in his head, a realisation that he was happy and content and at peace.

He slammed the car door shut, hearing the gravel drive crunch underfoot. Taking a deep breath, he pressed an intercom button on the gate, which opened after a second, a CCTV camera turning and focusing on him, like a beady eye following him as he walked up the path towards the house.

Marshall Roberts' home was not as grand as Jim might have imagined. It was large, but in a poor state of repair; the many millions he had extorted from businesses such as RedReef had clearly been ploughed into a Swiss bank account rather than his home.

Jim was met by a maid, who led him out to a porch that overlooked both the town and the sea. Baruda was almost completely flat, unlike the more rugged and luscious islands like St Lucia, but Roberts' house must have been at its highest point. Jim stood with one hand on the rail, consciously not turning his back to the house but keen to get some fortifying sun on his face. After a minute he heard footsteps padding through the property.

He had imagined a man with presence, perhaps with a gold tooth or some Prohibition-style fedora, flanked by sinister-looking henchmen. But Marshall Roberts was alone. He was an unremarkable-looking man, slim, of average height, in suit trousers and a pale blue short-sleeved shirt. His black hair was cropped close to his head and was flecked with wiry silver strands. He had a big gold signet ring on his finger and sandals on his feet, where the dark skin had cracked and paled around his toes.

'Sit down, Mr Johnson,' he said simply in a deep voice that carried more gravitas than his appearance. 'You wanted to discuss something with me.'

Jim nodded and perched on the edge of a wicker sofa.

'I'm impressed you had the balls to come and discuss things with me directly. So many don't.'

'I've dealt with people like you before, Mr Roberts,' Jim said. In fact he had never been at the sharp end of hotel management. His only dealing with gangsters was the time he'd played a gig at a pub in Manchester and some scallies had asked him for protection money. He had ended up buying them a pint and they were friends by the end of the evening. He wasn't sure it would go that way with Marshall Roberts. 'I generally find that we can both reach a mutually beneficial position.'

'I think I have what I want from you and your predecessor,'

said Roberts with a low laugh. 'Although since the new owner of RedReef is one of the richest men in the world, maybe it's time to renegotiate. A small uplift in the financial compensation for our services will be pocket change for Mr Desai.'

'Men like Simon Desai didn't get to where they are without watching every penny, Marshall. And without being ruthless. Extremely ruthless to anyone who tries to take advantage of them.' Jim tried to get the right note of threat into his voice. His palms had become clammy and his heart was beating twice as fast as normal, but he willed himself to stay cool and in control. 'Contributions to your business from RedReef will be stopping from this moment on. New management, new policy. I thought I would do you the courtesy of telling you that in person.'

'It's a shame,' said Marshall, lighting a cigarette. 'I heard RedReef was going to be the flagship hotel for your new chain. I thought you'd want to make it work. It has such potential, given the right conditions.'

'Simon Desai isn't Connor Gilbert, Mr Roberts. As you say, this hotel is important to him. Fuck with him and it will be the worst business deal you ever make.' Jim got to his feet decisively.

'You obviously don't realise how things work around here, Mr Johnson.'

'I think I do,' said Jim, edging towards the door.

'I control the people who control this island. And that makes me very powerful. More powerful than your boss Mr Desai, despite his billions.'

'We'll see,' he said as coolly as he could, before almost sprinting off the property and out to Gregor's car.

He half expected to hear gunshots follow him from the house, but he got back to the vehicle safely.

'How was it?' said Gregor, already starting the engine.

'Short, sweet. At least I escaped with my kneecaps intact,' replied Jim, staring straight ahead through the windscreen. 'Shit, I can't believe I threatened a gangster,' he added, glancing down and seeing his hands tremble.

'So what did you say?'

'I just told him we weren't going to pay any more. I mentioned Simon Desai's name a lot. Reminded him how powerful he is.'

'Not around here,' said Gregor, accelerating away from the house. 'Roberts owns this island. Not literally, but the police, the ruling council are in his pocket.'

'And what do you think might change their minds?' asked Jim, feeling hopelessly out of his depth.

'Maybe it's about time you went and asked them.'

'What, now?'

'The alternative is to call Simon,' replied Gregor.

'I don't want to get him involved,' said Jim resolutely.

'Then it's business as usual. We continue to pay.'

'We can't be the only people in this situation,' said Jim, trying to think. 'Perhaps if we all got together, put some pressure on the police, it would force them to take action against Roberts.'

'I'm sure it's been tried.'

'How do we know?'

'Have you spoken to Connor Gilbert yet?'

'No,' said Jim, not wanting to even think about him. If Connor had been avoiding him before, he certainly wouldn't be wanting a convivial chat any time soon. 'I want you to call Dean Davies. He was general manager before we bought the hotel. Find out what has been done about Marshall Roberts, if anything. And then get me a meeting with the mayor.'

'Welcome to the island,' said Leonard Martin, clinking his glass against Jim's.

St Sebastian's mayor and de facto chief of the island had taken Jim's call immediately, and had even suggested supper at his favourite harbourside restaurant to introduce himself properly. Jim had made small talk with the man over champagne and oysters, but now he wanted to find out if he really was screwed with the RedReef deal.

'It's good to be here,' he said, switching on the charm. 'The Omari group is delighted to be investing in Baruda. Simon Desai personally asked me to get in touch to say hello and just check we've got your support in making RedReef the most exciting new hotel in the Caribbean.'

'He did?' said the older man, obviously flattered. 'Well, you can tell him that we're thrilled to have you here. You've really got a beautiful stretch of beach over there. Did you know there's a wreck off Catseye Point? I don't know if you dive, but you should arrange to go down there next time you're here.

Maybe with Mr Desai. I could even come with you,' he offered.

Jim sipped his wine and assumed an expression of puzzlement.

'One thing,' he said, taking a strategic pause. 'One thing that has been worrying us is the influence of Marshall Roberts in the area. Seems to be the only supplier in the food and beverage chain, and we don't really find that a competitive way of doing business, to be honest.'

'We're a small island, as you can see,' said Martin, looking more uncomfortable. 'Some people do have the monopoly on various services, but the quality doesn't suffer.'

'In New York, Marshall Roberts would be called a criminal, Mr Martin.'

'I wouldn't say that.' The mayor began to stutter.

'He's a gangster and an extortionist. I hate to bring this up over a very convivial dinner, Leonard, but if his activities aren't stopped, then Simon Desai's investment in Baruda is going to be a very short one.'

Martin looked down at his swordfish and began to cut it up slowly and deliberately into small pieces.

'This island has worked the same way for a very long time,' he said finally.

'And you're not prepared to do anything to stop it,' said Jim bluntly.

Martin's face was unreadable. Jim decided that the best way to proceed was to flatter him into making him think he could make a difference.

'Roberts is extorting money from every single business on this island, Leonard. Businesses do not thrive when they are being squeezed by criminals. And if businesses don't thrive, Baruda isn't going to thrive.'

'I think we're doing all right so far,' he replied. 'For a tiny island with no airport.'

'But it could be so much more than a Caribbean backwater. Baruda could be the new Turks, the new Cayman Islands . . .'

He hesitated. He didn't want to be too provocative, but Leonard Martin was no pushover. Like all politicians, he had got to where he was in life by cosying up to the people who could do the most for him.

'I've done a bit of research about Baruda, Leonard. I know the police chief is your brother-in-law . . .'

'What are you implying?' Martin said with a frown.

'That your family has power, influence. If you choose to use it in the right way.'

Jim had no intention of stopping now.

'How does it work, Leonard? You turn a blind eye to Marshall's business in return for a kick-back?'

He didn't pause for the mayor to answer.

'You know, I don't blame you. It's how it works around here, isn't it? It's how it works all around the world.' He kept his voice low and level. 'But do you think this is going to end well for you, Leonard? What happens if you do something that doesn't please Marshall Roberts? If you piss him off? You go the same way as Daniel Verrander, one of our staff who was put in hospital by Marshall's men.'

'You've been watching too much *Miami Vice*, Mr Johnson,' said Leonard wearily, putting down his knife and fork.

'I know there's a better way to deal with men like Marshall Roberts. Better for you, for your brother-in-law, for the people of this island.'

'The system works.'

'For you and for Marshall perhaps.'

Martin leaned forward in his chair. His fist was clenched, his expression anxious.

'I can't,' he said urgently.

Jim saw a chink.

'Why not? You are the most powerful man on this island. Not Marshall Roberts. What you say goes. Marshall is one man and a team of goons. That's no match for your police force, your ruling council, the people of this island, who are sick to death of living in fear.'

Leonard's face hardened. 'And who supplements our losses?'

'Your losses?'

'How much do you think a public servant earns around here, Mr Johnson?'

Jim shrugged.

'I have a family with needs,' Martin said, as if that was a perfectly rational explanation for accepting bribes from a criminal. 'My wife wants a Mercedes, my son a speedboat. My daughter, my little girl . . . She wants Richie Hawkins to perform at her Sweet Sixteen party, although she's going to have to make do with a jeep. All these things cost money, and without Marshall's contributions who is going to pay for them? You?'

Jim tried to do some quick mental calculations, but then he had an idea.

'Your daughter likes Richie Hawkins?'

'She's his biggest fan,' Martin said, rolling his eyes like any weary parent of a teenage girl.

'And what would you say if I could get him to play at your daughter's sixteenth birthday party? It would be a dream come true for her, yes?'

'Get Richie Hawkins to Baruda and I'll be forever in your debt,' laughed the mayor, sipping his champagne.

'In that case, I'll sort out the rock star if you can cut Marshall Roberts down to size.'

Chapter Thirty

Jim settled back into his seat and accepted a glass of wine from the air stewardess. On other occasions he might have noticed how attractive she was, the curve of her hips under the dark pencil skirt or the brightness of her smile, but he was too busy checking his phone. He found a short message from Jennifer wishing him a safe flight home and smiled to himself. Many a time he'd teased his secretaries for obsessing about phone calls and messages from lovers and romantic prospects, and now here he was doing the same.

Without the luxury of Simon's private jet, he was travelling back to New York via Miami. He had made a call to Elan Models on the short layover and had managed to be connected to Celine Wood.

'You bastard, you never called me,' she'd laughed, before telling him he had missed his opportunity. Jim had apologised, then asked her if she could arrange for her new lover Richie Hawkins to come and play on Baruda. A short acoustic set would be fine. In return they could stay at the new Santai resort, RedReef, whenever they fancied, and she would be given one of the best suites at the Casa D'Or launch party. Celine replied that Richie would do anything she asked of him, and that a romantic Caribbean holiday might even hasten a proposal. Jim felt this was a win-win position for everyone.

The flight from Miami was a little over two hours. As he put his phone back in his bag in the overhead locker, he noticed the manuscript that Saul had given him the previous day. He wondered whether now wouldn't be the perfect time to read it.

Jim had always avoided his father's seminal novel. Back in his teens and twenties, he had been an enthusiastic reader, he remembered, thinking back to that slightly pretentious youth who loved art house cinema and Milan Kundera novels. But he had given Bryn Johnson's *College* a wide berth when it had hit the top of the best-seller chart, knowing that it would be folly to read it.

He did not particularly want to be reminded of the place where *College* had been written: Savannah, in the boathouse opposite Casa D'Or.

But there was another reason too.

Back when it was first published, Jim had had ambitions of his own to write the great British novel. Although he'd let his rock star dreams die after Savannah, writing, he appreciated, was something that could be fitted in around his corporate, money-making career. But it was tough living in the shadow of a literary lion, and the reviews and prizes and honorary doctorates that followed *College* only backed up Jim's fear that if he read his father's much-lauded and obviously brilliant novel and compared it with his own scribblings, he would never write another word.

These days there were more mundane reasons why he had never opened the book. He barely had time to read the *FT*, let alone get stuck into a four-hundred-page novel, but now, as he looked restlessly out of the window, he knew he had run out of excuses.

He sat back and put a pillow behind his head. The manuscript wasn't particularly easy to read. It was a long book, and the pile of pages was at least three inches thick. There were no acknowledgements or dedications. The type had faded, and there were white stripes of Tippex where his father had made mistakes. It was quite alien-looking, and strange to think that this was how people had worked only twenty years ago – an era that didn't seem so distant when he considered it was his university days, a time he could remember with nostalgic clarity.

He already knew the broad strokes of the story. Set in Cambridge, it followed the inappropriate relationship between a fifty-something don, Peter Colt, who had just been passed over for a professorship, and a beautiful young student, Cecile. Even from the first few pages it was obvious that this was going to be a beautifully drawn character study. Jim was immediately gripped. It was a book about ego, about masculinity, about wrong choices. Colt was not a particularly sympathetic character; he was jealous of the friends who had successful careers in the City, vengeful against his university colleagues who he believed had gained unmerited promotion. But despite this, his father had made it easy to understand where the character's anger and frustrations were coming from. They were an exaggerated and articulated form of many feelings experienced by men of a certain age.

It was easy to whip through the pages. It was the best type of literary novel – not weighed down by verbosity or pretension, yet smart and insightful with its observations about academic life.

It was literary legend that Bryn Johnson had written the book in less than three months, which made its quality even more impressive, and Jim grudgingly admitted that the inspiring surroundings of Savannah and the Lake House must have helped.

His father's particular skill was his creation of characters; people who jumped off the page – whose charms you wanted to identify with, whose flaws made you look into your own dark corners. At the heart of the book was the theme of obsession and the transference of Colt's volatile emotions to the beautiful Cecile, the daughter of one of his colleagues who had won undeserved promotion. Colt had started off wanting to impress the young woman, who was considered an intelligent scholar, attempting to point-score and show off, but their relationship had eventually become sexual.

Although he was tired, and could do with a nap after the drama of Baruda, Jim pushed on with one more chapter.

Peter and Cecile were spending their first night together. They had already kissed, and he had taken her to a cottage out of town, ostensibly to talk about Molière but really to consummate their relationship. Jim felt a twinge of embarrassment reading the powerful sexual imagery in his father's words, and glanced around the aeroplane cabin to make sure he wasn't being observed. The scene was certainly quite graphic for a mainstream novel, as the literary couple progressed from kissing over the French texts to soixante-neuf on the floor. Now they were lying post-coital in front of the fire.

> Peter kissed her shoulder, noting the red blush where his teeth had grazed her, moving down into the small of her back, stopping only when he reached the diamond-shaped mole at the base of her spine. 'This is mine,' he murmured, his lips pressing into her pale skin. 'This jewel is mine.'

Jim tried to swallow but couldn't. He blinked, read the lines again, his heart dropping like an untethered lift. A diamond-shaped mole at the base of her spine. It couldn't be, could it? It had to be a coincidence. *Had* to be.

An announcement came over the tannoy for passengers to fasten their seat belts in preparation for landing. Jim put the manuscript back into his bag and sat down, desperate to get back to New York.

He was up and moving the moment the seat-belt sign clicked off, running along the air bridge, straight through immigration. He stopped at the first bookshop in the arrivals hall and crossed to the 'J' section on the fiction stands. There it was: Bryn Johnson, *College*, a staff pick labelled 'A classic of late-twentieth-century sexual politics, a must-read for any woman who wants to understand men, or any man who wants to understand himself.' It had a fresh-looking red and black cover, presumably to attract a new audience.

Jim flipped to the chapter he wanted, his eyes wide as he scanned the text. Peter and Cecile go to the cottage, Peter turns on the charm, seducing the young Cecile. There was no mention of a diamond-shaped mole.

He reminded himself that the manuscript he had read on the plane was a first draft. Jim himself had never written a first draft of a novel, never got that far, but he could remember what it was like to write. He thought suddenly about his first girlfriend, Samantha Archer, a breakup that had affected him much more than it should have – almost derailed him from his English A level, in fact – when Samantha had delivered the fatal blow that she wanted to go out with one of his best mates at school, Peter Jackson.

Despite his laid-back nature, Jim was as vulnerable as the next person and had spent the entire summer listening to Smiths songs, writing poetry and letters to Samantha that had never been sent. It was a summer of wasted introspection, but the one thing he remembered about all those written words was their honesty. They were a transference of thoughts and feelings directly on to the page, unfiltered and raw.

But somewhere between the first draft of *College* and the

finished product, the diamond-shaped mole had been taken out.

If it had stayed in the published novel, Jim might have been able to convince himself that it was pure fantasy or wish fulfilment, but now? Its wilful removal was like a confession. A confession of what his father had done with Jennifer.

Chapter Thirty-One

His parents were renting a brownstone on the Upper West Side. For all of Bryn's fantasies about being close to the heartland of sixties beatniks, his desire to be near Columbia University was even stronger. Jim had only been here a handful of times before; Bryn and Elizabeth had adopted the Manhattan standard of socialising away from home, although the house was the sort of thing someone who had grown up in the fifties would want from New York: elegance, poor air con and the sense that Dorothy Parker might pop in at any moment.

He paused before he rang the bell, all the words that he had carefully crafted in his head on the way over here suddenly forgotten.

Bryn answered the door, and Jim had to resist the urge to swing at him. Keep calm, he told himself as his father, looking surprised, asked him to come in.

'I didn't think anyone just popped in any more,' he said as

Jim followed him through to the kitchen.

'Where's Mum?' asked Jim. He didn't want any confrontation to be in front of her.

'Gone down to the venue. I gather the chocolate truffles haven't arrived. I have no idea what we need truffles for at a party at my age. Half the guests are going to be diabetic.'

Bryn got two glasses from the cupboard and put them next to a bottle of wine on the counter. 'I've opened a nice claret to get me in the mood. Do you want to help me get rid of it before your mother comes back?'

'It's fine,' said Jim, holding up a hand.

Bryn poured two glasses anyway and passed him one.

'Apparently there's a couple of hundred people coming tonight, which I think is fairly impressive seeing as we've only been in the city two minutes. I've invited a few people from the faculty. Salman's coming, I think.'

'I saw Saul yesterday,' said Jim finally.

'How is he? You know he's not coming tonight?' Bryn added with a note of indignation.

'He's about to move into a home. He wanted me to give you this.' Jim reached into his bag and placed the envelope on the bar. His father eyed it suspiciously.

'What is it?'

'The first draft of *College*.'

A smile played on Bryn's face.

'Still got that? Sentimental bugger.' He reached out and touched it with one finger, as if worried it might disintegrate. 'What's he given it back for? To display at the party?'

'I need to ask you something,' said Jim.

He didn't want to ask. Didn't want to edge nearer the truth.

'Who was the inspiration for Cecile?'

Bryn shrugged slightly, taking a mouthful of his wine.

'What's this about? You sound like a reviewer for the *TLS*.'

'And if I was, what would you say?'

Bryn topped up his glass.

'The same thing that I did tell a writer from the *TLS*. That she was a glorious figment of my bourbon-soaked imagination.'

'She has a diamond-shaped mole at the base of her spine.'

Bryn frowned. 'A mole? Who?'

'Cecile. In the first draft she had a mole at the base of her spine. She doesn't in the version that got published.'

'Mole? What mole? I can't remember something I wrote in a first draft twenty-odd years ago.'

'Jennifer Wyatt was your inspiration for Cecile, wasn't she?'

'Who's Jennifer Wyatt?' said Bryn, drinking more wine.

'Don't tell me you don't remember,' Jim said, his voice hardening.

'The girl from Savannah?' Bryn said finally.

'You do remember. Jennifer Wyatt has a mole on the base of her spine,' said Jim, feeling his anxiety heighten.

'Well, good for Jennifer Wyatt. I assume you've been in contact during your stay in America. Close contact, it appears.'

'Jennifer was your inspiration for Cecile, wasn't she? I didn't notice it at first, but when you have one part of the puzzle, the comparison becomes obvious.'

'What puzzle?' Bryn said with irritation.

'Just admit it.'

His father's cheeks were beginning to colour. Jim wasn't sure whether it was from the claret, from shame or from anger.

'I can't remember who inspired every character in every story I've written. Maybe there's a writer in you yet, son. Your imagination seems to have gone into overdrive.'

'Bullshit!' snapped Jim. 'You write about a beautiful young girl with a mole exactly the same as the girl who was living in the house next door – that's supposed to be coincidence? Tell me, Dad!' he said through gritted teeth. 'I need to know.'

'What?' growled Bryn, turning his familiar aggression on his son.

'Jennifer was your inspiration for Cecile. And you knew she had a mole in an intimate place. Tell me how you knew that.'

'What are you saying, James? You want to know if I screwed her?'

'Just admit it!' roared Jim.

They both fell silent for a moment. The pressure in the room seemed to pop like a balloon that had been blown too full.

'Sure, I screwed her,' Bryn said, leaning back against the countertop and folding his arms in front of him. 'Is that what you needed to know?'

Jim blinked, feeling all the rage drain from him. Only moments ago he had wanted to strike his father; now he felt like he himself had been punched in the gut. He perched on a stool, his hands falling limp in his lap.

'Jim . . .' said Bryn. 'God, son. I didn't know how strongly you felt for the girl. I thought you were just friends, that's what you told me and your mother a dozen times.'

Jim looked at him. 'So that made it OK? It made her fair game for you?'

He closed his eyes and felt his head swim. When he opened them again, his father actually looked contrite.

'Look, I'm not proud of myself, but she made herself available to me, and I took advantage of that.'

'So it was all Jennifer . . .'

'She'd come to the Lake House, looking for you if I remember. I was in the boathouse, she came in, we started chatting about something or other. Wasn't she doing some documentary? And, well, one thing led to another.'

Jim shook his head with fury.

'I don't believe it,' he hissed under his breath.

'What don't you believe, Jim? That a twenty-something woman actually found me attractive?'

Of course he could believe that. His mother's constant vaguely anxious expression was the result of living for fifty years with a man that all other women were attracted to. And he couldn't deny he'd been jealous of the way he had seen Jennifer look at his father. The way she hung on his every word. It was easy to be seduced by Bryn Johnson. Very easy.

'I'm not particularly proud of myself for cheating on my wife, your mother, but the girl flattered me.'

'You like that, don't you?'

'How do you think it felt for *me* that summer, Jim? One

minute I'm king of the world, the next minute I'm the man who was. I liked to think I was in glorious exile in Savannah, but I was no fool. I saw the panic, the pity in Saul's eyes when he sent us to the Lake House.' He took a deep breath, a frown line appearing between his brows.

'Why you?' asked Jim, the question echoing over and over in his head.

Bryn looked ashamed. 'Because I was just a bit older, wiser and more famous than the boy next door.'

'I was in love with her.'

'I didn't know that. You have to believe that much. I was a middle-aged man who liked the attention and wanted an ego boost. Don't pretend it hasn't happened to you: someone young and beautiful presents themselves on a plate and you take it.'

Of course it had happened to Jim before. The gorgeous junior PR executives, the interior design assistants. Hell, he remembered the first time he'd had sex with Melissa; she'd been a lawyer at the firm he'd been doing some work with.

'Jennifer Wyatt is a beautiful woman,' continued Bryn, 'but she was brought up in a certain way . . . brought up to believe that she could use her beauty and charm to manipulate men, to get things from them, money, position, pleasure—'

'She's not like that,' Jim said.

'Isn't she? Then why did she choose Connor over you? Why is she sleeping with you, the successful, dynamic you, when she is, I assume, still married? That girl is trouble, Jim,' Bryn said intensely. 'She always has been. She's a prick tease. Look at how she led you up the garden path for weeks. Look what she did with me – that wasn't just about my connections or my status, it was a fuck-you to her mother—'

'What do you mean?'

Bryn looked hot and uncomfortable. He wiped his mouth and sank down on a kitchen chair. Jim could see sweat beading at his temples.

'Are you all right?'

'I'm fine. Probably had a bit too much to drink,' he said, resting his elbows on his knees. 'I started at lunchtime . . .'

'Do you want a glass of water?'

'No.'

'Are you sure you're all right?' Jim asked as his father seemed to sway.

'Actually, I feel a bit strange.'

'Should I call a doctor?'

'No, it's fine,' Bryn said, looking up. His face had now completely drained of colour.

'Dad, it's not fine.'

'I feel sick.'

'I'm calling an ambulance.'

As Jim pulled out his mobile, Bryn lurched forward and fell to the floor with a crash, the chair landing on top of him.

Jim crouched down and rolled him over gently. His father's face was ashen, and there was blood dripping down his chin from a cut on his lip. Ceramic floors were not a soft landing.

He grabbed his phone and started stabbing buttons.

'Mum, it's Jim. Get home now.'

'I'm just on my way. I'm in a taxi—'

'It's Dad,' he said, cutting her short. 'He's collapsed. I think it's a heart attack. I'm calling an ambulance.'

He cut her off and dialled 911 immediately.

Bryn's breathing was so shallow it was barely there. Jim was not familiar with this part of town. He had no idea where the nearest ambulance had to come from. A siren screamed somewhere in the distance. Jennifer, Casa D'Or flashed in his mind, but then it was gone, his attention focused on his father as he willed him to stay alive.

Chapter Thirty-Two

The doctors were serious and the nurses sympathetic and efficient. You couldn't really fault them; everyone did everything right. The ambulance had arrived within minutes and broken every traffic law getting Bryn to the emergency room. Jim had sat in the back, holding his father's hand, watching his grey face behind the oxygen mask, urging him to live.

Bryn had been wheeled straight into the treatment room, the gurney bumping through the double doors. Elizabeth had arrived half an hour later, white as paper, her cheeks stained. Jim couldn't remember seeing her cry before. Three hours later, a doctor had informed them that a stabilising procedure had been a success, then explained that 'success' simply meant that Bryn had survived the procedure; his survival beyond that was not guaranteed. 'We just have to watch and pray,' he had said.

'Go home,' said Elizabeth now, putting her hand on her son's shoulder. 'Get a few hours' sleep.'

'I dozed a little,' said Jim, forcing his eyes to snap open.

He had not left Lennox Hill hospital from the moment he had arrived in the ambulance the day before. Now he glanced out of the window and saw that the sun was rising, a whole night had disappeared and he had not left the tiny, sterile hospital room, although his mother had gone home around midnight when she had been told her husband was stable.

'Come on, Jim. You can come back later. We can rotate. Take the keys to the brownstone if you want. It's closer.'

'Are you sure?' he asked, thinking how much better he would feel if he had even just a couple of hours' sleep and a shower.

'Just go,' she whispered as they both looked towards Bryn lying in the hospital bed. His skin was ghostly pale; a drip fed from his arm to an IV bag held up on a rack. The sound of the respirator was slow, steady, but despite everything, he looked peaceful.

He got a taxi downtown, back to his apartment. It was a dark, wet morning, the streets of New York a sea of commuters and umbrellas, a jigsaw of colour on the rainy streets.

The events of the past twenty hours didn't make sense to him. His father had always been such a vibrant man. He'd turned seventy that year but he had the energy of someone twenty years younger.

The first consultant Jim had met after their arrival at Lennox Hill had told him that his father had gone into a brief but complete cardiac arrest, which had limited the flow of oxygen to his brain. He knew the doctor was trying to break the news that his father might have incurred some sort of brain damage, though it was too soon to tell if this had been the case. The idea of Bryn Johnson without his mind, without the full range of his faculties, was unthinkable. His intellect and wit were what he prided himself on, what defined his very being. Given the choice, Jim knew his father would rather not wake up.

His phone vibrated. He picked it up without even looking at the caller ID. He recognised Jennifer's voice instantly.

'Hello,' he said, feeling his voice tense.

'I thought I'd call. I thought you'd be back from the Caribbean.'

'Yes, I'm back,' he said briskly.

'Are you OK?' She knew him too well, and he was too tired to create the charade of being nice.

'Something's happened.'

'What? Is everything OK?' she asked with concern.

'My father has had a heart attack.'

'Oh Jim. I'm so sorry. How bad is it?'

'He's at Lennox Hill. He's stabilised. That's all we really know for now.' He was aware how clipped his voice sounded.

'Where are you?'

'In a taxi.'

'Going where?'

'Home.'

'I'm coming round,' she said more urgently.

'Jennifer, please. It's fine. I just need to sleep, and then I'm going back to the hospital.'

'Jim . . .'

'We'll talk tomorrow,' he said, and before he knew it, he had ended the call.

His apartment had never seemed so small, the four walls of the living room like a cell.

He kicked off his shoes and took the short walk to the bedroom, pulled down the blinds and sat on the edge of the bed with his head in his hands. Guilt, regret made his throat thick. His body was crying out for sleep but he could not even lie back on the bed.

He ran the argument with his father over and over in his head.

If only he hadn't gone to Saul's apartment, if only he hadn't been given the manuscript and read it, or seen Jennifer's mole and put two and two together.

His shoulders slumped in hopelessness. He wasn't even sure what hurt most any more. Certainly the fact that Jennifer had slept with his father had lost its force. It was only a paper cut now, not the fatal wound it had felt like the day before.

Too restless to sleep, he stood up and went to make some coffee. Every second seemed to stretch out interminably, but he found strange comfort in the simplicity of grinding the beans, filling the machine with water, listening to the glug of the coffee filter through to the jug.

He was pouring the black liquid into a mug when the intercom to his apartment buzzed. It made him jump, then panic made his heart thud hard. He put down the jug and pressed the intercom button.

Jennifer's voice brought some relief, although she was the last person he wanted to see.

'Shit,' he whispered under his breath as he buzzed her up. The night they had spent together just two days earlier felt like another lifetime.

'I'm sorry for coming over. I just had to.' She had a nervous gentleness in her expression. As if she wanted to hold him but something was keeping her back.

'I'm fine,' he said quickly. 'I just need to sleep.'

She took a step forward but he felt himself instinctively flinch away.

Neither of them said anything for a few moments.

'Can I do anything? How about brownies to go with that coffee? I can run down to Molly's Cupcakes . . .'

'No, it's fine, honestly.'

Another long silence. He almost felt sorry for her until he thought about Chapter 37 in *College*.

'What happened?'

Jim shrugged. 'He had a heart attack last year, but he still drinks, smokes . . . Infallible Bryn Johnson, or so he thought.'

'Did it happen at the party?'

'No. A few hours before it started, although I think he might have quite enjoyed the drama of collapsing in front of New York's finest.'

He snorted lightly, then shook his head at the macabre humour.

'We were at his house,' he said quietly.

'What? And he just keeled over?'

He closed his eyes and knew he had to tell her.

'We had a disagreement.' The words were right there on the tip of his tongue, but they wouldn't come out.

'What about?'

'Nothing.'

'I hope you're not blaming yourself.' She tried to catch his eye but he would not let her fix her gaze on his. 'It's not your fault, Jim,' she said.

'Look, Jen, I don't want to be rude, but I should get some sleep. I was at the hospital eighteen hours straight and I have to be back by eleven o'clock so I can swap shifts with my mum.'

She nodded tightly, then her face softened and she reached out and touched his shoulder, stroked the cotton of his shirt.

'I'm here if you need me.'

'Thank you,' he said crisply.

She headed for the door, then turned back.

'It doesn't matter, not now, but you should know that I've left Connor.'

She paused as if she was waiting for an answer, then opened the door.

'The argument was about you,' he said.

She closed the door slowly. He instantly regretted saying anything. But it was done, and it needed to be said. Her expression was like stone until her lip began to quiver. Right then he wanted her to feel pain. The pain he had felt, that his father had felt.

'Me?' she said finally.

He inhaled sharply, wiped his dry lips with the palm of his hand.

'I read his book. *College*. The first draft. The one he started when he was in Savannah. And the character, the beautiful brunette, she had a mole. A diamond-shaped mole, just like yours.'

He looked at her but she remained quiet. A tiny tear glistened in the corner of one eye.

'He told me what happened. I know it didn't mean anything and I understand that he's an irresistible man,' he said with a note of sarcasm. 'But you have to understand how it hurt me and I'm not sure how easy it's going to be for me to get past it. Not now.'

Her lips were pressed together, full, trembling.

'We shouldn't let what happened twenty years ago spoil things between us again.'

'How can it not?' said Jim, feeling his own emotions rise again at her tacit admission. 'How could you do that to me? I was in love with you.'

The tear had escaped and was trickling down her cheek.

Jim shook his head. 'Why does everything have to be so difficult between us?'

'It doesn't have to be,' she said, inhaling audibly. 'Please, Jim. Let's talk about it.'

'Just get out,' he said quietly. 'If you care about my feelings at all, just go.'

She nodded and walked with purpose out of the apartment, not looking back. As Jim listened to the fading sound of her footsteps in the stairwell, he heard another noise – the insistent ringing of his mobile phone.

He snatched it up. At first he heard nothing, just a cavernous silence, and then the small and defeated voice of his mother, uttering the words, 'Your father is dead.'

Chapter Thirty-Three

Casa D'Or was finished. The paintwork gleamed, the marble shone and the linens on the king-sized beds practically crackled when you lay on them. The old house was almost unrecognisable from the sagging wreck Jim had seen that day he had bumped down the driveway. All those potholes had been filled, of course, the trees forming the avenue expertly trimmed, the gardens primped and planted to look as if an army of gardeners had been carefully tending to the grounds since the twenties. Not that Jim was seeing any of that. There was less than thirty-six hours to go before the bells-and-whistles party to launch the resort was due to begin, and there were a thousand things to see to before then: the wine, the catering, the crooner who would serenade the VIP guests as they arrived, and who was currently stuck in Reykjavik.

In the six weeks since his father's death, Jim had let work be his saviour.

He had returned to London for his father's funeral and

spent a week's compassionate leave with his mother. Simon Desai had been incredibly understanding and had told him to take as long as he wanted. But Elizabeth's sister and brother-in-law had moved into the Hampstead house to be with her, and when she had insisted that he return to America, Jim had decided it was for the best.

'Just go and finish that property,' she had said when she had waved goodbye to him at the airport. He knew exactly what she meant. He wanted to put it all behind him, and had thrown himself into the final preparations for the Casa D'Or launch with a fervour that even the most zealous workaholic would have found tiring.

'Excuse me, Mr Johnson, you have a visitor.'

Jim was having a final inspection of the spa, which had been created in the style of a boathouse on the far reaches of the property. He was wondering whether to ask to actually try out a massage himself – his back seemed to be a series of knots these days – when Liane, one of the receptionists, came to find him.

'Who is it?' he frowned, glancing at his phone, where all his appointments and calls for the day had been logged. He had nothing scheduled for that moment.

'Says her name is Marion Wyatt.'

'Oh,' said Jim more brightly. 'She used to own this place. Bring her to the terrace and send over a couple of glasses of sweet tea.'

He wrapped up his conversation with the spa manager, and

by the time he got back to the house, Marion was waiting for him at one of the white wrought-iron tables under the shade of a linen parasol.

'Hello, Marion,' he said, kissing her warmly on both cheeks.

'How are you, Jim?' she said, squeezing his hand. 'I was so sorry to hear about Bryn.'

Jim sat down and nodded at the reminder of his father's death. He had been trying so hard to shut it out, but whenever someone mentioned it, or whenever he stopped working and caught his breath, he was knocked sideways by a wave of grief and emptiness.

'Thank you. I guess you know what it feels like,' he said quietly, remembering David Wyatt's passing.

Marion nodded. 'I don't think it ever goes away. Every hour of every day I still stop and feel displaced, and for a split second I don't even know why something feels so wrong, until I realise it's because David isn't ever coming back.'

She looked around the grounds and smiled sadly.

'They'd have adored what you've done with this place. Both of them.'

'My father loved it here,' said Jim honestly. 'It's why he enjoyed working in the boathouse. The whole view of Casa D'Or was so inspiring, and I guess you only see how amazing it is from the other side of the water. Like looking at the Manhattan skyline from Queens.'

'Maybe you should have bought the Sittenfields' place,' smiled Marion.

'Maybe,' he said, wondering if that would actually have

made life simpler. Had he bought the Lake House rather than Casa D'Or, he might never have met up with Jennifer and his father might still be alive . . . but he didn't want to torture himself with that now.

'How's your mother?'

'As well as can be expected. She's coming to the launch, actually. I'm about to go and pick her up from the airport. I think it will do her good to get out of London.'

'Well, I just wanted to come and see what you've done with the place. I've heard so many rumours about how fabulous it is, and they've not been wrong.'

'You're not coming to the launch party tomorrow?' he asked with disappointment.

'Perhaps,' she said in a tone of voice that suggested she would not. Jim didn't want to push it. He'd had the same dilemma with his mother. He knew that a week in the sunshine would do her good, but there were so many memories attached to the grand old house that he was still worried how she would react.

'At least let me show you around,' he offered.

Marion didn't reply.

'You've changed the name,' she said eventually.

'Yes. The Plantation House,' said Jim awkwardly. 'Casa D'Or was your name, the family house name. I'm just glad you had faith in me to do it justice.'

She fell silent again, and when he looked over at her, she had dropped her head and was staring at her glass.

'Are you OK?' he asked after a moment. He was conscious of the heat of the afternoon and wondered if she wasn't suffering from a touch of sunstroke.

'I'm afraid I've not been entirely honest with you,' she said finally.

Jim pressed his lips together. He had a feeling he wasn't going to like what he heard next.

Marion looked away as if she had regretted starting to tell him.

'There was a reason why I sold you the house.'

Jim frowned.

'I was having an affair with David Wyatt. Before Sylvia died.'

'For how long?'

'Not long.'

'Did she know?'

Marion shrugged. 'I'm not sure. But I've always wondered . . .'

He gave an encouraging nod for her to continue.

'Sylvia had been diagnosed with depression. She'd taken an overdose twice in Jennifer's final year at college.'

'Did Jen know?'

'No, they wanted to keep it hidden from her. They weren't serious attempts. But still.'

She took a drink of iced tea and her hand was trembling.

'That's why David went into hiding after Sylvia's death.'

'The guilt?' asked Jim softly.

'He always wondered if he'd done enough to help her. Sylvia was a proud woman. She hated taking medication, and refused to go to therapy. Her condition got brushed under the carpet. It was easier to think that she was just a little bit difficult, and perhaps that's why David kept the house. To remind him to be a better man. Yet for me it was always a reminder of how we betrayed her.'

Somewhere in the distance the band was doing the sound check.

'I should probably go,' Marion said quickly. 'I'm sure you're busy. I can come back another time.'

Usually he would have tried to convince her to stay, but he knew it was right to let her go.

'I'm glad everything worked out for you. Truly,' she said, and she lifted a tender hand to his cheek. He put his own palm over it for a moment, both of them united by the sadness of the past.

After he had walked Marion back into the house and said goodbye to her at the front door, he went into the library, which had once been David Wyatt's study. A trolley of drinks, fine brandy and whisky in crystal decanters, tempted him. He never usually drank at work, but now he poured himself a measure of bourbon and tipped the lot down his throat before sitting down on one of the big cream sofas and tuning out the background noise.

Richard Steel, the Plantation House's general manager, knocked on the door and stepped tentatively into the room, holding an old shoebox.

'Have you got a minute?'

'Sure, come in,' said Jim, standing up and hoping he couldn't smell the alcohol on his breath.

'Liane said the previous owner of the house was here.'

'She's just left,' replied Jim, glancing out of the window, but Marion's car had already gone.

'I meant to give you this before. One of the decorators found it a few weeks ago in one of the classic rooms in the eaves of the house.'

Jim nodded. It was strange hearing the nooks and crannies of the old house being referred to in such corporate and sterile terms. Jennifer's old room was now the Magnolia Suite, redecorated and remodelled, all traces of its former occupant erased. The pink paint had been covered with de Gournay wallpaper, and the room had a canopied bed and a shelf full of artfully created books there to be seen but not read. This transformation had been replicated everywhere. Casa D'Or was gone.

'Let's have a look,' said Jim with curiosity. 'Where was it? I thought all the Wyatts' belonging were moved out and put into storage when the sale went through.'

'They were. This was found behind an air vent. We didn't discover it until we tested out the heating system.'

Jim took the box and sat back down on the sofa as Richard left the room and shut the door. He perched it on his lap and took off the lid, which was covered in a layer of dust that coated his fingertips.

An air vent, he thought, with a troubling sensation of guilt. It was clear that whatever was in the box was of great importance to someone; something personal that they wanted to keep hidden.

He put the lid on the floor, careful not to get dust on the pale furniture, although his trousers were now streaked with long flecks of it. Inside the box was a pile of papers and envelopes. He picked up one of the envelopes, cream vellum, addressed simply to 'B'. There were two sheets of matching paper inside. Jim began to read.

No one forgets a summer spent at Casa D'Or. You remember them so clearly you don't even need to close your eyes to recall the heavy warm breeze, the smell of azaleas, and the air that sticks to your sun-kissed skin.

At first he wasn't sure what it was. Some poetry, perhaps, or creative writing. But as he read on, it became obvious that it was a love letter. One written with great intensity and in the sort of overblown language that would sound odd if you tried to say the words out loud, but that on paper was romantic and lyrical like a sonnet.

I can feel a storm in the air, and dark clouds are gathering over the lake. The light in your room is on – I spot it twinkling across the water, and if I narrow my eyes I can make out your outline tempting me with your forbidden promise. I want to see you before it rains.

The letter stopped abruptly, as if it was not finished. It wasn't signed off with a name, or even properly addressed to anyone. But as Jim stared at that 'B' on the envelope, a sad resignation overwhelmed him and he knew with absolute certainty that this letter was meant for his father. As for its author . . . he remembered Jennifer telling him once how she relished the idea of writing love letters.

He gulped in misery. Bryn and Jennifer's confession that they had been intimate with one another had crushed him underfoot, but he'd gained some consolation from the fact that it was a one-off occurrence. Yet there were at least a dozen letters in this box. How long had their relationship been going on? he wondered, feeling himself shiver with shame. What a fool he'd been. All that time he'd spent with Jennifer, trying to pluck up the courage to do something, say something.

He could remember that evening they had been to Tybee Island as clear as day. He'd almost kissed her then, but had been disturbed by a disapproving Sylvia Wyatt on the steps to the house. He'd driven home and stayed up all night to write Jennifer a song, a song that would leave her in no doubt about how he felt, then spent every penny he had hiring a four-track Tascam Portastudio to record it. And yes, the night he'd given her the compilation tape was a night he had never forgotten, never would forget.

But all that time it had been his father she had been interested in.

He picked up another letter with masochistic curiosity.

This one didn't have an envelope. It was a plain piece of paper folded into quarters, and it was typed rather than handwritten, which immediately gave it a more clipped efficiency than the soulful letter he had read a minute before.

An electric summer fades. It's one that I will always remember. The very thought of you across the lake has made my words bloom and my heart smile. Your touch, the secret taste of you, has kindled a passion for love and life I thought had long been extinguished, and for that I will always be grateful.

But my flight home leaves tomorrow and please accept that we must part. Your plan for a future together is bold, reckless, flattering, but as I told you at the party, my life is in London and yours is here. Let's not wring out what has come to its sweet conclusion and ruin the fun memories of what we had. Let us preserve this summer, our secret, in amber.

Yours, Bryn

Jim's heart was beating hard as his eyes trailed to the top of the page.

The letter was dated the final day of his summer in Savannah. And it was addressed to Sylvia.

Chapter Thirty-Four

The party was packed to the rafters with the great and the good. Everyone was here, New Yorkers, Hollywood stars and Georgia's richest and most celebrated. A walkie-talkie in Jim's pocket kept him up to date with problems – so far there had been few niggles to deal with. American *Vogue* had sent a photographer, who said the hotel was one of the most picturesque places he'd ever seen and he would be recommending it as a location shoot to the magazine, whilst Richard Steel had reported a five hundred per cent increase in forward bookings.

Flitting between rooms, Jim checked that everyone was happy. Celine Wood was here, and had teased him that she might ask him to organise her wedding to Richie Hawkins. Their stay in Baruda had gone swimmingly well. Not only had her boyfriend proposed after his one-hour acoustic set for the mayor's daughter's birthday party, held around the swimming pool at RedReef, but Celine had had a meeting with Gregor Bentley, who had agreed that the range of swimsuits and sarongs she had been developing over the past year could be sold at the hotel's on-site boutique.

'I'm fucking forty,' she'd told Jim over a glass of champagne on the terrace. 'I don't want to be a model any more. I want to be the new Diane von Fürstenberg.'

Jim thought it was an excellent idea, and they pencilled in an appointment to discuss Celine taking a small unit at every Omari property to start her empire, which seemed like a win-win situation for everyone.

Elizabeth Johnson and her sister were sitting at a table by the lake with an expensive bottle of wine. Jim knew that his mother wasn't in the mood to party, but it had been good to see her all dressed up: a smart new outfit, some make-up on her face and a softer, happier expression than she had worn in the weeks since Bryn's death. In a flash of recklessness, he had also invited Sarah Huxley.

'How are you, Johnson?' she grinned as she came towards him holding a bottle of Krug.

'Are you going to drink all that, or is it just a fashion accessory?'

'Swig?' she asked, offering it to him.

He shook his head.

'Thanks for inviting me,' she said after a moment. 'An evening's worth of quality gossip might make up for the way you broke my heart. Celine Wood told me she's launching a fashion company in the new year and has a chain of stores raring to go. She says I can even sell the story to the *New York Times*.'

She grinned at him playfully and he felt a note of sadness. Sarah looked great tonight, he thought with a fleeting moment of desire. With her long red hair and wearing an emerald-green dress, she looked like a very sexy leprechaun. He didn't doubt that with another bottle of Krug and a few choice words he might be able to win her round again, but that wouldn't be fair to anyone. No, he was married to his work now. That was the way it had been for the past twenty years and it was a way that worked.

He had planned a week's holiday in the new year in Patagonia, where he planned to trek and walk and climb, something he had wanted to do for years. Then he had the Santai empire to launch and the Omari group to expand, and perhaps in a few months, when the wounds had healed, he might be able to start dating again. Maybe one of his football mates knew someone nice. In fact, in the days after his father's funeral, a couple of them had taken him out for a drink in Highgate and one of them had mentioned that his wife had a friend, a single mum at the school gates, a cracker by all accounts, who they thought Jim might get on with. 'You know, when you're ready.'

Twelve months ago, Jim would have smiled politely at the suggestion, horrified at the thought of being fast-tracked to cosy domesticity. But now the thought of a stable relationship, without the highs of a Manhattan romance with someone young and beautiful, or the complexities of an affair with the love of your life, was an appealing one. There was comfort in the ordinary.

'So what happens next? Now this place is finished?' said Sarah, putting the bottle down. 'Are you staying in New York?'

'No, I'm heading back to London tomorrow, actually. I'm officially the new CEO of the Omari group.'

'That's amazing,' said Sarah, giving him a hug.

'It's what I've always wanted,' he said, not convinced by the words coming out of his own mouth. 'Besides, I can't turn an opportunity like this down.'

'What does Jennifer think about it?' she asked cautiously.

Jim took a sharp intake of breath to compose himself. After his father's death, he had made a resolution to put Jennifer Wyatt completely behind him, which wasn't easy, especially given that he was renovating her old home. It had been particularly difficult finding Bryn and Sylvia's love letters the previous day, a discovery that had unleashed a mixed bag of emotions.

He remembered something his father had said to him – was about to say to him – just before his heart attack: *Look what she did with me . . . it was a fuck-you to her mother . . .*

At the time, Jim hadn't known what he meant, but now the knowledge of Bryn and Sylvia's affair helped him make more sense of what had gone on that summer. Perhaps it confirmed that Jennifer had had no real feelings for Bryn; that it had been a one-off affair. Her relationship with her mother had always been complicated, and so sex with Sylvia's lover could well have been some twisted cry for attention that hurt all of them.

But right now, it brought little consolation to Jim, reflecting badly as it did on both Jennifer and his father, two people Jim had adored. His feelings about his father were especially complex. Bryn had always been both his tormentor and his hero, but since his death, Jim could barely countenance any negative thoughts about him, even though he knew how unfaithful he had been towards his mother. Death had exonerated his wrongdoings. No, it was best to forget everything about that summer.

'It didn't work out between us,' he said finally.

'I'm sorry to hear that,' replied Sarah, touching his shoulder.

They were distracted by the appearance of Simon.

'My new CEO,' he said, striding over and slapping Jim on the back. 'What an amazing party. I never doubted for a minute you could do all this.'

'Well here we are,' said Jim, grateful for the supportive words.

'For one moment, I thought I saw Connor Gilbert,' Simon said, glancing back towards the crowd. 'It wouldn't surprise me if he had the bare-faced cheek to turn up here.'

Jim smiled nervously at the mention of his nemesis.

'I heard about Marshall Roberts,' said Simon, looking at him over the rim of his glass.

Jim glanced at Sarah, hoping she would take the hint to leave them alone, but she stayed rooted to the spot.

'It was all sorted,' he said diplomatically.

'So I hear,' chuckled Simon. 'I thought that showed the sort of initiative I expect from my CEO.'

Jim felt his shoulders sag with relief. Whatever Simon knew about RedReef clearly no longer mattered. He had no idea how his boss had found out about the extortion that was going on at the hotel, but the fact that he had sorted it out had obviously earned him some brownie points.

'As for Connor, let's just say I've dealt with him,' said Simon, leaning in more closely. 'Nothing too serious, just enough pressure to make him sweat with his condo development.'

'Whatever you've done to put that slimeball in his place isn't enough,' said Sarah, brazen in her eavesdropping.

Simon roared with laughter. 'Know Connor Gilbert then, do you?'

'Unfortunately,' she snorted.

'Simon, meet Sarah Huxley,' said Jim, introducing them.

'I know who you are,' said Sarah, extending an eager hand. 'I just wanted to say how much I loved the cover feature on you in *Forbes*. I didn't realise you were from Jaipur. I did my university dissertation on the reign of Man Singh II, the state's last maharaja.'

Simon's eyes lit up and the pair began to talk animatedly. Suddenly Jim felt painfully alone.

'Excuse me,' he said. 'I'll be back in a minute.'

He stepped out on to the back lawn and walked down towards the edge of the lake, to the restored pavilion. He glanced back at the house, which looked magnificent with every window blazing with golden light. He tried to lock the memory in: Casa D'Or in all its glory. He knew he was unlikely to ever come back.

He turned and faced the lake again, watching the moonlight ripple across the inky black surface.

'Jim.'

He heard a voice behind him and turned.

At first the backlight from the house made it difficult to see. Then his vision came into focus and he realised it was Jennifer.

Chapter Thirty-Five

'Jen,' he said with total shock.

'I've gatecrashed,' she replied in a voice so small he could hardly hear it.

Her smile was apologetic. It made Jim felt ashamed. This was her house, her past, and he hadn't even invited her. He also acknowledged that it had taken some balls for her to be here. His silence over the past few weeks had surely sent the message that he didn't want to see her or speak to her again.

'Don't worry. Marion gave me her ticket, if you want to know how I wriggled past security.'

His heart was beating hard. He felt caught out and unprepared.

'How are you, Jennifer?' he said after a moment.

'Getting there,' she said slowly. 'The divorce is going through. Connor isn't contesting it. He wants it done quickly too. And I have a new place. In the East Village, believe it or not. I'm still not sure whether it's a little too young and edgy for me down there. What's that expression I heard you use once? I feel like mutton dressed as lamb. But it's great. The apartment takes dogs, so I've got Mars Bar with me. And it's right near Prune. They do the best Sunday brunches.'

'I've been. And the best Bloody Mary menu in town.'

'For a long time I drank too much. I don't any more,' she said quietly. 'Although the odd glass of champagne might tempt me tonight,' she added as if she were trying to not be too sombre.

'Well, I can recommend the non-alcoholic cocktails. The virgin mojito is excellent,' he said as briskly as he could.

He took a moment to observe her, and watching her, eager and nervous, made his heart soften.

'I can't believe you came tonight,' he said, unable to stop the crisp questioning note in his voice. He knew that his heart would probably always skip a beat when he saw her, but he couldn't forget the day they had last spoken. The day she had admitted a sexual relationship with his father.

'I wasn't going to pay to see the house,' she smiled, a moonbeam lighting up her face in the softest, most beautiful way. 'This way I get to have a snoop around without having to book a room.'

Jim shrugged, unable to shake off his discomfort. 'I would have sorted you out with a visit,' he said, inhaling deeply, hoping that the faintly salty air would get rid of his own sudden desire for a drink.

'It was difficult to come back today,' she admitted.

'I was going to get in touch,' he said, surprising himself.

'There's something I need to tell you.'

'I have something to say to you first,' she said, closing her eyes as if to steel herself.

He heard her inhale deeply, then she opened her eyes and looked at him directly.

'Don't say anything, otherwise I might not get the words out,' she said. 'This is something I should have told you a long time ago.'

He hesitated. 'Go on.'

She shook her head, then looked up at the sky.

'That day,' she said, her voice cracking. 'The day you left Savannah. I was raped.'

Jim felt as if he was falling through a trapdoor as pieces of a terrible puzzle began to fall into place.

'Raped?' he said, feeling uncomfortable even saying the word.

Jennifer stared at the ground intently. It was a few moments before she looked up again.

'You remember the day after my twenty-first party,' she said softly. 'I left the barn, I left you, and went to see Connor to tell him it was over. He wasn't happy; he almost hit me, in fact. But I did it. I did it because I wanted to be with you.'

'Your letter . . . you said that you loved Connor . . .'

She took a deep breath before continuing.

'I finished with Connor and I came to the Lake House to see you. I came to tell you that we could be together. But you weren't there.'

Jim gave the smallest shake of his head, memories of the day tumbling back like a waterfall.

'No one was home. I saw Bryn in the boathouse. He said you'd gone into the city and invited me in to wait for you. He gave me a drink, some gin, and we chatted . . .'

Jim closed his eyes. He felt sick at the thought of what she was going to say.

'He asked about my documentary,' she continued. 'Told me how talented I was. I suppose I liked hearing that. The sun was shining through the window and I was happy. I remembered the way you'd made me feel the night before, and hearing your father, the big-name author, flatter me . . . it was almost as if I was in a movie, and I was a more lovely and clever version of myself. He asked me to have a look at his manuscript, and I suppose I didn't think anything of it when he shut the door of the cabin behind him.'

Jim felt dazed, as if the whole world was spinning.

'Stop, please,' he said, his voice barely making it out of his throat.

'His papers were on his desk and I started to read them,' she continued. 'My back was turned and then I felt him behind me and he was kissing my neck, just here.' She touched a little patch of flesh behind her ear. 'I was embarrassed and I told him to stop. He said, "Why settle for the boy when you can have the man?"'

Jim thought he saw the glint of a tear in the corner of her eye, but it could have been the moonlight.

'I said no, but he didn't listen,' she said, dipping her head.

'And then I stopped saying no because it was going to happen anyway.'

She fell silent for a moment, as if there were barely any words left to say.

'I went and hid,' she said at last, still looking down. 'I wanted to hide until I had worked out what to do. But nothing felt right. How could I tell you? How could I not tell you?'

Jim didn't speak for a moment. A cool breeze rustled through the bulrushes behind them.

'Why are you only telling me this now?' he asked finally, his emotions in turmoil.

'I loved you, Jim. So I figured . . . I figured it was better to keep quiet. Better to write you a letter, tell you it was over, and for us not to see one another again. If I saw you, if I told you what your father had done, it would have forced you to pick a side. What was the point in pursuing it? Who would have believed me if I'd reported it? Was the young, impressionable girl really going to say no to the handsome, successful author? And even if I had pressed charges, how would that have turned out? It would have destroyed your family. You needed money, you needed a father, not a man locked in a foreign jail cell.'

'I can't believe he would do that,' he said, his confusion almost making him feel dizzy. 'You said . . . you said that you had sex with him. Why are you telling me a different story now?'

'Because your father was in the hospital—'

'And now he's dead,' he roared, spinning around and letting his eyes settle on the darkness of the lake. In the distance he could make out the silhouette of the boathouse, and he squeezed his eyes shut.

'My father is dead,' he repeated more quietly, turning to face her, his voice shaking with emotion. 'Don't do this. Don't come and tell me this. You can't,' he said, the thickness in his throat making it difficult to breathe.

Jennifer didn't take her eyes off him.

'It wasn't just my mother's death that kept me away from Casa D'Or, that kept me apart from you. It was Bryn. And I knew that if I didn't say anything, if I never gave us one last chance to be together, then he's won. They've won.'

'No one has won, Jen,' said Jim so quietly he could barely hear himself.

For a moment they stood there gazing at one another. And then he felt a swell of anger that almost knocked him to one side with the force of its surprise. He didn't want to believe her; he couldn't let himself believe her. He owed that to his father, to his father's memory.

He took a step away from her, and she nodded as if she got the message.

'I just thought you should know,' she said, her voice cracking.

She turned and disappeared back towards the big white house glowing like a spectral face in the darkness. Back to the Plantation House. For Casa D'Or was gone now, and so was she.

Chapter Thirty-Six

1994

It was past two o'clock by the time Jennifer reached Casa D'Or. She parked her car on the driveway, and as she slammed the door of the vehicle behind her, she wiped her clammy palms on her skirt to steady herself. Glancing up at the big house, she wondered whether to go inside. On the drive over from the Gilberts' house, she had steeled herself for another confrontation with her mother. Her showdown with Connor had not been easy, but it had given her the confidence to see this through. But as she stood in the shadow of Casa D'Or, she felt quite small, and a little less brave.

She heard a rustle behind her and turned anxiously. Relief made her sigh when she saw it was just Marion, coming from the direction of the walled garden carrying some tools.

'Hey,' she grinned, shielding her eyes from the sun.

'Just been pruning some of the roses,' Marion smiled.

'It's so warm for the flowers out there.'

Jennifer looked up to the sky and shrugged.

'Not sure we're going to have any rain this afternoon.'

'News says there's a storm coming,' said Marion, putting her trowel in the enormous front pocket of her apron.

'Your mama's gone out,' she said after another moment.

'Good,' said Jennifer without even thinking.

Marion gave a soft smile that suggested she agreed with her.

'Did you have fun at the party last night?' she asked.

'It was incredible,' Jennifer said, unable to hide a small, giddy laugh.

'Feels good, doesn't it?' said Marion, looking intently at her.

'What does?'

'Being in love.'

Jennifer felt her cheeks flush, but she couldn't help but smile.

'Why do you say that?'

'I saw you with Jim Johnson last night. I'm glad you two finally sorted it out after all this messing around.'

'Messing around? Is that what you call it?' she asked.

'First night you ever saw each other, I knew what was going to happen. Didn't think you'd leave it quite this late, though.'

'You knew he liked me?' Jennifer said, grinning more broadly.

'And you him. It was obvious.'

Jennifer glanced over towards the lake, which she could see through a tiny clearing in the gardens.

'I wouldn't exactly say I've sorted it out yet,' she said, grateful to share her thoughts. She wasn't particularly close to Marion. Although she had known her all her life, the fifteen-year age gap between them had always seemed too big for them ever to be friends. But suddenly she found strength in the housekeeper's presence and wished that they could have shared confidences earlier.

'Be brave and you will,' said Marion with wise authority.

Jennifer walked around the lake to get to the Sittenfields' house. The heat was still fierce and the water shimmered. Telltale tongues of orange had begun to appear on some of the foliage, but otherwise there was no clue that it was almost fall and summer was drawing to a close.

She watched a sandpiper peck for worms in the silt along the shore and wondered if she would ever walk this route again. There was really no need unless you were going to the Sittenfields', and although Jennifer was in a hurry to tell Jim that she had ended her relationship with Connor, she wanted to savour every step to draw out the summer just a little bit longer.

She felt a flurry of nerves as the Lake House grew closer. Marion had been right when she said it was a good feeling being in love. Jennifer felt an excitement that made her want to shout from the rooftops, and a reassuring sense that things had just fallen into place. But she could feel something else too. Fear. Anxiety. She'd made no proper plans with Jim that morning. They had both been too giddy to even think about any strategy beyond Jim changing his flight to a later date. Now there was a palpable sense of the unknown, but reminding herself how much she trusted Jim, she dismissed it.

She was by the boathouse now and could see a shadow moving inside. She smiled at the thought of Bryn Johnson working until the final moment he was due to leave for the airport, and didn't blame him for wanting to soak up every last minute of the glorious view.

Picking up her pace, she almost tripped over a canoe that lay carelessly on the grassy slope leading to the water. Hoping that Jim hadn't been gazing out of the window at that precise moment, she ran the rest of the way to the back door, knocking hard as she waited for someone to open it. There was no response.

'They went into town,' called a familiar baritone from behind her.

She spun around and saw Bryn Johnson watching her from the balcony of the boathouse.

Bryn's voice might have been loud enough to cross the length of the Sittenfields' back lawn, but Jennifer didn't want to be rude and holler back. She put her hands in the pockets of her sundress and walked towards him.

'Know when Jim will be home?' she asked as she got closer.

She took a minute to observe him. His feet were bare and a white shirt fell loose over the waistband of his beige trousers. A suntan from the warm Savannah summer had brought out the blue of his eyes, and Jennifer found herself wondering if this was what Jim would look like in thirty years' time.

Bryn shrugged. 'Left a while ago with Elizabeth. They should be back any time. Better had be. We have to leave for the airport at six.'

Jennifer felt uneasy. It was obvious that Jim's father still thought his son was flying to New York with them that evening, before their onward journey to London. But a voice in her head told her to trust Jim and dismiss his remark.

She looked back across the lake towards Casa D'Or, debating whether to hang around.

'Come inside and have a drink while you wait,' said Bryn, as if he were reading her thoughts. 'You can tell me what you think of my opus.'

'You don't want my opinion,' she laughed.

'An arts graduate from Wellesley College? I'd say you're better qualified than anyone to give me some feedback. So long as it's not too critical, of course,' he laughed.

She had always felt a little bit scared of Bryn Johnson. He was a formidable character, and now there was the added pressure that he was her boyfriend's father, and she wanted to impress him. But Bryn seemed to be in an affable mood as he ushered her into the cabin.

'Have you ever tried gin and tonic?' he asked as Jennifer looked around.

She had never been in the boathouse before. It was small and sparsely furnished, with large glass windows that overlooked the water, although the blinds were down to keep it cool in the heat of the day. A desk displaying all the signs of creative chaos – strewn papers, coffee cups and a solitary typewriter – was pushed against one wall. A leather armchair sat in another corner next to a teetering pile of books and a drinks trolley, the whole scene in stark contrast to the groomed perfection of Casa D'Or.

Bryn picked up an almost empty bottle and examined it.

'We should get a couple of measures out of this,' he muttered as he poured them both a glass.

He handed one to Jennifer, who sniffed the unfamiliar liquor.

'I guess you're old enough to drink now,' he said, leaning against the desk and looking at her.

'Being twenty-one?' she smiled, tilting her head to one side.

He nodded and knocked back his tipple.

'How's the documentary? Jim told me about it. Said you'd taken some of my sugestions on board.'

'Your idea of interviewing parents was fantastic. It's really added another layer to the narrative.'

'I only threw a few things out there. It's your talent that will make it as good as it can be. Remember, when you're ready, get in touch and I'll show it to some contacts in New York.'

She sipped her gin and motioned towards the desk.

'So how's your book coming on? Is it finished?'

'Not yet,' he snorted. 'I put myself under a lot of pressure to get things just right. The curse of success,' he said more ruefully.

'I'm sure it's brilliant,' smiled Jennifer, feeling warm in the lazy stream of sunlight coming in through a skylight overhead. 'What's it about?'

'Desire,' he said simply.

'I wish I could sum up my documentary in one word like that.'

'You can. Hope.'

He put his drink on the desk and turned around to gather some of his papers.

'Here,' he muttered. 'I need an objective opinion on this scene.'

Jennifer came towards the desk, her arm brushing against his shirtsleeve as she stood next to him. She could smell that strong juniper scent of gin again, and realised it was on his breath. As he touched the paper with his fingertip, one of the straps of her sundress fell off her shoulder.

She adjusted it quickly and began to read, not noticing that Bryn had gone to lock the door of the boathouse behind them.

Chapter Thirty-Seven

The woods on the Casa D'Or estate had been largely untouched since the plantation days. It was not a particularly dense forest – the mix of pine, poplar and palmetto let in streaks of sun through the canopy of twigs and leaves – but still, Jennifer had always found it a haunting place. Slave cabins once stood in the clearings, and although her grandfather had pulled them down decades before, the thought still made her feel uncomfortable. She was sure the only reason her father kept the woods was to make the acreage of the estate sound more impressive, and she generally avoided coming here. But that afternoon, after the boathouse, it was the first place she had thought of. She had found a tree and curled up against the rough bark of its trunk, the skirt of her dress pulled tightly over her knees, arms hugged around her shins, and she had sat there for an hour, maybe two, tears rolling down her cheeks until they dried on her skin.

There were no more tears left now. No emotion either. She

felt empty, hollow – a husk that just wanted to run on auto-pilot. But although she felt numb, she knew she could not stay here for ever. Slowly she got to her feet and brushed the soil and leaves from the fabric of her dress. Her watch told her it was a little after five, but it was dark overhead; the blue sky had turned a malevolent shade of pewter. Marion had said there was a storm coming and she'd been right, thought Jennifer as a drop of rain plopped on her head and the breeze picked up in the trees around her.

She began to run, her sneakers crunching the carpet of twigs and leaves underfoot. The temperature had dropped, and there was some comfort in feeling the wind slap across her face. It was strong now, cold and damp, but it was not powerful enough to erase the memories of the past few hours. She ran faster and faster, but still images of Bryn Johnson popped into her head like a nightmare.

The trees were thinning now, as lightning flashed overhead, followed by the deep grumble of thunder. She knew she had to get to shelter quickly. She saw Marion's cottage just a few hundred metres away. It was on the outskirts of the more manicured grounds of Casa D'Or, behind the old smokehouse, in the shade of one of the largest oak trees on the estate.

Once she was out of the woods, the rain soaked her to the skin. Panting hard, she ran on to the porch of the cottage and collapsed into an Adirondack chair underneath the window as another fork of silver lightning flashed across the sky.

The door of the cottage opened and Marion stood there, pulling a sweater on over her head.

'Get inside,' ordered the older woman. 'It's filthy out there. The storm will drown you before you reach the big house.'

Jennifer got up and followed the housekeeper into the cottage.

It was a single-storey building, the doorway leading straight into a living area dominated by a sofa, dining table and sideboard. Jennifer came in here rarely, but she noticed that there was a bigger television since the last time she'd visited, and a few more framed photographs on the bookcase.

Marion disappeared for a few moments and reappeared with a towel.

'Dry yourself off,' she instructed.

Jennifer towelled her hair, then pressed the fabric into her face to compose herself.

'Where've you been?' asked Marion kindly.

'Just walking,' Jennifer said, scratching her arms, her nails digging into the skin harder than was necessary.

'Knew there was going to be a storm,' observed Marion, looking up to the heavens. 'Coffee?'

Jennifer shook her head and looked at the older woman's kind face. She wondered if she should tell her, and took a breath to steel herself, tears swelling behind her eyes, but as her mouth opened, she could not find the words to even begin to describe what had happened to her.

A wave of shame engulfed her. She felt dirty, stupid, afraid. The consequences of even hinting at what had gone on in the boathouse were too awful to contemplate. No one would believe her, and even if they did, there was unlikely to be any sort of happy ending. How would anything make it better? What was done was done.

A tear leaked down her cheek and she blinked it away.

'Are you OK?' said Marion. She moved closer and put her arms around Jennifer. For a split second, Jennifer flinched at the touch of another person, but as she relaxed into it, it became clearer what she had to do. She had to forget.

'I will be,' she muttered into the housekeeper's shoulder.

'You can still write to him,' said Marion softly. 'Just because he's going home doesn't mean you can't see each other again. I hear London is beautiful in the fall,' she chuckled.

'I won't be going to London,' said Jennifer quietly.

'Oh,' said Marion more awkwardly.

Jennifer pulled away and used every ounce of her self-control to stay strong.

'Do you have paper and a pen?' she asked.

Marion nodded and went to get them. She put them on the small dining table in the corner of the room, then discreetly left Jennifer alone to write her note.

In the woods, Jennifer had been so confused that she hadn't known what to do, how to proceed. But now she had some clarity. There was only one way out of this mess, and however much it broke her heart, she knew it was the only thing she could do.

She kept it simple.

Jim,

It's been a wonderful summer but you should catch the

plane to New York. Tonight. I love Connor. We are engaged, and last night should never have happened. Just go back to England, Jim. If you are truly my friend, you should do what is right for all of us and not contact me again.

Jennifer

She folded the paper in half, ashamed of her lies, sickened at the thought of Jim's bewilderment when he read them.

'Marion. Could you do me a favour?' she asked simply.

'Of course.'

Jennifer handed her the letter.

'Can you drop this off at the Lake House? It's for Jim.'

Marion looked at it.

'I'll fetch an envelope and go as soon as the rain dies down,' she nodded.

Storms came and went quickly in this part of the world. Jennifer gave the towel back to Marion and said her goodbyes. The Wyatts' housekeeper didn't push, didn't question Jennifer's melancholy mood any further, and if she had noticed that the younger woman hadn't looked her once in the eye, she didn't say so. Jennifer was grateful for her unwillingness to pry.

She closed the door of Marion's cottage behind her and started walking back to Casa D'Or, across the gravel drive and the lawns that led to the house. The clouds were beginning to clear, and the rain had softened to a gentle spit. Suddenly she could smell flowers on the breeze, as if the whole world had been infused with a springtime freshness that was in contrast to her own despair.

There was only one thing she wanted to do now, and that was to shower the filth of the day from her body. She felt shivery and weak. Her stomach was grumbling but she felt nauseous, as if a pool of vomit had collected at the base of her throat.

The Wyatts rarely locked the front door to Casa D'Or – there was no need to on the Isle of Hope – and Jennifer pushed it open. The house was silent, all traces of the party gone except for the fragment of a gold balloon in one corner of the hall. She began to walk up the sweeping staircase, holding the oak banister to steady herself. Every step seemed an effort. She felt exhausted, although her mind was a frantic whirl of thoughts. She imagined Marion walking to the Lake House right now, her shoes squelching in the wet grass, and wondered if she would see him on her way over – the monster in his boathouse lair.

'Where have you been?'

She recognised her mother's voice instantly. The Southern inflections that were so syrupy on most people in this town sounded in Sylvia's tones clipped and brusque.

Jennifer was a few feet from the top of the stairs. Her mother stood on the mezzanine that overlooked the hallway, holding on to the balustrade so tightly her knuckles had turned white.

'Just out,' said Jennifer, not looking at her.

'Where?' pressed Sylvia.

'Why does it matter?' she said, clutching the banister harder.

'What were you doing at the Lake House?' asked her mother after a moment.

Jennifer's heart was thudding hard now. Her throat felt tight, her palms started to bead with sweat. She knew it was her opportunity to say something, to shout out the truth. Sylvia Wyatt was her mother. She was on her side.

Or was she?

A voice of doubt echoed in her head.

'I went to see Jim,' she said finally, her heartbeat almost banging out of her ribcage.

'Jim phoned here,' challenged her mother. 'He hasn't seen you.'

She took a moment to think, but she could come up with no convincing excuse.

'I've been walking,' she said at last, her voice shimmering with emotional restraint. It wasn't exactly a lie.

'What were you doing at the Lake House then?'

Her mother's voice sounded odd. Jennifer knew the signs. Knew what was coming next. That the volcano was ready to erupt.

'You were with Bryn Johnson, weren't you,' she said. It was an accusation, not a question.

Jennifer turned and started to walk back down the stairs, counting her steps as she tried to control her breathing. She knew she had to get back outside and run. She had no idea where to.

'Weren't you?' screamed her mother from the mezzanine.

'I have to go,' said Jennifer, quickening her pace, not daring to turn around.

'Where are you going? Come back here this minute and tell me where you were!' cried Sylvia, her voice echoing around the cavernous atrium space.

Jennifer was at the bottom of the stairs now, her eyes fixed on the front door. Suddenly she heard a thud behind her, and then another, a toppling domino chain of noise that made her stop in her tracks. She turned in time to see her mother bounce twice off the final few steps, landing on the hard walnut with a sickening crack.

Jennifer screamed and ran towards her. Throwing herself to her knees, she touched her mother's cold face, recoiling in horror as she realised that Sylvia wasn't moving.

'Mom!' she cried, looking around frantically, spotting a slipper on the stairs and then a trickle of blood oozing on to the brown floor.

Her hands were shaking. She ran to the phone on the cabinet in the hall and dialled 911, screaming at them to come to Casa D'Or as quickly as they could. Still trembling, she tried to contact her father, but his secretary told her that he had left for the day.

Tears were streaming down her face as she kneeled back down, desperately wondering what she could do. Only minutes before, she had thought her life could not get any worse, that she could sink to no further depths of misery, and yet touching her mother's neck, feeling the pulse get weaker and weaker, she felt as if her own life was being drained out of her body.

Sylvia's face was ghostly pale, and quite beautiful, like the moon.

'Mom, please. Stay with me. I love you,' whispered Jennifer. It was such a clear and definite thought, she wondered why she had not told her mother so every day of her life.

She heard the sound of tyres on the gravel but could not move. She took hold of her mother's hand and did not let go until she heard footsteps behind her.

'Oh God!' cried her father as he ran across the hallway.

'The ambulance is on its way,' said Jennifer, getting to her feet to meet him.

'What happened?'

'I don't know. I was coming down the stairs. She was behind me, standing at the top.' She pointed to the mezzanine. 'She was upset.'

David Wyatt took a sharp intake of breath, then squatted down on his haunches to stroke his wife's forehead.

Jennifer felt as if the world had stopped turning, as if she were suspended in space. She closed her eyes, wishing she had super-powers, that she could make the earth spin back on its axis and rewind time, but when she opened them again, she saw her father hunched over her mother's body, and it was the saddest thing she had ever seen.

Somewhere in the distance she could hear sirens.

She went to the door to wait for them, as if staring down the oak-lined drive would make the ambulance come quicker. At last she saw a flash of red light coming closer and closer.

Perhaps it was not too late, she thought, the beat of her heart speeding up.

'Hurry. Hurry,' she whispered, closing her eyes.

She barely registered Marion's arrival at the house, and then she was surrounded by people and noise. A stretcher was wheeled into the hall, and although the wail of the siren had stopped, the scarlet light of the ambulance seemed to cast the house in a fiery glow, as if she were in hell.

She felt Marion's reassuring hand on her shoulder. When she turned, she noticed that the housekeeper's eyes were glassy with tears.

'What's happening?' she whispered.

'It's too early to say,' replied Marion soberly.

Jennifer walked slowly, as if in a daze, to the porch, resting her hands on the ledge as she looked down at her grass-stained sneakers.

'Jen.'

A voice disturbed her. She looked up and saw a figure standing outside the house. Through her clouded vision, it took her a moment to recognise Jim Johnson.

'What's happening? Tell me,' he pleaded as he came up the stairs towards her.

'My mother. There's been an accident.'

'Oh God,' he said, glancing towards the inside of the house then coming to put his arms around her.

She shrugged him away.

'Don't,' she said, stepping back.

She looked at him and it was as if she were looking at an

old skin she had just shed. There was no point mourning it, no matter how beautiful it had once been, for it had gone.

'I've got a new ticket,' he said, trying to catch her eye.

'Didn't you get my letter?' she said, her voice barely a croak.

The paramedics wheeled the stretcher on to the porch. Her mother was lying there, attached to tubes and wires, her father moving alongside her, his hand gripping hers, as the two men lifted the stretcher down the steps.

'I'm going to the hospital,' said David, glancing at Jim.

'I'm coming too,' replied Jennifer quickly.

'I'll take you,' said Jim, a quaver of desperation in his voice.

She sighed, and her breath shook in her throat.

'Catch your plane. Go back to England,' she whispered.

He came to her and grabbed her hand, tears welling in his own eyes.

'I'm here for you, Jen. Just tell me what you want me to do.'

She summoned all her courage and looked straight at him.

'You've read my letter. Go back home, Jim,' she said as she followed her father into the back of the ambulance.

Chapter Thirty-Eight

2015

Jim felt horrible. He stood there for a moment, listening to the breeze. Everything Jennifer had said made sense, and yet it was the most vicious and vile story he had ever heard.

He remembered vividly where he'd been on the afternoon following Jennifer's twenty-first birthday party: in Savannah, trying to change his airline ticket. His mother had gone downtown too, wanting to buy last-minute presents for everyone back in London, and a little something for Saul Black, whom they were due to meet the next day in New York. Jim had driven them both there in the truck, and on the way he'd confided to Elizabeth that he wanted to stay in Georgia just a little while longer.

'You're in love with her,' his mother had teased.

'I think I am,' he'd smiled, wanting to get back to the Isle of Hope as quickly as possible.

Everything had taken for ever. The drive into town, the queue in the travel agent's, where they had eventually confirmed Jim's suspicions that he would just have to buy a fresh ticket if he wanted to postpone his trip back home. His mother hadn't met him at the time she'd said she would, and then she wanted to stop on the way back for one last slice of her favourite key lime pie from a bakery on Abercorn Street.

Jim had got back to the Lake House at around four o'clock. Their bags were already packed and his father was upstairs, apparently pulling together his notes to show his agent in New York. It was the lazy time of the day, when Jim would usually sit on the pontoon with a book or his guitar, but his mother had asked him to help do a final tidy of the house. He'd been grateful for the opportunity to keep busy. He was anticipating a knock on the door, or the ring of the telephone in his room. He was waiting for Jennifer to get back in touch, and he didn't quite believe it when he didn't hear a peep.

He remembered, quite clearly, calling Casa D'Or, only to be told by Sylvia in crisp and certain terms that her daughter wasn't at home. She'd sounded upset, even peeved, and at the time Jim thought it was because she absolutely hated him. But now, armed with the knowledge of Bryn and Sylvia's affair, he suspected other reasons.

He imagined his father typing his Dear John letter to Sylvia. Imagined it being left under a stone or in the pavilion, like a Cold War drop of secret intelligence, perhaps even brazenly slotted into the Casa D'Or mailbox itself. He imagined Sylvia watching the Lake House from a window at Casa D'Or. Imagined her seeing Jennifer disappear inside the boathouse and not come out for thirty minutes or more, and speculating what had happened. Jim did not know how long Bryn and Sylvia's affair had been going on, but judging from the dated letters he had found, it had been at least a month, and knowing how intensely he himself had felt about Jennifer after just a few short weeks, he had a good idea of how hurt Sylvia had been by it all.

It was quite easy for Jim to imagine everything, except what had gone on in the boathouse. He could not let himself accept the version of events that Jennifer had told him, even though the voice in his head told him it was all true.

He squeezed his eyes tightly closed to help him think more clearly, and when he opened them, he could see the shadow of someone standing by the door to the pavilion.

'Mum,' he said after a moment.

'It was always the quietest and most lovely spot out here,' Elizabeth said.

He groaned silently, feeling sickened at the thought that she might have overheard his conversation with Jennifer.

'I'm sorry. I didn't realise you two were down here,' she added, almost apologetically.

He didn't reply, and the silence seemed to stretch on for ever.

'So that's what happened. That day in the boathouse,' she said at last with crisp resignation.

He glanced across at her, noting the look on her face. Firm, stoical – the army officer's daughter that she had been brought up to be.

'She's emotional,' he muttered, looking away.

'So you don't believe her?'

'I don't know what to believe any more.'

Another silence that seemed to make the night air vibrate between them.

'I do,' said Elizabeth eventually, stepping out into the moonlight. 'I believe her.'

'What?' whispered Jim incredulously.

His mother's face had paled so that it looked ghoulish.

'I remember that day,' she said, moving towards him. 'It was hot, sticky. We'd come back from Savannah and your father was in the shower. At four o'clock in the afternoon.'

Jim didn't remember that detail.

'You said it yourself. It was hot . . .'

'Your father was a man of routine,' she replied, shaking her head. 'A glass of claret, a bath, a cigar in his dressing gown . . . Not a shower in the afternoon.'

She paused and looked out towards the inky lake.

'I'd suspected him of seeing someone for weeks. He was different, pleased with himself. I knew it wasn't the work, his book. I'd seen his notes, and believe me, there wasn't much of it. I wondered if it was Sylvia Wyatt, but then I knew how much she disliked us. Or perhaps the housekeeper, Marion. She was certainly appealing. So I went down to the boathouse. I don't know what I was looking for – a sign, a smell, a clue, something . . . and then I saw it.'

'What?'

'A necklace. A thin gold chain with a little hummingbird just here,' she said, touching her throat. 'I remembered Jennifer Wyatt wearing an identical necklace at the party. I tried to tell myself that perhaps you and she had been fooling around in there, but in my heart of hearts I knew something had happened.'

'It doesn't mean he . . . it doesn't mean he raped her.' He struggled to say the word.

'No, it doesn't,' she said sadly. 'But I heard Jennifer just then, and she wasn't lying. Besides, your father had form . . .'

'Form?'

It was another minute before she spoke.

'Saul had an assistant. Julia. Beautiful thing. Very similar in looks and poise to Jennifer. She made allegations . . .'

'What sort of allegations?'

'That your father assaulted her. Sexually.'

'People didn't believe her, did they?'

Elizabeth didn't speak.

'Say something,' pressed Jim. 'Was she trying to blackmail him? I'm guessing this was after his success with *College* . . .'

'Saul had the allegations buried,' said Elizabeth, shifting uncomfortably. 'Bryn was the biggest client the agency had. *College* was on its twelfth printing. It was one of the biggest global hits of the decade. No one wanted that bandwagon to stop rolling, and besides, there was no concrete evidence. Not that there ever is . . .'

'I don't believe it,' he whispered.

'We'll never know the truth. About Saul's assistant, about Jennifer. But yes, your father had his demons; all this self-confidence and yet he never quite believed he was good enough.'

Elizabeth took a moment, as if she were collecting her thoughts.

'We were never really happy together,' she said finally. 'Certainly after the business with Saul's assistant I could never sleep next to him at night without wondering if the allegations were true. But I stayed with him. I took the easy option, even if that meant being dishonest; dishonest with myself, dishonest with the world about what I knew about Bryn Johnson.'

'The truth hurts,' replied Jim quietly.

'Yes, it does. But at least it's the truth. Lies always catch up with you in the end.'

She stepped forward and took her son's hand.

'Go and find Jennifer. Trust her. Trust your feelings for one another.'

'I can't. Not after everything I've done, everything I've said,' said Jim, feeling wretched. All he had ever wanted was to be with Jennifer. Protect her. Even the acquisition of RedReef had been to help her, and yet when it really counted, he had turned his back on her.

'Jennifer was right. If you don't go after her now, he's won.'

Jim squeezed his mother's fingers, then wrapped his arms around her in a hug that had never been more full of affection and support.

'Go,' she whispered, and he released her and ran up the lawn towards the house.

As he pushed through the crowd, he vaguely registered the scene. In one corner he could see Simon Desai still deep in conversation with Sarah; in another, Celine Wood was sitting on her fiancé's knee. A couple kissed by the pool, a waiter topped up the fountain of champagne to shrieks of delight, a seventy-something socialite was laughing with Nina Scott, the travel PR. For one night at least, happiness was everywhere, except in his heart.

He ran through the house towards the front of Casa D'Or. Already a line of black Town Cars was queuing down the drive to whisk away the earliest-departing guests. He ran along, banging the window of each one, calling her name, until one pulled away and he saw her. The back of her dress, her dark hair fluttering in the evening breeze. Her hand was stretched out for a white Savannah taxi.

'Stop. Don't go!' he shouted. He could feel his heart thudding in his chest.

The driver of the cab held up his hand, but Jennifer shook her head, and with a disgruntled expression he went to park and wait for another fare.

They stood there for a moment, just looking at each other.

'I was wrong back there,' he said finally. 'I didn't want to believe you. I couldn't let myself.'

'It doesn't matter,' replied Jennifer in the quietest of voices.

'It does,' said Jim more passionately.

He took another tentative step closer to her.

'I'm sorry. I'm so sorry.'

He was ashamed of even trying to justify his actions, but he wanted her to know.

'Bryn was my father, my hero,' he said, bowing his head. 'And now he's gone. Part of me blames myself for his death, and that's the reason why I behaved like I did back there. But I guess he wasn't the person I wanted him to be.'

'I think we just have to accept that people are flawed. We all are, in our own ways.'

'Will you forgive me?' he asked.

For a second, Jennifer didn't say anything. Time seemed to drag on for ever, and Jim had a fierce and dreadful sense that he had just lost everything.

'Please,' he whispered.

'Only if we have no more secrets,' she replied, and his shoulders sagged with relief.

'No more secrets,' he agreed, holding out his hand, and when she took it, he drew her into his arms. He inhaled deeply, smelling the fresh scent of her shampoo, never wanting to let her go, and she rested her head on his shoulder as if, against all the odds, she felt the same.

'You know you shouldn't blame yourself for what happened to your father,' she said into the fabric of his dinner jacket. 'That doesn't end well, and I should know.'

He pulled away and looked at her.

'About that . . .'

He saw a wave of anxiety creep across her face and thought about Sylvia's box of letters sitting in a drawer in the house.

He had spent half the night tossing and turning, wondering what to do with them, and had woken up deciding that it would serve no purpose to tell Jennifer about her mother's affair with Bryn. He had stood there in front of the roaring fire that the housekeeping staff had lit and taken the letters out of the box, imagining them disintegrating to ash and taking the memories of that summer with them.

But something had stopped him.

No more secrets, repeated a voice in his head.

'You shouldn't blame yourself for your mother's death either,' he began.

'I know,' agreed Jennifer quietly. 'But it's not easy to do. We had words. I went down the stairs. She must have followed me and slipped . . . If we hadn't argued . . .'

'I don't believe it happened that way,' said Jim with conviction.

He looked away, and wiped his mouth, knowing that he was doing the right thing.

'Sylvia and Bryn were having an affair,' he said gently.

'What?' said Jennifer incredulously.

'I found love letters they had written to each other. I've got them upstairs.'

'An affair?' she repeated, her face crumpling into a frown. 'For how long?'

'I'd say a month or so, from the letters. Your mother's were very eloquent, passionate. I think she had intense feelings for Bryn, or perhaps they just felt intense at the time,' he continued carefully. 'But I'm not entirely sure they were reciprocated.'

Jennifer was looking down at her shoes.

'Bryn called it off the night of the party. I think she was distraught.'

Jennifer nodded slowly. 'It makes sense,' she whispered, as if she was lost in the past. 'She screamed at me that day – "Where have you been? What were you doing at the Lake House?" I thought she was upset about Connor, our relationship, my reputation . . .'

'Did you see her slip?' asked Jim, trying to catch her gaze.

'No.'

'She had been diagnosed with depression.'

Jennifer looked at him. 'Depression?'

'They wanted to keep it from you. But there was a reason why your mother could be cold and difficult. She was ill. Seriously ill. In your final year of college, she took an overdose. Two, in fact.'

Jennifer was wide-eyed with horror. 'She tried to commit suicide?'

Jim shook his head. 'She didn't want to kill herself,' he said, remembering what Marion had told him. 'It was a cry for attention.'

There was another silence. Jennifer's expression was stricken. Jim moved towards her in the dark to reassure her. He knew how bad she felt about her mother's death; he knew because he felt the same about his father. But now he just wanted to convince her it was not her fault.

'Maybe she fell that night, Jen. Maybe she was miserable, maybe it was another cry for help. But it was an accident, an accident that could have happened at any time because her illness wasn't under control,' he said, stroking her cheek.

'It doesn't matter how it happened, Jim. The fact is, she died.'

'And you don't have to carry that guilt around for the rest of your life.'

'Nor do you,' she whispered, this time taking his hand in hers, holding on as if she would never let go.

Epilogue

'Best-looking bride I've ever seen,' grinned Jeanne as she squeezed Jennifer tight.

'Some might say you're biased,' giggled Jennifer, smoothing the cream lace over her curves.

Jennifer realised she had turned into a cliché, but she couldn't stop smiling whenever she caught a glimpse of herself in the beautiful gown her old friend had found for her big day. She had originally got in touch with Jeanne to complete her documentary, now tentatively called *Twenty-One*, and had not been entirely surprised to discover that Jeanne no longer worked in the Seven Eleven but owned Savannah's most celebrated vintage clothing store. When she had invited Jeanne to her wedding, her friend had insisted that she would find her the perfect gown, and had flown to London three months later with the most exquisite dress Jennifer had ever seen, a delicate creation of pale silk and lace that had made her feel like a goddess from the second she put it on.

Jeanne took Jennifer's hand and led her to the dance floor.

'Are we going to boogie, then?' she giggled as Jennifer's Aunt Donna waved at them from across the room.

Jennifer's divorce had been uncontested and had been quickly finalised. Jim had taken her to Salcombe in Devon shortly afterwards, promising a weekend of good food and sailing, and had proposed during a walk on the headland.

She had fallen in love with the English seaside town, loved its pace of life and the silver light that glistened over the sea, so much so that it seemed like the perfect place to exchange their vows. Through Jim's property contacts, they had found a gloriously faded hotel on the outskirts of town. It had views of the estuary and the boats bobbing in the harbour, three acres of English country gardens, and a ballroom that could not only fit a hundred guests but whispered of a glamorous past – art deco era dances and flapper girls – that Jennifer found intoxicating. Savannah would always be Jennifer's home, but it represented her past, not her future, and in this small Devon town, she knew she had found a place where she could plot and dream and sail and be happy.

She spun around on the dance floor, feeling giddy and light-headed as the song faded.

'This one is for my beautiful wife,' said a voice from the stage.

Jim's eyes met Jennifer's through the crowd, their gaze connecting as if no one else existed. She felt her heart lift like a balloon, full of love, lust and joy. The most handsome man in the room – in the world – was on stage and he was singing a song for her.

'I love you,' he said into the microphone as Donna held her hand to her chest and gave a dramatic sigh.

'Four husbands in and I've never had anyone look at me the way your sexy man has just looked at you,' she laughed to her niece, as Frank grabbed her playfully and told her he would rectify the situation in the bedroom later.

As Jennifer swayed to the music – a cover version of a Mamas & the Papas song – she admired her husband on stage. Jim had the big job at Omari Hotels now, but since Jennifer had moved to London to be with him, he didn't seem to spend as much time in the office as a CEO might.

Their lives had settled into a comfortable and contented rhythm. By day, Jim worked at the Omari London office, while Jennifer developed her fledgling film company in between short courses at the National Film School in Beaconsfield. They lived in Jim's North London flat and went out most nights – to jazz clubs and museum late openings, to restaurants and dinner with Jim's old friends – but somewhere in the middle of all that, Jim had found time to reconnect with his music, and had become the man she had loved all those years ago, the Jim she thought might have disappeared when she met him again in New York.

The song faded and he jumped off the stage. He came to her and wrapped his arm around her waist.

'How was your rock star moment, then?' she laughed.

'Forty-one and I think I've still got it,' he grinned, and Jennifer smiled to herself about the wedding present – one of them – she would give him later. A vintage Les Paul guitar she had found at auction and knew he would love.

'Come on. We should go,' he said, taking her hand.

'Go where?'

'To our room,' he whispered into her ear.

She felt puzzled as he led her outside into the garden. A chill had settled into the English summer evening air, and Jim took off his suit jacket and put it over her shoulders.

'Jim, our suite is upstairs,' she frowned, looking back at the hotel.

'We're going somewhere else,' he said mysteriously as he beckoned her to follow him down a path that led to the coast. She had found the trail earlier in the day. It snaked down the hillside to the harbour, and at some point one of the event planners had lined it with lanterns that cast a golden glow over the track.

Jennifer had thought getting married on Midsummer Eve was romantic enough, but as they walked in the moonlight, hearing the sound of the waves, the cow parsley tickling her arms, there was something especially magical in the air. Or perhaps it was just the idea that she was now Mrs Jim Johnson.

'Here,' said Jim as they reached the harbour.

She laughed out loud when she saw the fishing boat tethered to the dock. It had tin cans strung from the stern and a wonky hand-painted sign that read *Just Married*.

'Where are we going?' she grinned, as someone waved from the cabin.

'Climb on board. We're going for a spin.'

'Jim, our wedding . . .'

'We'll be back. Go on. I just want to show you something.'

She took off her heels and hitched up her skirt and did as she was told.

Cushions had been laid out along the seat at the back of the boat. Sunset was fading to dusk and the sky floating above the estuary had darkened to saffron-streaked violet.

The fisherman operating the boat cast off and the vessel chugged to life, the noise of the cans rattling against the stern as they carved through the water.

Jennifer curled into the space between Jim's arm and his chest, consumed by the warm and peaceful feeling of coming home. She didn't fool herself that she was a young woman any more. She would be forty-three soon. Almost certainly in the second half of her life and she had lines on her face and the scars of experience to prove it. And yet, as they powered down the estuary, watching the village recede into a series of lights, there was a sense of possibility, excitement and new beginnings that had seemed inconceivable a year earlier, when, living with Connor in her grand town house on the Upper East Side, she felt as if she was just treading water and slowly sinking.

'What are you thinking?'

'I'm wondering where we're going. It's exciting,' she said softly as Jim gave her shoulders a squeeze.

She heard the engine of the boat begin to slow.

'We're here,' said Jim, getting to his feet.

She realised that they had anchored just off the opposite shore to Salcombe. It was a short distance to the beach, and a small tender lowered them from the bigger boat to take them there.

She was careful not to let salt water splash the hem of her dress and, barefoot, she followed Jim across the sand. He took her hand and led her away from the beach, past rocks covered with mussels and seaweed towards a small white cottage set in a thicket of trees.

'It's a micro-climate around here, so exotic plants can grow,' he said, pointing out a perfumed myrtle, a magnolia bush and a banana plant.

'Magnolia,' sighed Jennifer, recognising all sorts of subtropical blooms from Savannah.

'I know we were going to wait until after the wedding to buy a new house, but I saw this and thought it would be perfect as a weekend place.'

'It is,' she said. She didn't have to go into the cottage to know that it was just right. 'It's my dream house. The red door and the magnolia bush. How did you know?'

'I've always known you,' said Jim, his voice full of love, and he took her hand and led her inside.

Acknowledgements

My gratitude as ever goes to the fantastic team at Headline, especially my editor Sherise Hobbs, Beth Eynon (goodbye and good luck!), Mari Evans, Jo Liddiard, Caitlin Raynor, Yeti Lambregts and copy-editor Jane Selley. Also the sales team, both at home and overseas.

My agent Eugenie Furniss is a star. Also Isha Karki, and Liane-Louise Smith, who knows that without stamped envelopes my business wouldn't function. Thanks also to Richard Best.

My fantastic friends help get the word out there about my books and can always assist with a plot point or know someone who can. Phillip B provided detail on hotel investment and Carlota P brainstormed Spanish names for the Savannah House. My great mate Bella Andre is a source of inspiration and kindness – I will never forget my sunrise workathons on the wine country deck!

Continued love and thanks go to my family for all their support, especially Fin, who never complained when he was dragged around another big old Deep South house for 'mum's research', and John, who makes everything possible.